FIRST FIERY TOUCH

Abby saw the shadow move from the doorway. His profile was unmistakable as he stepped into the silvery moonlight. She gasped to realize that he was naked from the waist up.

"Good evening," he said, as if they were conversing on the street in daylight.

"It's late, Mr. Carlson," she replied. "Is there something I can do for you?"

Come to my bed, he wanted to say. *Let me taste your lips just once to see if they are as soft as they appear.* But he only smiled and stepped closer.

Abby felt her chest grow tight; suddenly the urge to flee was paramount. But before she could move away, Chris wrapped his arms around her. Before she could realize his intentions, he planted a firm kiss on her lips. The kiss deepened, and she felt her senses reel. But when she opened her eyes, he was gone. . . .

Abby stood trembling as she reached up to touch his lips. If she closed her eyes, she could still feel the pressure of his flesh on hers. Her mind spun in confusion. She felt as if she'd been struck by lightning. And deep within her soul, the flames of passion sparked for the first time. . . .

CAPTURE THE GLOW OF
ZEBRA'S *HEARTFIRES!*

Rainy Kirkland
Ecstasy's Flame

ZEBRA BOOKS
KENSINGTON PUBLISHING CORP.

ZEBRA BOOKS

are published by

Kensington Publishing Corp.
475 Park Avenue South
New York, NY 10016

First printing: November, 1992

Printed in the United States of America

TO EDIE
FOR CONSTANT SUPPORT AND GENEROUS
ENTHUSIASM—BUT MOST OF ALL
FOR GIVING DAD BACK HIS SMILE
WITH MUCH LOVE
RAIN

Chapter One

August, 1698
Middle Plantation, Virginia

The sun blazed down in all its glory on the small graveyard on the far edge of town. Flies and mosquitoes danced about in the thick humidity but the minister, the Reverend Jeffers, remained undaunted. He raised his voice to be heard over the boisterous weeping and droned on about the torments of hell and damnation until the last shovel of earth was tamped firmly in place.

"Amen," he pronounced as the two servants stepped back to lean on their shovels. Turning to the slender woman wrapped in a black woolen cape he squinted against the sun's bright glare and realized for the first time how well Abigail Barclay's face was hidden behind her widow's veil. For the briefest moment he pondered her age. More than nine summers had passed since he had heard of her marriage to Malachi Barclay. His brow wrinkled. Barclay had been a heathen in their fair community, refusing to attend services despite the numerous threats heaped upon him by the town fathers. Looking now upon his widow, the good reverend concluded that she

7

must be heathen too, for he had no memory of ever seeing her face. He stepped around the grave to stand beside her. "I think it was a grand service." His voice carried pride that his words had so deeply touched the two that stood weeping before him. "And God certainly blessed us with some fine weather for the event." He watched her hand tremble as she reached into her reticule. Then he struggled to contain his astonishment as she silently handed him a pocket watch. The casing was gold with a handsome design.

"It works," she said quietly.

Carefully he studied the gift. An expensive piece to be sure, at least five times his usual fee, but then nothing about this funeral had been usual. Hastily he pocketed the watch lest the griefstricken widow suddenly realize she had given him too much. Tipping his hat, he backed away. "You have a good day now, Mrs. Barclay," he called as his feet hastily carried him from the graveyard.

Abigail Barclay watched the man disappear from view before a muffled cough pulled her attention back to the task at hand. Turning to the two waiting servants, she offered gold coins.

"Mrs. Barclay," the younger of the two black men stammered. "Nobody gives this much just to see kinfolk dug under."

"You both did a fine job," came her soft reply. "Thank you." Having offered once and not really wanting to return the outrageous payment, the pair silently nodded their thanks and quickly departed.

Abigail then turned back to the two sobbing women who stood on the other side of her husband's grave. Taking a deep breath, she gathered her heavy cloak to hide the shabbiness of her dress and stepped around the grave toward them. Carefully she took

8

their hands, discreetly leaving a gold coin in the palm of each as she did.

"Thank you for coming today," she said softly. The noisy weeping stopped immediately.

"Mrs. Barclay, we can't . . ." The stout woman's words ended with a gasp as her companion's elbow caught her sharply in the ribs.

"You're a generous lady, Mrs. Barclay," the taller woman said quickly, taking her friend's arm in a tight grasp. "We'll be on our way now. Good day to you." Then giving an awkward curtsy the two turned away, clutching their coins, arguing as to how they should spend their new found wealth.

Abigail shaded her eyes through the dark veil and looked about the deserted grounds. This isn't right, she thought wearily. The sky should be dark, filled with black clouds and streaks of lightning. Thunder should crack and the wind should howl. But as she looked up, the sky was a bright azure blue. The trees that edged the clearing stood as proud, silent mourners and even the song birds maintained an unearthly hush. Death was in the air. She could feel it, and its presence in the bright sunlight seemed even more sinister. Her eyes lingered for only a moment on the freshly packed earth that rested over her husband.

"It is a hot day today, Mr. Barclay." Her foot crept out from beneath her cloak to push a clump of dirt firmly back into place. "But if there be any justice in this world . . . where you are is even hotter." With her final good-by hanging in the humid air, Abigail Barclay began her solitary walk back to town.

Three-quarters of an hour later, Abigail reached the back steps of the Stag's Head Tavern. She had passed many townsfolk on her way, but no one had stopped to offer condolences or even tip their hat in friendly sympathy. She hadn't been offended, indeed she would have been more than surprised if they had.

Shrugging out of her cape, she hung it carefully on a peg by the door. Sweat trickled down her back but now, without the cloak's oppressive weight, she felt an odd sense of freedom. With a sigh she removed the large pins that had held her widow's veil and that, too, found a resting place on the peg.

Abigail stopped before the small, cracked looking glass and reached for her mob cap that hung on its corner. She didn't need to see her reflection to wind her waist-length hair back into place, for if truth be known she avoided the glass whenever possible. Malachi had recited her flaws so often that she knew them by heart. Her light brown hair had too little color and the golden streaks were constant proof that she must have worked in the garden again without her bonnet. Her brown eyes were too big and her cheek bones too high. Abigail turned from the glass and resisted the urge to wish for a pleasant face. She had given up wishing the summer she was but ten-and-four. The oldest of thirteen children, her father had sold her into marriage with a man forty-nine years her senior. The day after the wedding Abby knew with certainty that dreams never came true.

Carefully, she pulled her thick locks into a tight bun, meticulously tucking each stray hair into place. It was not an easy task, for her hair fought to escape whenever possible. It mattered not how many pins she used, stray wisps would always slip from beneath her cap to curl about her face, causing her husband to grow wild with anger. "You look like a harlot ready for the streets," he would scream, and then the pain would begin.

Abigail shuddered. He's dead, she chanted silently,

10

but still her fingers struggled to push each hair into place.

"Miz Abby?"

Abigail jerked about, bumped into the corner of the hall table, and tried to still the rapid beating of her heart. Rubbing the sting from her hip she smiled at the elderly black slave who stood in the doorway. "I'm sorry, Obadiah, I don't seem to be myself today. What did you say?"

His concern for her well-being was evident in his tired eyes and he searched for a way to ease her burden. "Is we 'specting folks," he questioned gently, "or do you wants me to take that punch away now?"

Abigail glanced uneasily toward the parlor. She hadn't expected anyone to come, indeed she had known they wouldn't. But for some foolish reason at the last hour her thoughts had turned. What if there had been someone that Malachi had not offended, she reasoned. One single soul he had offered a gentle word to. And if that one soul arrived on her doorstep to pay their respects and she had nothing to offer . . .

"You may take it out to the back and share it with the others, Obadiah. I doubt there will be a need for it now."

She fought back the wave of weariness that washed over her. She had had the parlor cleaned from top to bottom, then through the night she had sat beside the coffin of her husband, hoping for one last chance to think a kind thought about him. None had come. The black man nodded and turned to go but her words halted his steps.

"Did you send for Mr. Danvers as I asked?" With hands that trembled with fatigue she tied a well-worn apron over her gown.

Obadiah shifted uncomfortably. "Miz Abby, why

11

you wants to go talking with that man? You know he be no good."

Abigail pulled her shoulders back and took a deep breath to steady her nerves. "I learned one thing from Mr. Barclay, Obadiah. If paid enough, Mr. Danvers will do anything he is told to do. The man has the manners of a goat, but he'll not offer advice that's not wanted and I need his pen as an attorney. Now, did you send for him?"

The slave nodded solemnly. "The man be coming at one of the clock this very day."

"Good." Abigail rubbed her hands nervously against her apron. "I'm going to see to Mr. Barclay's things now. You call for me when Mr. Danvers arrives."

Three hours later, her meeting with the attorney concluded, Abigail returned to the bedchamber her husband had occupied. For the first time in nine years, she hesitantly pulled the drawers from his chest-on-chest and carefully removed the contents to sort upon the bed. Within moments she stood before the largest collection of clothing she had ever seen in her life. There were four coats of blue the exact same cut and color, three green jackets, five coats of brown and six more of black.

Abby stepped back from the bed. She had known her husband had owned more than she, and the notion of it had never troubled her. But now, seeing the magnitude of his greed, the reality hit her for the first time. She possessed two gowns, the one she wore, and an extra in the same troubled state of disrepair. Malachi could have changed his garments every day for a month and never worn the same piece twice. A shudder of revulsion brought gooseflesh to

12

her arms as she remembered their last confrontation. He had flown into a rage when she had gathered the courage to show him the worn fabric on her shoe. She had already stitched it twice herself, but further mending was no longer possible. Malachi had lectured her for the remainder of the day and then whipped her soundly at the woodpile for not taking better care of his property.

The chamber door creaked open and Abigail jumped like a guilty child with fingers caught in the biscuit bin.

"Oh, Obadiah," she gasped pressing her hand against the frantic beating of her heart. "I thought you were him."

Obadiah entered the room on silent feet. "I sure didn't mean to give you a fright, Miz Abby, but I do know what you mean." His eyes scanned nervously about. "I keep waiting to find out that it was all a prank, and he ain't really dead. I keep thinking he's going to come marching round the corner with that riding crop and say 'Obadiah, get yourself out to the woodpile boy, you ain't pleasing me today'."

Abigail wrapped her arms about herself. Despite the heat of the day she was freezing. "Well he's dead. My eyes watched him be hammered into that coffin and put down under the earth." She rubbed the chill from her arms. "Now I just wish I could get my mind to remember it." For several moments the two stood lost in thought, then Abigail drew herself erect. "Obadiah, take those clothes out to the back and burn them. I'll look upon them no more."

Obadiah nodded, but as he reached for the garments, his hand slowed. "Miz Abby," he hesitated then turned back to face his young mistress. "I know you don't wants to see these, but it would be a sin to waste all this good cloth when

13

there be those who could surely use a new jacket."

Abigail looked at the old man before her. His shirt was just a washing from the rag barrel and his breeches not much better. "You're right, Obadiah. Take all that," she gestured to the huge mound of clothing, "and place it on the table in the dining hall. Get all the others together and tell them to meet me there directly."

Obadiah nodded. "You wants Effie and Nanny too?"

Abigail smiled and for a fleeting minute her fine features reflected the excitement of a child with an unexpected gift. "I want to see everyone. And get Willie to help you so you don't have to make so many trips up and down those stairs. I know your knees are giving you pain today."

The servant nodded and offered a smile for her kindness. "Things is gonna work out fine, Miz Abby," he said quietly. "There's a soft breeze a stirring from the south and I just know it's gonna bring good days ahead."

"Obadiah, get out of here with that fortune telling. You're getting as bad as Suzannah, thinking you can call out what hasn't even happened yet."

The old man took no offense, but sent his mistress a wink as he reached to gather the discarded clothing. "Something good's a coming for you, Miz Abby. I can feel it in my bones."

Abigail waited until all the clothing had been removed before shutting the door. Obadiah got the strangest notions in his head, she thought. With her back pressed against the smooth wood she surveyed the room. The large tester bed stood before her, its cream colored counterpane tight and smooth the way Malachi liked it. A narrow shaving table stood on the far wall and Abby swallowed hard as she stared

14

at the leather strop that hung so innocently from its hook. The chest-on-chest was empty now, yet the room still carried her husband's stale scent. Abby reached behind to turn the key and when the lock clicked into place her heart lurched within her chest. Her eyes pressed closed as the sound that marked the entrance to hell echoed through the room.

"He's dead," she chanted over and over, trying to erase the fright that seeped steadily into her veins. "You saw him buried . . . he's dead." On legs that threatened to buckle with each step, Abby slowly made her way across the room to the massive hearth. The stones felt cold and rough beneath her palm and she took comfort in their solid form. Her fingers traced over the mortar that held them in place. Slowly, ever so slowly, her hand traveled the seams until she felt it — the slightest shift beneath her questing fingers. Carefully she examined the stone. Then taking a determined breath, she pulled it free. Its weight was more than she had anticipated and her hands struggled to maintain their grip. Flopping down onto the floor with the stone securely in her lap and her heart pounding wildly in her ears, Abby stared across the room at the locked door. Had he heard her? Were those his footsteps? Her eyes glued to the door, she struggled to steady her breathing. "He's dead," she whispered to the empty room. "He can't come back because he's dead." But her eyes never left the door latch as she heaved the stone from her lap onto the floor beside her.

Taking a deep breath, Abby brushed off her hands and scrambled to her feet. Glancing around, she spied the low stool that stood near the bed. She had just set it into place before the hearth when the door latch turned with a click.

Abby jumped back, her eyes wide with fright, her

scream locked in her throat. Terrorized she watched the latch turn slowly up and down. Her fist clenched until her knuckles whitened. "He's dead!" Her mind pleaded with the reality of what she was seeing. "He's dead . . ."

"Miz Abby, you still in here?"

Abby felt her legs buckle, then like a puppet whose strings had been slashed she was sitting in a heap at the foot of the hearth. Gasping, she let her head fall to her knees as she struggled to find her breath.

"Miz Abby?"

"I'll be down directly, Obadiah," she called, desperately hoping he wouldn't hear the frightened tremor in her voice.

"Miz Abby . . . is you feeling poorly? Do you want me to fetch somebody?"

Abby looked up from her place on the floor. Oh Obadiah, she thought with a strangled laugh, who would you fetch? Gathering what was left of her dignity, Abby pulled her shoulders back and took a calming breath.

"I'm fine, Obbie. I just need to be alone for a few minutes. Will you wait below stairs with the others?"

"I'm going 'cause you say go, Miz Abby, but you sure don't sound fine. No you don't sound fine at all."

Abby waited until she heard his retreating steps before she forced herself up off the floor. Bracing herself she stepped onto the low stool and peered into the dark hole. She could see nothing. Carefully she reached inside and the tips of her fingers brushed against something soft. She had to strain, pressing her entire shoulder against the stone before her fingertips could catch enough of the cloth to pull it forward. The edge of the brick bit under her arm but

16

she refused to ease up until she had a firm grasp on the velvet pouch.

Abby stepped off the stool and, clutching the pouch, walked unsteadily to the bed. It took her trembling fingers more than a moment to untie the leather lacing; then Malachi Barclay's hidden fortune tumbled onto the smooth coverlet.

She stared in wonder at the gold coins. They felt hard and cold as she scooped them into her hand. "How many years did it take, Malachi?" she challenged the empty room. "And how many lives did you ruin on your quest?" Silently she counted the coins as she placed them back in the pouch. Relief soared through her as she realized that what she now held would be sufficient to see her plan to fruition. Abby closed her eyes with satisfaction. It was not a great plan, but it had come to her just after midnight while she sat at her dead husband's side. And somehow that made it all the sweeter.

Minutes later, Abigail joined her household in the back dining hall, her husband's clothing an obscene pile on the wooden table. They were all there; white-haired Nanny with her youngest grandsons who had just seen their sixth summer, the housemaids Effie and Celie, and all the others who helped with the running of the tavern.

Abby read anxiousness in every face as she hurried to take her place at the table. She set down the packet of papers the attorney had prepared and plopped her husband's pouch on top.

"First I want to thank each of you for all your help these last hours," she began softly, looking from face to face.

"Miz Abby, with the master dead, we belong to you now." Obadiah said formally.

Abby frowned. "That's just it, Obbie. I don't want

17

to own anyone." She felt a moment's hesitation. What if it wasn't a good idea after all? How would she ever live with herself if something were to happen to them because of a foolish notion on her part? Fighting back her uncertainty, she reached for the stack of papers.

"You're not slaves any more," she said quietly handing the packet to Obadiah. "I had the attorney, Mr. Danvers, write these up. They say that you aren't slaves any more so you don't belong to me."

"You giving us our freedom?" Harley stepped forward and folded his massive arms across his wide chest. "Why you doing this, Miz Abby?" His dark eyes narrowed suspiciously.

Uncomfortable being the focus of their attention, Abby shrugged. "Mr. Barclay wasn't always a decent sort," she murmured, her eyes on the floor as memories filled her with humiliation. "It just seemed to me that his death should have some meaning."

"Then this paper says we can leave and no one can hunt us down and bring us back?" Abby looked up at Thomas. His quick temper had often been on the receiving end of her husband's vindictiveness. She recalled all too well the time Malachi decided to cure Thomas' wayward tongue, as he put it. He had had the slave tied spread eagle in the barn and then he had personally scraped every inch of Thomas' skin with the curry brush while he forced the entire household to watch. Abby felt her chest grow tight with the memory. Thomas had held his cries, even when Malachi used handfuls of coarse straw to further abuse the raw skin. But her husband had not been content. Determined to break Thomas' spirit, he had then rubbed lemon juice over the man's entire body. Abby closed her eyes, for in her mind she could still hear Thomas' tortured screams. Swallow-

18

ing back the bile that rose in her throat, Abby looked up at the large man before her.

"I made Mr. Danvers read it to me twice." She held Thomas' dark gaze. "I can't change what went before, but I have the means to see that it never happens again."

"But where would we go?" Effie interrupted.

Abby turned back to face the group again. "You're welcome to stay here and make the tavern your home. But this paper means that if you ever decide to leave, you don't have to ask me to do so. You can make your own decisions."

"But if you don't own us," Thomas challenged, "how you gonna whip us when we don't do right?"

Abby drew herself erect and gave the slave a hard stare. "We're none of us children, Thomas, save little Willie and Wesley. We don't need to be beaten to know what's right. You want to stay under my roof, then you do your share of the work. You don't want to help out, then you leave and find another who will take you in."

Thomas' brow narrowed in thought. "This ain't no trick?"

Abby felt her energy begin to drain away. "It is no trick, Thomas, go or stay as you see fit."

Obadiah still could not fathom the consequences of the master's death, but one thing he did know and that was the mistress was growing paler by the minute.

"Miz Abby." Gently he took her arm and led her back to her chair at the table. "You need to go and rest for a spell and stop worrying about other folks."

Nanny peered long and hard in her direction before heaving herself off her stool. "You need a cup of Nanny's special cider, child, before you plum fall over."

19

"Wait," Abby halted the old woman's slow movements. "While everyone's still together I need to say more."

"You'll have your drink first," Nanny stated firmly, and neither Abby or anyone else in the room uttered a protest as the old woman shuffled out and returned with a full pewter mug. She stood at Abby's side until she was satisfied that more than half the contents had been consumed.

Abby glanced to the table beside her. "These are Mr. Barclay's clothes." She struggled to keep her revulsion hidden. "You may take what you wish as long as each gets a fair share." For an instant no one moved, then like a field of sweet corn beset by a swarm of grasshoppers the mound of clothing was devoured.

"Now I would barter with you." She smiled, relieved that the ache in her head was finally abating. "Thomas, what would you call the value of those breeches and jacket?"

The man's dark eyes again narrowed in suspicion. "You want these back?"

Abby nodded and dumped the contents of the pouch on the table. "Would you say that this gold piece would be a fair price?"

Thomas' eyes grew wide. "Miz Abby," his words were flustered. "You kin have these back if you wants them. You don't have to pay me for them."

Liking the carefree feeling that was easing the aches from her tired limbs, Abby smiled. "The choice is yours," she said lightly. "If you wish the coin then dump the garments over in the corner. If you prefer to keep the cloth that choice is yours to make."

It didn't take long for Abby's small hoard of coins to disappear while the pile of discarded clothing on

20

the floor grew in size. No one wanted a remembrance of Malachi Barclay.

"Miz Abby," Obadiah eased himself onto the chair beside her, the events of the morning almost more than he could comprehend. "You just gave away all your money. What you gonna do now, child?"

Abby smiled with a vacant look to her eyes. "Don't worry, Obadiah, I have a plan."

Obadiah looked skeptical. "And what's you want me to do with all this clothing that you just bought back?"

Abby rose unsteadily from the table, her bright smile somewhat lopsided. "Take them out and burn them."

Nanny stood slowly and faced the stunned group. "Now you all gets. There's chores awaitin' and they ain't gonna get done by themselves. Thomas, you and Harley see to these here clothes. Miz Abby wants them burned, so you burn them till nothing's left." She gave Thomas an affectionate cuff on the shoulder. "Now you get and stop standing around like you got nothing to do."

Thomas grinned and patted the gold coin and folded paper that rested in his pocket. "I'm free, old woman. You can't be telling me what to do."

Undaunted, Nanny gave Thomas a withering stare. "And if you planning to eat any of my chicken an' dumplings for your supper, you'll get yourself gone."

Thomas hesitated less than a heartbeat before moving to scoop up the garments. "And Thomas," Nanny called as he reached the door. "I've got your favorite, fresh rhubarb pie for dessert." Nanny turned back to her mistress. "Ain't good to give a young buck like Thomas too many choices, Miz Abby. He's likely to choose wrong. Now, we need to get you up to bed. Effie, you see Miz Abby up to her chamber. And you Missy," she shook a crooked finger at Abby. "You go to bed and stay there until I climb those stairs and tell you the dark lines is gone from those eyes of yours."

Abby struggled to argue, but her eyes felt so tired. "I can't lie abed while the sun is shining."

"You most certainly ken," Nanny took her arm and gently helped Effie guide her to the stairs. "You done more work about this place than any three people, then last night you sit up for all those hours with that coffin. Child, what you been through would send a hearty man to his knees, much less a tiny wisp of a thing like you. Now you get and don't sass Nanny back. When I tells you sleep, then you sleep."

Nanny waited until the pair was out of sight before turning back to follow her husband out to the cook house. There she eased herself onto her stool and reached for the wooden bowl that held the potatoes for the evening meal. With a practiced hand she cut the peel in thin strips while she watched Obadiah fold the papers that granted their freedom and tuck them inside his shirt.

"Obadiah, I'm not leaving Miz Abby, so don't even let that notion enter your head."

Obadiah reverently patted the folded paper, liking the crinkling sound. "I don't see how we could even if we wanted to." He poured the coffee beans into a shallow roasting pan and set them near the fire. "Miz Abby's a hard worker, but even she can't run this tavern all by herself. What ken she be thinking of, Nanny? That child's done gone and gived away most all her money."

Nanny's weathered face pulled into a scowl. "I think the master done hit her one time too many and now her mind be all scattered. That poor babe's got a heart of gold, but the common sense of a nit."

Obadiah nodded in agreement then moved to the door.

"Obbie, where you going?" Nanny questioned, her sharp eyes taking in the excitement that seemed to radiate from the aging bones of her husband.

Obadiah stood in the doorway, silhouetted by the bright afternoon sunlight and flashed a smile that shone even brighter. "I'm gonna burn me some clothes."

Chapter Two

Christopher Carlson sat in his father's study and stared at the letter that held his name. The lump returned to his throat and his eyes grew misty as he read. The writing, the bold hand of his father, had comprised most of the message, but at the bottom his mother's delicate scroll had been unmistakable. His fingers smoothed over their signatures as he pictured their image. Just weeks ago they had been happy and carefree, joking with each other over the breakfast table, sharing secret smiles and glances. Now, they were dead, victims of the dreaded summer fever.

Wearily, he pulled the formal white wig from his head and tossed it irreverently onto the desk beside him. Then with eyes that burned, he reread their message, feeling again their pain at knowing that the end was near. Heartsick, he refolded the parchment and slipped it into his coat pocket as he heard the door to his father's study swing open.

"There you are." Julie Carlson Morgan swept into the room pausing to glance at her reflection in the looking glass as she passed by. Black makes me look too washed out, she thought with a frown. Leaning close she pinched color back into her cheeks and scowled at the red rings that still lined her eyes. No more crying, she decided firmly. Turning, she spied her brother's wig lying on the desk.

"Honestly, Christopher," she looked pointedly toward the discarded hair piece. "That cost a fortune. The least you could do is wear it for the full day. You know how Mother always harped, 'a man of station is not completely attired until his wig is securely in place'."

"Mother never harped, Julie. I wore that cursed thing to the service this morning out of respect for her, but I'll not wear it a minute longer just to make a damned social statement."

Julie sighed as she perched carefully on the edge of the settee. Life wasn't fair, she thought angrily. Her brother thumbed his nose at the dictates of fashion but nobody seemed to care. She looked down at her dark skirt and grimaced. She needed soft colors that complemented the porcelain white of her complexion. Black made her look like a ghost, while Chris, who cared not a wit, wore black and looked magnificent. It accented the golden tan of his skin and the sun streaks in his blond hair.

Her eyes narrowed with frustration. "Just because things haven't gone your way, you can't stay in here and sulk," she declared sharply, causing her brother to raise a brow. "There is too much to do. Besides, Marigold Thurmont, Betsy Alders, and Elizabeth Johnson are all but panting at the door for your return." Julie rose and brushed at her skirt. "Honestly, Chris, how could you invite all three of your mistresses to the same event? What were you thinking of?"

Caught up in her tirade, Julie missed the darkening of her brother's eyes. "It's a funeral, little sister, not some social gathering. And those women are friends, nothing more."

Julie rolled her eyes, then decided to try a different tack. "Christopher, I know you're upset about the will," her voice took on a pleading tone. "But I need you out there now." Her black taffeta skirt swished as she crossed the room to stand before him. "Another wagon load of people have arrived and we are almost out of food."

"That's impossible." Christopher gazed out the window. From where he sat he could just see the top of the fence that surrounded the family graveyard. Had his father focused on that plot as he penned his final words?

Her patience gone, Julie began to pace. "Chris, they've consumed more than ten gallons of spirits, including two of your favorite brandy."

He waved aside her protest. "There is more in the cellar. Send one of the boys down to fetch it for you."

"But they're eating me out of house and home!" she wailed. "Cook has already prepared a sheep, a pig, and more turkeys than I care to count. Mazie carries in a full tray and before I can turn around it's empty again. I don't know what to do."

"You know the smoke house is well-stocked, just tell cook to send someone for more. What can be so difficult about that?"

Julie turned on her brother in anger. "It's well and fine for you to say, but it's not your food that is being devoured."

Chris felt his patience strain to the limit and wondered yet again why his parents had never realized that a spoiled little girl would turn into a vain, selfish woman. But he was just as much to blame, he reasoned, for had he not been devoted to her complete happiness since the day she was born? Yet now, as she turned from beguiling vulnerability to chilling viciousness before his eyes, he felt sickened.

"Sister, you are one of the richest ladies in the entire colony of Virginia. Surely you can't begrudge a simple meal for those who traveled so far?"

"The Wilsons live just down the road. There was no need for them to stay, and with all their children. You can't turn around without stepping on one of them."

Christopher stood so quickly that she jerked back in fright. "Enough." The quiet tenor of his words sent chills down her arms. "I will not allow you to disgrace our parents on the very day we have buried them. Now, you will go out and tell cook to take whatever she needs from the cellar or the smoke house or the buttery. She will continue to fill the platters until the last guest has departed. Do you understand?"

Completely taken aback, Julie paused with uncertainty, never had she seen her brother so angry. "I understand how you must be feeling," she tried to pretend sympathy. "I'd be madder than a wet hen if they had cut me from the will. But Chris," hesitantly she stepped closer and placed her hand on his arm. "I would never force you from your home. You could stay here and rent the house from me. You still have money and I'd not set a price above your means, you being my brother and all. Why if you just give it a little thought, this could work out quite nicely."

Christopher shook his head, unable to believe what he was hearing. "You wish me to pay rent to stay in the house that I have lived in for most of my life?"

Julie smiled, pleased with herself for thinking of

27

such a grand plan. "Well it does belong to me now and Clarence would probably be grateful if you would act as his overseer. He's never going to manage if he has to run back and forth between our place and this one."

Christopher stepped away, suddenly repulsed by his sister's touch. "I hadn't planned to tell you this way, or even mention it today. But since you've brought the subject up you may as well know the truth. I shall be leaving for Middle Plantation as soon as I can make arrangements."

"Leaving? You can't mean that."

Chris raised a brow. "As you so kindly pointed out, this is now your house."

"But I need you here," Julie wailed, letting tears gather in her eyes. "Clarence can't manage on his own, he's a stumbling fool."

"He's your husband," Chris replied quietly. "Perhaps with your help the man could make a go of things."

Julie whirled around and stomped her foot. "I don't believe this. How can you abandon me this way? What will you do?" Her eyes narrowed. "Surely you don't think to become a tradesman. You fashion silver as a hobby. Did Nick Beaumont put you up to this? I saw you two talking," she accused wildly.

"Julie, the man was offering his condolences."

Her foot began to beat an agitated rhythm on the hard wood floor. "He didn't bother to come over and chat with me at length. Ever since he married that Puritan he's been afraid to speak to me."

"The man is civil to you, little sister, and truly that's more than I would expect. Have you conveniently forgotten that your meddling almost got his wife killed?"

Julie shrugged. "Nothing happened. You and

28

Nick managed to save her, so what harm was done?"

"What harm? Julie, Sarah was accused of witchcraft and put in prison. If we hadn't gotten there in time she would have died!"

"Well don't blame me. I wasn't the one who accused her. If the fault lies anywhere it's with her brother. He's the one who said she was a witch."

"You, dear sister, were the one who convinced her to return to Salem where you knew she'd be in danger."

"But you and Nick got there in plenty of time. As I said before, no real harm was done. I don't understand why you and Nick continue to carry such a grudge about it."

"Julie, Sarah almost lost her life from your childish prank. Do you feel no remorse at all?"

Julie shrugged and glanced back over her shoulder at her brother. "If dear Sarah is as sweet and innocent as you both think she is, why didn't she come with Nick?"

Christopher smiled for the second time that day. "In just a few weeks, Sarah's going to make Nick a proud papa again."

Julie flopped down on the settee, the delicate features of her face pulling into a pout. "She's going to turn into a brood mare from all those babies," she muttered, then her eyes brightened. "And in a few more years she'll look like a cow and then Nick will realize he should have married me."

Chris shook his head and walked toward the door. "Nick had the good sense to follow his heart," he said quietly. "And now I shall at last follow mine." He didn't wait for his sister's reply, but closed the door firmly behind him.

"Well my boy, that's that." Walter Johnson laboriously added a flourish to his signature then reached to replace the quill in its silver holder.

Christopher Carlson hid a smile. At thirty and eight he hadn't been called a boy for some time, but he couldn't contain the childlike excitement he felt as he looked about the well-equipped shop that was now his.

Walter rose slowly from his chair and handed Chris the document. "I wish you all the best, young man. But you heed me well, and always insist on ready money. Won't matter how talented your hands are if your heart gets in the way and you start allowing credit." Walter moved about the shop with a halting step, cursing the aching bones that were forcing him to give up the craft he loved so dearly. "No, don't you go giving credit. Ready money or tobacco vouchers, that's all you accept."

Chris watched emotions fill the old man's face, and felt an anxious knot returned to the pit of his stomach. Looking down at the deed to the silver shop, he hesitated, then raised his eyes to the old man. "Sir, are you having a change of heart?" Reluctantly, he offered the parchment.

Walter Johnson waved aside the document with a jerk of his hand. "No, no, my boy. You bought it and now it's yours lock, stock, and barrel so to speak. Although," his eyes began to twinkle, "the only stock I leave is silver, none of the four-legged variety is about."

Chris smiled as relief coursed through him. For a fleeting moment he had thought his dream was going to vanish. Now he held it securely in his hand. "You mentioned an apprentice." Chris looked toward the back door. "Is he about?"

Walter eased himself back onto his chair and reached for his cane. "Jimmy Richardson. In fact,

30

the lad was recommended by friends of yours, the Beaumonts."

Chris nodded. "I've been staying with them until our transactions could be completed."

"I envy you my boy." Walter gazed out the window in thought. "Pretty little thing, that Mrs. Beaumont. Came in one morning with Jimmy tagging behind. Smiled at me with those eyes of hers and I was a goner. Would have given her the shop if she had asked."

Chris bit back a grin. "Then maybe I should have engaged Sarah to negotiate these transactions for me."

Walter cleared his throat and straightened abruptly in his chair. "No, no, my boy, what's done is done. Now, as to Jimmy Richardson, he's a bright boy, a bit over enthusiastic at times, but a bright boy. Off making a delivery at the moment. The lad's got so much energy that sometimes he gets in his own way. Whenever that happens, I send him off to fetch or carry."

Chris watched the old man's eyes suddenly fill with tears.

"Well, there's nothing left for it," Walter sniffed and stood slowly. "My ship leaves in less than three hours and if I want to get settled, I'd better get on my way to Jamestown."

Chris reached for the leather case that stood waiting beside the door. "Are you sure you don't want to take your hammers with you? I've brought my own you know."

Walter Johnson gave a heavy sigh and shook his head. "These old hands just don't do what I want anymore. Besides," he let Chris help him out the door and into the waiting carriage, "I don't plan to do any more smithing. Since my Martha died last year, I've had a yearning to see my home in England again." He settled back on the carriage seat with a grunt and despite the heat allowed Chris to help him secure a lap robe around his legs and feet. "Do you know I've a brother that I've not seen for thirty years? Old mule would never even come for a visit. Said the colonies were too savage." Walter laughed out loud from the thought and then with a signal to the driver, the carriage was moving. "You take care my boy," he called. "Just remember—NO CREDIT. . . ."

Chris watched until the carriage was no longer in sight before turning back to his new shop but the excitement he felt was short lived when he glanced at his timepiece and realized the hour. If he didn't hurry, he'd be late and Sarah Beaumont would have his head.

"To the most talented silversmith in Middle Plantation." Sarah raised her glass and smiled bewitchingly at her two companions.

"My thoughts exactly." Nicholas Beaumont lifted his glass to join his wife's toast.

Chris looked across the table at his two closest friends and felt his cheeks grow warm in pleasure. "I fear you may not be wrong," he started slowly. "For at the moment," he paused and winked, "I am the *only* silversmith in Middle Plantation."

Refusing to diminish the importance of their celebration, Sarah shook her head. "If that be so then I shall simply change my declaration. To Mr. Christopher Carlson, the most talented silversmith in all of Virginia."

Nick smiled in agreement, but Chris set his crystal glass down on the table.

"I appreciate your support, Sarah, but don't you think that's going just a little too far?"

Sarah gave him her sternest look, the one she saved for the children when they were particularly rowdy. "I am the mistress of this house, Mr. Carlson. And if I say that you are the most talented silversmith in Virginia, then you are. Now if you wish to take exception to my words, I simply must give the matter over to my husband."

Chris watched the way Sarah's eyes sparkled as she turned to Nick and he wondered yet again if he'd ever find a woman who would look on him with such unconditional love.

"I'd not challenge her my friend," Nick patted his lean stomach, "for I'm too content to wish a duel. Besides, I agree with her completely. You've been tinkering with those hammers of yours for as long as I've known you. It's about time you put all that talent to use. And," he reached to take his wife's hand, "there's talk again of moving the Capitol from Jamestown."

Chris shook his head. "It will never happen. The new statehouse was just finished, not to mention the church and the powder magazine."

Nick shrugged. "The Governor himself is in favor of the move. And now that construction on the college has started . . ."

"But what difference would it make?" Sarah interrupted.

Nick drew her hand to his lips for a kiss. "If the Capitol is moved to Middle Plantation, our town will surely thrive. And more people can only mean more business for a silversmith . . . although if the number of female callers who have graced our parlor during the last fortnight is any indication, the only rival his business will have is his social life."

33

Chris groaned. "I'm sorry for the inconvenience, especially since you have extended your hospitality to me, but I shall be out of your way first thing in the morning."

"It was no inconvenience, and you know it Christopher," Sarah stated firmly. "The children loved having you here and so did I. But I am concerned that you're leaving too soon. You just signed the documents, things can't possibly be ready for you to move in."

Chris smiled and felt his excitement begin to grow again. "The house attached to the shop is more than adequate for a bachelor like myself, and the work area behind is crying for my attention. Walter left several orders that have not yet been completed and as much as I have enjoyed being with you, I am anxious to get started."

Sarah turned her gaze back to her husband, silently bidding his support. "I think Christopher should continue to stay with us until the ship brings his order back from London and the business is firmly established."

Nick smiled at his wife and again raised his glass to his friend. "I'd lay heavy odds that the women of our fair city aren't going to be content to wait until the ship has returned from London. And if they are half as determined as you are, my dear, the Carlson Silver Shop will be thriving in no time."

Christopher ushered the last customer from his shop and sighed with relief as her skirt cleared the doorway. Latching the door securely, he turned and leaned his long frame against it. Just hours ago his shop had been organized and tidy; now it lay in chaos. A stack of new orders spilled over and covered the front counter; two broken quills lay discarded on the floor, and the display cases were nearly empty. He took a deep breath of satisfaction and smiled. The air within the small shop still carried fragrant reminders of the morning customers but now that the hour was well past noon, the mouthwatering aroma of freshly baked bread mingled with the scents of costly French perfumes.

"Zounds! Look at all this food." Jimmy Richardson tried to inconspicuously edge the red checkered cloth from the corner of the covered basket nearest him. The delicious scents intensified as did the noisy rumblings from Jimmy's stomach.

Chris stretched, then shrugged out of his well-tailored coat of black satin. "You pick." He gestured toward the baskets, smiling at his apprentice's undisguised enthusiasm. Jimmy Richardson had turned out to be a lanky lad of ten-and-four, with sandy hair, a ready smile, and feet three sizes too big.

"I knew it!" Jimmy squealed with delight as he peeled back the red checkered cloth. "Peach pie, I knew I should have laid odds." He sniffed again with obvious pleasure. "Fried chicken and peach pie." He gave Chris a curious glance. "Miss Thurmont must think you're really special. Her peach pies are legendary and she don't give them to just anybody." Jimmy lifted the chicken from the basket and then blushed to the roots of his hair, suddenly realizing that he might have said the wrong thing.

"Miss Thurmont was just being neighborly," Chris replied easily, taking a chicken leg and biting through the crispy coating to the succulent meat inside.

Jimmy rolled his eyes. "Nobody was ever this neighborly to Mr. Johnson. Why you had more customers in this one morning than all the time I've been here. And what about those?" He gestured toward the baskets that lined the back shelf. "Counting the one that Mrs. Beaumont sent down with Ruby this morning, you've got five different lunches to choose from."

Watching the boy devour his second piece of chicken, Chris could only shake his head. "Well, at least we won't have to worry about going hungry." He saw Jimmy's hand reach for a third piece then hesitate. "Here," he pushed the plate closer to the boy. "Eat all you want."

Jimmy scooped the fine china plate onto his lap and wiped the grease from his mouth with his shirt sleeve. "This is better than snitching pies at the Governor's reception. You think this is gonna happen every day?"

Chris tossed his chicken bone into the waste bin and reached for one of the linen napkins that Jimmy had pulled from the basket. "I rather doubt it."

Jimmy nodded, his mouth full of chicken. "Yea, they didn't mean to just leave them here." He hesitantly reached for the other napkin, wiped his hands, then refolded the linen square to match the one Chris had tossed on the counter. "I think them ladies meant for you to take them courting or something." He missed Chris' darkening gaze as he continued to root through the basket. "But if you was to ask me, I'd give you good odds that each of them is real sweet on you, if you know what I mean." He looked up and gave Chris an exaggerated wink.

Not eager to further the discussion of his love life with his young apprentice, Chris unbuttoned his waist coat and removed the lace collar and cuffs to his white shirt. "You finish eating." He pointed toward the other baskets. "Just save me a piece of the gingerbread from the one Mrs. Beaumont sent." He folded the waist coat and placed it on the end of the

36

counter with his coat. "I'm going to get started in the back. We have a busy afternoon ahead of us."

"Yes, sir," Jimmy declared, already poking through the next basket. "Zounds! Look at the size of this apple. Old Betsy Alders must have gone clear to Jamestown to get this."

"Jim!" Chris said no more but the look on his face was all too clear.

"Yes, sir, sorry sir," Jimmy stammered. "I'll be right along, sir." He waited until Chris was no longer in sight before quickly flipping the cloth from the smallest basket. His eyes grew wide and despite all the chicken he had consumed his mouth began to water as he lifted out two delicate crystal glasses. "Sir," he called loudly. "Did you truly mean that I could eat anything that's here?"

"Just save me the gingerbread," came the muffled reply.

Jimmy poked through the basket and found the tiny silver spoons that he knew would be inside. Holding the crystal to the window, he let the sunlight pour through the two layered desert. "Syllabub," he whispered reverently, taking a spoonful and letting the tart lemon cream melt on his tongue. His spoon dipped deeper the second time to gather some of the brandy that waited on the bottom. Closing his eyes he savored the delicate blend of flavors. If there was something more delicious than syllabub, he had yet to find it. A clang from the work room broke through his dream and within seconds he had devoured both goblets of the lemon dessert. I've died and gone to heaven, he thought, quickly tossing the glasses back into the basket and refolding the cloth on the top. I'll learn a trade that shall make me rich, and women will fight to see who may bring me lunch. Determined to get started as soon as possible

37

on the road to fame and fortune, Jimmy hurried to join his new master.

Chris scowled as his tin snips bit into the tarnished silver bowl, then with a practiced hand he cut the metal into small pieces that could easily be melted down. It was the only part of his craft that he disliked. It mattered not how damaged the piece was, he simply hated making scrap out of something someone else had created. He dumped the first handful into the crucible and wondered if the English Parliament would ever allow the colonies to import silver ingots.

"The fire is ready, sir."

He scooped the last of the scraps into the crucible and turned. Even from where he sat he could tell the coals weren't hot enough, and he wondered if the fault was in the boy's understanding or in Walter Johnson's teaching.

"I think the bellows require more of your attention, Jim. It will take twice as long if the temperature is not ready."

Jimmy quickly moved back to his place by the fire. He needed to reach his full height to grasp the bellows handle and the fire hissed and spit from the uneven gusts of air.

Chris sighed then stepped behind and placed his own hand on the handle. "Keep the pressure even." He pressed the lever down then controlled its upward swing. His hand stayed in place for two more strokes until he was sure that Jim could feel the motion.

"Thank you, sir." Jimmy maintained a steady hand. "I think I have the knack now."

Chris watched in silence for a moment and then smiled with approval. "That you do. But tell me lad, how is it that you apprenticed with Walter Johnson for some three months and still can't . . .

"Three months?" Jimmy gasped with a start. "Sir, I don't know what Mr. Johnson told you but I've been here just under three weeks."

"Still, in three weeks you should have already mastered the fire." Chris watched Jimmy's youthful face crumple with dismay.

"I'm sorry to be a disappointment, sir." Jimmy fought against the catch in his throat and his words came out in a croak that made his face blossom with color. "But if the truth be known, and with no disrespect to Mr. Johnson, most of my time with him was spent on errands and such."

"Ah ha," Chris nodded. He watched the steady hand that the boy maintained. "Well, I know we've had an unusual morning, but what say we get started? I think you're ready for your first lesson."

"Oh, yes, sir." But in his haste to join Chris at the work bench Jimmy's feet tangled with the rope handle of the water bucket and before he could blink, he and the bucket had both spilled onto the floor."

Chris struggled to keep a straight face as he watched the boy scramble awkwardly to his feet.

"I'm sorry, sir," Jimmy stammered, his face now a deep beet red.

"No harm done. But the water bucket needs filling before we move on. With smithing there is always the chance of fire. You must always be ready for the unexpected."

"Yes, sir." Jimmy grasped the soggy handle and darted out the opened back door with the bucket banging against his legs.

Chris allowed himself the briefest of smiles as he took the broom and began to sweep the water toward the door. *His* door, *his* shop. A tune came to mind and he began to whistle. The broom swished in time with his melody, but when he reached the doorway

39

and gave a mighty swing, Jimmy stepped into the line of fire and caught the broom's spray head on. For a moment the two stared in silence, then Jimmy slowly reached up to wipe a drip from the tip of his nose.

"Is this a christening of sorts, sir?" His voice sounded serious, but his eyes sparkled with merriment and Chris could contain his laughter no longer.

"Mr. Richardson, do come in," he chuckled. "I think we are going to do just fine."

For Jimmy the hours that followed only heightened his enthusiasm. He learned how to grease the iron ingot molds with tallow, and to hold his breath when Chris sooted the molds and the excess whale oil burned off. Fascinated, he kept the bellows steady as the crucible was positioned in the coals. An iron rod was placed into the crucible to act as a temperature gauge and when the rod was withdrawn from the red hot liquid, he gasped as sparks shot off in all directions.

"That tells me that the silver is ready for pouring," Chris said, carefully dumping a small shovel of sand to float onto the crucible's molten interior.

"Sir!" Jimmy gasped with disbelief. The only thing that he had learned from Walter Johnson was that dirt was the silversmith's worst enemy. He had polished the hammers and various shaped anvils for days on end, even when Mr. Johnson hadn't touched them. "Sir," Jimmy cleared his voice. "That's sand you've dumped in."

Chris set the small shovel to the side and reached for the tongs. "The sand will bake on the top and keep the air out. If we didn't do this the silver would absorb the air and when the ingot finally hardened, it would be full of holes."

Wide-eyed Jimmy watched as Chris carefully

tapped a small hole in the sand's hard surface then tipped the crucible to fill the waiting molds. He couldn't stop his gasp of dismay when a small piece of crusty sand broke off and fell into the mold.

"It's not a disaster, Jim," Chris said patiently, never taking his eyes from his work. "The sand will float to the surface as the metal cools. We have only to scrape it away." He set the red hot crucible back on the edge of the hearth and turned to watch the silver harden. "Did you mix the pickle solution like I asked?" Jimmy nodded vigorously, and Chris wondered how his neck managed not to snap.

Deciding that the time was right, Chris knelt down next to the sand-filled box on which the molds rested and using his tools carefully opened the first to withdraw a round silver ingot nearly an inch thick.

"Zounds," Jimmy reached for the shiny piece that was nearly the width of his hand.

"No!" Chris snapped, raising his voice for the first time. Taking the tongs, he carefully lifted the piece from its bed of sand and crossing to the far wall, lowered the ingot into the pickle solution. Steam rose to hiss and spit as the hot metal hit the water.

Jimmy looked down at his outstretched hand and his forehead wrinkled. "I didn't realize it would be so hot."

Chris turned back to the second mold and opened it like the first. "Metal that's hot enough to pour one minute might look cool the next, but it isn't. Just remember that you never touch anything sitting in the sand box with your bare hands. He lifted the second ingot with the tongs and it joined the first in the pickle barrel. "You have only to follow the procedures and you'll not have an accident. But if you find yourself in doubt, don't take the chance, use the tongs." When the third mold was tapped out and dumped into the pickle, Chris withdrew the first.

Relieved that the master didn't appear angry over the near mishap, and completely baffled as to how the thick disk of silver was going to turn into a coffee pot, Jimmy edged closer for a better look. "Does the water make it cool off faster?"

Chris turned and the two collided with Jimmy bouncing off Chris' hard chest to again land on the floor.

"A good apprentice has to learn not to sit down on the job," he teased, extending his hand to pull Jimmy to his feet. "The pickle solution contains sulfuric acid. It quenches the metal, making the silver more malleable as well as increasing its durability and cleaning the surface."

"Pickle juice can do all that?"

Chris slipped a leather apron over his head. "Come, give heed, for this will be your task starting with that second ingot."

Jimmy watched his new master perch on a low stool and spread his knees so the leather apron was stretched under the press. Carefully he cleaned the silver's edges of sand and then, with the disk secured in the press, he worked to smooth the surfaces, catching the silver scrapings he filed off in his apron so they could be saved. When the surface met with his approval, it was placed back in the coals until the silver turned a bright, cherry red.

"How did you know that was ready?" Jimmy demanded, taking the tongs from Chris so he could hold the disk secure on the anvil.

Chris raised his sledge hammer with both hands and struck hard on the disk's edge. "Although it seems impossible in the beginning, there will come a day when you'll know all the shades of red and the temperatures they indicate.

But for right now, just keep that disk in place."

Jimmy anxiously chewed on his lip as a thousand questions sprang to mind. How long would it take before he recognized what the red hot colors meant? When would he be allowed to work on his own projects? Could this flat disk of silver truly become a pot for coffee? And how ever did one gain the interest of so many ladies? Deep in thought, he didn't realize that his hands had gone slack on the tongs until a stroke from the hammer sent the piece skidding off the anvil to roll across the floor.

"Godamercy!" Jimmy dove after the twirling disk as it clanged along, the sound as loud as a cannon, announcing his failure to the world. The clattering seemed to last an eternity before he managed to grab the disk, but as his hand closed firmly around the metal, the heat of the silver startled him and with a yip his fingers flipped the disk away onto the sandbox. Gasping hard, and rubbing his hand against the coarse fabric of his breeches, he looked up to find Christopher standing over him, the sledge hammer still in his hands.

"Are you burned?"

Unable to speak, Jimmy shook his head. This is it, he thought, watching his dream disappear, and for a heartbeat he wondered if he'd be flogged or just bashed over the head with the hammer to be done with it. In petrified silence he watched Chris retrieve the disk and examine its surface. Deciding he could face the thrashing better if he was standing, Jimmy scrambled to his feet.

Chapter Three

Chris checked the silver, his gloved thumb rubbing the edges to test its smoothness. "You need to keep your mind on what you're about," he said quietly, placing the disk back into the coals. Bending, he scooped the tongs from the floor and handed them to his trembling apprentice. "A piece of silver can be repaired or replaced, but if your hand had slipped under the hammer, or melted onto the ingot, it would be a lot harder to repair those fingers."

"Yes, sir," Jimmy stammered. The two stood silent, watching the metal within the flames until again it turned a bright red. Chris placed it on the anvil and stepped back to raise the hammer.

Taking the tongs in a death grip, Jimmy's brow knotted with concentration and his knuckles grew white as he clutched the tongs to keep the silver piece secure. He had almost ruined an afternoon's work with his daydreaming but he hadn't been flogged, or even given a good set down. Cautiously looking up, he watched Chris raise the hammer to his shoulder. His muscles flexed and stretched from the weight, and with each stoke of the hammer the silver metal resting on the anvil moved ever so slowly to do the master's bidding. And with each stoke of the hammer, Jimmy's admiration grew.

The sun had long since started its homeward path before Chris set down his hammer for the last time. He winced from a twinge between his shoulder blades but the discomfort disappeared as he lifted the flattened ingot from the anvil. He let his hand run the surface, pleased with the even thickness of the piece.

"That's amazing," Jimmy's tone was hushed and filled with question. "I thought it was to be a coffee pot, but you made a perfect dinner plate."

Chris set the piece on the workbench. "A coffee-pot is indeed what it shall become, but it will take more than a week and your ears will ring from the noise before we're through."

Jimmy drew himself erect. "I ain't afraid of no noise. I'm gonna be the best apprentice you've ever had."

"Then now's the best time to start." Chris looked about the workroom with a feeling of satisfaction. "After you tidy up in here, join me in the front. I've some deliveries that you can see to while I try and sort through the orders that came in this morning."

"Yes, sir," Jimmy declared solemnly.

Chris was only half finished with his sorting when Jimmy emerged from the work room. "That was fast."

Jimmy grinned. "I'm speedy when I know what I'm about and my ma taught me to clean before I was tall enough to see over a wagon rut."

Chris made a silent note to introduce himself to Mrs. Richardson at the first opportunity. He reached for a pair of ornately worked silver buckles and slipped them into a velvet pouch of midnight blue. "Do you know Malachi Barclay?" He checked the name on the parchment. "We need to get these buckles to him."

Jimmy took a step backward. "That's gonna be real hard, sir," he stammered.

Chris looked up from the papers that covered his desk. "You don't know the man? Well no matter. According to the receipt he resides at the Stag's Head Tavern just down the road."

Jimmy took a deep breath and twisted his hands together. "I don't think Mr. Barclay is much worried about them buckles, sir."

Chris checked the order again. "Of course he is. The man paid a handsome price for these and for some reason Walter had him pay in advance."

"It was probably a good thing then, cause old Malachi Barclay is dead."

Chris looked up in surprise. "What?"

"About a week ago, I think. I didn't go to the funeral or nothing so I couldn't say for sure. But I know he's dead and it weren't no loss if you was to ask me."

Not anxious to become involved in town gossip his first day in the shop, Chris stared down at the pouch in his hand. "Well, that does make it take a different tune. Wait, was Barclay married?"

"Yes, sir, but I don't know the lady."

"Then we must deliver these buckles to her. She'll be pleased to receive them if only as a keepsake. Walter did excellent work on this pair and they're one of the most costly sets I've ever seen."

"So you want me to take these over to the tavern and see if I can find the Widow Barclay?"

Chris tied the draw strings and handed the small pouch to Jim. "Deliver these and offer condolences on behalf of the shop. I'll have the next delivery ready by the time you get back."

Jimmy gave a mock salute. "Aye, aye, sir." Then with a slam of the door the boy was off and running down the street.

Turning his attention back to his paperwork, Chris continued to sort through the scattered pieces of parchment. Betsy Alders had commissioned an ornate coffee pot, a copy of the one that had graced his mother's table, and when Marigold had glanced down and seen the order, she had changed her needs to encompass a complete coffee service with both sugar and creamers as well as the silver buckles she had originally wanted as a gift for her father. His expression turned grim as he realized the magnitude of the work before him. He scanned the names again, Betsy, Marigold, Catherine, Elizabeth. He had expected their support, indeed even welcomed their enthusiasm, but this was ridiculous. Did they really know him so little that they thought to buy his affections? And would their enthusiasm last once he made his choice of partner for the Governor's Ball? The thought left a sour taste in his mouth and his delight in the morning's business faded. Slipping the commissions into a cubbyhole within his desk, Chris stood and stretched again. His stomach rumbled and as he pulled on his waistcoat, his eyes found the baskets that still rested askew on the back counter. Thoughts of spicy gingerbread brought back his good humor. Ruby had hinted that Mrs. Killingham, the Beaumonts' cook, had made something special for him and now his mouth watered in anticipation. He had been stealing pieces of Mrs. Killingham's gingerbread ever since he and Nick had returned from school together. Even though a score of years had passed, the memory still warmed him. Poking through the baskets, he grinned again at the size of the apples Betsy had procured. Lifting one, he was surprised to find its mate. He would have placed odds that Jimmy had devoured it, seeds and all.

The door to the shop swung open, setting the bell above on a merry dance. Chris turned to find Jimmy leaning against the doorjamb clutching a daisy. "That was fast. Did you make the delivery?"

Jimmy looked up, confusion written all over his young face. "I found her, but she wouldn't take them." He took a deep breath and glanced about the shop as if seeing it for the first time.

Chris frowned as he motioned the boy out of the doorway and tossed him an apple, bringing a lopsided smile to the apprentice's flushed face. "You told her the pieces were paid for?"

Jimmy bit into the apple and nodded.

"Did you show her the fine craftsmanship? Mayhap the design didn't suit."

Jimmy chewed quickly and gulped. "I never showed her what was in the pouch, sir. When she said she didn't want them, I guess I was so surprised that I just left."

Chris relaxed and leaned back against the counter. "That must be the answer. Go back and show her the fine workmanship, but tell her that if they are not what she desires we can alter them to fit a ladies shoe if that would better suit her needs."

Jimmy wolfed down the last of the apple and his eyes brightened. "You want me to go back again tonight?" He glanced at the fine wooden clock that rested on the shop's mantel.

Chris reached for his coat and the basket that contained his cake. "Aye, deliver the buckles then get yourself home and have a good night's rest. I'll expect you come first light tomorrow morning."

"Yes, sir." Jimmy slipped the velvet pouch and the daisy into his pocket and his palms began to sweat.

"Ah, sir? Might I ask a question of you?"

Chris watched his apprentice blush to the roots of his sandy hair. He waited, but the lad only turned a brighter shade of crimson. "It's growing late Jim, and you still need to see to the widow before your day is done. Do you wish to postpone this chat until the morrow?"

Jimmy's head snapped up. "No sir, it's just . . . sorta personal."

Chris folded his arms across his chest and took in the boy's bedraggled appearance. His shirt might once have been white, but was now a sorry shade of gray and tucked into breeches that would have fit a man twice his size. "Do you need money, lad? Did Walter Johnson not purchase you a suit of clothing?"

Jimmy looked down at his breeches and shirt, the nicest garments he had ever owned. "Oh, no sir, I mean Mr. Johnson did give me these, sir."

"Then what is the problem, lad?"

Jimmy looked down at his feet and took a deep breath. "I was wondering, sir, please don't think me forward or nothing, but, I ain't got no Pa, and well I was wondering, did you really like them ladies bringing you all that food?"

"What?"

Jimmy gulped and rushed on, his words tumbling one after another. "I mean all that food . . . peach pies, syllabub, apples . . . is food what you give to someone if you want them to take notice of you?"

Christopher felt a grin begin to tug at his lips. So Jim Richardson had a sweetheart. Careful to keep his eyes from betraying his amusement, he gave the matter serious thought. "I would think that anything, no matter how small, if given from the heart would be most appreciated."

Jimmy heard the words of wisdom echo over and over in his head. "Then you don't pay no mind to how dear something is?"

"It's the thought and the reason behind the gift, Jim, that one needs to take to heart."

Lost in his dreams, Jimmy reached for the door knob. "Thank you, sir," he mumbled.

"Jim, don't forget to stop at the Stag's Head before you start home."

"The Stag's Head, sir?"

Chris' expression turned stern. Young love was one thing, but not if it interfered with the boy's work. "I'll be vexed if on the morrow I find that you've forgotten to stop and deliver those buckles to the Widow Barclay."

Jimmy blushed again as his head bobbed in silent apology. "I'm on my way, sir," he stammered reaching for the door knob.

"Jim, wait." And as the boy turned, Chris tossed the other apple. Jimmy's bright eyes flashed gratitude before he was gone again, slamming the door behind him.

Chris shook his head and wondered who was leading his apprentice on such a merry chase. He opened the windows and secured the shutters before closing and latching the windows for the night. He locked the shop's front door and then with the basket in one hand and his coat slung over his shoulder, he opened the door to the private quarters that occupied the side of the shop.

The September air was too warm for a fire, but Chris lit two lanterns and placed them high on their pegs. His stomach growled again as he used the cloth from Sarah's basket to cover the table then laid out its contents. His eyes took in the thick slices of cold meat and cheese but it was the grand slice of gingerbread covered with lemon glaze that his hand reached for. Not bothering with a plate or fork, he took a hearty bite of the tempting fare. His foot hooked the room's only chair and pulled it to the table. Lowering his lean frame onto the straight wooden seat, he let the tart lemon icing melt on his tongue. His shoulders held a pleasant ache from his afternoon's work, for his responsibilities at his parents' plantation had seldom offered a complete day that could be spent on his craft. He popped the cork from the wine Sarah had included and drank it straight from the bottle. Now he could work at his silver for hours on end if it suited him, not steal moments here and there only to feel guilty that another chore was going unattended. He thought of his parents, the memory of their passing still fresh with pain. "How is it that you knew me better than I knew myself?" he wondered. Wiping his hands, Chris reached into his waistcoat pocket and withdrew a heart-shaped silver locket. It was old and dented, but well polished. His fingers smoothed lovingly over the piece, the first one he had ever completed, and his first gift to his mother. "I would have buried this with you," he whispered to the empty room. "But how glad I am you left it for me." He looked about the stark room, bare save for the small wooden table and the chair on which he sat. "It's not much to look on at the moment, but in time . . ." He let his thoughts wander.

The crickets began their night song, the stars winked in lazy patterns overhead, and still clutching his mother's silver locket, Christopher Carlson fell asleep on his hard backed wooden chair.

Abigail sat at a corner table in the empty dining room. It was well past the dinner hour and she glanced longingly toward the mug of steaming coffee Obadiah had placed before her, but the energy to reach for it had abandoned her. Why had she never realized just how many tasks needed to be performed each day to keep the tavern running smoothly? She had freed Malachi's slaves only to become one herself. The garden needed tending, there were cows to milk and butter to churn, floors to sweep, laundry to hang, indoor chores, outdoor chores, the list seemed endless. Her head dropped forward and she took a deep, fortifying breath of the aromatic coffee. Obadiah and Nanny had been the only ones who chose to remain at the tavern. And although they willingly tackled as many extra chores as possible, Nanny's time was necessary in the cookhouse and Obadiah's thin shoulders were not meant to take over the heavier tasks and Thomas' carefully tended woodpile had eventually been depleted.

Abigail looked down at the blisters that lined her palm. She had chopped enough wood to supply the cookhouse for the day, but the responsibility had roused her from her pallet before dawn and consumed more hours than she cared to count. Her shoulders ached, and the entire process had to be repeated again on the morrow. The blisters stung, and she struggled against the despair that of late threatened to be her constant companion.

Obadiah finished wiping down the last table and scowled at his young mistress. "You gots ta eat something and then get some rest, Miz Abby, cause if you get much thinner, I 'spect one day soon you'll just blow away like the wisps on a dandelion seed."

Abigail slowly reached for the coffee. "I'm fine, Obbie. You go on and tell Nanny not to start washing those dishes before I get out there."

"Miz Abby, you been working all day without

stopping. Now those dishes can wait. I'm gonna bring you a big helping of okra soup and I don't wants you getting out of that chair until the bowl is licked clean." He gave her an appraising stare. "What you really need is to eat some meat, but the gentlemen done ate all the tongue and utter."

A tired smile crossed her face. "It's Nanny's ginger gravy that keeps them calling for more and if all is gone then we must have done better than I thought."

Obbie shoved a tattered gray rag into his apron pocket. "Got two handfuls of shillings in the box."

She felt a moment of satisfaction before the memory of irate merchants shoved it aside. Demanding payment and clutching fists full of overdue notes, they had descended on her like a flock of vultures to pick the bones clean. She had reasoned and pleaded for more time, but in the end had doled out the last of her tiny hoard of coins. Now, her only ready money was the small box of shillings from today's dinner. Despite the pain from her blisters, she clutched her mug tightly with both hands.

"My real money is safely hidden in my book." Malachi's taunting words ran through her mind again and again, and her brow wrinkled with thought. Twice she had overheard him bragging. "I'll never want for money in this town. There's enough in the book to keep me in style for the rest of my life."

Enjoying the steam that rose to greet her as she blew on her mug, Abby took a small sip and then another. "I'm going to make a success of things, Mr. Barclay," she declared softly. "Despite what you've done, I'm going to survive. It won't matter that I can't find your blasted book. I'm going to succeed on my own."

"Beg pardon, Miz Abby?" Abby only shook her head and took another sip of her coffee. "Then you just sits there while I gets this last tray into the cookhouse. I'll be back with your dinner before you can blink twice and count backwards."

True to his word, Obadiah reappeared with a bowl of steaming soup and a basket of freshly baked bread. Knowing better than to say she wasn't hungry, Abby lifted a spoon of the hearty soup thick with okra and tomatoes from her garden. It had yet to reach her mouth when a loud banging sounded at the front door.

"I'll see to it," Obadiah said quickly. "You eat before that cools."

Gratefully, Abby sank back onto her chair and again lifted her spoon. The soup was hot and delicious, and suddenly she realized she was ravenous. Pulling off a hunk of bread she dipped a corner into the spicy mixture then sighed with pleasure as her teeth bit into the tasty morsel.

"It was the young Richardson boy from the silver shop again," Obadiah stated pulling the door closed behind him. "I told him that you was eating so he said he'd wait around back."

Feeling her appetite vanish, Abby slowly placed her spoon on the dark wood table. "I wish you had turned him away."

Obadiah looked up from arranging the wine bottles for supper. "You want me to tell him to come back tomorrow?"

I don't want him to come back at all, she thought wearily. Carefully refolding her napkin, she pushed back her chair and took a deep breath. Would she never be rid of remembrances of her husband? "No, I'll see him now and have done with it."

"But Miz Abby, you ain't finished eating. The boy don't have no problem with waiting. Why don't you finish that soup?"

Abby shook her head and wondered if the churning in her stomach would ever truly settle. "He's come about those buckles again, I just know it. It was probably a mistake when he told me they were paid for and now he wants his master's money."

"What you want me to do?"

For a moment she savored the thoughts of Obadiah simply sending the boy away. But in her heart she knew he'd just be back again and each time a knock sounded at the door, she'd jump and wonder. Squaring her shoulders, she tucked a stray curl back under her cap. "You finish in here, Obbie. I shall deal with the boy." She started to remove her apron then remembered it covered the unsightly patch on her skirt. With a shrug of her shoulders Abby made her way down the back hall. Then she heard it, the rhythmic sound of an ax biting into wood. Her hand flew to her heart with anticipation, had Thomas or Harley returned? Her step quickened but the sight that greeted her in the doorway stopped her cold. The errand boy from the silver shop had draped his coat over a tree limb and was splitting her wood. Totally confused Abby crossed the wide porch and flew down the stairs.

"What are you doing?" she called. Startled, the boy missed his swing, burying the ax deep in the stump he used for a base.

Jimmy swallowed hard and forced himself to turn. He could feel the heat creeping up his neck. "You had wood that needed splitting," he stammered, praying his voice wouldn't squeak. "I thought I'd do some while I waited. I didn't mean no harm or nothing."

Abby shook her head trying to make sense of what was happening. "You just decided to split those logs because you were waiting here?"

He nodded nervously and wished he hadn't let go of the ax cause now he didn't know what to do with his hands. Desperately, he tried to picture what his master would do at a moment like this. Mr. Carlson was always so at ease when the ladies came to call, laughing, chatting, smiling. He gave Abby a sheepish grin. When she hesitantly returned his smile, Jimmy felt his insides melt like butter too long in the sun. Lordy, she was beautiful. Her skin was pale; no, delicate, he decided; no, angelic. She was just what he had always thought an angel would look like, 'cept maybe she'd be dressed in white. He could see the stray wisps of golden hair that had slipped from her cap and wondered if they'd feel like silk on his fingers. Then her smile faded and his heart stopped beating.

"I can't pay you for this." She gestured toward the wood he'd already split.

Jimmy gulped and tried to get his Adam's apple out of his mouth. "I didn't expect no pay, ma'am. I mean, it was just sitting there so I thought I'd keep busy."

"I appreciate your kindness, Master Richardson. But . . ."

"Jimmy," he interrupted, feeling his face grow hot again. "You can call me Jimmy. I . . . ah . . . I brought you something."

Spinning so quickly he nearly tripped over his own feet, Abby watched as his hand dove into the wide square pocket on his coat. Folding her arms across her chest, she stood her ground. She was not going to pay for Malachi's ridiculous silver buckles. Jimmy Richardson could just take them right back where they came from.

"I brought you this . . ." tentatively he turned, balancing a large red apple in the palm of his hand.

He gave the fruit several swipes across his shirt before offering it.

Stunned, Abby could only stare in silence at the boy's gift.

"Ah, well."

She watched the pleasure fade from his eyes and the hand holding the apple dropped to his side.

"You probably already got enough apples. You'd probably rather had an orange or something."

Hesitantly she stepped forward and touched his sleeve. "Actually," she replied softly, "I have quite a fondness for apples. But wherever did you find one so large?" She smiled in question and watched the boy's face grow pink.

"I think it came up from Jamestown," he stammered, not willing to tell a lie, but unwilling to admit the truth.

"Well, it was more than thoughtful of you to bring it to me. Thank you." She took the apple and held it reverently with both hands. "I don't think I know what to make of you, Master Richardson." She tipped her head to the side as if to better study him. "First you come and chop wood for free and then I find that the real reason for your visit is to bring me a treasure. What am I to make of that?"

Jimmy gulped and shifted from foot to foot. What would Mr. Carlson do? His mind scrambled frantically, but his brain had turned to corn mush and his mouth went dry as she continued to smile at him. Shoving his hands into the pockets of his breeches and trying desperately to appear aloof, his fingers touched the velvet pouch and reality came back with a jolt.

"I know when we spoke before you said you didn't want your order from the silver shop," he mumbled as he withdrew the pouch. "But Mr. Carlson said

57

that I should have showed you the fine workmanship and stressed that you really must take them."

"And you're here to deliver and collect payment?"

Concentrating on the impossible task of untangling the drawstrings, Jimmy missed the chill that touched her words. "No, madam, your husband already paid in full. Mr. Carlson, my master, thought you'd care for these as a keepsake and said I was to give you condolences from the shop." Pleased that he had remembered each of his instructions, he looked up and was startled to find she had turned away and was moving stiffly toward the porch. Damn, he swore silently, what had he said?

"You may tell Mr. Carlson I appreciate his thoughts on the matter, but he's mistaken." Her voice was cold and her back straighter than a ramrod. "I didn't want the buckles before, I don't want them now, and you can assure him that I won't want them tomorrow." Fueled by anger, Abby climbed the steps.

"Mrs. Barclay."

"The answer is no."

"Mrs. Barclay, please . . ."

The pleading tone of the young boy's voice caused her to pause and then turn slowly at the top of the steps.

"Please, Mrs. Barclay." Desperately Jimmy looked down at the pouch then took a step toward the porch. Her eyes were bleak her face pale and tense. She still misses her husband, he thought miserably. "Mrs. Barclay, I've only been with Mr. Carlson for a day. I already messed up more times than I can count and if I go back with these buckles again . . ."

Abby felt her resolve begin to crumble. She knew only too well what it was like to work for an unappreciative and unyielding master. Her toe tapped an agitated rhythm on the wooden floor. "It's important that you make a good impression on this Mr. Carlson then?"

Jimmy nodded enthusiastically. "My family, well they really need me to have this position. If I come back again like I did before . . ." Jimmy crossed the fingers of one hand behind his back and hoped he wouldn't be damned to hell for telling such an outlandish untruth. "Mr. Carlson, well, he might not want to keep an apprentice that can't even make a simple delivery. You gotta help me, ma'am. Please!" His last word was almost a cry of desperation.

Abby sighed with resignation then motioned the boy onto the porch. Holding the pouch by the strings she let the small velvet bag swing from her fingers. "There are two silver buckles inside?"

Jimmy nodded, standing close enough to learn that she smelled like spice. "I'm sorry the string's so knotted."

She brushed aside his apology. "If these are mine now, free and clear of debt, I may do with them what I wish?"

"Yes, ma'am. Mr. Carlson said that if you don't like the design he'd do them over for you. He's real good, ma'am."

Abby grimaced. "I care as much for Mr. Carlson's talent as I do for his advice. Now, listen to me, for I'll not say this twice. These are mine, so I am giving them to you." She reached for the boy's hand and closed his fingers around the soft pouch. "Consider them a thank you for splitting that wood."

"But I didn't even chop half a cord," Jimmy stammered. "And these are costly buckles. Mr. Carlson said he'd never seen a more expensive pair."

"If you won't take them as payment," she paused uncertainly, then her eyes glowed with satisfaction.

59

"You may consider them a gift, Master Richardson. A gift for the kindness you've shown me today. Now you must forgive me but I've much to attend to. Supper will be served shortly. Good day."

"But . . ." Jimmy's protest fell silent when Abby turned and entered the tavern. Well this is a fine pickle you've gotten yourself into, he muttered. What is Mr. Carlson going to say? Slowly he descended the steps and reached for his coat. He had seen the fresh blisters on her hands and wondered why they were there. Surely she hadn't been trying to chop wood. He dismissed the thought as quickly as it came. She owned a tavern, and tavern owners didn't chop their own wood. Still, she had been doing something to get those blisters.

He eyed the woodpile and the scant amount he had already split, then his fingers closed over the velvet pouch in his hand. Slipping the pouch into his pocket, he tossed his coat back over the branch. No stranger to wielding an ax, Jimmy had a rhythm going in no time. He paused only once when the whack of the back door sounded and she magically appeared. She thanked him again for the apple, then with a smile she vanished back into the tavern. Before the sun had fled from the sky, the Widow Barclay had a wood stack that would see her through the week.

Exactly when the idea had come, Jimmy would never be sure. But his plan gave a swing to his step as he started home. He would give one of the buckles to his mother, but the other, the other he would take to the silver shop. He withdrew the pouch as he walked down the dusty road. They were a weighty pair. If he took one for himself, he could melt it down and then make the Widow Barclay a gift. He smiled thinking of how pleased she had been with

60

the apple. And if a simple piece of fruit would make her smile that way, then what would she do if he gave her a solid silver brooch that he had designed himself? Heady with the notion, Jimmy didn't even mind his long walk.

Chapter Four

"She did what?" Chris turned from the design he was perfecting to face his apprentice.

"I gave them to her just like you said, sir. I even remembered to tell her you thought they would be a fine keepsake. Well, she took them and then she said that she was giving them to me for chopping the wood."

Chris set down his thin charcoal stick and began to scrape away excess clay from the model he was sculpting to match the design. "And just how much wood did you have to chop?"

Jimmy shrugged. "That's the bite of it sir, she didn't seem to care. That's when she said they were a gift from her to me."

Had grief made the widow lose her reasoning? Chris wondered, molding the clay to produce the shape of a leaf. He knew only too well how deeply pain and loneliness could cut. Mayhap he had erred in sending the boy when he should have gone himself. "How is the widow faring?" he asked.

Jimmy's eyes slid closed as he leaned boneless against the counter. "She's beautiful," he sighed, a wistful smile touching his mouth. "She's so beautiful."

"I asked how she was faring, not how fair she was."

Jimmy jerked upright from the tone in his master's voice. "I'm sorry, sir," he stammered in embarrassment. "It's just that . . ." Jimmy couldn't find the words. How did he explain that he had found the girl of his dreams, but she had married another. He had tried to guess her age, but no matter how he ciphered, the odds that she would wait for him to finish his seven year apprenticeship were never in his favor.

"I think she's still very much in love with her husband, sir," Jimmy straightened and tried not to show how much it hurt to state the fact aloud. "Each time he was mentioned she seemed to go all queer and shuddery. I think her loss is so great that facing the memories is more than she can bear. Did I do wrong, sir, by taking the buckles? It just didn't seem right to press her further when she was already so upset."

Chris rubbed his hand over his smooth jaw and wondered why life could never be simple. "No, lad, you did the right thing. But my concern is that a fortnight from now when the pangs of grief are not so strong, the widow might regret her decision."

"You think she might want the buckles back?" Jimmy felt his heart begin to pound with disappointment. His mother had been so pleased with the buckle, then panic set in. If he returned the silver, he wouldn't have the means to make Mrs. Barclay a gift. Unless, his mind raced on . . . her gift was already made when she asked for the buckles. Excitement churned through his limbs. He could copy one of Mr. Carlson's designs, and they were going to pour molds that very morning. He'd commit to memory each move the master made. It wouldn't be hard to come back to the shop at night, especially if

63

he had the design already chosen. His heart soared with the possibilities. He'd make the grandest brooch she had ever seen. She'd be so overcome by his gift, she'd forget all about her dead husband and smile again. Maybe she'd be so pleased she'd not take to heart how young he was. The thought of her smile made his knees go weak.

"Jim," Chris snapped. "Have you heard a word I've said?"

Jimmy looked about in confusion and spied the empty water bucket sitting by the hearth. "Yes, sir, I'll have the bucket filled in no time."

Chris stared at his new design and prayed for patience. Was the widow overcome with grief like the boy said, or was she the type to dally with the affections of a lad just ten and four? Making a mental note to stop by the tavern later in the day, Chris added another flourish to his design. He'd meet the Widow Barclay and make his own decision. Until then he'd be too busy to think about it. But think about it he did, each time he looked up and caught Jimmy's love-sick grin staring into space. What kind of woman could she be, he wondered. The boy hadn't seemed the least affected by the other beauties that had glided through the shop. Just what was it about the Widow Barclay that made her so special?

Abigail counted the small handful of coins for a second time as Nanny entered the dining room, tying a red kerchief about her white hair. "I wish you and Obadiah didn't have to travel clear to Jamestown to purchase supplies," she said, placing the money back in their small wooden box and handing it to the elderly woman.

"Don't you fret, child," Nanny clucked. "You

know that we ken get better down in Jamestown. Obadiah's got folks that don't mind our company for the night and this way we be there for first light."

Abby looked out at the dusty shadows of the night. "I just wish you didn't have to travel in the dark."

Nanny shook her head. "Now you don't go getting yourself all worked up again. Old Sallymule knows the way so good we could probably send her by herself if she could say what she wanted when she got there."

The absurdity of the notion made Abby chuckle in spite of her misgivings. "If Sallymule knows the way so well, I still don't see why I can't go and leave you both here to rest."

Nanny tucked the money box deep within the folds of her cape. "Now, Miz Abby we've been over this so many times that I know it by heart. It ain't proper for you to go off to Jamestown at night by yourself, child. What people gonna think about you, you go and do a fool stunt like that?"

Abby's chin lifted stubbornly. "Nanny, I don't give a hoot what people think."

Nanny sighed and patted Abby's cheek. "But you'd care if they stopped coming to dinner. We ain't had no overnighters since way before the Master done got himself killed. If people stop coming for their meals then none of us would have any place to go, and Obbie and me, we are just too old to start off with new masters."

"But you're not slaves anymore," Abby argued. "You have the papers that say you're free."

Nanny harumphed and made her way slowly toward the back door. "Freedom's only a state of mind, child. I been free since the day the master died. I don't need no paper to tell me so. Now you, on the other hand, you still don't know that you free. You're like a little bird so long in a cage that now the door be open, you be afraid to fly away."

The mule brayed and Nanny pulled her cape snug against her ample hips. "I best be getting now. Once old Sallymule gets it in her head to start walking it ain't the time to tell her to wait."

"Please be careful," Abby whispered.

Nanny moved slowly down the steps. "I 'spect we be back by breakfast but there's corn chowder and bacon ready if we late. Obadiah ground the coffee, just don't add too much chicory like you did last time. And when we gets back, I don't want to find you with them dark circles under your eyes. You take to your bed and sleep, child. Obadiah already checked all the doors, so you only got to lock this one. Now, I'm gone, so you find your bed."

Abby followed the old woman out onto the back porch and watched as Obbie helped her onto the wagon. Then with a click of the tongue old Sally-mule was moving. Turning back toward the beckoning doorway, she began to tick off the chores that stood between her and her pallet, but before she could take a step, she froze as a shadow moved on the far end of the porch. Her heart stopped beating and her mouth went dry. Obadiah had told her there had been break-ins. Someone had stolen into the Brackstone's root cellar, and that was but three doors down.

"Who's there?" Abby stammered, pulling her shawl closer about her shoulders and praying no one would answer. "You just go away now, or I'll . . . I'll fetch my husband." She felt the word catch in her mouth and nearly gagged.

"Then 'tis not true and he's still alive?"

Abby frowned and kept her eyes firmly fixed on the corner. "Who's there?"

"Abby?" the voice was halting and familiar. "Abby, it's me, Suzannah."

Relief was pushed aside by anger as Abigail Barclay marched to the end of the porch to find her younger sister huddled near the corner. "Suzannah Forester, what are you trying to do? You scared me so you near turned my hair as white as Nanny's."

"Is it true he's still alive?" Suzannah's eyes darted about with fright. "We heard he was dead!"

"He's dead, Suzannah, I just said that to frighten off any would-be robbers." Taking her sister's hand Abby pulled her into the tavern. Carefully she locked the back door and then lit another taper to push the shadows from the room. Her sister's dark hair flowed in tangles about her shoulders and her eyes were wild and haunted. Abby recognized the look and a feeling of dread seeped back into her tired bones.

"Suzannah, what's happened?"

Suzannah tossed her thick main back from her face and shrugged out of the dark cape that had concealed her so well in the shadows. Her chemise slipped, revealing the rounded curve of her pale shoulder but she ignored it. "I've run away," she declared defiantly. "I'm through with listening to men and I'll be damned if I'm going to be a doormat any more."

"Suzannah, hush," Abby gasped, pushing her sister's chemise back into place. Her eyes darted nervously about the deserted back room. "Don't speak so harshly."

Suzannah's eyes flashed with anger. "I'll not hush. I'm not like you, sister, content to be a quiet little mouse and do as I'm told."

67

Abby felt her own anger spark. Maybe she hadn't possessed the strength to stand up to her father or her husband, but she had survived hadn't she? Surely that had to count for something.

"Malachi is dead but you're still afraid of empty shadows," Suzannah taunted. "Well, not me. Father has decided he no longer needs me as his house-keeper so I'm to be sold in marriage to a man named Fiddler Smith."

Abby watched tears well in her sister's eyes and her heart went out to her. "Mayhap it will be a good thing, Suzannah. I know since mother died you've yearned to be away from father."

"That's the twist of it," Suzannah sniffed back the hated tears. "I want to be on my own, not married to some horrid old man. He's had three wives and each has died; and under circumstances that are more than curious. The last one, Lucy Parker, was youn-ger than I by two years. She fell down the steps and broke her neck."

Abby pressed her palm against the frantic beating of her heart. "Surely, Father won't marry you to someone with such a questionable reputation."

"He married you to Malachi Barclay, didn't he?" Watching her sister's face grow pale, Suzannah felt her frustration turn to regret. Dearest Abby, who al-ways tried to protect the world when she couldn't even protect herself. She had always been slender but now she looked positively frail. Dark smudges ringed her eyes and her face was taut with worry. And now I've added to her burden, Suzannah thought misera-bly. "Abby, I'll be twenty-and-one this very summer and I've no dowry. No man of genteel qualities is go-ing to present himself a-begging to take me to wife. So I've decided to run away."

"Does father know?"

Suzannah began to pace. "No, but this is the first place he'll think to look." Wearily she dropped onto a side bench and looked up at her sister. "I would never have come to see you but I needed to warn you."

Abby edged down on the bench beside her sister. "You ran away from home to warn me? Of what?" She closed her eyes and remembered back to a warm summer day when they had played as children. High in the loft, away from Father's angry belt, they told stories and made up dreams of their future. "Miss Whiskers is going to have kittens tomorrow," Suzannah had declared. "You can have the white one but I want the one that's got orange stripes."

"You don't know that," she had challenged, angry that her younger sister, who was not yet four, had known something she hadn't. "You're just guessing."

Suzannah had set her jaw and stared in that stubborn way of hers. "I know what's going to be," she said firmly. "And if you don't believe me, just wait." The next day they stole off to the barn each chance they got. Suzannah had been right. Miss Whiskers had her kittens in the exact colors predicted. Abby stared in awe at her younger sister. "I just know things sometimes," was all she would say. But Suzannah didn't always know everything, and later that day, when her beloved orange kitten had died, nothing Abby did would console her.

"You've had another of your 'visions?' "

Suzannah nodded slowly. "Abby, I saw it as clear as I see you before me. It's a fire. People screaming and shouting, but the flames just dance higher against the dark night sky. I've seen it twice now. That's why I knew that even though father would probably follow me here, I had to come and warn you first." Her eyes hardened. "I took money from

69

his room. Do you know that I've more than fifty pounds?"

"Fifty pounds?" Abby gasped. "Where would he get such a fortune?"

Suzannah stiffened suddenly. "The danger, it's close." Her eyes grew wide with fright. "Dear God, Abby we need to find it; put it out. I can smell the smoke."

Abby grabbed her sister's shoulders and gave a hard shake to get the sanity back in her eyes. Suzannah terrified her when she got this way. "Where? Suzannah, where is the fire?"

Suzannah blinked. "I don't know," she looked about in confusion. "I can feel the heat starting."

"Then we shall search," Abby said firmly, fighting to keep the fear from her voice. "We'll just start on the top floor of the tavern and work our way down." Suzannah nodded mutely and took the candle holder Abby pressed into her hand. But as they reached the stairs in the main hall, both women screamed in fright as a loud knock sounded at the front door.

"Oh God, it's father." Suzannah dropped to the stair like a small trapped animal. "I'll never get away now."

"Is there trouble in there?" called a deep, masculine voice. "Mrs. Barclay . . . are you all right?"

Abby bit on her knuckle to keep from crying out in relief. She knew not the owner of the voice, but it definitely wasn't father. "Who's there?" she called leaning closer to the wooden door.

"Mrs. Barclay, my name is Christopher Carlson. We've not met but I'm the new proprietor for the silver shop down the road. I know the hour is late, but might I speak with you a moment?"

Abby let her forehead drop against the door. No wonder young Jimmy was so apprehensive of his master, she thought. The man was as tenacious as a hungry dog with a bone. "I told your apprentice, sir, I . . ."

Like one possessed, Suzannah scrambled past her sister and turned the latch. "We need him to help us look," she cried, fumbling with the lock. "We're never going to find it on our own."

Christopher stepped back as the door flew open to reveal a raven-haired beauty. Grabbing his arm, she tugged him inside. "Mrs. Barclay?" he smiled, taken aback by her forwardness. No wonder Jimmy was so enchanted.

"We don't have time to waste." Her dark eyes were wide with fright. "You must help us." Dropping his arm she started up the main stairs.

"Mr. Carlson, I'm Abigail Barclay. That is my sister Suzannah Forester."

Christopher turned and realized a second woman stood beside him. Raised to believe that all women deserved his respect, he struggled to keep the surprise from his voice. "You're Mrs. Barclay?" Surely this could not be the one Jimmy Richardson had lost his heart to. Despite himself, he stared in wonder. It wasn't that she was homely, her features were good, but in a quiet way. Her hair, unlike her sister's, was completely hidden beneath a ridiculous cap, but he knew without a doubt it wasn't the same rich dark color. Realizing what he was doing, he cleared his throat with embarrassment. "Mrs. Barclay, I beg pardon for calling so late, but I heard a scream. Is there a problem here?"

Abigail struggled to find her voice. Never had her eyes feasted on a man with such striking looks. His face held concern, and his eyes . . . she felt her heart skip a beat. His eyes were the same shade of blue as the robin's egg she had once kept so carefully. She

71

felt her mouth go dry. How often had she crawled away to the back nook of the woodshed to escape from Malachi's abusive temper after a beating, to cradle the tiny egg in the palm of her hand and wish for a different life. It had become a talisman of sorts, until Malachi had crept up on her one day and found her holding it. He had tormented her unmercifully then the robin's egg and the last of her dreams had been soundly crushed beneath the heel of his boot.

"Mrs. Barclay, are you ill?" Chris watched with alarm as her face grew paler still. "What can I do?" He reached to steady her, but the widow deftly sidestepped his touch.

Abby tried to recapture her scattered thoughts. How did one tell a gentleman that the color of his eyes haunted her memory. That the breadth of his shoulders was intimidating. That his presence was not welcome. Desperately she struggled to find the words that would make him leave; knowing that to tell him of Suzannah's vision would be to condemn her sister to public ridicule . . . if not worse.

"Mrs. Barclay . . ." he prompted.

"There is naught amiss here, sir." Abigail struggled to keep her voice even. "We were just on our way above stairs when the sound of your knock gave us a start. I fear you have called at a most inconvenient moment." She clenched her hands tightly before her.

"Abby come quick . . ." Suzannah's terrified cry echoed down the stairs. "It has started, the fire has started . . . I can feel the heat."

"Dear Lord, Suzannah where are you?" Abby gathered up her skirts and raced up the stairs like one chased by the devil. "Suzannah?"

Hearing the word "fire," Christopher took the stairs two at a time, crowding past Abby to reach the top before her. Following the sound of a panicked cry, he found Suzannah Forester standing in the middle of a wide communal bedroom. Snatching the candlestick from her trembling fingers he scanned the room but could find no threat.

"Are there boarders?" Not waiting for an answer he moved about the room with quick efficient motions, pulling beds from the wall and lifting spreads to peer at the floor hidden beneath. He found nothing.

"Suzannah, where is the fire?" Abby pleaded.

Suzannah continued to stare with her eyes locked wide in horror. "Can't you find it?" she cried. "Oh God, Abby I can smell the smoke growing thicker."

Leaving the two women in the middle of the room, Christopher quickly checked the remaining bed chambers, but his search was fruitless. The evening still contained the stifling heat from the day so no fires had been lit. There were no boarders so no candles burned, beckoning the weary traveler to his bedside. Confused, he made his way back to Mrs. Barclay and her sister.

Taking a firm grip on the widow's arm, he ignored her startled gasp as he pulled her out of the doorway and into the hall. "I've checked all the chambers on this floor and found nothing. Now why is she babbling about a fire?" He saw her flinch and instantly his tone softened. "Mrs. Barclay," he cajoled. "I'll not be able to help you if you don't share with me what is wrong. Is she touched in the head?"

Abby looked up at the sympathetic expression on his face and, despite her resolve, began to tremble. Did she dare confide that Suzannah could predict the future . . . sometimes. Or would they fare better to send the imposing Mr. Carlson on his way? Her thoughts ran in all directions and she twisted her

73

hands in frustration. Then his expression changed before her eyes and in that moment her worst fear came to pass.

"She has the gift of sight?" His words were more statement than question, and Abby could only nod her head in confirmation. Chris let out a low whistle between his teeth. He had heard of such things but never had he experienced it first hand. "Is she always right?" he challenged. "I can't . . ."

Lightning flashed, illuminating the hallway, exposing all its shadowy corners. Abby bit back her scream but the crash of thunder that followed propelled her into Christopher Carlson's arms.

The last rumble of thunder faded and Abigail stood frozen in terror. Dear Lord what had she done? She was completely enfolded within the arms of a stranger, her cheek pressed tight against the soft satin of his coat. Her heart began to pound wildly. She could feel his chin brushing against the top of her cap and the arms that encircled her were hard and muscled. The clean male scent of his body engulfed her and her mind started to reel. She felt his hands rub gently against her back and realized for the first time that she was clinging to him. Mortified by her behavior and terrified of the consequences, she let her arms drop and tried to step out of reach, only to find the gentleman reluctant to let her go.

Moonlight streamed in the window beside them and Chris watched the emotions play across the delicate features of her face as she looked up at him. Had the silvery light heightened the gentle curve of her cheek, or had he just not noticed before how clear her complexion was? Her eyes were huge and filled with anxiety and silently he cursed himself. Less than a fortnight had passed since the poor woman had put her husband in the ground, and here

74

he was wondering what she would taste like. Unable to resist, he traced a knuckle down her cheek before he released her.

"Well," he cleared his voice and looked down at the candlestick. "We seem to have put out the fire." He lifted the extinguished taper and held it between them hoping to coax a smile from her trembling lips.

Abby felt as if the flame from the candle now glowed from her cheeks. She could still feel the touch of his hand on her skin. It had been warm, not cold and clammy like the touch of her husband. "I'm sorry," she stammered, trying to edge further away, but the wall blocked her retreat.

Wondering why the urge to pull such a plain woman back into his arms was so strong, Chris smiled and tried to reassure her. "No harm done, besides the thunder startled me too."

Abby looked down at her feet and wondered what to say next. She had never had time to converse with the tavern's patrons so she continued to study the stains that marred the hem of her apron.

Knowing he had to move, but strangely reluctant to do so, Chris took a deep breath of night air. "Well," he sighed slowly. "It appears that your sister is only human after all, although I must admit for a minute she actually had me smelling smoke." He watched relief soften her features then her nose wrinkled and her smile vanished.

"I do smell smoke," she gasped.

Having taken another breath, Chris could only agree. "Outside," he snapped. "Get your sister and get outside. Start filling buckets." Waiting only long enough to be sure the women were on their way down the stairs, Chris moved back to the window and sniffed again. There was definitely a fire, but it wasn't inside the tavern.

Taking the stairs two at a time, he flew out the front door and sailed over the front step. Mindful of the shrubbery, he leaped over anything in his path as he circled the tavern. The moonlight showed the well house clearly but he only saw one of the women. Suzannah, raven hair streaming down her back, held the wooden bucket and struggled not to let the water slosh over the sides.

"Where is your sister?" Then he saw her, running from the opposite side of the tavern. Her cap had slipped low over her forehead and reaching up to push it back, she almost stumbled over an exposed root.

"It's not the tavern," she gasped, pressing a hand against her heaving chest. "But something is aflame."

"Look," Suzannah pointed and as they turned Chris felt his stomach lurch.

"Bring the buckets," he commanded, running toward the orange glow that was now creeping into the dark night sky. The church bells sounded their urgent plea as he rounded the hedge that edged the tavern's property. His eyes strained as he propelled himself down the rutted street, joining others that had been roused from their beds by the clamoring noise. Clad in assorted nightdress they came, carrying buckets, shovels, anything that might give aid against their most dreaded enemy.

He was less than a block away when he realized it was the silver shop. "Dear Lord, no!" his mind screamed. How could this have happened? He knew with a certainty that he had left no lanterns burning, and the forge by its very nature was flameproof. Yet something had started the inferno. As his steps drew him closer he watched flames lick at the roof of his new home, leaping into the darkness of the night to

76

do their deadly dance of destruction. Darting toward the well at the back of the property, he found his neighbors had already formed a makeshift brigade, passing buckets from one to the other. Grabbing a full bucket Christopher tried to edge closer to the building where the water might do the most good, but the intense heat burned his eyes and drove him back. Reality came swiftly, the pitiful splashes of water were like teardrops against an ocean of flame.

"Mr. Carlson!" He turned to find the elder Mrs. Getty, clad in her nightrail, clutching a shawl tightly about her shoulders and tugging on his sleeve. "Around front," she gestured frantically. "They need you around front."

Not bothering to ask why, Christopher took off and rounded the corner to see Suzannah standing apart from the others. Her finger pointed toward the front of the shop and the sight before him made his heart stop beating. Abigail Barclay had pulled a shawl about her head and was moving along the front porch.

"Someone is in there," Suzannah cried.

Dumping the bucket he carried over his own head, Chris took off at a run and prayed that he'd reach her in time. The shutters had pulled free, and the glass could explode at any moment from the heat. Each shard would become a deadly missile. Horrified, he watched as the widow struck the window with a bucket. The pane shattered, then she was half leaning, half climbing into the opening. Damn it all, did the woman have a death wish? Did she see this tragedy as a way to join her husband? Blinking against the thickening smoke Chris grabbed her by the waist and tugged. The widow didn't budge. Then he saw what she clung to.

Half in the window, Abby gave another desperate

jerk and Jimmy Richardson struggled to his knees. Desperate to be free of the inferno but disoriented from the smoke, he climbed unsteadily to his feet. Abby managed to grab both his arms and pulled with all her might. She felt the hands and offered a silent prayer when they reached past her and grabbed for the boy.

"Let me get him," Chris shouted, giving up his air and taking in a mouthful of smoke.

Knowing she had not the strength to get the boy out on her own, Abby leaned back. It gave Chris the room he needed to find purchase, then all three were falling from the window. Neighbors rushed forward to help carry Jimmy to safety, but as Abby tried to scramble to her knees she found herself trapped. Her eyes stung, and her skin burned, but she couldn't move. Her lungs hurt too much to take a breath and her arms collapsed beneath her. She felt the tug, heard the rip of fabric then she was floating away from the hell that had tried to consume her.

Her head dropped against a hard chest as she struggled to take a breath, but her lungs burned from the effort. Away from the heat she was lowered unsteadily onto the cool grass. A dipper of water was pressed against her lips and she drank greedily, only to have her stomach rebel and reject the offering along with the soot she had swallowed. Spasm after spasm shook her slight frame, then she was shivering uncontrollably.

Hands that trembled wrapped a blanket about her shoulders then supported her as a wet cloth wiped the soot and ash from her face. Abby sighed in pleasure, but the sound came out as a croak.

"Are you burned?" She blinked up to find Christopher Carlson, staring down at her through red rimmed eyes.

"Is the boy? . . ."

"He's going to be fine thanks to you." Chris punctuated his words with dry coughs that wouldn't be calmed.

Finding a full bucket of water at her side Abby reached for the dipper and pressed it back into his hand with a hoarse, "Drink." She watched in silence as the limp body of Jimmy Richardson was placed on a board and loaded into a wagon. Then angrily she turned on Christopher.

"You had him working at this hour of the night? He should have been dismissed at sunset. Where are they taking him?" she struggled to her knees.

Chris closed his eyes and wished he could dunk his entire head in the bucket. His eyes burned, his throat hurt, and he had no answers to her questions. Jimmy had left the shop well before he had. His hand rubbed against his neck. It felt like he had swallowed a live coal each time he tried to take a breath. "They're taking him home," he choked out. "His mother is the best one to care for him now."

"Oh, God, Abby, I didn't know you would be hurt." With tears streaming down her face, Suzannah dropped to her knees before her sister. "It's all my fault."

Abby glanced nervously about them, but all eyes were riveted on the burning building. Only Mr. Carlson sat close enough to hear her sister's garbled confession. "Hush, Suzannah," she croaked in a dry whisper. "You know how fickle a crowd can be. I'm not hurt."

Suzannah turned and clutched Chris's hands, ignoring the wince of pain that crossed his face as she pressed them tightly between her own. "I'm so sorry," she sobbed. "If you hadn't helped us at the

79

tavern, you might have been home in time to prevent the fire."

Unwilling to admit he had been thinking those exact thoughts, Christopher stood and took an uneven breath. "It would be prudent for you to hold your tongue about this." Then on unsteady legs he walked back to the crowd that stood in hushed silence before his shop. Buckets and shovels hung from defeated hands, and as the roof crashed down, showering sparks and ash, Christopher felt a hollow knot form in his chest; first his parents, then his home, now this. The weight of depression descended and his shoulders slumped in defeat.

Chapter Five

Like mourners, the group stood until the last wall of the building folded inward to be consumed by the greedy flames. Only the two slender columns of the chimneys remained standing, like arms reaching toward the heavens, pleading for salvation. Lightning flashed, competing with the brilliance of the fire and thunder shook the ground on which they stood, but no one moved until the clouds opened.

Christopher acknowledged the words of consolation and offers of a dry bed, but as the townsfolk edged quietly away to seek shelter, he remained alone in the rain. The fat drops felt blessedly cool against his parched skin and he tipped his head back to let them splash against his face and become the tears he refused to shed. Smoke mixed with the rain and the acrid smell burned his nose, but at last the bright flames of the fire began to spit and hiss in protest. The rain continued to fall steadily, and Christopher watched until the charred remains of his shop were no more than fading embers.

Abigail waited silently until the last of the townsfolk had departed. She had urged Suzannah to return to the tavern, and now she stood, weighted by her own uncertainty. Rain soaked through her thin clothing, cooling her fevered skin then leaving it chilled. She wrapped her arms around herself to stem the shivers and desperately wished to be warm and safe in her bed. But try as she would, she found she could not walk away and leave him standing there.

Quietly, she studied the sharp chiseled planes of his face. At some point in time he had lost his jacket and now he stood in breeches and shirt, soaked to the skin. This was not a man who sat idle. His body was powerful and well muscled. Hesitantly she stepped closer, careful to keep more than an arm's length between them lest he decide to vent his frustration in her direction.

"Mr. Carlson?" He turned and Abigail nearly lost her courage. She had expected to see despair etched deep across his proud features. Instead she found strength. It would take more than a fire to beat this man, but she wondered if he'd yet to realize that fact. "Mr. Carlson, would you come back to the tavern with me?"

Chris turned. He had felt her presence even before she spoke and the gentle tone of her voice soothed the raw pain that filled him. He glanced about, realizing for the first time that they stood alone before the ruins of his shop. The rain continued and yet she made no move to leave. She had lost her cap and her hair hung in knotted strands about her pinched face, her lips nearly blue from cold. His thoughts of going to Sarah and Nick's vanished in the growing mist. He certainly couldn't let the widow see herself home in the dark.

"Come." His words were more clipped than he

meant, but a wave of exhaustion washed away the last of his patience. Had it not been for her, he would have willingly made a pallet on the grass and slept with the night as his only cover. He reached for her arm and scowled as she neatly stepped back.

"I can manage," she said quickly, starting down the road. "As you know we have plenty of beds . . ."

And I've peered under every one of them, he thought darkly.

"So you can have your choice." She struggled to keep her teeth from chattering.

Great, he thought, lengthening his stride. I get to spend the night in an empty tavern with a widow and her crazy sister. "Just what good is it for your sister to see a fire if she can't tell what's going to burn?"

Abby jerked at the suddenness of his words and lost her footing. One minute she had been looking at the dark stranger beside her, the next, she was sitting in the mud and looking up at him from the ground. She heard it then, the barely controlled anger, and instinctively she tried to scoot away from the hand that reached for her. "I'm sorry," she stammered, scrambling awkwardly to her knees. "I know my sister should keep her own counsel, but she meant only to help."

Christopher's hand dropped as he watched her struggle to her feet. What was wrong with the wench? She acted as if his touch carried leprosy. Annoyed, he took a step closer and watched her take a step back.

"I have no money to offer for your rebuilding," her words tumbled one over the other as she

83

started off again. "But you are welcome to keep free lodgings at the tavern for as long as necessary."

Free lodging? Christopher took off after her retreating shadow. Did she really believe he would take money from her? There were names for men that lived off women and damn it he wasn't one of them. "I still own a shilling to pay my own way, Mrs. Barclay."

"I would not take your money." She stopped, but he took two full steps past her before realizing.

Arms akimbo he turned back to her. "And why the hell not?" He thought he saw her flinch, but the night was dark and he was too angry to care. "Do you find my money as distasteful as my touch?"

"I'm sorry," her fingers linked together anxiously, the skin tender. "I didn't mean to cause offense."

Christopher looked up at the clouded sky and prayed for patience. "Will you stop saying you're sorry!"

"I'm sor . . ." Abby bit her bottom lip and wondered how everything had gone so wrong. She had just wanted to help a neighbor, something Malachi had never allowed, yet now she felt as if she held a bull cow by the horns.

Chris took a steadying breath. He was acting like an absolute jackass and he knew it, but damn it he had reason. His livelihood had just gone up in smoke, nearly taking his apprentice with it. But try as he would, he could find no cause for the widow's prickly attitude. He took in the stubborn set of her chin. Mayhap, she was a shrew like his sister. He shuddered at the thought and wondered yet again why he was planning to spend the night under her roof. He pictured the soft bed and hearty brandy that would greet him at the Beaumont's, not to mention clean clothes, and decided it would be worth the walk back through town. But as the lanthorns before the tavern beckoned, his steps grew slower to match hers. And by the time they had climbed the stairs to the front door, Christopher decided he didn't care where he slept.

Thankful that Suzannah had already taken to her bed, Abigail led her reluctant guest up the stairs. But he turned in the opposite direction when they reached the top.

"Mr. Carlson, the rooms are this way."

But Christopher was in no mood to sleep in a common room, or to wake in the morning to find another traveler had decided to share his bed. His step carried him to the large private chamber at the far end of the hall.

Protecting the flame of the taper with her hand, Abigail scurried after him. Her mouth opened to tell him the room belonged to her husband, but as she watched him plop wearily on the bed and begin to tug at his boots, her protest fell silent. Her eyes darted nervously about the shadowy corners. Surely there could be no harm in it; after all it was the best chamber in the tavern. She'd let him spend the night here and then move him to a different one in the morning.

"If you'll place your clothes outside the door," she said softly. "I'll see them cleaned for you."

Christopher stood and nodded as he reached for the hem of his shirt. Words seemed too much effort. He watched the widow hastily retreat then pulled his shirt over his head. Discarding his breeches and stockings, and dropping them in a

85

heap outside did much to clear the air in the room.

The rain continued to beat a steady pattern against the roof and, naked, Christopher sank back onto the comfort of the horsehair mattress. He knew he should wash, for he could still smell the fire. But his eyes, once closed, refused to open, and within minutes he was sound asleep.

Christopher awoke to the song of a mockingbird. Turning his head on the pillow he gazed at the hazy pink light that filtered through his window. It was just past dawn and the sound of the bird was sweet and persistent. His eyes traveled about the room and he frowned at the unfamiliar surroundings, then the smoke that clung to his hair and skin invaded his senses and reality came crashing back. His eyes closed in defeat. The silver shop was gone before he had even had a chance to make a start. Thoughts of returning home to the plantation seeped into his mind, but he pushed them aside and forced his body to sit on the edge of the bed. His lungs ached when he drew a deep breath and the skin on his hands was tender to the touch. But no one had been killed, he thought with relief. Wearily he ran his hand through his hair and grimaced from the smell. What had Jimmy been doing in the shop? The question played over and over through his mind like a tune that couldn't find a home.

Chris stood and slowly made his way to the wash basin. Pouring water into the porcelain bowl his eyes grew wide as steam rose to greet him. His hand touched the water to find it still pleasantly warm. The Widow Barclay certainly ran an excellent household he thought, gratefully taking the small bit of soap from its pewter dish. The servants had even provided a fresh sassafras twig so he might clean his teeth.

Feeling decidedly better with the grime washed from his body, Chris turned and realized that his clothes had also been attended to. Washed and pressed, they rested on the chair by the door. His mood lightened further as he donned the fresh smelling garments and as he fastened the ties at his knee, his thoughts turned back to the widow. Had she discovered yet how it ached to take a breath or did she still lay in peaceful slumber? A frown tugged the corners of his mouth as the image of the flaming shop leaped into his mind. She shouldn't have tried to get the boy out by herself. But as he relived the night before, he realized that no one had rushed to help her. She alone had reacted to Suzannah's cries. Thoughts of Suzannah, eyes dark with passion, made his blood quicken. How unfair, he mused, absently twisting his stock into a fashionable knot, for one sister to be a striking beauty leaving the other pale and bland by comparison.

Standing before the small looking glass, he used the small ivory comb to bring some semblance of order into his hair before pulling it back into a queue. Then, with more spring to his step than he would have thought possible, Christopher opened the door to his room and looked into the shadowy hallway. At the end of the hall the common room stood quiet, still he stepped lightly as he made his way down the stairs.

How strange there were no servants about. Quietly he peered into the dining room. It was well appointed, but the chairs stood awkwardly atop the tables. He passed through the room, surprised at the absence of stale tobacco smoke and poked his head into the tap room. It too was empty. He continued to explore, through the game rooms and the private dining chambers, the wooden floor creaking beneath his feet. Still he found no one. Deciding there'd be servants near the cookhouse, Christopher made his way down the back hall to the door that led to the porch. It stood open, but as he went to step through it, he stopped short.

Surely his eyes were playing tricks on him, for sitting on a stump near the woodpile was the Widow Barclay. Hair the color of ripe wheat shimmered down her back as she pulled her comb through its golden masses. She wore only a nightrail, a tattered gray shawl forgotten on her lap. Her head tipped back exposing the slender column of her neck and as she turned her face to the warmth of the sun, Christopher smothered a gasp. She looked almost ethereal in the rosy glow of the morning light. Her features were delicately carved, her eyes closed as her lips smiled at some imagined pleasure.

His pulse leaped, his mouth went dry. Why had he ever thought her plain? The woman looked like an angel. An angel that had darted headfirst into hell he thought, remembering how she had danced with the flames.

Chris cleared his throat and noisily stepped onto the porch. He suppressed a frown as she jumped to her feet and grasped her shawl, pulling it tightly about her shoulders. "I didn't mean to frighten you," he said easily, coming down the steps to stand before her. "But I couldn't find any of the servants about." He watched her knuckles turn white, and smiled when the shawl she pulled frantically about her did more to reveal than conceal her slender curves.

"Was there something you needed?" she stammered. "We don't break the fast until eight of the clock." Her eyes darted nervously toward the sun to check the time; surely it was not yet half past six.

Lost in thought, Christopher pictured waking to find her face snuggled close upon his pillow. What she would taste like, he wondered, if he pulled her from sleep with kisses? He had meant only to thank her for the bed and clean clothes, and then be on his way. Yet as he watched her bare toes peek out from beneath her gown, he imagined her clad only in his dressing robe.

"Last night, you offered lodgings," he hesitated, wondering even as the words left his mouth what he was thinking of. "Did you mean that?"

Her head bobbed slowly, her brown eyes wary.

"Then if you have no objections, I would like to stay, until my shop is rebuilt."

Abby ran her tongue over her lips to moisten them. "That could be a long time." Her soft voice rolled over him like honey and he found he couldn't stop the smile that tugged at his lips.

"A very long time," he said quietly.

Her head nodded again in agreement but words refused to come.

Chris stepped closer and realized that rings of fatigue circled her eyes. Indeed she seemed to be growing paler with each passing breath. "Mrs. Barclay, are you quite all right?"

Abby blinked with confusion. Dear Lord what had she done? Suzannah had disappeared, her father could arrive at any moment, and she was standing in her nightrail conversing with a man in broad daylight. Her eyes darted anxiously about. If anyone should see them, she'd be punished for certain. Tension tightened like Malachi's leather belt around her forehead.

Convinced she was going to faint at any moment, Chris reached to steady her only to see total panic cover her face as she struggled to evade his touch.

"Easy," he whispered, "just sit down and rest for a moment." Taking her arm, he pushed her firmly back onto the splitting stump and knelt before her. Despite the humidity that hung in the air, her skin was cold and clammy to the touch. His fingers tucked a lock of silken hair back behind her ear and he felt her flinch again. "I think perhaps you should return to your bed. I don't think you've completely recovered from last night."

Embarrassed to admit that she had not yet seen her bed, Abbey tried to find her wits. "I need to start the morning meal," she stammered, wishing he wouldn't stay so close.

As if reading her mind, Christopher stood. "Where are the servants?"

"On their way back from Jamestown Market."

"All of them?" He watched distress etch deeper on her frail features and instantly cursed himself. The woman needed her bed, not him badgering her about how to manage her household. Besides hadn't he already decided that his every need had been anticipated and attended to? "I know 'tis none of my business," he said gently, "but surely the house servants can set out the morning meal on their own. I really think you should retire for a few more hours sleep. You look exhausted."

Abby swallowed hard and wondered why it hurt to hear him say she was unattractive. She knew her face carried no beauty, but for him to state it so plainly made her eyes sting.

"So will you rest for a while?"

Realizing he had given her the perfect escape, she nodded and stood abruptly. The band of tension around her forehead tightened further and for a sickening moment everything began to spin. Gasping for breath, she didn't even notice that he had slipped an arm about her waist to support her trembling body.

"Definitely a few hours in bed," he said gently, leading her toward the porch. But when they reached the first step, Chris felt her stiffen.

"I can manage." Her fingers took a death grip on the railing.

Reluctantly he released her and watched her stiff, awkward movements as she climbed the stairs to the porch. When she reached the top she paused and turned back.

"Will you see Jimmy Richardson today?"

Chris nodded.

Taking a breath, and relieved by the space now between them, Abby rushed on before she could lose her nerve. "You'll not deal too harshly with the boy . . ." She remembered Jimmy's agitation when she wouldn't take the buckles, and now, as she gazed down at Mr. Carlson, she knew the source of his fear. The snug fit of his breeches emphasized the strength of his legs and without the cover of a jacket, his shirt molded itself to the wide expanse of his chest and shoulders. This was a man she would never want to anger. "You'll take into consideration that he tried to stop the fire . . ." Her plea faded as she watched his eyes narrow.

"Madam, you make me out to be the villain in this piece. Why would I berate my own apprentice when he nearly lost his life trying to save my shop?" Chris propped his foot on the bottom step and didn't miss the way her fingers tightened convulsively around the door latch. "I have questions, and I dare say that even you would agree that I deserve some answers. The first of which is why young Richardson was out at that time of night. He'd been dismissed at least two hours prior."

Abby's brow wrinkled in thought. "Might he have forgotten something?" she ventured.

Chris shrugged. "That is the only explanation I can think of. But what could have held such importance that he could not wait till the morrow? And what in heaven started the blaze to begin with?" He looked up and found the widow leaning against the door, her eyes nearly closed in sleep. "At any rate, I plan to visit the Richardsons directly after breaking the fast, which by the way, I shall not be doing here this morning."

Abby struggled to keep her eyes open and felt herself stiffen with rejection.

"By now my friends will have heard about the fire," he continued easily. "I need to reassure them that the only thing lost was my shop."

"The only thing," she gasped. "It was your shelter . . . your livelihood. How can you dismiss it so lightly?"

His easy smile faded completely. "Don't misunderstand me, Mrs. Barclay. God saw fit to strike me a blow, and it has cut deep. But no one was seriously hurt and for that I am grateful. If I find young Jim in good spirits this morning then all shall be well."

"But you lost . . ."

Chris cut her off with a wave of his hand. "It was wood and stone that burned. With effort and a strong back it can be replaced."

"But all your silver . . ."

Chris rubbed his hand across his chin. "Aye, that is the worst of it, losing the hours of workmanship that Walter Johnson put into the pieces already finished. But even that carries a bright side, for the silver itself can be reclaimed by carefully raking though the ashes. Now I am off and you are to bed. Agreed?"

Abby felt herself nodding even as she wondered what sort of man could still find a smile when his entire livelihood had just been snatched from his grasp. Fascinated, she leaned her forehead against the door and watched until his step carried him from sight.

Chapter Six

Nicholas Beaumont reached for the decanter of brandy that sat on the corner of his desk. "How is the young Richardson lad faring this morning?"

Christopher stretched out in his chair and wearily crossed his boots at the ankles. "He's still unconscious." Gratefully he accepted the offered drink. "Mrs. Richardson said he stirred several times during the night, but until he wakes up, we'll not know the true extent of his injuries." Chris swirled the brandy in his glass then downed the contents with one gulp. The fiery liquid burned his raw throat but brought a soothing numbness in its wake. "The boy has some wicked burns on his hands and arms and his hair's been badly singed but, thank the Lord, his face was spared. Under the circumstances, I fear we must be grateful that he's still alive."

"Just what are the circumstances?" Nick prodded. "I can understand the speed in which the fire spread; with wooden houses we all live in fear of lightning. But from what you tell me, the storm had yet to start. Did anyone actually see lightning hit the building?"

Chris shook his head. "We only know that young Richardson was the first to discover it. His mother said it was well after supper when he told her he had to return to the shop. She assumed he had forgotten something since he offered no other explanation."

Nick's eyes grew thoughtful. "I know the lad well. My guess would be that rather than calling for help, he must have thought to impress you by extinguishing it on his own."

"Only it spread too quickly." Chris reached for the brandy and poured himself another hearty drink. "Where do such foolish notions come from? The lad could have gotten himself killed."

"Don't be too hard on the boy." Nick said slowly. "I can remember a time when you were anxious to win the approval of a dainty Miss Prudence Mayfield."

"I was a child," Chris defended. "Green behind the ears and in love to boot."

"A child of young Richardson's age if I recall correctly," Nick continued. "You climbed, how high was it, to rescue her cat?"

A sheepish grin tugged at the corners of his mouth as Christopher shifted in his chair. "High enough that when I fell, I broke my damn arm." He shook his head. "I'm at her feet with a broken arm, she's cooing poor kitty, and you stand there laughing." Absently he rubbed his hand over his chest. "I wonder now which caused the deepest pain, the broken arm, or discovering that dear Miss Mayfield cared more for her cat than she did for me . . ."

"The point is your arm healed, and young Richardson will do the same," Nick said firmly. "Although the lad will probably be terrified when he realizes how much his error in judgment has cost you. A good thrashing would not be out of line here."

"Thrashing be damned," Chris rubbed his hand over his eyes. "The boy could have lost his life. My only concern now is that he recovers."

"And while he does, what are your plans?"

Chris flopped back in his chair. "I'll reclaim what silver I can from the ashes, then rebuild the shop." He stared down at the amber liquid in his glass, then straightened his shoulders. "I've waited more than thirty years to have the opportunity to do something with my life that truly pleases me. I'd always thought my silver work could be no more than an amusement, for there was never the time to allow it more." He looked up at his friend. "It's a setback to be sure, but patience shall become my virtue, at least for the next few months."

"If you wish, I can recommend some good men to help with the rebuilding, and you know you're welcome to move back in with us for as long as you wish."

Chris smiled in thanks and took another sip of his drink. "Actually, I was thinking of staying at the Stag's Head Tavern." He paused. "What do you know of the Widow Barclay?"

"I can't say that I've ever met the woman." Nick frowned with thought. "I did know her husband, though. A sour bastard, well up in years, always looking for the fastest way to make a coin."

"Gambling or smuggling?"

Nick's eyes narrowed. "I can't speak with certainty, but in my own case, about five years ago, I found he was trying to buy favor with the crew of the Merry Chaser. The man thought that he could bribe someone to change the manifest and then sell the excess cargo directly to him."

"Increasing his prophet margin a hundred fold."

"Exactly. It was a clever enough plan, but Barclay's own greed caused it to fail."

"And when you confronted him?"

Nick's smile of satisfaction vanished. "The evidence connecting Barclay to the deed was destroyed before I could press formal charges."

"I know you too well to believe you let the matter drop," Chris challenged. "Especially if Beaumont Shipping was involved."

Nick shook his head and his eyes darkened with the memory. "I had no problems confronting Barclay directly. I apprised him of the consequences should he ever presume to be so foolish again. The man whimpered and cowered at my feet like an old woman. He had the backbone of a slug. Then . . . ," his voice trailed off.

"Go on."

"I heard later that same day, the bastard beat one of his slaves to death right there on the wharf."

"My God."

For several moments neither man spoke. Nick turned his gaze out the window to where Sarah and the children sat in the shade of the giant oak tree to escape the sweltering heat. "I must confess," he admitted, his voice touched with pain, "it's played on my mind more than once that if I had handled the situation differently, mayhap that young man would still be alive."

"You can't take the responsibility for that," Chris chided. "From what you say, Barclay was a bastard through and through." He thought of Abby embracing such a man and his skin went cold. "How did he die?"

"Carriage accident just over a month ago." Nick reached for a clay pipe, then changing his mind set it back on its dish. "He was well past seventy, but I don't think anyone, save his wife, was particularly grieved to hear of his passing."

"Seventy!" Chris rose and began to pace. "How

97

could she have married someone that old?"

Nick looked at his friend with amazement. Christopher had always been a favorite with the fairer sex. His easy charm and kind ways would have made him popular even if his striking looks had not already done so. The result was a harem of beauties that pursued him endlessly. Nick's eyes narrowed and he steepled his fingers together to gaze over them. Sarah had always said that Chris was just waiting for the right woman to come along. Now, as he watched his friend's anxious pacing, he couldn't help but wonder.

"Mayhap she had no choice," he offered. "Barclay may have made a business arrangement with her father. It's a common enough practice."

Chris visibly shuddered. "The thought of someone that reprehensible touching her makes my skin crawl, yet it's plain the woman's still in mourning. What qualities could a man like Barclay possess that would garner such devotion?"

Nick shrugged. "Who's to say what one sees in another? Besides," he teased, "I thought you were always the one with all the answers when it came to the ladies. Could it be there is finally a damsel who has tossed an obstruction in your path?"

Chris resumed his pacing. "I don't know what she's done but I tell you plain that I don't like it. I saw her only briefly this morning, yet I can't force her image from my mind."

Nick smiled knowingly. "You always did manage to ferret out the beauties."

"Actually she's rather plain," Chris paused, "but her hair is the softest color of golden sunlight I've ever seen." His mind drifted back to the dawn where she sat like a goddess carved from the finest alabaster. "She's a tiny thing," he muttered, "reaches no more than my shoulder . . . but her eyes," he frowned. "Her eyes haunt me."

"A blue-eyed blonde," Nick teased. "I should have known."

Chris looked up with a start. "The widow's eyes are brown."

"Well there's a contradiction."

Chris missed the teasing note in his friend's voice as his frustrations began to grow. "No, I'll tell you of contradictions. The woman owns a tavern yet she clothes herself like an ill-kept slave. She invites me to spend the night, then won't let me touch her to help her off the ground."

Nick suppressed a grin. "You meant to take her on the ground? Really, my friend, I gave you credit for more finesse. No wonder the lady's not interested."

A scowl marred Chris' features. "She made that plain enough. But why should I care if she chooses to cling to the memories of an old man? She means nothing to me, we met only yesterday." His angry strides carried him to the window, but he turned back a moment later. "Do you realize that woman caused me vexation even before we met?" he challenged. "Young Richardson had to make two trips to the tavern before she'd even accept the damn buckles."

Intrigued, Nick struggled to stem his laughter. "Yes, I can see where that would cause insurmountable problems."

"The best work I ever saw from Walter Johnson's shop on the costliest buckles this side of London and what does she do with them, this woman whose apron has a rent the size of my foot? She gives them away."

Convinced that there was more to the story, Nick decided to pursue a different course. "I've never known you to be possessive of your work once it was delivered."

"Walter Johnson's work," Chris muttered. "And it was beautiful."

"But what does it matter?"

Chris threw up his arms in frustration. "She gave them to my apprentice."

Nick sat forward. "She gave the buckles to Jimmy Richardson?"

Chris nodded. "That's why I wasn't at the shop when the fire started. I had gone to the Stag's Head to speak with her about the situation."

"Ah, now we get to the root of the problem. My friend, you are jealous."

"What!" Chris exploded. "Have you lost your senses completely? How could I possibly . . ." He looked up to see Nick rocking back and forth with silent laughter. "I'm not jealous, but I am acting like a jackass, aren't I."

For once in his life, Nicholas Beaumont had the good sense to remain silent.

———

Abby pressed a hand against the growing ache in her back as she leaned over the hearth. Meticulously she scooped away the brown scum that swirled about the pork joint. The water boiled furiously in the great kettle, and steam billowed up to mix with the perspiration that ran freely down her flushed cheeks.

"Child, ain't that pork broth gone clear yet?"

Wearily, Abby rubbed her face against the side of her arm. "Almost, Nanny. Why is it that when a pot needs watching, it takes twice as long? If I was to put this joint on to cook and then walked away, it would have boiled in no time."

Nanny tossed another peeled apple into the bowl.

"And if you didn't get all that scum off before it set you'd have a pork joint that tasted like cow dung." Turning to her young mistress, Nanny's dark eyes filled with alarm. "Child what in the world . . ." Stepping quickly to the hearth she grabbed a handful of Abby's skirt from behind and gave a hearty tug, making her stumble back with confusion.

"You get much closer and you might as well climb right in the kettle with that old pig. What's you thinking of, leaning over that far? You gonna ruin that back of yours for sure."

Grateful to be even slightly away from the fierce heat, Abby tried to straighten and grimaced from the motion. "I was just doing like you taught me."

Nanny harrumphed and steered Abby away from the hearth. "Honey, I also taught you not to stand too close to the flames. Why if you was to lean in half a breath more, we wouldn't need that old pork joint to go with the turkey, we could have just had you since you'd already be roasted."

Abby shuddered. "I didn't realize . . ." Taking the corner of her apron she wiped the sweat from her face and neck as she watched Nanny give the kettle a final stir. The heavy lid was secured in place and then the kettle was shifted to the corner where it would simmer for the next three hours.

Nanny scowled at the violet rings of fatigue that circled Abby's eyes. "You go and peel those potatoes," she nodded her head toward the far end of the table. "And you sits yourself down while you're doing it. You look ready to plum fall over. You never should have stayed up half the night a-washing that man's clothes."

"I had no choice," Abby muffled a yawn. "Everything reeked of smoke." Glancing up she saw the stubborn scowl on the old woman's face. "Nanny,"

101

she cajoled. "The poor man doesn't even own a wig. He's new in town and last night he watched his entire shop burn to the ground."

"Miz Abby," Nanny eased her bulk back on her stool, "you can't go filling up the tavern with strays. People ain't the same as those pups you're always trying to save."

Abby's tired eyes flashed with pain and anger. "Well at least Malachi isn't here to drown him. Nanny, the man needs a helping hand until he can get on his feet again."

"Honey, you can hardly stand on your own feet, so how you gonna help another? You know we can't keep this up much longer. Obadiah and I just ain't young enough no more, and you be wearing yourself out trying to take on so much."

Abby clenched her jaw. "Nanny, the man stays and as our guest. I'll hear no more about it. Besides Suzannah . . ."

"Don't you go talking to me about that sister of yours. You got enough on your plate without taking on Suzannah's problems," Nanny scolded. "Now, if Miss Suzannah wants to come and tell about a fire, that's her business. And if you was to ask me, since it was Miz Suzannah's fire, she should have been the one staying up doing the washing."

"But . . ."

"Honey, there just ain't no buts about it. Miz Suzannah got her free bed and board and then she done flied away leaving you, like always, to clean up behind her."

Knowing it was an argument she'd never win, Abby retreated. Besides, she reasoned, Suzannah was well on her way to who knew where. Dear Lord, she thought desperately, just keep her safe and don't let father find her. For if he did . . .

102

Abby gave herself an abrupt shake, there wasn't time to worry over Suzannah now. She had diners coming in less than four hours and there were still carrots to peel for the pudding and potatoes and onions to chop for Nanny's onion pie.

Turning to the table she reached for a large bowl of potatoes, but her feet refused to cooperate and she stumbled again. Landing on her wooden stool with a swoosh, she blinked and tried to straighten as if nothing had happened. She couldn't afford another mishap. Nanny had said nothing when she had clumsily dumped the bucket of wash water on the floor creating a muddy mess for them to walk around, and she had even kept her silence when Abby dropped the fresh plucked turkey on the ground outside the cookhouse door. The old woman had merely looked toward the well and then had gone back into the wooden building that was her domain.

The coarse rope had stung her fingers as she had hauled another bucket of water to clean the mud from the fowl. She had had to dunk the naked bird several times to remove the grit. Shaking from fatigue she decided it would probably be the cleanest turkey her patrons had ever consumed. Hefting the twenty-five pound bird into her arms, she had carried it into the cookhouse and plopped it on the work table. But as she released the bird, her elbow had bumped a tray of clean pewter forks, dumping them onto the floor.

Abby shuddered. She definitely could not afford another mishap. With slow deliberate motions she pulled the bowl of potatoes closer and began to peel.

"That's it, child you're going to bed."

Abby jerked at the sudden sound. Confused she looked up to see Nanny standing before her.

103

"What's the matter?" she stammered.

The old woman pulled Abby's hand up for closer inspection and scowled at blood that dripped slowly from her finger.

Abby's eyes grew wide. "When did that happen?" She looked to the knife in her other hand and then to the bowl in her lap. Dots of red were sprinkled over the white potatoes. "I didn't even feel anything," she gasped.

Nanny pinched the cut with a rag and the bleeding stopped almost instantly but the old woman was far from satisfied. "You and me don't always agree on seasoning, but I draw the line at blood. Now I don't want no arguments. Upstairs to the loft! Obadiah's put a fresh pallet in there just yesterday in case one of the others was to come back. You go on up and lay down for just a little while."

Abby rubbed her hand wearily over her eyes. "Maybe I should, but I'll go to my own room."

Nanny shook her head as she steered the girl to the back stairs in the kitchen. "No, you don't. That room of yours ain't got no window and the heat in there will be fierce. No, you just take yourself upstairs, there's a nice cross breeze up there to cool you off. Go on now."

Satisfied, Nanny watched as Abby climbed the narrow stairs. She knew better that to let her mistress go back into the tavern, for the child would have been sidetracked by a million chores. Now, at least, she'd know just how long the girl slept, for the only way out of the loft was down the same set of stairs. The old woman reached for the carrots and, once settled again on her stool, her deep voice broke into a gentle lullaby. The song of the birds accompanied her as did the constant buzz of the flies that soared freely in and out of the cookhouse.

Still amazed that she had slept completely through dinner, Abby closed the door behind the last patron. She turned the key in the lock, then went into the dining room to face the clearing up.

Obadiah and Nanny had done a magnificent job and she felt her chest swell with pride at their accomplishment, but guilt ate at her pleasure. Dinner had consisted of spicy pumpkin soup, roast turkey, sliced pork with gravy, carrot pudding, onion and potato pie in a buttered shell, two green vegetables and crusty bread. For the sweet Nanny had managed a flaky apple pie as well as a lemon cheese cake to go with the usual jellies.

Determined to do her share, Abby started to gather the plates onto her tray. With quick, efficient motions she cleared the last two tables as she continued to make mental notes of what needed her attention first. They were nearly out of butter, so she'd see to the churning as soon as the cleaning was finished.

Obadiah entered the dining room with a mug of hot chocolate and a steaming bowl of pumpkin soup. "Miz Abby, you stop that now you hear? I can take care of these dishes. Now you sit yourself down."

"Obbie, I just got up."

"That might be so but you ain't put nothing in your stomach all day."

Realizing that the leftover aromas from dinner had made her ravenous, Abby allowed herself to be seated at her usual corner table and smiled in gratitude as Obadiah placed the steaming bowl before her.

"You and Nanny did a magnificent job, Obbie," she praised.

"Nanny and me got a good night's sleep," he chided gently. "But if my count's not off, Miz Abby, we had a full hand more today than yesterday. And I think two of the folks were from the college."

Abby tried to contain the growing excitement that started in the pit of her stomach. "Word of Nanny's fine cooking is starting to spread and being so close to the college is bound to be good for business. Maybe soon we'll have patrons to spend the night too."

"No doubt," Obbie beamed with satisfaction. "We already got one, and even though he be only a guest, maybe he'll tell others and that's a start. Why," Obadiah was interrupted by a loud pounding on the front door. "I'll get it," he nodded for Abby to sit. "You finish before it cools then I'll bring your dinner."

Abby leaned back on her chair and tried to curb her elation. If Obbie was right and business continued to grow, everything would work out. Carefully she ticked off the figures in her head. If she was frugal, she'd soon have enough to offer wages, and another pair of hands would go a long way to easing the burden. Despite the thought her brow wrinkled with worry. Nanny had been right to say she and Obbie wouldn't be able to keep up the pace. Then I go and sleep the entire morning, Abby shook her head in self-disgust. Well the first thing we'll do is get Nanny help in the kitchen. Abby smiled with satisfaction. She could certainly manage to keep the tavern and the gardens, while Obbie did his regular chores. But the thought of chopping wood brought her soaring spirits down with a jolt.

"Miz Abby." Obadiah edged hesitantly into the dining room closing the door to the hallway firmly behind him. "Miz Abby, Mr. Bloom has come to

106

call. He says it's urgent he has a word with you."

Abby frowned and searched her mind for a face. "Is he a merchant?"

Obadiah shook his head. "He be gentry."

Abby slowly pulled her napkin from her lap and placed it on the table. "Did he state his business?"

"No, ma'am, but let me tell him that you're in the middle of dinner and he should call back later."

Filled with uncertainty, she looked down at her soup. "No, it's best that I see to his needs first. Will you tell him that I'll . . ."

Abby never finished as the door to the dining room swung open and Cyrus Bloom stepped through. Startled by the sight, she could only bite back a gasp at the image the heavy-set man presented. The flared skirt of his red satin coat reached his knees and the buttons that ran from collar to hem were left open as was the fashion. But in Mr. Bloom's case, it was the wide girth of his middle that kept them apart and his tight fitting breeches looked dangerously close to losing their seams. The man poised with one foot slightly forward then doffed his hat, causing its feather trim to flop precariously.

"Mrs. Barclay, I do hope that I have not called at an inconvenient time but my schedule is so pressing that this was the only moment I could spare. And now I can see that you are in the middle of your dinner. Well no matter. Boy," he turned to Obadiah. "You may bring me a serving of soup and a mug of your finest punch. I'll join your mistress. Hurry now so her meal doesn't cool and see that mine is hot or I'll have your hide."

Obadiah had learned years ago how to keep his face expressionless. He turned toward Abby. Her eyes were wide and filled with apprehension, but she gave him a slight nod.

107

Completely taken aback by the man's forward behavior, Abby watched in stunned silence as he pulled a chair close, then wedged his bulk between its arms.

"What can I do for you Mr. Bloom?" she questioned. The chair groaned in protest as Mr. Cyrus Bloom rested his weighty elbows on the table.

"It's not what you might do for me, Mrs. Barclay, but what we can do for each other. Ah yes," he grunted with satisfaction as Obadiah placed a steaming bowl before him. Like one who had not eaten in days, he devoured his soup with lightning speed and then called for more.

"I am afraid I must appear slow witted, Mr. Bloom," Abby struggled to keep her amazement from her voice, for never had she seen one consume food so quickly. "But I do not know your business."

"Madame," he snapped with reproof. "It is exceedingly bad manners to engage one in conversation while he is in the process of dining. I'll thank you to remember that. Is there meat and vegetables?"

Abby felt her heart start to pound with anxiety as she shook her head. "All the turkey was consumed at dinner but there might be a bit of pork left."

Bloom gave a knowing grunt and called for a third serving of soup while he consumed the last of the bread. When he had finished, he made a grand show of daintily wiping the corners of his mouth, completely missing the stain of broth that still marked the center of his thick chin.

"It's just as I thought," he declared, tossing the napkin to the table. "You have not the experience to keep the tavern functioning." He sighed with exasperation at her startled expression. "Mrs. Barclay, you have just proved my point. If you were doing an adequate job, you would not have run out of meat."

"I beg your pardon," Abby stammered hesitantly.

108

"But I was not aware that we did. Obbie, was there not sufficient meat to serve those who dined here today?"

Obadiah stepped to the table and reached for the man's empty dish, frowning at his mistress's full one. "Yes, ma'am," he said politely, refilling Mr. Bloom's mug with punch. "We had plenty for all who wanted."

Abby turned back to her guest with a questioning look.

"If you had sufficient, Mrs. Barclay," the man spoke slowly as one who might instruct a dim-witted child, "you would have had fowl to serve to me, would you not?" Clearly not expecting an answer. Bloom pushed his weight from the chair and began to pace the room examining tables, touching the pewter sconces that lined the wall. "I can see now that you are in even greater need than I originally thought. And being the generous man that I am, I find it my Christian duty to help you."

Abby looked to Obadiah with questioning eyes only to see him shrug and shake his head. "But in what manner do you propose to help me, Mr. Bloom?" she questioned hesitantly. "I still do not know your business."

"My dear lady," Bloom puffed out his chest and gave his shoulder length curls an arrogant toss. "I come from one of the finest families in Virginia. I do not engage in business." He grimaced as if the word left a sour taste in his mouth. "I am here to propose an arrangement that will be of vast interest to you. I must admit I had misgivings at first, but now my mind is set. I shall take you to wife."

"You want me to marry you?" Abby gasped with disbelief and flopped back in her chair too stunned to reason.

109

"As I see it," Bloom began to pace again, "you have only to gain from such a union. My family name is well respected, indeed revered throughout the colony. And clearly, you cannot handle the business of this inn." He turned and gave Abby a hard stare. "You're rather on the plain side and much too thin for my taste, but one cannot be choosy. I am willing to make the sacrifice."

Abby gripped the arms of her chair so tightly her knuckles turned white. "You must forgive me Mr. Bloom," she stammered, "but I have no plans for marriage."

"Of course you don't, with your husband so recent in the ground. But a woman in your position cannot afford to make a show of mourning. Granted there are those who will talk, but I shall soon squelch any rumors that might arise." His thumb pressed hard against the table as if killing a bug and Abby couldn't help but wonder if he would seek to squelch her if she did not comply.

Her knees threatened to buckle as she pushed herself from the table. Her stomach churned dangerously but she drew herself erect. "I know I should be grateful for your charity, Mr. Bloom, but I fear I must refuse your offer." Her palms grew moist as she watched the stunned look of disbelief cross the man's face. His eyes narrowed and she felt her pulse leap with fear.

"My dear young woman," he sneered, "don't you have any idea who I am?"

Abby could only shake her head and the simple gesture made his mottled skin turn redder.

"Then I think I should warn you that going against my wishes is not the best way to start a marriage."

Abby struggled to keep her voice firm. "Sir, with

110

all due respect, I . . ."

"I'm sorry I'm so tardy, I hope I'm not causing too much inconvenience."

Abby spun around as Christopher Carlson entered the room.

"You'd do yourself a service to leave, sir, for as you can see you are interrupting." Cyrus Bloom took one look, then appraised and dismissed in the same glance. The man wore no top coat and his shirt was stained with sweat. He was well built, but he sported no wig. Cyrus looked pointedly toward the door as he clutched his lapels and rocked back on his stacked heels.

Chris raised a brow. "Sir, I don't believe we've met."

"Cyrus Bloom here." His expression clearly stated he expected the man to fall at his feet in apology.

"How good to meet you. Christopher Carlson, at your service. But tell me, good sir, why should I wish to leave? I've only just arrived." Chris briskly rubbed his hands together. "And I'm in dire need of nourishment."

"Then I fear you'll be sorely disappointed for there's no meat. My advice to you, young man, is that you take yourself home at once."

Chris couldn't help but grin for, if anything, Bloom was probably a year or two his junior and a poppinjay to boot. "But, sir," he said as he feigned surprise, "this is my home." With a twinkle in his eye he turned to the widow. Confusion was written all over her face. "Am I intruding madam?" he asked gently. Their eyes met and held and Chris felt his mouth go dry.

"Sir, you are a guest and as such could never be an intrusion."

Chris realized he was holding his breath and exhaled on a slow easy smile. Lord, but she was beautiful. Turning to Bloom he shrugged a shoulder. "It seems, sir, that you are mistaken."

Bloom drew himself erect and sent a withering glare in Abby's direction. "I find it impossible to continue our discussion," he looked down his nose at Chris, "under the present circumstances. I shall call on you at a more opportune time when we may finalize the arrangements."

Abby's head jerked back and her eyes grew wide. "Sir, feel free to call as you wish for we serve dinner at two of the clock and supper at half past seven. But know here and now that we have no arrangements to discuss."

Bloom continued to glare. "As I said, madam, we shall continue this discussion at a later time. Good day to you."

Ignoring Chris completely, Bloom turned to go but Obadiah stepped deftly to his side holding the box that contained the shillings from dinner. "You didn't get no meat, but you had soup thrice over, so I 'spects you'll think that half a shilling is a fair price for your meal."

Cyrus Bloom puffed out his chest, his cheeks blotchy red with indignation. "I do not intend to pay for that."

Obadiah held his ground. "This be a public tavern, sir," he kept his voice soft yet firm. "Them that eat their dinner here pays a shilling. It's posted right on the wall."

"I ate my dinner with my family," Bloom sneered. "Trout, and ham, and beef." He brushed aside the slave and moved toward the door.

"Then I got to tell Miz Barclay that you didn't pay and she's got to tell the magistrate." Obadiah struggled to keep the smile of satisfaction from his face.

112

"The magistrate, why he be more than partial to Nanny's cooking and he wouldn't take kindly to someone getting it for free."

Bloom paused in the doorway, his eyes filled with contempt. "I was a guest of your Mistress, boy, and I know she'll not say otherwise. But I'll tell you one thing that's firm and certain, you and I are going to have a lengthy reeducation session when I become master here. One that's long overdue, if you ask me."

Obadiah resisted the urge to fling the news of his freedom in the man's face as another loud knock sounded at the door. For a heartbeat the room stood in silence, then Cyrus Bloom turned with a flourish and snatched his hat from the table.

He jerked the front door wide only to lose his balance as a tall unkempt man stumbled into his path. The unlikely pair collided in a heap with Bloom's massive girth taking the brunt of the fall.

"Get off me, you oaf," he hissed, as the two struggled to right themselves. Awkwardly climbing to his feet, Cyrus grimaced when the unmistakable sound of splitting fabric filled the air. "Now see what you've done!" he bellowed.

"I don't give a damn whether your fancy arse is covered," the other man stretched to his full height and glared eye to eye with his opponent. "But if you value your life, you'll tell me where the bitch is."

Chapter Seven

"Oh no," Abby groaned. Taking a step backward, she collided against the hard chest of Mr. Carlson. His arms caught her shoulders to steady her as they viewed the commotion in the foyer.

"Do you know that man?" Chris felt her body stiffen beneath his hands, then she straightened and slowly took a step forward.

"Father," she said stiffly. "How nice of you to come to call."

At the sound of her voice, Lucas Corbin spun around in his tracks, his previous adversary forgotten as he glared at his daughter. His dark hair spiked in all directions giving an ominous appearance to his unshaven face. He wore no shoes, and mud from his journey caked his feet and legs which were bare to the knees.

"Where is she?" he snarled, his eyes flashing with fury.

Hesitantly, Abby took another step closer. "Father, come in and rest yourself. I'll have Obadiah fetch you a nice draught of ale."

With the speed of a striking snake, Corbin's hand reached out and grabbed Abby by the arm, jerking her close. "Don't get fresh with me, chit, yer not too

114

old to feel a taste of me belt. Now where is she?"

Christopher felt rage start at his toes and surge upward until every muscle in his body was taut with anger. "Perhaps if you told us whom you were seeking," he said tightly, "someone could offer you assistance."

Corbin never took his eyes from Abby's tense face. "I'm looking fer my daughter as this one well knows," he sneered, enjoying the way her lips thinned white with fear. "And if she knows what's good fer her she'll tell me fast. Where's yer sister?"

"I haven't seen her," Abby squeaked as the pressure around her arm became a band of pain.

"Don't lie to me, girl. Ye know I ken always tell when yer lying. Where did ye hide her?"

"She said she hadn't seen her," Chris said.

Lucas Corbin missed the menacing threat in the softly spoken words. "Oh she'll talk all right. It might take a while with the strap for she's a stubborn little thing, always has been. But I ken tell when she's lying and when I'm through she'll tell me where her sister is."

"Are you perhaps referring to Suzannah?" Chris leaned nonchalantly against the door jamb.

Lucas Corbin dropped his daughter's arm and gave a suspicious glare. "Then ye know of her, do ye laddie?"

Chris shrugged. "Dark haired beauty with flashing eyes?"

Corbin turned back to his daughter. "So she was here." His hand lashed out so fast Abby had no chance to defend herself and the backhanded blow sent her crashing into the wall. But as Corbin stepped forward to strike again, he found his wrist grasped in a vise of iron that spun him about and pinned his arm high up behind his back. Face to face

115

with an enraged Christopher Carlson, Lucas Corbin tasted fear for the first time in his life.

"That was a very unwise act, Mr. Corbin," Chris said softly. "Let me escort you out to the back. I'm sure we can find a solution to your problem." Chris jerked the arm further upward, drawing the man to his toes lest he hear his bone crack.

Abby tried to step forward, but the motion sent the world spinning and she grabbed the wall for support.

"Obadiah," Chris snapped, "see to your mistress." Then with his unwilling partner in tow, Chris moved purposefully down the hall to the back door.

Abby gingerly touched the lump forming on her forehead and grimaced. Pain was starting to spread, but she knew that to give in would only make it worse. Blinking to clear her vision, she tried to smile when Obadiah's troubled face finally came into focus and thankfully stayed steady.

"I'll be all right, Obbie." Her breath came in hiccoughing gasps. "I'd forgotten . . ." Her words faded as horrors of the past surged forth. The world tilted again and gratefully she accepted Obadiah's arm for support. "I've got to find out if Suzannah confided in Mr. Carlson." She fought back the panic. "If he knows and tells father, Suzannah's doomed unless I can find out where she is and warn her first."

"Miz Abby," Obadiah gently nudged her into a chair. "Your father's gonna hurt you bad if you get near him again. Why don't you just let Miz Suzannah fight her own battles?"

Despite her pain, Abby's face turned cold. "I'm the only one in the world Suzannah can depend on, Obadiah. I'll not desert my own sister."

116

The wizened face pulled into a frown. "I guess it don't matter then that Miz Suzannah's always deserting you? Besides," he pleaded as she tried to rise, "you can't go nowhere, Miz Abby. You're hurt." His fingers gingerly touched the swollen side of her face. "Your lip is cut and you're bleeding."

Abby's reply died on her lips as the back door slammed and footsteps echoed down the hallway. Her knuckles turned white as she gripped the wooden chair. Slowly she forced herself erect to face her father, and as the shadows emerged from the darkened corridor, her anxiety grew.

Mr. Carlson's arm encircled her father's shoulders in a benevolent fashion and he chatted easily about the price of ale. The pain of betrayal settled deep within but Abby refused to acknowledge it. Her own survival and her sister's safety were her first concern. But as the unlikely pair edged closer, she blinked with confusion. Mr. Carlson seemed to be supporting much of her father's weight.

"Your father's just stopped back to bid his farewell, Mrs. Barclay, before he's off again." He gave the man's shoulders a hearty squeeze. "It's indeed a pity but he's just remembered pressing business that needs his immediate attention. Isn't that right, Corbin?"

Lucas Corbin looked at his daughter. His face, now several shades of gray, was slick with sweat. "Off again," he mumbled. "Needed . . . back home . . . right away . . ."

"Such a shame you can't stay longer," Chris continued easily. "But if it can't be helped, then there's no more to say." He turned to Obadiah. "My wagon is secured near the shed and one of my men waits with it. Why don't you see Mrs. Barclay's father set-

117

tled and then instruct the driver as to the proper direction." He gave the servant a knowing wink. "I'm sure Mr. Corbin would be most grateful for the kindness."

Obadiah's troubled scowl vanished. "I ken do that, sure enough, Mr. Carlson."

Completely befuddled, Abby tried to step forward. "Father?"

Corbin's eyes darted nervously from Chris to his daughter and then back again. "Gotta get home."

Chris stepped to the widow's side as Obadiah helped her father from the room. "Here," he pressed gently on her shoulder. "You need to sit down. Your lip is bleeding."

She flopped back in the chair only to spring up like a top. "Did you tell him where to find Suzannah?"

His hand pressed again on her shoulder and this time stayed to keep her in place. "I wouldn't tell that man the time of day. Besides, Mrs. Barclay, I don't have the foggiest notion as to where your sister might be."

"But you said . . ."

Chris placed his finger to her swollen lips. "Hush," he commanded gently. "I haven't seen your sister since the fire last night. Now will you be still?"

Like one stricken of mind Abby watched in amazement as he dug in his back pocket and produced a handkerchief stained with dirt and sweat. He scowled and the fabric was hastily shoved out of sight. Then spotting her discarded napkin on the table, he scooped up the cloth and dipped the end into the water pitcher.

Chris felt his chest swell with pain as he knelt beside her chair. A thin trickle of blood ran from her

118

lip and a lump the size of a quail egg had appeared on her forehead. Gently, using the cloth, he wiped the blood from her pale skin.

"You're going to have quite a shiner, in the morning, Mrs. Barclay," he said softly moving the cloth over her forehead, grimacing when she winced.

"A shiner?" Her speech slurred from the swelling.

Chris reached for the water jug and again dunked the napkin. "Aye, a black eye. Here, can you hold this for me?" He placed the damp pad he had fashioned from the napkin into her palm and guided it to her forehead. She flinched from the initial touch, but he was persistent. "I know it hurts, sweetheart," he soothed. "But the coolness should help the swelling, just try to keep it in place for a few more minutes."

"Oh, my poor poor baby," Nanny crooned, carrying a small covered dish she waddled through the doorway. "Obadiah told me what happened," she huffed. "That wicked man should be shot dead, and I don't care who hears me say so." She gave Mr. Carlson a challenging stare. "Now let me see . . ." Setting down the dish her fingers poked here and there against her mistress's bruised flesh, leaving white impressions that faded slowly. "The cheek is just bruised," she declared finally. "And there's not much to be done for it, but the forehead is different. I think you did the most harm by dancing with the wall, Miz Abby." Her fingers pressed the lump on Abby's forehead. "The leeches ken help with that."

Chris knelt in silence beside the widow's chair and watched her face grow paler still as the old black woman uncovered the dish filled with sluglike creatures. "Wait." His hand reached out in protest.

"You men all the same," the old woman clucked,

119

"you can take it yourself but it tears you apart to watch it a happening to someone else. Now, be a good lad for Nanny and hold the little one's hand here. She's always been a bit squeamish about the leeches."

"I really don't think they're necessary," Abby pleaded, her voice thin. But Nanny would not be put off. Carefully she lifted a small, slimy creature from her dish. Unable to face the inevitable, Abby pressed her eyes tightly closed and prayed for the ordeal to soon be over.

The widow grimaced as the leech was placed on her forehead and Chris felt her shudder. Her fingers tightened involuntary around his. "Does it hurt?" he questioned gently, her hands felt like ice within his own and he would have laid odds that she was going to faint at any moment.

Nanny leaned over to peer closer at her work and grunted with satisfaction. "When the blood's still running under the skin, like 'tis here, then the leeches does a body good. Problem is that people wants to use them for everything. See . . ." She ran her fingers lightly over the girl's forehead where the swelling was already noticeably reduced. "Almost over, Miz Abby," she soothed.

"But does it hurt?"

Abby kept her eyes tightly closed. "It makes me feel . . . queer," her voice shuddered.

The creature had grown to more than three times its size before Nanny was satisfied. "I think that one will do it this time, Miz Abby. Now you just hold still a minute longer."

Chris watched in amazement as the slug dropped off in the old woman's hand. This time, she had said. Did she mean that this type of confrontation

120

happened often? He watched the woman drop the engorged leech back in her dish. "It's barbaric," he stated.

"But it works," Nanny declared. She reached over and gave his shoulder a reassuring pat. "It didn't cause her no pain, Mr. Carlson," she said firmly. "The little one here just gets a bit squeamish thinking on a leech drinking her blood. I thought she'd grow out of it but I guess not. You might put that cloth back on her cheek though, the leeches ain't gonna do her no good there."

"Thank God for that," Abby mumbled.

"You just rest here for a while, Miz Abby." Nanny picked up her tray and waddled toward the door. "I got things to see to in the cook house."

Chris rinsed the napkin again in the water pitcher and gently placed it against her bruised cheek. Her skin was so pale it almost looked translucent-like fine alabaster, he thought. What kind of madman would deliberately abuse something so precious? His eyes narrowed, he would pay a visit to Lucas Corbin on the morrow and settle this account once and for all. Daughter or not the man had overstepped his bounds. This, he swore silently, looking at her bruised cheek and cut lip, this was never going to happen again.

With the leeches gone, Abby's eyes fluttered open. She savored the gentle touch of the cloth against her bruised flesh, but its cooling dampness did little to calm the tremors that were now threatening. He was too close, her mind screamed in panic. She could see the fine lines at the corners of his eyes and the dark lashes that fringed them. Gently he stroked her uninjured cheek with his knuckles as his soft voice wove a spell around her.

Despite her fear, Abby felt herself begin to relax.

"That's the way," he praised gently as he felt the tension begin to leave her slender frame. "Why don't you just rest your head back and close your eyes. You've had quite a shock."

Abby almost smiled. Calm she was, crazy she wasn't. Her eyes took on a challenging, if somewhat lopsided, slant. "What did you say to make my father leave so abruptly?"

Chris lowered the cloth he'd been holding against her cheek and rinsed it again. "We just had a friendly chat," he said easily.

She raised a brow. "Just talk?"

Chris sighed and took her hand again, holding it loosely in his despite the stiffening of her fingers. "Let's just say we had a little discussion. I asked him to describe the pain he thought he'd given you and when he couldn't, well, I gave him something to compare it to."

"You *hit* him?" Stunned, Abby could only stare in amazement. Even Malachi, with his quick temper, had never dared to strike her father.

Chris struggled to look remorseful but without success. "Sweetheart, I'm sorry. I know he's your father, but that doesn't give him the right to . . ."

"He left because you hit him?"

Chris shrugged and looked down at their clasped hands as he balanced on the balls of his feet. "Not exactly. I just asked which was more important, finding your sister or keeping his kidneys. All things considered, I think he made a very wise choice."

He grinned and Abby felt the heat shoot straight to her stomach.

"So, now that all the commotion is over," he leaned back on his heels. "What's the chance

122

of getting fed if you miss the dinner bell?"

"It ain't no problem 'tall, Mr. Carlson," Obadiah entered the room with a large tray that carried two steaming platters. "Nanny said to tell you there's more of anything that you wants and her special lemon cheesecake is awaiting on you when you're done." Deftly he set two places at a clean table and motioned for the pair to sit. "Miz Abby here is partial to chocolate, but I thought you'd prefer ale, although we do make a fine rum punch."

"Ale will be fine." Chris took the widow's elbow and helping her stand, guided her firmly to the chair opposite his.

Abby looked down at the heaping portions of pork and turkey in confusion. "I thought you told Mr. Bloom that there was no meat . . ."

Obadiah shrugged and tucked the tray under his arm. "Nanny was saving this for Mr. Carlson. She said since she'd never fed the man she didn't know how much he'd be needing."

The platters that filled the table held enough meat to satisfy six hearty appetites and despite her swollen lip Abby tried to grin. "Obbie, I think you did that on purpose."

The old man raised a brow but his smile said all. "Don't see how it matters much since the man wasn't paying no way."

"But in the future . . ."

"In the future," Chris interrupted, giving the servant a wink, "I shall arrive on time and thus the problem will be no more. Now, if you would be so kind as to join me, Mrs. Barclay, I really am famished."

Obadiah discreetly disappeared and the two ate in companionable silence for several minutes. Abby,

123

hampered by the pain in her lip, nibbled at her food and tried to watch her guest as inconspicuously as possible. He had filled his plate with undisguised delight and then set about doing justice to the lot. He didn't slurp or belch constantly as Malachi had been so fond of doing. All in all she decided, his manners were perfect. His plate was nearly empty when he looked up and caught her eye. He grinned and Abby felt a hot blush rush into her cheeks.

"You're not eating much," he observed.

She shrugged. "The weather this time of year often takes my appetite."

And a drunken lout for a father certainly doesn't help, he thought darkly. He pushed aside his empty plate. "Does your lip hurt overmuch? Mayhap you'd deal better with soup until the swelling goes down. I'd be happy to go . . ."

"I'm fine, Mr. Carlson," she interrupted, as he made to rise, and his look forced her to continue. "In fact, I was dining on soup when Mr. Bloom arrived."

And ate two mouthfuls, Chris thought with a frown. "I don't mean to pry, but does Bloom dine here often?"

She leaned back in her chair her fingers absently pressing against the ache in her forehead. "I'm not always in the dining room, but today was the first time I ever remember speaking to the man."

As if by magic Obadiah appeared. The dinner dishes were whisked away, though he scowled at Abby's full plate, and two generous portions of cheese cake were left in their place. Chris grinned and immediately pulled his close and took a bite, sighing with exaggerated delight.

"Obadiah, you can tell Nanny that her reputation

124

as Middle Plantation's best cook is no exaggeration. I thought my mother made the best cheese cake, but even she would take pleasure in this one."

Obadiah's eyes flashed with pride. "She'll be right pleased to hear that, Mr. Carlson. If you be needing anything else, you just let old Obadiah know."

"Well, when my driver, Jason, returns from his errand do you think you could find him a meal?"

"Nanny already put some aside, sir. And she said to tell you that dinner is served prompt at half past the hour of seven this evening."

"Ouch," Chris grinned. "I guess that means I'd better be on time."

"Unless you're busy, sir. If that be the case we'll be sure to save a little something to tide you over."

"I think you've made a conquest," Abby said slowly as Obadiah departed. "Nanny takes a great deal of pride in her cooking, but to be true, I've never known her to care if someone missed a meal. She let Harley go hungry once because he didn't show up on time and he was her own flesh and blood."

Chris shifted and eyed her untouched piece of cake. "The woman is one fine cook," he said solemnly. "And when you get to know me better, Mrs. Barclay, you'll know that I don't give compliments lightly, and when I do, I mean them."

Abby felt a strange sensation start deep in her stomach. His eyes raked over her, and her skin began to tingle like the air before a thunder storm. Never had she seen a man so fascinating. His thick blond hair was neatly tied back and his face was clean shaven. And even though his shirt was stained and he wore no wig, he appeared more the gentleman than Mr. Bloom with his satin breeches and fine brass buttons. A wicked smile began to tug at her sore mouth and she watched Mr. Carlson's brow raise in silent question.

"I know it's unkind of me to have such thoughts," she said, smothering a giggle, "but I was just thinking of poor Mr. Bloom and wondering how he managed with the rent in his breeches."

"I'd almost forgotten." Chris' eyes filled with laughter as he imagined the red faced man scurrying down the street with his backside bare. "Now, I'm not one to take my pleasure in someone else's misfortune," he chuckled, "but in this case, since the man didn't pay hard coin for his meal, I don't think he'd mind us having a laugh at his expense."

This time Abby did chuckle, but the movement hurt her jaw and her laughter died as quickly as it had come. For a moment, the need to share Mr. Bloom's strange request was on the tip of her tongue, but years of caution made her force it aside.

Chris wondered what thought had taken the joy from her face, and he leaned forward in his chair bracing his elbows on the table. "Mrs. Barclay, I truly appreciate your generosity in providing me with a place to stay, but I would ask an additional favor of you." Abby watched him shift as if he wasn't quite sure how to continue. "Would you take offense if I asked to provide my own bed?" he hesitated. "It's just that, well, I'm a good head taller than most and the bed upstairs is about a foot too short."

"Oh, dear," The memory of his unclad body draped across her husband's bed came instantly to mind and Abby felt her cheeks grow warm. She hadn't meant to pause, she had intended only to replace his cleaned garments and fill the pitcher with warmed water. But as he lay sprawled in careless

126

abandon above the covers, she could not help herself. His skin had been golden in the early morning light, not blue-white and flaccid like Malachi's; and smooth as it rippled over muscles then tapered to his waist. Never had she seen shoulders so wide. But he was right, his feet had hung over the edge of the bed and when he had groaned in his sleep and started to shift, she had made a hasty exit.

"I have no objection if you provide your own bed, Mr. Carlson," she stumbled over the word, "but surely it did not survive the fire."

"The only things that survived the fire, Mrs. Barclay, were the two water buckets that Jimmy forgot to put way." He gave a deep sigh. "But I can't complain. As the fates would have it, I had not moved any of my own furniture into the building. It's stored in a wagon at the home of friends."

"Then you must transport it at your convenience." Abby struggled with the urge to flee, as she felt the warmth in her cheeks continue to burn. "Did you receive any news of young Jim?"

The bright blue of his eyes darkened with concern. "I've been to the house twice but the lad's still unconscious. The doctor says that's normal with a fright like the one he had, and that, it will probably take hunger to rouse him."

"Then he won't wake until supper?"

"Possibly not even until tomorrow morning. Although at his age I remember being constantly hungry. My mother once accused me of having a hollow leg," he grinned.

Abby felt her cheeks grow hotter still for she knew only too well that his legs were not hollow but straight and well corded with muscles that curved neatly onto his hip.

127

"But I will confess," he continued, "I'd feel much relieved if the lad were to wake sooner than later."

"Nanny has some calve's foot jelly put by, would you take a crock to Mrs. Richardson next time you go?" she offered.

Chris smiled. "That's very thoughtful, but why don't you come with me this afternoon."

Abby's eyes dropped to her lap and settled on the stains that covered her apron. "I don't think that would be possible," she said quietly. "Besides, Mrs. Richardson has enough on her hands without having to deal with a stranger arriving at her door."

"Hardly a stranger," he argued, realizing how much he wanted to stay in her company. "You are the one who saved her son's life. The woman will be eternally grateful."

The widow looked up with a start. "I did no such thing and I'll thank you not to spread such tales, Mr. Carlson. We both know it was you that pulled the boy from the flames, so don't you go telling that boy's mother otherwise."

"Don't distress yourself so m'lady," He moved to take her hand, but Abby quickly slid it out of reach and stood.

"I must beg your pardon, Mr. Carlson, and take my leave. I've much to see to for the evening meal. I'll have Nanny set the jelly out for you." Before his words of protest could be uttered, she scooped up her dishes and disappeared down the darkened hall.

Christopher leaned back in his chair and watched her retreating form, enjoying the gentle sway of her skirt as she moved. She certainly was a flighty little thing, he thought. His fingers thumped a rhythm on the table. She had bolted when he'd reached for her hand and blushed like a school girl when he had but

128

mentioned a bed. His eyes narrowed. "You do your cause no service to tempt me too far, Mrs. Barclay," he whispered to the empty room. "For there's nothing I enjoy more than a good chase." Rising, he patted his firm stomach, then reaching into his pocket, tossed a shilling onto the table. "And as any would tell you," he grinned toward the hallway, "I am always the victor." With thoughts of their next encounter already spinning through his mind, Chris quietly took his leave.

Chapter Eight

Christopher stretched out in bed and wondered why he couldn't shed the foul mood that, of late, seemed his constant companion. Folding his arms back under his head he stared at the ceiling as the tall, cased clock ticked away the minutes. There was no logical reason for his irritation, he thought darkly. True, he was maintaining a back-breaking pace, but he had never been one to shy away from a challenge and things were proceeding better than he had planned. He had coaxed his father's old carpenter, Nigel Williams, out of retirement to act as overseer for the shop's restoration and, with William's reputation as a craftsman, it had taken no time to assemble a crew. More than eighty percent of his silver stock had been recovered and now rested in buckets awaiting his attention. And even Jeremy Knapp, the blacksmith, had been willing to rent him a corner of the livery to work in while his shop was being rebuilt. Young Richardson had recovered and was back at work and although completely subdued in spirit, the lad seemed none the worse for wear.

Chris gave a sigh. It was not his circumstances that constantly pricked at his good humor, he reasoned, but his frustration with the elusive Abigail Barclay. That first evening he had arrived late on purpose, hoping she would again take her evening meal with him. The widow had not appeared. And as the days slowly passed he managed no more than an occasional glimpse of her retreating form, no matter how he tried to arrange otherwise. Christopher scowled at the full moon that filled his room with its silvery light.

Several of his crew now took their lodging at the tavern and it seemed the widow's name was a constant in their conversation.

"The Widow Barclay mended this shirt for me," one would say. "And did you taste that ginger gravy . . ."

"The Widow Barclay made a poultice for my sore tooth . . ." another would add. On and on it went until he felt like lashing out at the very sound of her name. Why, he wondered, was she accessible to everyone but him?

"You need to take some time away," Nick Beaumont had counseled. "Do yourself and your men a favor and make yourself absent for the afternoon."

Deciding to take Nick's advice he had invited Betsy Addlers on a picnic. He rolled his eyes at the ceiling as he thought of the disaster it had turned into. Nanny had provided him with a basket fit for royalty and at first he had found Betsy's adoration a balm for his bruised ego. But as the afternoon wore on, so did his nerves. Why had he never noticed how much she chattered, he thought darkly. She had commented on everything from the weather, which was certainly damp, to the holly berries that surely weren't as lush this year as last.

And so it went, Betsy found a way to pick at everything. They had scarce reached their destination by the river before his head was aching. The chicken, she complained, was a tad too greasy for her delicate stomach, and yes oysters were her favorite, but didn't these taste just a bit too spicy. . . .

Disgusted with himself, Chris sat up on the edge of his bed. Why had he even bothered to show her the plans of his shop? Standing, he slipped into his breeches and tied the knee straps. Betsy had stared hard at the drawing and then, batting her lashes, which were thick and dark, asked him what color he had planned to paint the bedroom. He had tried to explain the plans, hoping to garner some enthusiasm, but it soon became clear that Betsy thought him a fool for wishing to work when his financial situation didn't require it. She had gazed at him blankly when he tried to explain the joy he felt when he fashioned the metal. Then she let it be known that she wasn't sure if she could be happy having a tradesman for a husband, and didn't he want to reconsider?

Shaking his head, Chris stretched and walked to the desk. Bathed in the moonlight he studied the rough floor sketch of his shop. Why, he wondered, had he ever thought a picnic with Betsy would solve his problem? He added a notation and then turned back to the bed, but tonight sleep was as evasive as the widow.

Pacing the room, Chris cursed himself as a fool. Never had a woman caused him such vexation. Hell, he had even picked flowers for her, and he had felt like a school boy too shy to plead his own

132

case when he had handed the bouquet to Obadiah.

"For your mistress," His voice had been clipped, but the old man had only smiled.

Chris rubbed his hand across his cheek feeling the new growth of beard. He was going to have to think this through from a different angle.

At first the sound was so soft, he thought he'd imagined it. But cocking his head to the side, he listened again. Silently his feet carried him to the corner window. Looking down he felt his pulse leap. Sitting on a chair just outside the cookhouse door and bathed in silvery light, was the Widow Barclay. Silently he stood, drinking in the sight of her. Wishing he could sweep away the ridiculous cap that concealed her golden hair, he watched the rhythmic motion of her arms as they worked the butter churn. Leaning closer to the window, he found he could just make out the melody of her song as it blended with the night sounds.

Without a moment's hesitation, Christopher found himself striding toward the door. Pausing only long enough to retrieve the plans to his shop, he quickly made his way down the darkened stairs. A foolish grin covered his face, for in the brief moments he had watched her, he realized that his gift of flowers now rested on the stump beside her as she worked.

Abby saw the shadow step from the doorway, and instinctively knew it was not one of the patrons on his way to the privy. Mr. Carlson's profile was unmistakable as he stepped into the silvery moonlight. She swallowed a gasp when she realized that he was naked from the waist up. The muscles of his broad shoulders and chest were clearly visible, yet as he approached she realized she felt no fear. This was the man that had dared to strike her father. Despite her desire to be a respectful daughter, a smile touched her lips each time the image came to mind.

"Good evening," he said pleasantly, as if they had been conversing on the street in the daylight instead of by the cookhouse door as the hour approached midnight.

"It's late, Mr. Carlson," she replied gently. "Is there something I can do for you?"

Come to my bed, he wanted to say. Let me taste your lips just once to see if they are as soft as they appear. Instead, he stood before her with arms akimbo. "There's a new girl serving in the dining room yet you still find no time to share a meal with me."

Abby raised a brow, for his tone and posture clearly indicated he was put out. "Effie is hardly new, Mr. Carlson. She's Nanny's daughter. She and her family have served at the Stag's Head longer than I." She glanced at Thomas's well-stocked wood pile with relief. "But I did mean to seek you out and thank you for the flowers." She smiled at the thick bouquet of hearty mums.

Chris found himself staring at the constant up and down motion of her arms and wondered if she did it just to torment him as desire akin to pain twisted in his gut. "I'm glad they pleased you." He searched for something to say. For days all he had wanted was to speak with her and now he stood tongue-tied like a fledgling youth. "Ah, I wanted to thank you, too, for the picnic lunch . . ."

Abby shrugged and tried not to think of the

134

beautiful lady that had leaned on his arm as the carriage had made its way slowly out of town. "It was Nanny's doing, but I'll be sure to pass on your appreciation. Did you have a pleasant afternoon?" Instantly, she bit her tongue. Shut up you fool, her mind screamed. Do you want to hear him prattle on about another woman?

Chris felt his pulse leap at the tone in her voice, was it only polite conversation, or had there been just the slightest hint of jealously? Encouraged he sat on the step beside her chair. "Actually, it was a disaster," he smiled up at her. "I had other . . . things on my mind."

Abby felt her chest grow tight and suddenly the urge to flee was paramount. Her hands grew slippery on the wooden handle of the butter churn, and she struggled to find something to say. "How is the new shop progressing?" she stammered.

Chris took a deep breath and relaxed for the first time in days. "The men continue to amaze me with their speed," he said easily. "It's hard to believe that a shop and house once stood on that spot for Mr. Williams has had it completely cleared. The finished sketches were delivered today and await my final approval."

"You are going to lay a different floor plan?" Her voice carried her amazement as she shifted slightly to look at him. How could he even think of such a ridiculous notion? The man had not enough spare shillings to purchase a wig, yet he was willing to redesign a shop he had yet to establish. Concern drew her brows together. "Is that a wise decision?" she questioned, hoping she wasn't overstepping her bounds.

135

"Would you like to see?" he offered. "Maybe you'll notice something that should be done differently."

Abby's eyes grew wide in disbelief. Never in her life had she been called upon to voice a thought over anything more pressing than the amount of starch for the table linens. "You wish my opinion?"

Chris spread out the sketch on the step. "This would be the entrance way." Eagerly Abby looked down at the strange lines, but her excitement drained when she realized the night shadows did not allow a clear view. Even bending closer as she churned, she couldn't make out what was what.

Realizing her problem, Chris stood and placed his hands on the butter churn gently nudging her to his place on the step. "If you sit closer," he urged, "I think the moonlight will suffice."

For a moment Abby could only stare, for she had never seen a man work a butter churn, but his steady rhythm could not be faulted, and his grin was disarming. Feeling her cheeks grow warm, she quickly dropped to the step and carefully spread the parchment across her lap. He had been right, for now the moonlight fell directly on the paper and as she looked her excitement grew as she realized she understood the odd assortment of boxes and lines.

Eager to share his ideas, Chris launched into a detailed explanation as Abby took her finger and traced a path through the shop and into the living quarters. "Would this give you adequate space?" she questioned pointing to the corner near the window that would be his work area.

For the next quarter hour, they discussed and argued the various placement of the rooms. "The dining room is too far from the cookhouse," she had insisted. "You will never eat a warm meal under that roof." Grudgingly he had conceded she was right.

Feeling a strange burst of confidence, Abby turned her attention back to his work area. "I still think you should allow for more space. And this amount of space for an entrance to your private quarters is totally wasted. 'Tis a business you're building not a grand mansion. Now, if you were to push this wall back to about here, you would almost double your work area. If you are to be a thriving silversmith, Mr. Carlson, you must convey that to your customers. I think . . ." She stopped when she realized that her suggestions had turned into a tirade and he was silently grinning down at her. She felt her skin go hot and sticky with embarrassment and her eyes instantly dropped to her lap. "I'm sorry," she stammered, in a whisper.

Puzzled, Chris watched her sudden mood shift. One moment she had been bright, and dynamic with her points, now she sat almost huddled within herself as if she expected some type of revenge to be taken upon her person. An uneasy feeling stirred within him, but eager to recapture their earlier comaraderie he pushed it aside.

"My mother would have liked you," he said suddenly, not at all sure where the words had come from. "She was always partial to a woman who could look at a situation and state her opinions plainly. And I'm beginning to realize that I am too."

137

Abby fought the emotions that seemed to atta⸱ her from every side. He wasn't angry? Slowly t⎹ tight muscles of her shoulders began to rela⸱ "Your mother has passed on?" she asked, her voi⸱ the barest whisper.

Chris sighed and his hands on the butter chu⎹ slowed. "Aye nearly two months. I lost both h⸱ and my father the same week."

Abby looked up at him as he gazed off in⸱ space and wished she had the nerve to touch h⸱ shoulder and offer comfort, for she could feel h⸱ pain. He's lost so much, she thought, yet ⎹ doesn't rant and rave, cursing God for his misfo⸱ tune. Hesitantly, she stood and placed her har⸱ over his on the churn. "You speak as if you car⸱ for them very much."

Christopher felt the jolt the moment her fle⸱ touched his but all his instincts warned him to pr⸱ ceed slowly. "I think I cared even more than I re⸱ ized at the time." For a long moment he was silen⎹ his eyes thoughtful. "I grieve for my own loss ⸱ them," he said carefully. "But they had a hap⎹ life. It was not always easy, but I'm beginning ⸱ realize that their love carried them through. I dor⎹ think one would have wanted to live on without t⎹ other."

Fascinated, Abby remained silent. She had on⎹ the vaguest memory of her mother and no memo⸱ at all of her father caring for anything other tha⸱ himself. Reluctantly, she withdrew her hand fro⸱ his. "You were indeed very fortunate." The twink⎹ returned to her soft brown eyes as she gazed ⸱ him. "I'll bet you were a little terror."

His sheepish grin told her she had hit the na⸱

square on. "I'll admit I spent my fair share of time bent over the fence," he chuckled. "But more often than not I could charm my way out of it. But my mother," he chuckled, "she had her ways and sometimes I would have preferred my father's belt than the chores she'd set out for me. Once, I chopped wood for three straight days." Absently he rubbed his shoulder while one hand continued with the churn. "That time I definitely would have preferred the belt."

Lost in his own memories, Chris missed Abby's shudder for she had tasted the belt, the cane, and the switch more times than she cared to remember. Her father had been adamant that a beating wasn't over until he had drawn blood or flayed her near unconscious.

"I think this is ready," he said noting her shivers. "And I'm thinking we deserve a treat for working this late." He looked up at the silver moon as if to prove his point.

Abby stood in silence, having no idea what he was speaking of. Giving her a wink, he hefted the churn and then brushing past her he entered the cookhouse. She had left one lantern burning on the work table and its shadowy light glowed in the center of the room. Chris set the churn beside the table.

"You get the bread," he whispered, already prying off the churn's top and looking for something to scoop inside.

Abby realized what he was about and she almost laughed out loud at his antics. "You want something to eat?" she whispered.

Nodding, he grinned and pointed to his muscular

thigh. "Remember . . . it's hollow. Where's knife?"

Mesmerized, Abby found she could not move The lantern light bathed his naked chest in golden glow and she found her mouth had gon dry from the sight. His arm brushed lightly agains hers as he reached around her to retrieve the bread She couldn't take her eyes from his hands as the carefully sliced two thick pieces, then generousl lathed both portions with the fresh butter. He ex tended his arm and offered her a piece with courtly bow. Then taking a large bite of his ow portion, he gave an exaggerated sigh and closed hi eyes in ecstasy. "Delicious," he declared. "Definitel worth all the hard work."

"But Nanny's going to be furious in the morn ing," she warned, looking toward the cut loaf.

Chris only grinned and carefully rewrapped th loaf replacing it exactly on the shelf. "She'll neve know who," he continued to whisper. "She'd neve think me bold enough and you're so tiny it's obvi ous that you never snitch food."

Abby took another bite and wondered when sh had ever tasted anything so tempting. "I don' know," she said slowly. "Nanny's very clever. wouldn't be too surprised if you came down t break the fast and found only egg shells on you plate." He swallowed the last of his bread and hi grin turned to a full smile that snatched her breat away.

"Then I'd just have to prevail on the mistress o the tavern to meet me at midnight." He touched finger to her chin and noted gratefully she didn' flinch as he raised her face to his. "I know th

140

woman," he continued softly. "She possesses a heart that's pure gold and makes the best butter I've ever tasted." Before she could realize his intentions, Chris planted a firm kiss on her lips. His arms ached to pull her close and his body throbbed to take her, but reluctantly he stepped away. Taking in her stunned expression he could only smile. "The best I've ever tasted," he said backing out of the cookhouse door with a wink.

Abby flopped down on Nanny's stool. Her fingers trembled as she reached up to touch her pulsing lips. If she closed her eyes she could still feel the pressure of his flesh on hers. Her head spun in confusion. What had the man been thinking of? And why did she feel so queer? She rubbed her hands over her arms for suddenly she felt the night's chill. Slowly she stood, forcing her attention back to the chores that wouldn't let her rest. But her hands trembled as she scooped the butter from the churn into the waiting crock. And her steps were less than steady as she made her way though the silvery moonlight to the small dairy house.

Christopher shed his breeches and eased back on his bed. The scent of fresh linens made him smile when he thought of the hands that had spread them. He folded his arms behind his head and felt his body pulse with an aching need. It took no effort to picture her image; soft brown eyes filled with innocence, the gentle curve of her cheek, and her lips . . . her lips had been even softer than when he dreamed of her. The tall, cased clock struck one and for the first time in days, Christopher closed his eyes in sleep, eager for the dreams that he knew awaited him.

141

Cyrus Bloom angrily paced the length of his study and back again. Filled with cheap port and righteous indignation, he cursed the fates that had brought him to such desperate times. His scowl deepened as he scanned the bookcase. The rosewood shelves had once boasted an expensive collection of rare books. Now they housed an odd assortment of chipped porcelain. Cyrus poured himself another drink from the side bar. He hadn't actually minded selling the family heirlooms, for he had never understood the ridiculous value placed on books when life offered so many other stimulating diversions. No, it had been the humiliation of dealing like a tinker with boorish colonials too ignorant to recognize the rare finds he was offering that had set his teeth on edge. He still chafed at the thought of the paltry sums he had been forced to accept. But as his gaze moved over the dusty shelves, he had to admit Mrs. Gaffney had done an admirable job of finding castoffs to fill in.

With a calculating step he moved about the room. The missing pictures had been the hardest to deal with for the walls still carried their ghostly silhouettes as a constant reminder. But here he had prevailed and a smile tugged at his lips when he thought of the coins the gilded frames had brought in. It hadn't mattered in the slightest than the frames had been deemed more valuable that the paintings of his ancestors.

The sun dipped lower in the sky and as dusty shadows began to invade the room, Bloom's eyes grew critical as he surveyed his surroundings.

Things might just work out after all, he reasoned. Carefully he repositioned the winged back chair he had carted down from his bedroom. Mrs. Gaffney had had the forethought to cover the worn places with lace doilies and all in all the effect was quite stylish. Carefully he viewed the room from all directions then again repositioned the chairs. The sun moved lower still and the room took on a golden glow as the shadows lengthened. He smiled with relief. To the untrained eye the room would still carry the flavor of wealth and prestige, and he was risking all that his visitor would not be able to tell the difference.

Taking a seat behind the small desk, he artfully arranged the papers that bespoke of a thriving business man, then he leaned back in his chair to wait.

Waiting was not what he did best, but for the past year he had had no choice. Now all had changed. Providence had stepped in and gifted him with a solution. The faintest smile creased the corners of his mouth as the image of the Widow Barclay came to mind. And his satisfaction, like his smile, grew when he thought of the revenue he'd have at his disposal when he owned the tavern. He steepled his fingers and rested his pudgy chin on their tips. Thank God she wasn't hard to look on, he thought, and teaching her her place would surely have its pleasures. But his smile turned menacing when he thought of the slave that had dared to insult him.

A loud rap on his study door pulled Cyrus from his musings. All things come to he who waits, he thought with satisfaction. Then leaning back in his

143

chair he bid entrance.

A hulking servant with fists the size of smoked hams ushered in a reluctant Lucas Corbin.

"Come in, come in," Cyrus greeted cordially. "How are you faring my good man?"

"If I be yer good man," Corbin sneered, jerking himself free from the servant's grasp. "Then hows come ye had yer lackey here drag me through the back door?"

Cyrus raised a brow. "Surely, Mr. Corbin," he mocked, "you did not expect someone of my standing to admit a drunkard like yourself through the main doorway to my home where anyone who was passing by could see?" He looked down at the mud spattered clothing with disdain.

"Well ye wants me here enough to send yer carriage clear to me shack to fetch me. So's I can't see why ye'd be a caring which door I'm a coming through."

Cyrus gritted his teeth. "You may go, Toby," he gestured impatiently toward the servant. "I'll speak with Mr. Corbin in private."

"Private is it now?" Corbin flopped down in his chair and tried to keep the tremors from showing as his eyes quickly scanned the room for something to filch. "What's a fancy peacock like yerself a wanting with the likes of me?"

Cyrus smiled as he recognized the nervous tremors for what they were and realized the man's desperation could only help his cause. Slowly, deliberately, he stood and moved to the side bar. "Perhaps you'd like some liquid refreshment, Mr. Corbin, to wash the dust from your throat before we get down to business?"

144

"I won't say no to a nip or two," came the hasty reply.

With the precision and flare of one serving royalty, Cyrus poured two generous tumblers. But he settled himself behind his desk before slowly passing Corbin his glass. The man gulped the entire contents then blatantly looked for more.

"When we've finished our discussion," Cyrus said easily, enjoying his guest's discomfort.

Lucas Corbin stared hard at the popinjay that sat across from him and every inch of his body throbbed with anger. Bloom knew how much he needed another drink, God damn his black soul. Yet there he sat, like a king on his throne with his big ass stuffed in bright red breeches.

With the insolent grace of one who knew he had nothing to lose, Corbin rose and stepped directly to the sidebar. He almost laughed aloud at the startled expression on his host's face.

"Now we both know ye didn't have yer lackey drag me all this way to discuss the weather, Mr. Bloom," he said easily pouring himself another drink. "And I ain't some young sapling that don't know the way the wind's a blowing." He returned to the chair with his filled glass in one hand and the crystal decanter in the other. "Now," he set the decanter on the desk with a thud. "Why don't ye just stop this game of cat and mouse ye be playing and tell me what yer want?"

Cyrus gripped his chair so hard his obese form threatened to snap the delicately carved arms. "How dare you," he sputtered.

Corbin only shrugged. He could already feel the tremors starting to ease as the alcohol seeped into his blood and the relief made him heady. "It was you what sent for me, Mr. Bloom. I didn't come a begging." He stood, made a courtly bow and wondered if he'd make it out with the Chinese figurine that was now snug in his pocket. "So if ye ain't got nothing te say, I'll just take my leave."

"Enough theatrics, Corbin," Cyrus leaned forward and his voice went cold. "I'm willing to admit I'd underestimated you, but I'm also willing to lay odds that you're too smart a business man to walk out that door without first hearing my proposal."

Corbin flopped back in his chair and poured himself another drink. "And jest what would someone like yerself," he glanced about the room, "be needing with someone like me?"

"Your daughter," Cyrus stated.

Corbin choked on his drink and pounded himself hard on the chest as tears filled his bloodshot eyes. "Ye wants Suzannah?" he gasped. "Do ye know where she be hiding then?"

Cyrus shook his head. "No, no, I'm speaking of your daughter, Abigail. How tragic the fates to steal away her loving husband, leaving her alone in her bereavement."

"Ye want Abby?"

Cyrus nodded. "As her father I'm sure you want only the best for her."

Snorting with disgust, Corbin poured himself another drink. "So ye want to take Abigail to wife." He drank deeply and then belched. "What's it worth ta ye?"

Cyrus slowly leaned back in his chair as if contemplating the situation for the first time. "I had rather thought that I would be asking that question."

"What? Ye expect me ta give that girl a dowry? Ye must be daft. She ain't my responsibility now. The chit was married to Barclay for over nine years."

"Oh," Cyrus sighed with feigned disappointment. "That certainly creates a ticklish situation." He waited the space of three heartbeats then sat forward with his revelation. "But wait," he exclaimed. Skillfully, he laid his trump card on the table. "What if I was to offer you fifty pounds as compensation for the hand of your daughter in marriage?" He held his smile as Corbin's eyes nearly bugged from his head.

"I'd say ye done right well fer yerself, son." Corbin tried to take in his good fortune. "Have ye asked the wench? Is she agreeable te the match?"

Now Cyrus frowned in truth. "Actually, I did mention the thought to her in passing, but I'm afraid she wasn't too keen on the idea. Lord only knows why. My family is one of the most respected in the colony. And she'd have a beautiful home to preside over." He glanced about the room and prayed the shadowy evening light would hold just a little longer.

"Ye ken just leave the wench ta me," Corbin stood. "She's a feisty little thing, but I know hows to talk ta the girl." He patted his worn leather belt. "When were ye thinking of posting the banns for the first time? No sense in letting the grass grow under yer feet," he urged.

Cyrus fought down his smile of triumph. "I rather thought I'd speak with the good Reverend Sunday next. I've business that calls me out of town this weekend."

Lucas Corbin rubbed his hands together with undisguised glee. "And just when would you be imparting with this compensation ye was talking about?"

Cyrus rose and moved to the study door. "Why don't I give you ten pounds the day we sign the marriage contract and the remaining when the deed is done?"

"Why don't ye give me ten pounds now in good faith?" Corbin bargained, feeling the Chinese figurine bump against his leg. "After all, we're te be family the two of us."

"Why don't I give you five pounds now in good faith," Cyrus countered reaching for his money pouch to indicate the dickering was over. "I'll speak with Mr. Danvers first of next week when I return from Yorktown, and then we shall speak with your daughter."

Corbin wiped the spittle from his mouth with the back of his sleeve as Bloom carefully counted out five pounds. "It's a pleasure to do business with you, Mr. Bloom," he chortled, wondering how much more he'd receive for the figurine. "It's a blooming pleasure to be sure."

Chapter Nine

Abigail Barclay sat in stunned silence as the words of Magnus Webster became her worst nightmare. She had been surprised when the message had arrived that the well respected attorney wished to meet with her, and if four of the clock was not inconvenient, he would await her at his office. All afternoon her mind had anxiously anticipated the reason. Her eyes dropped to her clenched hands that rested in her lap. How foolish of her to conclude that the man had wanted to arrange a private dinner, just because the tavern now served a handsome crowd at each meal. She almost smiled from the irony of it all.

"So I'm sure you understand why I can not allow this situation to continue, Mrs. Barclay," he stated formally.

Abby turned her attention back to the case at hand. Webster had a kindly face, but his eyes were hard as he gazed at her over his wire-rimmed glasses. "I don't understand," she said, trying to keep her voice from trembling. "I thought that Malachi owned the tavern. Now you are telling me that he only rented?"

The portly attorney nodded. "Your husband was

more than a month behind with his payments when he died, Mrs. Barclay and since you have not made a payment since, your debt has continued to grow these past months."

"But why did you not send for me sooner?" she struggled to remain calm. "Why did you wait until the debt was so enormous that I would have no hopes of payment?"

Webster shifted uncomfortably in his chair and pushed a coil of chestnut curls over his shoulder. "For that I do apologize madam," he said carefully. "But the truth is that shortly after your husband's untimely death, the ownership of the Stag's Head changed hands. The new owner had instructed me to maintain his properties but then there was . . . well that's of no matter." The attorney cleared his throat, clearly embarrassed that he had nearly divulged private information concerning one of his clients. "But now that I have the situation in hand, I find myself in a dilemma, Mrs. Barclay. I wish you no ill will, but I find I must demand payment in full of all monies owed my client."

"Mr. Webster, I fear the dilemma is mine. It's not that I don't wish to pay, but I don't have the kind of revenue of which you speak at my disposal. Is it possible that some type of plan might be worked out between myself and your client?" She tried to cipher a solution in her mind, but her scattered thoughts made dealing with numbers impossible. "perhaps I could resume the required monthly rent," she offered desperately, "and pay off the outstanding amount a little each month. You would have my word that I would pay as much as possible."

Webster pulled off his glasses and folded them carefully before placing them on his cluttered desk. Damn but he hated dealing with females. They took everything so personally. "Madam," he said impatiently, "I do not doubt your integrity and I truly am sorry that circumstances have become so overwhelming for you. But my client finds himself in need of ready cash and has instructed me to review all of his accounts for outstanding balances. And yours madam is the largest."

"But what shall happen if I can't pay?" Despite her resolve her voice trembled.

"I can be lenient to a point, Madam," Webster said gently. "For I do feel responsible for allowing the situation to go unchecked. Therefore, I shall extend you a fortnight in which to secure the back payments. Then you can continue your monthly payments. It would be most convenient if you would send the monies here rather than waiting for me to come and collect them."

"Two weeks," Abby gasped and felt her head grow light. The amount he had quoted had been staggering but the thought of finding it within two weeks was inconceivable. "You must give me more than two weeks," she stammered.

"I'm afraid that's not possible." Webster stood abruptly, anxious to have the widow out of his office before she collapsed. Her skin had grown pale and her eyes looked unusually bright. "My client has been most explicit in his needs, therefore my hands are tied." He took a step toward the door but the widow didn't move. Nervously, he mopped his brow with a wide handkerchief and prayed she would not resort to tears.

151

"Perhaps I could meet with your client," Abby pleaded desperately. "If I could explain in person, mayhap he would find it in his heart to be more lenient and thus grant me more time."

Adamantly the attorney shook his head sending the curls of his chestnut wig a-tremble. "That would be most inappropriate, madam. Business is best kept to business. That is why my client employs me, so he won't be bothered by mundane trivialities.

Abby felt her frustration turn to anger. "I would hardly call putting me out of my home a mundane triviality. What will happen to my household if I can't find the money?"

Webster rocked back on his heels, his hand still resting on the door knob. "The eight slaves are part of the estate, and as such would stay with the tavern." he said easily. "They are, after all, the property of the new owner."

Abby felt a sickening dread seep into her bones. "Malachi owned none of them? Nanny, Obadiah, the others . . .

"Your husband did possess their papers at one time, but their ownership transferred when the deed to the tavern transferred. I am afraid your husband mortgaged everything he possessed, Madam. And now the responsibility for that debt rests on your shoulders. I wish there was something I could do for you Mrs. Barclay, but as you can see my hands are tied." He opened the door and stood impatiently.

Filled with panic, Abby rose from her chair. "I must speak with the new owner," she demanded, but the words came out in a plea. "There are cirumstances that I must explain."

Webster looked away and shook his head. "Impossible, madam. I would be happy to convey any message you wish, but a direct meeting is out of the question."

Abby swallowed hard and tried to imagine herself explaining the fact that she had given papers, declaring them free, to eight slaves that were not her property. She looked at the attorney's stiff form and shuddered.

"I don't mean to rush you, Mrs. Barclay," Webster opened the door wider. "But I am a busy man and I do have other business waiting."

Managing only the briefest of nods she left the office and stepped into the afternoon sunlight. Dear Lord, what had she done? Thomas and Effie had returned with the boys but Harley and Celie had not come back. Why had Danvers not known, her mind screamed? She had paid him dearly to write those papers and now they were worthless. Pulling her shoulders back and taking several deep breaths, Abby tried to gather her thoughts and fight back the panic that threatened to consume her. First to Danvers to get some answers she reasoned, as her breath came in fitful gasps. I'll confront him first and then worry about the money. Her stomach knotted with apprehension as she briskly made her way to Danvers' office at the rear of Mr. Wilkins store. The tree-lined street was a canopy of autumn colors, brilliant reds to the palest gold against the blue sky, but Abby never noticed. Her feet crunched through the dried leaves that coated the ground, and more than once she winced as a sharp rock pushed against the soft fab-

ric of her slippers, but her determination never fa[ltered]
tered.

She nodded briefly to the women that were lea[v]ing the store and tried to ignore their obvious cu[ri]osity as she made her way to the back of t[he] building. Crossing her fingers, she took a dee[p] breath and pushed the door open. Her luck he[ld] for the man was in, though his smile faded whe[n] he saw her.

"I've just been to Mr. Webster's office," s[he] blurted out forgoing the formalities of greeting. [" commissioned you to write some documents," s[he] lowered her voice, "yet now I find that they a[re] worthless."

The attorney rose quickly and anxiously peer[ed] out the back door to assure himself of their pr[i]vacy. Hastily he closed the door behind her the[n] pulled out a chair indicating for her to sit.

"Calm down, Mrs. Barclay," he scolded, as o[ne] might an errant child.

Abby pointedly ignored the chair and pulled he[r]self even more erect. "I want some answers."

Danvers returned to his own chair and lean[ed] back, his first flash of nervousness gone. "If y[ou] remember, Mrs. Barclay," he said easily, "I advise[d] you against such documents in the first place. [I] knew they were going to bring you trouble."

Abby felt her anger grow with each breath. "B[ut] you took my coin and produced them anyway."

"Only after you demanded that I do so, madam[.] Pray tell me what has happened to have gotten y[ou] so riled? Did one of your blacks steal a horse [or] get into some trouble?"

"Those good people are more honest than y[ou]

are, Mr. Danvers. But Mr. Webster just informed me that my husband didn't own those slaves. They belong to the tavern as part of the estate."

Danvers snapped his chair forward with a jolt. "Well that is a different kettle of fish as it were," he said slowly rubbing his hands on his worn breeches. "But wait," he looked up at her and the tension · eased from his body. "You told me that you owned the slaves. I believe I was most emphatic when I asked that question."

"Well I thought I did," Abby snapped. "But now I find out that I don't . . . didn't . . . therefore the documents you made for me are worthless."

Danvers had the nerve to smile and nod in agreement. "And just what is your point, Mrs. Barclay?"

"You . . . you robbed me," she challenged. "I paid for services that . . ."

"That went against my advice and that you demanded. Is that not right, madam?"

"But . . ."

"No, you let me finish," he rose and towered over her. "First you send for me to do what you would ask of no other attorney and I comply. Then, when you find that the deed no longer suits you, you storm into my office ranting like a fish monger and accuse me of thievery. I would be very careful if I were you, Mrs. Barclay, for if you continue this vicious attack on my reputation I shall be forced to take you to court for slander. You'd not like the consequences of being labeled a shrew," he continued grandly. "I believe the punishment is a day and night in the stocks with a public beating for good measure."

"But I'm right!" she gasped. "I paid for some thing that had no value. You should have advised me thus!"

Danvers waved his finger slowly back and forth "Tsk, tsk, Mrs. Barclay. You were the one who lied. You told me that the slaves were yours. Did you lie on purpose? For I think that there is a heavy penalty for that also."

"But . . ."

Danvers rocked his chair back again and smirked. "Be reasonable, Mrs. Barclay," he cajoled "You may take your claims elsewhere and even have me brought to court. But once there," he paused for effect. "Whom do you think the magis trates will believe? I am a respected attorney, well versed in the art of the law. While you . . ." he le his eyes roam insultingly down her frame.

Abby looked down and flushed with embarrass ment. Her cape had come open with her tirade re vealing her drab apparel. Her apron, while once white, was now dingy and stained beyond redemp tion, and her gown underneath sported more patches than original fabric. Carefully she pulled the frayed edges of her cloak together and held them in place with hands that trembled.

Danvers stood and smoothed the satin of his blue jacket. "I think my point is well made madam." He cocked a brow and looked blatantly toward the door. "As always your servant, I bid you good day."

Humiliated, Abby turned and left the office in a daze. The afternoon sun stung her eyes and the knot in her stomach tightened further. Dear Lord what was she going to do now? In two weeks she

needed to find more money than she had ever
known in a lifetime and tell the people she loved
most in the world that their freedom was a lie and
they were still bound into slavery.

The wind gusted and she found herself shivering.
They were not yet a week into October, but the air
already carried a winter chill. She pulled her cape
more securely about her trembling frame and with
the weight of the world and the fate of her entire
household resting on her slender shoulders, she
started the long walk home. She didn't hear the
friendly calls from the workers at the silver shop as
she passed. Lost in thought, she looked neither left
nor right but continued as she had all her life, putting one foot before the other and trying to pretend that the pain didn't exist.

Abby rubbed the grit from her eyes then straightened as the flames of the fire greedily consumed
the kindling and sprang to life. The downstairs
fires were now lit and although the desire to stay
and warm her hands before the growing flames was
strong, she wearily turned back to her morning
chores. She had spent the entire night pacing from
room to room searching for anything that she
might sell, anything of value that might aid her
cause. But as the night gave way to morning, she
was faced with the grim reality that all she owned
was a piece of fabric that she'd purchased to make
a new apron, and the tarnished silver handle from
a broken hairbrush. Anxiously she began to pace.
She had counted the coins from dinner again and
again, and although yesterday morning the amount

would have thrilled her, today it was insignificant.
She picked up a single plate and walked to the
table, setting it down with great precision before re-
tracing her steps. How was she going to tell them
their freedom was a hoax? She felt the pain in her
stomach tighten. Why had she ever thought herself
clever enough to accomplish such a feat? Hadn't
Malachi pointed out to her over and over how stu-
pid, ignorant, and clumsy she was? Her eyes
burned as she reached for the sugar bowl. But her
pacing stilled as Cyrus Bloom sprang suddenly to
mind. He had offered marriage, and he obviously
wished to oversee the tavern. But why would someone in his position want to become a tavern
keeper? her mind challenged. Did he think that to
wed her would grant him the tavern's ownership?
Slowly her pacing began anew. Once he finds that
the property is mortgaged, she thought, he'll probably want no part of it, especially since back payments are due . . . And even if he was still
interested, eccentric as Malachi was fond of saying,
that still wouldn't solve her problems with the slave
papers . . .

Christopher rose as the first streaks of light
broke through the night sky and quickly dressed
against the chill in the air. He knew Thomas would
be arriving soon with the coals to rekindle the fire,
but this morning he was not willing to wait. Determination filled him as he tucked his shirt into his
breeches. This morning she would not evade him;
for he wanted answers. Twice yesterday she had
walked by his shop, and not once had she stopped

to share a word or even offer a smile of encourage-
ment. Several of the men had called to her in
greeting but she had blatantly ignored them. Christopher splashed cold water against his face and
tried to erase the memory of a kiss that made his
blood ache from wanting. If she didn't wish his ad-
vances that was one thing, but he'd tolerate rude-
ness to his crew from no one. Carefully he
buttoned his waistcoat and slipped on the rust
brown jacket. The other tavern patrons would stay
abed for at least another hour, he reasoned, checking the time with the tall cased clock, and by then
he would have his answers.

He found her in the far corner of the main dining room as he expected, but something was very
wrong. For several moments he watched her and
his scowl deepened. Once, as a boy, he had captured a silver fox, foolishly thinking to tame it into
a pet. But after days of watching the animal pace
itself to near exhaustion, he'd been forced to admit
his folly and he'd set the creature free. Now as he
watched the widow, he recognized the same caged
energy. She turned in his direction just as he
stepped forward.

Jerking with fright, Abby managed to stifle her
scream, but the dinner plate slipped from her fingers, crashing against the wooden floor, the sound
a gunshot in the empty room. Her breath came in
choppy gasps while her hand pressed against the
frantic beating of her heart.

"Mr. Carlson," she stammered. "You gave me a
fright," she continued to gasp as she fought the
tremors that were threatening to over take her.

Chris took in the frantic look in her eyes and the

159

shadows that ringed them. Didn't the woman have any sense at all? It was obvious that she had left her bed too soon. How much abuse did she think her delicate form could take?

"I'll get that," he snapped bending to retrieve the broken plate. "Sit down before you fall over."

Too stunned to speak, Abby stood where she was and took deep steadying breaths. "You're down early," she said when he returned from the dustbin. "I didn't expect to see anyone standing there. You startled me."

Christopher nodded to a chair, and felt his mood soften when she perched on its edge without an argument. "What is wrong?" he questioned without preamble.

Abby shook her head and clasped her hands tightly in her lap looking more like an errant school child than the mistress of a tavern. Her mob cap concealed most of her curls but stray wisps had escaped and now curved enticingly at her temple. "All is well, Mr. Carlson. Is your shop progressing as you wish?" She made the mistake of looking up at him and her mouth went dry at the scowl on his face. His blue eyes were cold with fury and panic filled her. She swallowed hard and tasted fear the likes of which she had never known, for it was clear his anger was directed at her.

Christopher saw the bravado in her stiff carriage change to fear and watched the blood drain from her cheeks. Her soft brown eyes filled with apprehension as they awaited his next move. Damn it to hell, he thought, did she think he'd strike her for not extending a simple good day when she'd passed by? He stepped closer. She flinched but continued

160

to look up at him. Suddenly the image of her bouncing off the wall at the hand of her father filled his mind and another piece of the puzzle fit into place.

Slowly he dropped to the balls of his feet before her and gently placed one of his hands over her clasped ones. They were cold as ice and although he made no other move to touch her, he was gratified when she didn't pull away.

"I didn't mean to frighten you," he said gently. "And I'm sorry I scowled. I'm sometimes a bear in the morning."

Abby wanted to argue that fact for she'd never seen a man as cheerful as he. Malachi had rolled from bed with a belch and a fart, then cursed his way to the privy. If he spoke, it was to snarl, and if his joints were aching, the belt would become his vengeance.

Christopher felt her tremble beneath his hand and edged closer. "Come now," he coaxed gently. "Tell me what is amiss?"

Abby felt herself falling into the clear blue of his eyes. She felt the strength in the hand that warmed hers and strangely it brought comfort.

"Come," he squeezed her hands gently and propped his other on the chair beside her shoulder. "You were my ally when I lost everything. Share the burden with me and you'll carry only half the load."

Abby swallowed hard. "I've made a mess of things," her words came out in hiccupping gasps. In halting phrases she told him how much money she needed to find to pay the back rent, but she could not bring herself to share the potential di-

161

saster she had created for the slaves. One crisis at a time.

"And you say that Magnus Webster is handling the accounts?" Chris asked, coming to his feet. "I know the man, decent sort and very reliable. I'll speak with him if you'd like."

Abby shook her head. "It would do no good, for even if he extended the time by a fortnight, I'd still not be able to raise the cash he would require."

Chris rubbed his hand on the back of his neck. "Well, why don't you let me try to think of something?"

"Do you think you might get him to tell you who holds the mortgage?" she asked hopefully. "He wouldn't tell me a thing. Only referred to the man as his client."

Chris shook his head. "Webster's reputation is sterling and if his client doesn't want his business known, then Webster is the one to keep his secrets. No, I think there might be an easier way."

"To find out who the man is?"

"No," he chuckled. "To find the money. Why don't you let me think on it for a while."

Abby felt her spirits plummet yet she struggled to smile a thanks. Mr. Carlson had as much chance of procuring the money as she had, and she knew her chances were slim to none. "Maybe Cyrus Bloom is the answer after all."

She hadn't realized she'd voiced the words until she saw the startled expression on Mr. Carlson's face. "He's asked me to marry him," she explained quickly. She watched him stiffen and wondered why.

"And you've given him your answer?"

Abby shook her head. "I don't want to marry anyone." She jerked to her feet and began to pace anew.

"Then put Bloom out of your mind," he snapped. "Besides the match would be absurd."

Abby thought of Mr. Bloom's fancy clothes and aristocratic family name, then looked down at her own stained gown. She knew she held no hopes of bettering herself, but Mr. Carlson didn't have to voice his opinion so adamantly. "I might not have a choice," she said slowly, suppressing a shudder. But the thoughts of Cyrus Bloom touching her made her stomach knot tighten further and despite her resolve she groaned from the sharp stabbing pain.

Chris was instantly at her side. "Are you ill?" his hand brushed gently against her forehead then her cheek.

Ill from the notion of marrying Cyrus Bloom, she thought, and dizzy from the way you touch me. "I'm fine, Mr. Carlson. My stomach is just a little queer this morning." She stood as quickly as she dared. "I appreciate you listening to my problems, but to be honest, it might be wise for you to look for other lodgings."

"You're putting me out?"

"Of course not," she struggled with her silent burden. How many people, Dear Lord, were going to suffer from her ineptitude?

"It's just that I might have to take some drastic measures in the near future and I might not be at liberty to offer you free lodging."

"Like taking Cyrus Bloom for a husband?"

Abby fought down her own panic. It seemed so

163

much worse when he said it that way. But thoughts of Obadiah and Nanny in chains stemmed her protest. "Sometimes a person does what's necessary." She looked up and felt the intensity of his gaze shoot straight through her. "But until the deed is done," she said quietly, "you shall remain as my guest. Maybe your shop will be ready by then," she added on a hopeful note. "Then all shall be well."

Except you'll be married to Cyrus Bloom. Chris scowled, startled at just how bitter the thought tasted. "Promise me you'll do nothing until I can think on the matter." Her sad smile tore at his heart.

"You stop worrying about me, Mr. Carlson," she counseled. "You have a new business to establish. That's enough for anyone's plate."

Chris took her by the shoulders. "Promise me you'll do nothing rash."

Abby shook her head. "I'm not a rash person, Mr. Carlson. But I am going to be late with breakfast. You must let me go."

He told himself to back away, the widow was trouble with a capital T. But as she gazed up at him, he could no more have left her than cut out his heart. Throwing caution to the wind, he pulled her close. His lips settled firmly over hers and he sighed with the rightness of his possession.

Abby struggled to be free, but the fear that held her rigid was draining away and her hands gripped his jacket for support. The tip of his tongue traced the outline of her lips leaving a trail of delicate flame. His arms tightened, securing her position until she was enveloped by the heat of his body. Her mind emptied, her body strained closer then closer still, begging for more but of what she knew not.

"Miz Abby, the fires above stairs is all lit and happy," Thomas' voice boomed into the room. "You wants me to fetch the vittles now or wait a spell?"

Chris reluctantly took a step back as the servant entered the room.

"Good day to ya, Mr. Carlson," Thomas nodded. "You sure is an early bird this morning."

"Good day, Thomas." Chris's smile was strained. Every fiber of his being throbbed with the need to possess her completely. He watched her wide-eyed wonder as she slowly raised a trembling hand to touch her lips. She belonged with him, he knew that now with a certainty. And thoughts of another touching her brought back his dark mood. "Nothing rash," he commanded, holding her stunned gaze until she slowly nodded. "We shall speak of this again when I return. But for now . . ."

His kiss was brief, not more than the firm pressure of flesh against flesh, but Abby felt as if she'd been struck by lightning. Her skin tingled from its scorching heat and deep within her soul the flames of passion sparked for the first time. He drew back, then changed his mind and placed a fleeting kiss on her forehead. In stunned silence she watched him turn and stride purposefully from the room. Her hands trembled, her heart thumped wildly, and her mind soared until the soft lilting tune of Thomas's whistling broke through the haze of wonder that surrounded her.

"Old Obbie was right," Thomas said, watching in amusement as her eyes cleared and the faintest

165

blush touched her cheeks. "He looked up at that old sun this morning and said to me, 'Thomas this here is gonna be one fine day.' " Thomas gave her a knowing wink that made her cheeks go brighter. "Yes, sir, this is gonna be one fine day."

Chapter Ten

Anxiously watching the last two patrons in the dining room finish their meal *and* their second bowl of punch, Abby busied herself behind the bar. Cyrus Bloom's wide lace cuff dragged through the gravy on his plate each time he cut a piece of meat and the stain on his pink satin coat was growing larger with every mouthful. How could a man wipe his mouth so often, she wondered, noting his flowery use of his napkin, yet constantly miss his chin? As he mopped up the last of his gravy with a wad of bread, Abby felt her stomach tighten. The mere thought of his greasy fingers on her flesh made her skin crawl. Taking a breath, she wondered if she possessed the nerve to see her plan through to the end.

Obadiah entered the dining room and silently cleared the table. The servant was wizened and bent with age, yet there was a spring to his step, and deep in her heart, Abby knew the reason why. She shuddered and tried to imagine which would be worse, telling Obadiah and Nanny they weren't really free, or enduring a lifetime with Cyrus Bloom.

Her attention turned to Bloom's unlikely dinner

partner and she felt her nerves tighten further. She had been more than a little startled when her father had entered the tavern, but he had made no move to speak with her. Instead, he had insolently tossed her a shilling to pay for his dinner then taken a place at the table. She shifted her position behind the bar and wished she could make out their hushed words.

When both men pushed back from the table yet made no move to leave, Abby realized the moment of truth was at hand and a sickening apprehension filled her.

"Have ye no words of greeting fer yer own kin?" Corbin challenged. Bolstered by the hearty rum punch and his new-found fortune, he stood, weaving only slightly.

"Did you enjoy your meal, father?" Abby made her way around the bar, careful to keep at a distance.

Corbin shrugged. "The tongue was tough and the ham too salty."

"But you ate three . . ." She bit back the rest of her words and silently cursed herself for a fool. Why, after all the pain, had she still not learned he would never be satisfied with anything she did? And why, she wondered, did it matter.

Lucas Corbin stepped forward and felt a keen satisfaction when his daughter stepped back. "When a man's hungry," he said derisively, "he'll eat anything. Including the slop ye serve here. But I ain't here ta talk about vittles. I be here on business."

Abby watched Cyrus Bloom rise from the table and notice the large stain on his coat front for the first time. With irritated motions he tried to wipe the smeared gravy with his napkin, but succeeded only in making the stain more noticeable. With a growl of disgust he tossed the napkin down and turned to her.

"If I might interrupt." He looked down his aristocratic nose as if to say the blemish on his coat was completely her fault. "When I was here last, Mrs. Barclay, I mentioned a matter of the utmost importance. I trust you've had time to think on the situation."

Abby felt her heart leap into her throat and prayed she'd make the right decision. "And which matter are you referring to, Mr. Bloom?" Her nails bit into her palms and her stomach threatened to turn over as she watched his thick fingers lock on the edges of his coat. How would she ever endure this man?

"Darling, I'm late again." Abby spun around at the sound of Mr. Carlson's voice. "Will you forgive me?" Ignoring all else, he stopped directly before her and placed a fleeting kiss on her forehead. "Say you're not vexed with me."

Abby looked up only to find herself captivated by the blue of his eyes. Her head spun in confusion and desperately she wondered if this was a dream like the one she had had at daybreak.

Christopher placed a firm arm about her shoulders and turned back to their guests. "You must excuse me, gentlemen," he said with a grin. "But I find when I'm gone from this lovely lady it's more than I can bear."

Cyrus puffed out his chest, and his face went a blotchy red. "Sir, what is the meaning of this vulgar display? I demand you take your hands off the widow this very instant."

Chris had the grace to look completely confused then he taped his finger to his head. "Oh, darling forgive me." He turned to find the widow watching him with eyes big as saucers and prayed he was not too late. "Sweetheart, I know we agreed not to tell anyone, but when I saw your father here, naturally I assumed that you'd already spoken to him."

"Spoken ta me about what?" Lucas Corbin shifted uneasily from foot to foot. The young upstart had gotten the best of him once, but he wasn't about to let it happen again.

"Why the wedding of course."

"Wedding?" Chris almost chuckled as the three voices sounded in unison.

"Mrs. Barclay is going to marry me," Cyrus challenged, taking a menacing step forward.

Chris felt her shiver beneath his arm and pulled her closer to his side. "I don't think that's possible sir, since the lady has already agreed to marry me."

Cyrus sputtered in anger and whirled toward Corbin. "What is the meaning of this? We had an agreement!"

"I don't know nothing about no wedding." Lucas Corbin felt his world tilting away from him. Damn the wench. If he had to beat her black and blue she wasn't going to cheat him out of the money Bloom had offered. Desperation fed his courage and his eyes narrowed on the couple. "Ye ain't come ta me ta ask fer my daughter's hand and that's fer sure," he said slowly as his brain tried to find purchase.

Christopher struggled to mask his hatred. The bruises on the widow's cheek and forehead had faded, but the memory of her pain still burned clear in his mind. "Mrs. Barclay is hardly a child,

170

sir, in need of parental approval. As a widow she can own property, pay taxes, and oversee her own business."

"There is a breach of contract here," Bloom interrupted. "For I asked the widow nearly a fortnight ago to marry me and she replied that she wished to marry no one."

Chris threw one arm wide in triumph, keeping the other securely about Abby's trembling form. "Then by your own words the lady didn't agree to marry you. I'm sorry, but I just don't see how you can lay claim to her affections when they so clearly belong to me." He gazed down at her, relieved to see she wasn't going to contradict him.

"Affections be damned," Cyrus ranted. "Sir, this is a business arrangement. I demand to know just when this decision was made." He tossed a menacing look at his accomplice.

"I say there ain't no arrangement." Corbin gave his daughter a challenging glare. "I've known this brat since the first day she squalled and I'm telling ya true there ain't no wedding. I ken see it in her face."

A glimmer of hope sparked in Cyrus Bloom's narrow eyes. "Perhaps you'd like to tell us then, Mrs. Barclay, just when is this supposed wedding to take place?"

Abby felt the walls closing in about her. She looked up at Mr. Carlson, her eyes full of gratitude for what he had tried to do. But as he returned her gaze she was startled by the intensity of emotions so clearly visible on his face. As on the night of the fire, there was no defeat in this man, but a strength that seemed to seep from his soul into hers. Abby drank in all that he had to offer, feeling the heat of his body where they still pressed close together.

"The wedding is a week from Saturday," Chris said easily, fighting down the urge to ravish her on the spot for what she was doing to his insides.

"I asked my daughter," Corbin challenged. "Did he give ye a token yet?"

Abby took a deep breath and reluctantly looked back at her father. She felt the arm about her shoulder tighten ever so lightly and her courage strengthen. "Mr. Carlson's words are true, father. We are to be married a week from Saturday."

"As to the token," Chris reached into his coin pocket, of his waistcoat. "I can't think of two better witnesses." He withdrew a small silver locket in the shape of a heart. His large hands managed the delicate clasp with ease as he secured the chain about her neck and watched the familiar piece settle in the ivory hollow of her throat. "My gift, Mrs. Barclay," he said softly, wishing he could read the thoughts behind her eyes. "A week from Saturday?"

Abby found she couldn't speak. Never before had anyone come to her aid. Unable to cope with the onslaught of emotions that threatened, the briefest nod of her head was all she could manage.

"But what of banns?" Cyrus demanded. "There can't be a wedding, for no banns have been posted."

Abby looked back to Mr. Carlson. "Banns?" she questioned softly, wondering where he had gotten the necklace and marveling at his ability to create such a ridiculous story for her benefit.

Chris smiled, flashing straight white teeth against

he golden tan of his skin. "Special license," he said easily.

Abby cocked her head to the side and looked at him long and hard. Damn it, but she was starting to believe him. "Special license?" she echoed.

"Special license." He nodded, liking the way her lips curved in that funny half smile that was so uniquely hers.

"This is ridiculous," Cyrus snapped. "And I'll not stand here and be made a fool of. I say you're bluffing, Carlson, and I find no humor in this situation."

Abby watched Mr. Carlson's eyes go a deadly cold. "You mock something that is sacred to me, sir," his voice was soft but to Abby it carried more threat than had he shouted like a madman. She started to draw back, anxious to be clear of the hands that had cowed even her father, but his arm tightened, warning her not to move. "The widow and I shall be married a week from Saturday at the home of Nicholas Beaumont. A special license has been awarded and that is all you need to know. I'm sure you'll understand when I say that your presence at the ceremony will not be required."

Cyrus tasted fear from the softly spoken words and knew the moment was lost to him. Pulling together what was left of his dignity he gave the couple a dismissing glare. Much could happen during the ensuing days. He'd just have to reassess the situation and be patient a little longer.

"I fear you are making a terrible mistake, madam," he said from the safety of the doorway. "You've chosen a penniless pup over the good name my family has to offer. And you," he turned to Corbin now sulking near the window. "I'll settle

173

with you later." With all the grace his bulk would allow, Cyrus Bloom hastily made his exit with Lucas Corbin close on his heels.

Still pressed to Mr. Carlson's side, Abby fought back her panic. She could feel the anger that coursed through him and the rigid tension of his muscles. Yet this time when she tried to draw back, his arm immediately dropped away.

"Thank you," she said in a shaky voice. "I don't know what I would have done if you hadn't come and put them off the way you did."

Chris watched her like a hawk with his prey. "You don't need to thank me."

Abby swallowed hard. "Yes I do. I don't think Mr. Bloom would have taken no for an answer if it had been left to my own devices." She struggled to keep the tremors from her voice with little success for although she had put off Bloom, she still had no money for the back payment. Self disgust erased her relief.

"You didn't *want* to marry that man, did you?" Chris challenged, trying to understand the distress that clouded her eyes. He watched her shudder and breathed his own sigh of relief.

"I can't imagine letting that man touch me," she whispered her eyes on the floor and heat flooding her cheeks. "But then I've just realized that I'm quite weak in spirit and totally self centered."

Christopher snorted with disgust. "I find your logic completely at fault. Your own safety and well being should be your first concern. The running of this tavern and your late husband's debts must come second."

"But there are others . . ." Abby took a deep breath to stop her words. She could not allow her

174

ear to jeopardize Nanny and Obadiah's safety. "Oh wait," she reached up to unfasten the necklace. "Let me return this to you lest we forget."

Chris easily captured her hands in his. "There is no need madam. The necklace is a gift I would like you to have. The piece is very precious to me."

"All the more reason I should return it, Mr. Carlson. You should gift this to your wife." Her panic intensified when he refused to release her hands.

"I just have, Mrs. Barclay." He might have laughed aloud at the startled expression that covered her face, but his own emotions were too close to the surface. "Did you think I spoke in jest?"

"You're too kind to jest about my problems, Mr. Carlson, but you needn't turn your chivalry into fact."

Christopher raised a brow, as his blue eyes darkened. "I meant every word I said. You were contemplating marriage to Bloom for the sake of repaying your husband's debt and restoring his good name, were you not?"

For Nanny, Obadiah, and the others, her mind screamed. Never for Malachi. But her words would not come.

"Then you shall marry me instead." Chris reached into his coat pocket and withdrew a worn leather pouch. "Here is the money you need for the back payments as well as for the month we've just started."

Abby stared at the pouch in amazement then her eyes darted to his. "Where did . . ."

"It is not important," he interrupted.

"But you wish me to marry you? In return for the payments?"

175

Chris nodded. "A week from Saturday."

"But the banns," she whispered.

"Special license," he smiled.

"You actually procured a special license?" she gasped.

Christopher shrugged. "By this time tomorrow it shall be in my possession."

"But you told Mr. Bloom . . ."

"That he's not invited to the wedding," he finished for her.

Abby felt her knees grow weak and sank gratefully onto a straight back chair. "Your generosity has captured my tongue, sir."

Chris looked about the room as if assessing its value before his eyes came to settle on her. "From my vantage point it's a good investment. And I'm beginning to realize that I'm partial to those with long-term profits."

Abby struggled to make her mind work. "As I said, you have been more than generous. But you need not bind yourself with the vows of marriage to secure your investment. You have my word, sir, that I shall repay every shilling."

"I'd rather entertain the notion of marriage, madam," he said easily. "That way I can keep a constant watch over my concerns." The chief one being you, he thought silently. I want the shadows gone from your eyes and I never want to wake again to find you pacing over the lack of coin."

"But sir," she stood and grasped the back of the chair for support. "We hardly know each other . . ."

Chris watched her face flare with color. "Madam," he took a step forward but halted as her eyes flaired with panic. "I realize that this is rather sudden, but you were willing to entertain the situation with Mr. Bloom, were you not?" Her hand tightened on the back of the chair until her knuckles went white, and he pressed further. "My offer is this madam. The money is yours in exchange for your hand in marriage. If the offer does not please you, you have only to say so and I will withdraw my proposal and my funds."

Abby bit hard on her lower lip. "You would have it no other way?"

He folded his arms across his wide chest and shook his head. "I am not a hard man, madam, but an impatient one and will have your answer now for there is much to arrange."

Her head dropped forward, and her words were the barest whisper. "You would wish this to be purely a business arrangement?"

Chris raised her face with his finger under her chin and felt her tremors. "You may call it that if you wish, but make no mistake about this. You, will share my bed."

Unable to meet the intensity of his gaze, Abby closed her eyes. "Sir, before you make your final decision, you must know that I am barren. If it is your wish to have a family, a son to carry on your name, then you would be in grave error with this match."

Stunned, Chris drew back. In truth, he hadn't thought past the dreams of sharing his passion with her, but he had always known that someday he would have a family. Children to cherish and a wife to grow old with . . . these too were dreams.

"You are sure?"

She flinched from the tone in his voice and nodded, her eyes never leaving her shoes. "I was Mr.

Barclay's wife for nine years," her voice trembled from the memories. "But was never blessed with a child. Nine years is long enough to know what will be and what will not."

Chris frowned at the catch in her voice. "But do you dislike children?" he prodded.

The absurdity of his question pulled her eyes to his. "Who could not like children?" she questioned, then answered it herself with thoughts of Malachi.

"Good, then I take it you have decided to accept my offer?" Chris said slowly.

"But sir, even after what I have told you, you would still insist on marriage?"

Silently he nodded.

Abby took a shuddering breath and forced herself to look hard at the man who stood before her. Surely no one could be as bad as Malachi, her heart offered. He took on your father and won, her mind countered. But he's kind, her heart challenged. Who else has ever even pretended to care about you? It matters not her mind declared finally, you have no other choice. Abby pulled her courage around her like a well worn cloak. The safety of those she loved in exchange for a lifetime of bondage to a man who's eyes made her knees go weak. Her hand trembled only slightly as she extended it to him.

"We have a bargain."

Mr. Carlson took her hand. But when he raised it to his lips and pressed a moist kiss within her palm, Abby felt the shock of it clear to her toes. His eyes met hers. Her heartbeat quickened and desperately she wondered if she had made a bargain with the devil after all.

178

* * *

"And how are my two favorite ladies this evening?"

Sarah Beaumont beamed with pleasure as the handsome form of her husband entered the nursery. He placed a promising kiss on her upturned lips then gazed lovingly down at his sleeping daughter.

"Madam, I fear you have outdone yourself with this one." He let his knuckle brush against the baby's cheek and was rewarded with a sleepy smile. "When you gave birth to Ethan, I thought my life complete," he said softly. "Then you created Jonathan and I wondered how we ever existed without him. But this one . . ." With a practiced hand he took the infant and cuddled her close. "This one melts my heart each time she opens her eyes."

Gently placing his two-week-old daughter in her cradle, Nick turned back to Sarah. Taking her place on the chair he pulled her between his legs to sit on his lap. "What's wrong?" he questioned, nuzzling the side of her neck. "Did the boys tire you overmuch today?"

"You are too perceptive for your own good, Mr. Beaumont. But your conclusions are faulty. My sons are nothing less than perfect gentlemen at all times."

Nick snorted with laughter. "Madam, your sons are two and four years respectively and a brighter pair of troubles I've yet to see."

Sarah made no protest when he tipped her chin up to share a kiss. Looping her arms about his neck she hugged him close, reveling in the manly scent that was so uniquely his. "I'm so lucky to have found you."

Nick heard the catch in her voice and pulled her even closer. "If it's not my sons who have vexed you, then pray madam, tell me who is at fault?"

Sarah rested her head on his broad shoulder and again thanked the fates that had carried her to Virginia. "I met the Widow Barclay today," she said softly, mindful of the sleeping child. "Nick, something is very wrong here. Christopher is walking around like one afraid of cracking eggs and today I find the widow is just as miserable. I don't understand what is happening. Chris loves her, of that I am certain, for his eyes light up when he but says her name, and he was so excited when he came to share the news, yet now . . ."

Nick rocked her gently in his arms. "I know of what you speak," he said, "for I too met the widow today." He smiled at Sarah's startled expression and continued. "Did she tell you that she drove clear to Yorktown alone to meet me?"

Sarah shook her head. "She never mentioned a thing. But why would she travel to Yorktown when we live just down the road?"

Nick's eyes grew thoughtful. "It was a most enlightening meeting. She said she came to my offices at the dock so there would be no chance of Christopher seeing her."

"But why?" Sarah interrupted.

"It seems," Nick continued, "that the widow has no concept of Christopher's true wealth. She thinks him a struggling silversmith who has lost his shop."

Sarah wrinkled her brow. "But that much is true. Is she afraid he'll not make a fair living from his trade? Even if he had no other monies, surely she had only to look at his work to be satisfied of his talent."

"I don't think that talent has anything to do with it. It seems that Chris has loaned the widow a goodly sum of money and somehow the poor dear has gotten it into her head that Chris borrowed the money from me. She wanted to reassure me personally that Mr. Carlson, as she calls him, would never have asked for his own benefit and that I'm not to think less of him for borrowing such a grand sum. She assured me that although she'd be forever grateful, the money would be repaid as soon as humanly possible."

"And she traveled all the way to Yorktown to assure you of that?"

Nick nodded. "I must admit, madam, that I was most impressed with the lady. She looked frail enough for the wind to toss about and how she managed a team on her own is still a mystery, but she stood firm and looked me straight in the eye while making her declaration."

Sarah's brow wrinkled in thought. "No wonder she seemed so surprised when I arrived this afternoon."

"And what did you think of our friend's new bride?" he prodded.

"She's scared to death." Sarah gave her husband a puzzled look. "If she thinks Chris has extended himself for her benefit, then she should feel gratitude not fear. Yet this afternoon I could hardly get her to speak of the wedding and it's less than a week away. I know it will not be a grand social affair, but I did wish it to be special for them." For a fleeting second, Sarah remembered her own rushed wedding in the office of Nick's solicitor. There had been no cake, or well wishers, just the growing storm and a disastrous end.

181

As if reading her mind, Nick pulled her close and planted a searing kiss on her lips. "Have I told you today, Mrs. Beaumont that I love you?" he whispered, as his hand found its way under her skirt.

Her violet eyes twinkled in promise and the troubling memories were firmly pushed aside. "Do you love me enough to allow Julie to attend on Saturday?" she challenged, raising a brow.

Nick stiffened and his eyes went dark.

"Darling," Sarah gave him a beseeching look. "The tension between Chris and his widow is painful enough. Julie is his only family. We can not offer to host his wedding in one breath and then refuse to admit his sister with the next."

"Christopher would understand," Nick slipped her from his lap and began to pace. "That woman nearly cost you your life. How can you forgive her so easily?"

Sarah moved to stand before him and ran her fingers up the satin fabric of his waistcoat. "Darling, you found me, and in the end, all was well." Slowly she slipped the first button from its loop. "Besides, nearly five years have past since Julie played her foolish prank. Surely, as a woman grown, with a husband and thriving plantation to care for, she has left behind her childish ways. And surely we treasure Christopher's friendship enough to extend our hospitality to his sister, even if it's only for a few short hours."

Another button slipped free and Sarah smiled as her husband's eyes darkened with passion. There had been a time when he had terrified her, yet now just a glance sent her blood racing. Her fingers toyed with the last button. Mayhap tomorrow she'd venture to the tavern again and have a womanly talk with the widow about the joys of marriage.

"Enough," Nick snapped as the last button of his waistcoat lost its purchase. "You may have your way, as you always do. Julie may come to the blasted wedding, but if she utters just one insulting word . . ." Sarah stopped his threat with a well-placed kiss and gasped as he effortlessly swung her into his arms. Julie was instantly forgotten as Nick carried her easily into their private chambers. But even as he laid her down on the counterpane of their bed and began to remove her clothing, Sarah found she couldn't banish the Widow Barclay's haunted eyes from her mind.

Chapter Eleven

Hardly daring to blink, Abby looked down at the delicate ivory gown that fell from her shoulders. The neckline was square and low cut, while the stiff bodice sported the delicate lace of the same ivory color. She took a shallow breath, all that the tight bodice allowed, and the skirt of the gown shifted slightly making the beads that graced its full length shimmer with life of their own. The overall effect was stunning and Abby kept waiting for the dream to end. Cautiously, she looked over at her unexpected guest.

Sarah Beaumont was indeed beautiful, with eyes the color of violets, but she certainly was willful. They had met only yesterday but at that very first meeting Mrs. Beaumont had pressed her relentlessly for information about the wedding. Abby shuddered from the memory. Her nerves had already been stretched to their limit from her confrontation with Mr. Beaumont and then his wife had arrived. Abby hadn't meant to be rude, but the wedding was the last thing she wanted to think about. No, she hadn't decided upon a special dress, and no she hadn't any friends to invite. And did she have any special wishes? Just for this madness to be over, she had thought desperately. She hadn't been able to take a breath of relief until the woman made her departure, but by then the damage had been done and for the rest of the afternoon and evening, Abby found her thoughts constantly on the wedding.

Looking at her guest, Abby realized she should have known Mrs. Beaumont would not give up so easily. The afternoon meal had just been cleared away when she glanced up to find Mrs. Beaumont again on her doorstep. The woman labored under numerous parcels and was followed in by Madame Rousseau, the town's most revered dressmaker. Within moments the pair had selected a private dining room and had Thomas scurrying to build a roaring fire. Nanny, who was impressed with no one, had shuffled off to the cookhouse only to reappear with Effie and a huge tray of tiny, mouth watering cakes. A grinning Thomas gazed longingly at the cakes before being firmly ushered out. Nanny posted Effie at the door then gave a nod of consent to Mrs. Beaumont.

Abby, grateful only that she had finished her new apron just that morning, had witnessed the silent exchange but nothing could have prepared her for what had come next. One moment she was dressed and the next she was standing before the fire, clad only in her chemise. For a desperate moment she had thought they meant to strip that away too, but mercifully Mrs. Beaumont had stilled the dressmaker's hand. Mortified, Abby felt her body go rigid. Her eyes pricked with pain that she tried desperately to blink away. She knew Mrs. Beaumont had seen the scars that striped her back and recognized them for what they were and she'd braced herself for the woman's censure. They would pack up their mysterious parcels and depart with haste, condemning her to stand alone with her humiliation.

Never missing a beat, Mrs. Beaumont had merely shaken her head when Madame Rousseau had reached for Abby's chemise. "Let her keep that on for now," she had said calmly. "Mrs. Barclay can try the new one later." The dressmaker had started to protest, but Mrs. Beaumont was not to be put off. "Charlotte," she stated firmly, "I simply cannot wait another minute to see this new creation of yours."

Madame Rousseau had hesitated only for a moment before giving her shoulders a shrug. "Whatever you wish, ma chère," she said easily. Then the first of a dozen petticoats were lifted gently over Abby's head.

"I knew the color would suit," Sarah chatted easily, "but Charlotte, you've outdone yourself again. This gown is simply magnificent."

Abby looked down at the revered dressmaker in awe. Charlotte Rousseau's name was legendary yet she knelt before her to straighten the pins in the hem.

"Straighten your shoulders, ma petite," the seamstress ordered. "You must hold your head high when you wear one of my creations. Otherwise the gown will lose its lines."

Abby struggled to raise her chin, but her fascination with the dressmaker at her feet was much too tempting. She'd never owned a gown whose fabric and cut had been for style rather than service or durability. Now, as she felt the soft silken fabric against her arms, she tried to remind herself that it was only a costume for a masquerade, but memories of Mr. Carlson's kiss kept surging forth. She had felt hot and cold at the same time, and she wondered now how that was possible. Straightening her shoulders as the dressmaker demanded, her hand reached up to the silver locket that rested in the hollow of her throat. She had peered at it in the mirror after he had gone, and smiled at the image. It carried the shape of a heart, but the intricate design was rough and unpolished. She gave a sad smile and shook her head. It was probably a good thing that the tavern would bring in sufficient income to support them, for Mr. Carlson's silver work would be hard-pressed to keep food on the table.

"You must forgive me for staring, Mrs. Barclay," Sarah said suddenly. "But I've just noticed your locket. I know that piece. It belonged to Christopher's mother. He must love you very much to have gifted you with it."

Until Mrs. Beaumont had spoken, Abby didn't realize that her fingers were clinging to the locket like a lifeline. But she did realize that her company was on more intimate terms with her husband-to-be than she was, and each time they casually spoke his given name, her nerves stretched tighter.

Sarah watched the clashing emotions and recognized one too close to the edge. "I've had the good fortune to know your husband-to-be for the past five years," she said gently trying to put the girl at rest. "He and my husband were school mates in England and they carry a deep affection and respect for each other. I hope in the days that follow, you and I shall be able to enjoy such a friendship as well, and you must call me Sarah."

Abby stared uncertainly. Other than Malachi's slaves, she'd never had a friend; there had never been time or opportunity. As a young child, she and Suzannah had been close, but that had ended with her marriage, and Suzannah had never been dependable anyway. Emotions she could not explain pressed around her. Mrs. Beaumont didn't even know her, yet she had brought more gifts than she had ever received in her lifetime.

Her head gave the briefest of nods as she offered her own shy smile of gratitude.

Charlotte Rousseau stood, then walked slowly around her. A scowl etched deep lines around the older woman's red mouth, and her brows drew together with displeasure. Abby felt her apprehension heighten as the woman stared at her. Was she so lacking that even a dressmaker would not be satisfied? The silence in the room turned thick and Abby felt her stomach start to churn.

"Charlotte, stop being so critical, you are scaring the poor girl half to death," Sarah chided, watching anxiety cloud the widow's young face.

Abby felt the slim glimmer of hope die within her. "I'm sorry that I'm not suitable for one of your gowns, madam," she said, her voice thick with regret. "But this is the loveliest thing I've ever seen and just to have had the opportunity to try it on was a privilege I shall treasure, always."

Charlotte's head snapped up and her eyes filled with horror. "Ma petite enfant," she soothed, her words tumbling one over the other. "It is not you that is lacking — why your figure is one of perfection. Would that all my clients carried such fine proportions. No, it is the gown. It still needs adjustments to do you justice."

Stunned, Abby stood speechless as her eyes searched the dressmaker's face for truth.

"Your waist is so tiny," Charlotte continued, slipping a pin here, taking a tuck there. "When I have the opportunity to see one of my gowns on someone as perfect as yourself, or Mrs. Beaumont," she smiled at Sarah, "I have an occasion to show my creations in the best possible way. And I did not get to be where I am by not taking advantage of each op-

ortunity presented." She slipped in another pin and
hen stood back. "There," she turned to Sarah. "Will
he not make the most beautiful bride you have ever
een?"

Sarah nodded and beamed with pleasure. "The
own is truly magnificent," she replied easily. "And
ou, madame," she smiled at Abby, "you look like a
rincess from some far off land, waiting patiently
or her prince to come and carry her home."

Abby felt the heat of embarrassment seep into her
heeks as they stared at her. But she couldn't erase
er smile, for each time she moved, the tiny beads
hat covered her gown sparkled and glowed like dia-
nonds in the firelight. It was as if she had stepped
nto another's skin, walked into another's life.

"Oh, Miz Abby," Nanny sniffed loudly.

Startled by the sound, Abby looked up to find
Nanny's round cheeks covered with tears, and the re-
lity of her situation came crashing back. The wom-
n's shoulders shook with her silent sobs as she rung
er hands together.

Sarah stood and was instantly at the old woman's
ide placing a comforting arm about the trembling
houlders. "There there," she soothed, gently easing
er onto a chair. "Can you tell us the source of your
istress?"

Abby watched in stunned silence as Mrs. Beau-
nont wove her comforting presence about Nanny's
rembling form, and felt her reserve begin to melt.
Nanny?" she questioned.

The old woman gave her nose a hearty blow and
hen scrubbed at her eyes. "You look just like them,
Miz Abby," she glanced sideways at the two women
ho now flanked her with their care. "You look like
he grand lady you was always meant to be." The ser-
ant gave another healthy sniff. "You been through

189

so much child, but I think Obadiah be right when h[e]
said good things was finally coming for you."

Charlotte felt her own eyes grow moist from th[e]
love that poured from the old woman to the beaut[i]
ful girl before them. But ever practical, she swa[l]
lowed back her tears. "She is going to be a beautif[ul]
bride, Nanny." Charlotte gave the servant's broa[d]
shoulder a gentle pat. "But what are we going to d[o]
with her hair?"

The three women looked up at the same tim[e]
Abby blushed and tried with little success t[o]
straighten the mob cap that still sagged bedraggled[ly]
about her face but her efforts only caused the othe[rs]
to chuckle from the sight she presented.

"Charlotte, what would we do without your goo[d]
sense?" Sarah asked, discreetly wiping a tear fro[m]
her own eye. "Do you do your mistress's hair?" sh[e]
asked Effie, who still guarded the doorway.

"No, madam," she stammered, still not believing [it]
was Miz Abby who stood before the fire.

"No matter," Charlotte offered quickly. "I sha[ll]
send one of my girls over in the morning. Litt[le]
Daisy has quite a gift when it comes to hair. I'm su[re]
you'll not find her wanting."

Abby pressed her hands together tightly. "Than[k]
you," she stammered, "but I have no way to repa[y]
you for your kindness."

Charlotte flopped back on a chair and grinne[d]
"A glass of sherry and one of those cakes would go [a]
great way, ma chère."

"What a splendid idea," Sarah seconded, rising t[o]
make herself the server. "Nanny, I think we all d[o]
serve a glass, don't you?" Carefully she poured th[e]
amber liquid then passed the first to the old servan[t]
Abby took the opportunity to slip out of the ne[w]
gown and placed it gently over a chair. When th[e]

190

petticoats had joined the pile and she again wore her own patched gown, she carefully tied her new apron into place.

"Come, Mrs. Barclay," Sarah urged, offering a glass. "We cannot start without you."

Abby hesitantly stepped into the circle and perched on the edge of her chair. "Would you call me by my given name, Mrs. Beaumont?" she stammered.

Sarah smiled in pleasure. "Only if you remember to call me Sarah as we agreed," she challenged. "Now," she turned to the little group, "a toast to the new bride?"

"Here here," Charlotte chimed in. "May her life be long and filled with happiness."

"Lord knows it's about time," Nanny added.

"You was beautiful," Effie whispered in awe, glancing nervously at the others that made up the circle.

"To Abby, may each day be filled with joy." Sarah raised her glass.

"And each night filled with love," Charlotte added with a wicked grin, taking a deep sip from her glass.

"Thank you," Abby stammered, wondering why anyone would look on an impending marriage as something to celebrate. It was a contract, nothing more.

Nanny passed the cakes and the room fell into comfortable silence as each savored the sweet delicacies. Charlotte helped herself to another cake and poured a second sherry. "To the wedding night," her eyes twinkled with mischief. "May the passion and pleasure of that grand event last forever, but if not, may our new bride have a good memory to warm herself on cold winter nights."

Nanny chuckled under her breath and Sarah

191

choked with laughter. "Charlotte Rousseau," she stated firmly, "you make it sound like there is only one night to look forward to." Sarah's eyes narrowed in challenge. "But I know, from your own lips, that you are more than content with Mr. Bertram."

Charlotte had the grace to look sheepish for only a moment before the sparkle bloomed brighter in her eye. She turned to Abby. "I, like you, was a widow, mon amie," she whispered loudly as if confiding the most delicate of secrets. "But when I found and married my Bertram, oh la la." She rolled her eyes. "Let me tell you about craftsmen," she winked in exaggeration.

Moments later, Sarah and Nanny were in tears again. "Charlotte, stop," Sarah commanded, trying desperately to stem her laughter. "You are too clever with your words."

The dressmaker shrugged, not the least offended. "The man is a master," she sighed. "A true craftsman always pays attention to even the smallest details and that's what makes Bertram such a fantastic lover."

Nanny clucked her tongue and wagged a gnarled finger. "Madame Rousseau, you is one wicked lady, but you sure can sew."

Charlotte tilted her nose in the air with a comical wink of her eye. "I am French," she said drawing out her accent. "We are known for our creativity and our passion."

Abby could only stare at the unlikely group in wonder. Nanny sat easily between the town's most prominent seamstress and the wife of one of its most important men, as each expounded on the pleasures that were to be experienced on the wedding night. She thought of Mr. Carlson and her eyes grew dreamy as she pictured him standing in the moon light by the cook house. His muscles had rippled each time he had worked the churn and his smile . . . she fought back the memory as her hands grew moist. She tried to imagine him touching her, creating the rapture the others had alluded to, but when she did, images of Malachi returned with a vengeance, making her tremble. Her hand shook as she carefully placed her glass on the side table. She felt her stomach turn as she remembered all too clearly what had been demanded of her. Looking down, Abby clenched her hands tightly in her lap. How could anyone find pleasure under such humiliating and painful circumstances, she wondered. And how was she going to manage to tolerate it again?

By the time her guests had departed, all the final arrangements had been settled, and Abby felt herself losing control. Charlotte would arrive the next morning with Daisy to help her dress and to do her hair. They wouldn't hear of her walking to the wedding, so, much to her dismay, it had been decided that Nicholas Beaumont would collect her and deliver her promptly at noon.

Abby slowly undressed and eased down onto her pallet on the floor. The reality of what she was about to do washed over her leaving panic in its wake. Somehow, the easy chatter of the women that afternoon had kept her terror at bay. Their laughter and bawdy stories had soothed her nerves until she had relaxed enough to chuckle with them. But now, alone in the dark, there was no one to offer comfort, no one to ease her fears. The wind whistled and buffeted the tavern and Abby shivered. Pulling her thin blanket more securely about her shoulders she drew her knees up and locked her arms about them. Silently she rocked, trying to ease the tension. Desperately she looked about the small chamber, but found nothing that offered peace. "I just want to be warm," she whispered shivering in the darkness. "I want . . ." and suddenly she realized that what she truly wanted was to feel the heat of Mr. Carlson's arms around her. She hadn't seen him in two days; although flowers and delicate pieces of handmade lace were delivered nearly every hour from his messengers, she would have preferred to have seen the man in person. That notion is absurd, her mind argued. He's the source of this travesty to begin with. But he's been so kind, her heart would counter. There must be a way to persuade him not to relinquish his freedom. And so it went, emotions tugged her in every direction until exhaustion stepped in and bid her sleep.

Dawn came all too swiftly as Abby stood by her window. Anxiously, she watched the red streaks slowly break through the night's darkness and she prayed for them to halt in their dance across the sky. The autumn air carried a damp chill that would not burn away as the sun took its place and leaves, dried and brown, swirled about the ground leaving the trees as barren as she felt.

Abby pressed her forehead against the frigid glass. It was the first day in nine years that she hadn't been down to open the cookhouse and set the coffee beans on to roast. But there was no pleasure in leaving her chores to others this day. Gladly she would have done it all if only to avoid the coming hours. She heard the stirring outside her door and knew Thomas was busy lighting the fires. Her tiny chamber housed no fireplace, but today it mattered not for she felt numb both inside and out.

From her window perch she watched the comings and goings at the cookhouse and felt completely abandoned. She knew Nanny had meant well in declaring she should sleep, but she was used to constant activity. With nothing to divert her mind, she felt like a caged criminal. She'd been tried, found guilty, and condemned to marriage all because of Malachi's debts. The chill in the room did little to stem her shudders, for her imagination had already journeyed to the coming night. She tried to count her blessings: at least it was Mr. Carlson and not Cyrus Bloom she would be wed to. But now as the hour approached the difference offered little comfort. Pain from any hand was still pain. And when she thought of entering Malachi's old room and placing herself on his bed like a sacrifice at the altar, her stomach lurched in protest. Malachi's taunting laugh echoed in her mind until she felt she might go crazy from the sound. She could almost feel his panting breath on her flesh, the cold bone-like fingers that could create such humiliation. And as the dawn broke full to admit the new day, Abby prayed she'd have the strength to endure what she knew she must, when the daylight surrendered to the darkness of night.

Madame Rousseau and a pair of maids arrived much too soon, and Abby found herself bathed, perfumed, and groomed. She knew they had seen her scars, for the startled expressions on the young girls faces had said it all. And for a terrifying moment she feared she would be sick if they questioned her. It would be humiliating enough to expose her secrets to Mr. Carlson, but if she had to offer explanations to the maids, Abby feared she'd go mad.

Gratefully, Madame Rousseau had ignored their startled looks and her demanding pace left little room for idle speculation. Abby felt the minutes of her freedom slip away with alarming speed as she was commanded to move this way and that. Soft cream was rubbed onto her hands and arms while her freshly washed hair was combed dry then brushed until it shown and her head ached. The thick golden masses were pulled and twisted and pinned and braided, until Abby thought she would scream in frustration.

Her old chemise had disappeared and when Madam Rousseau handed her a new one, she could not contain her gasp. The fabric was softer than anything she had ever felt and delicate lace decorated the neckline where tiny blue flowers had been painstakingly embroidered. But Abby's startled expression was not from the fine workmanship. The fabric was nearly transparent. And as the garment was slipped over her head and the ribbon tied securely under her breast her worst fears came true, for the gossamer chemise did more to entice than to cover. She thought of the eyes that tonight would view her body and her knees went weak. Her feeble protests were muffled as the grand processions of petticoats were lifted over her head and tied securely into place.

Thomas and Obadiah carried in a long oval looking glass then stared in wonder at the transformation of their mistress. But Charlotte was still not content.

"You are still too pale, ma petite, it's a wedding not a funeral. Daisy, step lively and fetch me the syrup."

Like a marble statue and just as cold, Abby stood in rigid silence while the seamstress painted her lips with raspberry syrup. The temptation to lick it off before it dried was forestalled by the dangerous churning in her stomach. When the syrup dried, Madame Rousseau tipped her chin up and wiped her lips clean with a damp cloth, leaving only the faintest stain.

"There," she decreed, giving Abby's cheeks a gentle pinch to add to the color. "Look at yourself, my petite. You are magnificent."

Abby turned and gazed at the looking glass only to see a stranger looking back at her. It was not her in the mirror, she reasoned, for the creature there looked like royalty. Her hair, the color of dark honey, was intricately entwined with tiny seed pearls woven among the curls. The gown that flowed about her shimmered in the light and sparkled with her slightest movement, it's ivory color a surprising compliment to her hair.

"You is sure beautiful, Miz Abby," Obadiah said clutching his worn hat to his chest.

"I ain't never seen no one so pretty," Effie offered shyly, her eyes still round in awe.

Abby tried to accept their compliments and well wishes, but the last minutes of her freedom were flying by too quickly. And despite what they said, or how fancy they had decorated the outside, inside she knew she was still the same Abigail Barclay, clumsy, inept, and doomed.

Hair tousled and eyes bleary, Christopher entered the frenzied mayhem of the Beaumont's cookhouse and looked desperately for something to eat. For two days he'd worked almost non stop but it had been worth it. Now as the fruit of his labor rested securely in his pocket he turned his attention to his most pressing need, food. His mouth watered as he surveyed the work tables. Silver platters, many from his own hand, were piled high with a mouthwatering assortment of delicate pastries, and the tantalizing aroma of beef pies filled the air.

"Christopher where have you been?"

He turned to find Sarah, arms akimbo, standing

197

in the doorway. "You are to be married in less than an hour yet you steal into my cookhouse looking like a vagabond. Pray tell me you've not had a change of heart for if Nick finds that he's endured your sister's presence for naught, I fear the consequences will be great."

Chris grinned with undisguised delight. "I finished it," he said reaching into his pocket even as Mrs. Killingham smacked the back of his other hand with her wooden spoon.

"Those jellies are for your wedding, Mr. Carlson. You just get out of here and behave yourself," the old cook chastised.

He rubbed the sting from his flesh and gave the woman a disarming grin. "You'll have me fainting at the altar, my dear lady," he said easily, "for I've not eaten since noon yesterday."

"What?" He smiled as both women spoke in unison.

"Then you just sit down this minute," the cook chastised. "I'll have a plate of ham and biscuits ready in no time, and there's plenty of your favorite sausage gravy left from the morning meal. If you're good and clean your plate," she said as she waved the spoon in a menacing fashion, "I just might remember that I saved a nice hunk of my gingerbread from dinner last night. Now you sit and don't give me no sass."

Chris winked at Sarah as he pulled a chair to the corner of the table. His look reminded her of a little boy who had just discovered the delights of carrying a frog in his pocket.

"What have you been doing, Christopher?" Sarah raised a brow and gave her most challenging stare.

He fished into his pocket and withdrew a velvet pouch of midnight blue. With reckless abandon, he tossed it to Sarah, then turned his attention to the plate Mrs. Killingham had placed before him.

Sarah opened the pouch and cautiously slid the contents into the palm of her hand. A delicate ring fashioned in gold glittered in the sunlight that poured through the doorway."Chris, it's beautiful," she whispered letting her finger trace the ring's edge. But when she lifted the piece, the ring fell apart in her fingers. "Oh dear heavens," she cried. "Chris, what did I do? I'm so sorry . . ."

Not the least disturbed, Christopher motioned her closer, holding out his hand for the ring. "It's not broken," he said quickly, noting the sudden brightness of her eyes. "Watch."

Sarah stared in amazement as Christopher put the interlocking loops back into place and suddenly, before her eyes, the ring was once more whole. "Chris, how did you do that?" She lifted the piece from his opened palm only to have it fall to pieces again in her fingers.

"Try it," he urged, ravenously scooping the gravy from his plate with a biscuit.

Sarah stared hard at the tangled mass in her hand. There were four rings of gold each looped within the other, yet moments ago they had been a whole. Gently she slipped two of the bands into place marveling over the detailed workmanship that adorned them, and the intricacy in which they wove under and over each other. But her triumph was short lived for as she tried to maneuver the third band into place, the first two slipped from her grasp and once more she held a tangled mass.

"The design is often called the Sultan's puzzle ring," Chris said, setting down his fork, and retrieving the tangled hoops, with a smile.

To Sarah it seemed that she had only blinked but

the ring was once more whole and resting on his opened palm.

"Christopher, it's beautiful. I've never seen anything like it."

He beamed in pleasure. "Neither have I, but I heard a story once and it's always intrigued me."

Sarah pulled a stool close and sat down ignoring the chaos that bustled about them. "You designed this from a story?"

Chris slipped the ring on his pinkie. "On one of our many journeys home from England for the summer holiday, Nick and I had opportunity to book passage on one of the most antiquated ships that I've ever sailed. We took bets the entire voyage as to whether we'd even make it home."

"You know how I feel about gambling, Christopher," she said stiffly making his grin stretch wider.

"Anyway," he continued. "we happened upon a rusty, old, sea dog with the most fantastic stories. One was of a Sultan and his ring. God only knows why, but I've always been intrigued by the tale."

"Tell me," she urged impatiently.

"Well, as the story goes — There once reigned a Sultan in a kingdom far to the east. He was very powerful, very rich, and had many wives." He grinned as Sarah stiffened.

"I think this is a story for Nicholas," she said properly.

"Hear me out," he grabbed her hand as she rose to leave. "Out of all his wives there one the Sultan cherished more than the rest. Her name was Lark and although far from being the most beautiful in his harem, her grace and quiet charm had captivated him completely. But even with all his wealth, the Sultan was not granted contentment. He lived with the fear that one day Lark would fly from his heart, for she was very, very young and he was past his prime. So to test her loyalty, the Sultan commissioned his silversmith to fashion a special ring for his young bride. He knew that if she were to seek out the affections of another, she would remove his token, so he didn't tell Lark the ring's secret. The piece was designed to fall apart if removed from her finger. He dreaded the day she would come to him with the ring in pieces, for he knew that would be the day he would lose her forever. The laws of the land were very clear and to betray the Sultan meant instant death, even for a favored wife."

"That doesn't seem very kind," Sarah frowned. "And any man with more than one wife doesn't deserve loyalty." Sarah's eyes suddenly went wide with dread. "Surely you don't mean to test Abigail's faithfulness in the same horrid manner."

Chris patted her hand with affection. "Listen to the end," he said gently. "The Sultan called Lark to attend him and he presented her with the ring. The four bands, the old Sultan explained, represented the four seasons, and she would have his love for each as they passed one after the other. The interweaving design was a symbol of their lives, one pouring into the other, each depending on the other to create a whole. The story goes that little Lark was so touched with her gift that she fell in love with her husband, the Sultan, and from that day until the day she died at ninety-three, the ring never left her finger."

"Oh Christopher," Sarah blinked back her tears. "And from that story you fashioned this beautiful band?" Her finger traced over the gold that glimmered on his pinkie.

A flash of anxiousness crossed his handsome face. "I wanted to design something special for her, something beautiful and unique like she is. Then the story came to mind and I knew what I wanted to do." He shook his head from the memory of his frustration. "I just didn't know how. Do you really think she'll be pleased?"

Sarah saw his uncertainty and her heart went out to him. "Christopher, the ring is exquisite but Abigail will love it all the more because it was your care and talent that created it."

As long as it makes her love me, he thought silently.

Sarah stood and wrinkled her nose. "But she isn't going to have the chance to tell you if you don't make haste. You smell like a barnyard, and look even worse."

"Livery," he said, trying to swallow a huge piece of gingerbread even as he rose from his place at the table. "I've been using the forge at the livery these past two days."

She held her nose as he stepped closer. "You go up to the front room, and I'll have them start heating the water. Your clothes are already laid out and if you use the back stairs, with any luck you'll miss your sister."

Christopher grimaced. "She's arrived already?"

Sarah pushed at his broad shoulders to turn him toward the house. "About an hour ago. And I'm not exaggerating when I say that Nick is more than a little vexed with you for not being here to greet her."

Chris took two long strides out of the cookhouse then turned back to Sarah. Taking her shoulders firmly in his hands he leaned down and placed a hearty kiss on her cheek. "Thank you from the bottom of my heart," he said, his voice suddenly thick. "I know you've done much and with little notice, but I truly appreciate your intervention on Julie's behalf.

I know she's trouble and she drives Nick crazy, but . . ."

"But she's your only sister," Sarah finished easily. "You are a dear friend, Christopher," she reached up and patted the dark stubble that covered his cheek. "But at the moment you're a very dirty one. Now be gone with you or your bride will be thinking you've deserted her."

Chapter Twelve

The hands of the clock inched toward the appointed hour and Abby watched the sun disappear from the sky. Dark clouds gathered overhead and the brisk wind foretold the coming of a storm. From her perch on the window seat, Abby watched the droplets splash their pattern against the wooden floor of the porch. She tried counting the raindrops to ignore the confusion that buzzed about her, but the effort only made her head ache more.

The clock struck twelve and Nicholas Beaumont entered the tavern as the last chime sounded. Abby stood as one stricken of mind as everyone voiced their opinion as to how to get her safely into the carriage.

"The gown must not get wet, Nick," Charlotte commanded, dressing Abby in a satin cape.

"Oh, but do take care with her hair," Nanny cried, as the light hood was drawn forward. Amidst all the confusion, Abby remained silent. She stood when they beckoned and moved as they commanded and wished with all her heart that lightning might strike her.

She watched Mr. Beaumont's scowl grow darker and reasoned he didn't share his wife's enthusiasm for weddings, especially one in which fate decreed he must fetch the bride. He listened patiently to Charlotte's words, and gave Nanny a brief, reassuring smile, but Abby wasn't prepared when he suddenly scooped her into his arms. Before she could find her voice to offer protest, Abby found herself sitting in the waiting carriage with Mr. Beaumont climbing in beside her. Taking care not to step on her gown, he settled in to face her. Then, they were on their way. Desperately she wished she had been allowed to ride with the others, but Mrs. Beaumont had been quite insistent. The others would go ahead, and Nick would escort Abby. Rain beat against the leather casings on the windows, while inside a small lantern cast an unreal light on the carriage's plush interior.

Abby tried to take a deep breath, but the constricting bodice of her gown forbade it and she wondered why she had allowed them to fasten the stays so tightly. She clutched her hands in her lap and tried to maintain her balance as the carriage rocked to and fro. She felt as if her entire world had turned to glass, ready to shatter at the slightest touch.

Nick scowled as he watched her inner struggle. The joy of a new bride was definitely absent, but the grim set of her face forbade questions. He maintained his silence until the carriage drew to a halt before his home. She looked up then, and the panic in her eyes reminded him of another time and place and his heart went out to her.

"Mrs. Barclay, I would have but a word before we join your impatient bridegroom." She said nothing, but watched him in wary silence. "Somehow, madam, assumptions were made and I, by my silence, have led you to believe in their truth. I would rectify the matter if you would allow." He waited

205

until she nodded slightly. "You came to my office." He watched her chin drop and saw the heat of embarrassment that bloomed against her pale cheeks. Nick reached for her hand and found it freezing. Without thought he took it with his own as he would have with Sarah. "My admiration for you is great, madam," he said gently, watching her head snap up in surprise. "You showed me the courage and strength that Christopher speaks of so often. But I cannot allow you to believe a falsehood. Christopher did not borrow the money from me."

Abby's eyes grew wider still. "But if not from you, then . . ."

Nick rubbed her hands gently within his own. "Madam, Christopher has sufficient wealth to see his children, nay his grandchildren, in comfort for the rest of their days."

Preposterous, her mind challenged. "But he never wears a wig," her voice trembled. Her eyes searched Mr. Beaumont's dark gaze for truth when a sickening revelation hit with force. The man before her, one of the richest in the colony, wasn't wearing a hair piece of any type. Abby felt her world crumble about her. Mr. Carlson was a man of wealth? "I don't understand," she stammered, feeling ever more the fool.

"I'll tell you a secret," Nick said softly, trying to allay her fears. "But you must promise to keep your own council." He watched her nod solemnly then continued. "Christopher and I shared a vow never to wear wigs. It all started one night at Eton, when we were young and full of brandy. We decided that wigs were not to be tolerated and with great fanfare set our own aflame."

"Oh, my Lord," she gasped.

Nick only smiled in memory. "I think we had consumed too much brandy for the Lord to have counseled us on that night. At any rate, the story did not end there for, in our zest for adventure, we decided to sneak into the headmaster's house and steal *all* the wigs. We had no way of knowing that most of the masters had shaved their heads."

Abby couldn't contain the chuckle that bubbled forth. "What happened to you? Surely there were dire consequences for such mischief."

Nick shook his head, grateful to see the color back in her cheeks. "We were caned soundly before the entire school and then the prefects were allowed to shave our heads."

Abby tried to picture Mr. Carlson without his thick blond locks but the image refused to come. Instead she saw a young man flogged in humiliation. Her smile faded.

Dismayed, Nick wondered how he had erred in his story. Moments ago she had relaxed enough to smile, now she looked ready to burst into tears.

"Truly, it wasn't so bad," he offered. "We didn't sit for a day or two, but Christopher concocted the grand idea that we should keep our heads bare for the rest of the term. I never quite knew how he did it," Nick confided, "but Chris somehow managed to turn our bald heads into a symbol of bravery and courage. By the end of the week we were the envy of the class and all was well until we came home. My grandmother was the first to see our naked pates and flew into a tizzy. She threatened to cane us all over again, but Christopher, being a master of diplomacy, managed to get her to relent." Nick's smile turned sad as he thought of those now lost to them. Dear Gran, both of Christopher's parents . . . "Chris had the good sense to wait until his own hair was well on its way before he ventured home," Nick continued. "Although I dare say his mother was probably so glad to see him, the length of his hair was the last thought on her mind."

Abby's brows drew together. "If his parents cared for him as you say, why did they disinherit him?"

Mr. Beaumont's easy smile turned to stone before her eyes. "They did care for him," he stated firmly. "For a greater love between father and son I've never witnessed."

"But why . . ."

"They didn't disinherit him, they set him free." Nick interrupted. "His parents knew his heart didn't lie on the plantation. But Christopher was a dutiful son and never would have left on his own. With their death, they gave him the greatest gift of all. They allowed him to leave with a free conscience to pursue the craft he's loved all his life. Christopher is a talented silversmith, as I'm sure you're now well aware, and his work is in great demand. But until now, the joy of creating could only be a pastime with him."

Abby's hand reached for the silver locket that she wore as her only jewelry. "But . . ."

Again Nick interrupted her. "The locket you wear was the first piece he ever attempted. It was a gift for his mother and I know it was her most treasured possession. I believe he was ten and two when he made it. I tell you this only to reassure," he said gently. "I know you're frightened. I can see it in your eyes. But you are a beautiful bride and the time has come to set your fears to rest. Now give me a smile, or Christopher will have my hide."

Abby felt her heart knock painfully against her ribs as she struggled to smile. She couldn't imagine

Nicholas Beaumont letting anyone have his hide, friend or not.

The rain had momentarily ceased, and as he opened the door, Abby took a breath of the damp, frigid air. The clouds hung low, and the sky looked more of twilight than noon, an ominous setting, she thought looking towards the heavens. But she was not left to her musings.

Quickly ushered inside, Abby stopped dead in the foyer of the Beaumont Mansion. She stood motionless as Mr. Beaumont removed her cloak and handed it to a stiff looking gentleman he identified only as Wadsworth. Stunned by the elegant splendor that surrounded her, her eyes darted in all directions. Garlands of greenery scalloped the banister of the massive staircase and candles placed within flickered their greeting. Huge paintings in gilded frames broke the starkness of the pristine white walls and great bouquets of asters and marigolds were everywhere.

Abby blinked in wonder at the crystal chandelier that hung overhead. Here, too, the candles had been lit, and their light sparkled like sun-drops as they pushed back the afternoon shadows. No wonder Mr. Carlson had designed such a grand entrance way for his new home, she thought miserably. This was what he was accustomed to. She remembered vividly their discussion at the cookhouse steps. How utterly naive she must have sounded as she prattled on about changing walls. Yet never once did he explain. Feeling more than a bit betrayed, and completely out of her depth, Abby's panic intensified. The hum of voices droned in the background and somewhere the elusive tones of the harpsichord danced in gay abandon.

"I'll tell Sarah we've arrived," Nick said, ushering

her into his office. "Why don't you enjoy the peace and solitude in here for a moment while I fetch her."

Closing the door behind him, Abby found herself in a comfortable chamber well appointed with massive oak furniture. Books lined the walls from floor to ceiling and the faint smell of bee's wax and lemon oil lingered in the air. Here, too, the candles had been lit to push back the shadows and as she moved to stand near the deep window, she flinched as the rain started again and beat its fury against the glass pane.

The door behind her opened and Abby turned, expecting to see Mrs. Beaumont. Instead a petite woman clad in deep royal blue swept regally into the room.

"I can't say it's a pleasure to meet you," the woman said, her eyes dark with malice. "And my brother's a fool if he thinks I'll let him get away with marrying you."

Startled, Abby drew back. From the fair blond coloring and the vivid turquoise eyes, she knew this must be Mr. Carlson's sister Julie, but never had she anticipated such a vicious attack. "Miss Carlson?" she questioned.

"It's Mrs. Morgan to you," Julie snapped stalking around Abby's trembling form. "What have you done to bewitch my brother?"

"Bewitch . . ." Abby stammered, with indignation. She was the one being coerced into marriage.

Julie Morgan folded her arms across her chest and felt her hatred grow. It was bad enough that Nick's affections had been stolen from her by that conniving Puritan from Salem, but to lose Chris's devotion to a common tavern keeper was more than she could bear.

"I've done some checking," she taunted, lifting a delicate brow. "And though the time's been short, which I attribute to your scheming ways, I've made it my business to seek out your background. Shall I be frank and tell you what I've found thus far, my dear?" She sneered, not expecting an answer. "Your mother was no more than a common tart and died years ago, probably from the pox. Your father is a blackheart and a drunkard to boot, and your late husband left you in substantial debt." The smile on her face turned savage. "Not bad for a few days searching, wouldn't you say? And who knows what other scandals I'll find when I dig deeper?"

Abby drew herself erect and wondered how this vicious woman could be related to Mr. Carlson. "It is as you say, madam." Her voice was cold. "But a child is not to blame for its parents' circumstances. That my father drinks is my concern, not yours. As for my late husband, he's dead, so no more need be said."

"Hah!" Julie swirled and her blond curls danced about her shoulders. "You're a nobody playing dress-up and trying to fit in where you don't belong. Well I won't have it. I won't have a common tavern keeper in my family, married to my brother."

Humiliation kept Abby from laughing at the irony of it all, for in her mind everything Julie said was true. She was a nobody, yet for some ridiculous reason Mr. Carlson wanted to wed her. She gave Julie a desperate look. Mayhap if he heard the words from his sister's lips, he would finally realize the folly of his actions. "I think you should take your concerns up with your brother."

"Oh you'd like that wouldn't you," Julie sneered. "You'd like me to run to Christopher with my information, then you could play the innocent victim and weep on his shoulder. My brother was always pathetic when it came to strays. Well to me you are just another mangy she-cat he's brought home out of pity."

The hurt turned to fury and Abby straightened, her eyes ablaze with anger. "Then mayhap you should beware lest you feel the sting of my claws."

Julie hesitated for only a heartbeat. "I'll concede you the day, little cat. But never forget that the ultimate victory shall be mine. Until then, I'd be very careful with each of those nine lives of yours. For there's no telling just how true that old wives tale is."

Footsteps sounded beyond the door and Julie's eyes narrowed in warning. "I concede the day, slut, but only the day." Turning on her heels, she yanked open the door to reveal a startled Jimmy Richardson hesitating on the other side. Looking first from one to the other, her eyes narrowed in silent speculation. "My brother's wife and his apprentice," she said as a wicked smile touched her lips. "I wonder what I could do with that?" With her threat still hanging in the air, Julie Carlson Morgan made her exit.

Jimmy swallowed hard and stepped back as Mr. Carlson's sister swept by him. He'd already been on the receiving end of her temper once that day and it was an experience he chose not to repeat. Taking a deep breath he looked back at Mrs. Barclay and felt his heart stop beating. He had always thought her beautiful but now she made his mouth go dry. Her dress shimmered with each breath and her hair was a crown of gold atop her head. Mesmerized, he stared at the sway of her skirt as she beckoned him in.

"The nerve of that woman," Abby muttered. "Jimmy, come in." She offered her hand in greeting.

212

"It is good to see you again. How are your burns?" She turned his calloused hands over within her own. "You never even gave me a chance to thank you for chopping all that wood."

Jimmy felt the blood rush to his ears. He'd rehearsed for two days, but he hadn't realized she'd look so different. And when he touched the cool softness of her hand, his heart leaped to his throat making it impossible to speak.

Her fingers traced over the scars that covered the back of his hands. "These might fade with time," she said softly. "Do they still give you pain?"

Silently, he shook his head, trying to ignore the growing tightness in his belly. But when she looked up and smiled at him, Jimmy's passion pushed aside his common sense.

"You can't marry him," he blurted out.

Abby looked up at his freshly scrubbed face with confusion. "Jimmy, what are you talking about?"

The tremor in her voice was his undoing and in desperation James Richardson threw caution to the wind. "He's a good man. I more than anyone know that. But you can't marry him. You can't." His voice cracked and his last word carried the high pitched tone from his youth.

Abby watched his cheeks bloom with heat and felt her own senses begin to reel. Was the match so ill fated that even a young apprentice could see the fault with it? She dropped his hands and her own stiffened at her sides. Julie's words echoed over in her mind. "You don't belong . . . you're only playing dress-up." Desperately she wished she could draw a deeper breath, for the tightness of the stays and the weight of the gown were becoming more oppressive with each passing moment.

213

"He doesn't love you," Jimmy stammered. "I would love you forever. I would love you more than the air I breathe, more than life itself."

Abby's head snapped up, her eyes wide in shock. "Jimmy . . ."

"I know I have no money now, but I will some day. Please," he begged, falling to his knees before her. "I'll do anything you ask of me. Just say you won't do this. Say you'll wait for me."

"You want me to marry you?" she gasped. Completely unnerved, Abby could only stare in wonder.

Encouraged by her silence, Jimmy grasped her hands tightly within his own. "I'll chop all your wood, and travel to Jamestown everyday to buy the best apples you've ever seen." His eyes nervously dropped to their locked hands, and he wished he had the nerve to kiss them.

Eyes closed, Abby swayed unsteadily on her feet. "Jimmy, I can't marry you. When did I ever act to make you think otherwise?"

Jimmy scrubbed his sleeve across his eyes and sniffed hard, wishing he could name a time and place. "I know you don't love me now, but you do care for me. You wouldn't have sent the calve's foot jelly if you felt nothing. Right now it's enough that I love you. And I know in my heart in time I could make you care even more. You must wait for me. You'll never find anyone to cherish you as I do."

"Jimmy no," she stammered.

"Mr. Carlson doesn't love you," he interrupted quickly, unable to face rejection. "He has too many other women to love just one. I know I don't have as much money as him, but I'm saving. I even tried to make you a brooch but the fi . . ."

Abby felt the breath leave her body and prayed her

instincts were wrong. "Jimmy," her voice trembled apprehension. "Jimmy were you in the silver shop before the fire started?"

Realizing what he'd revealed, Jimmy's face blanched. "I didn't mean for it to happen," he choked, his eyes brimming with sudden tears. "I thought to melt down one of the buckles and create a brooch for you. I had the design and just that afternoon Mr. Carlson showed me how to pour a mold. He made everything look so easy." Tears now ran freely down his young face. "But I spilled the silver and the hay caught fire, and the water buckets weren't full and, oh God, I didn't mean for it to happen. I only wanted to make you a gift."

Abby's thoughts scattered in all directions. "We've got to tell him," she said, desperately trying to draw a decent breath. "We've got to tell him the truth about the fire."

"No!" Jimmy cried in terror. "You can't. I'll deny it. He thinks me a hero for trying to put it out. If you tell, then everything will go all wrong again."

"Jimmy," she pleaded, "don't you see? Everything is all wrong now."

Frantically he scrambled to his feet, his eyes darting about like a caged animal. "You must come with me now. We'll . . . we'll run away. We'll go somewhere where they'll never find us."

Abby pulled her hand from his tenacious grip. "Jimmy stop," she said sharply. "I won't run away with you. You're a fine lad but you're only ten and four. Jimmy, we must tell Mr. Carlson what happened that night. He's got a right to know."

Vehemently, Jimmy shook his head. "I . . ."

Lightning flashed and thunder cracked instantly in its wake. The glass window panes rattled in their cas-

215

ings as the entire house trembled from the force. Terror covered Jimmy's face.

"Come with me now," he cried, grabbing her hand and yanking her toward the doorway. "We've got to get away before Mr. Carlson finds out. I didn't mean to burn the shop down, I only wanted to make you happy. You must come with me or all will have been for naught."

Desperation intensified his strength and Abby felt herself tugged to the doorway. But as Jimmy careened around the corner into the foyer, Abby pulled back and crashed into one of the massive floral arrangements. She felt the tall slender table tip even as she grabbed for it. But as her arms filled with flowers the table toppled to the marble floor and the porcelain vase smashed with the sound of cannon fire. Regaining her balance, Abby looked up to find Sarah and Nick across the hall in the parlor's doorway. Mr. Carlson, his sister, and a host of wedding guests stood just behind. The front door slammed, but no one seemed to notice Jimmy's departure for all eyes were focused on her.

Abby felt a coldness begin to grow in the depth of her body. She looked down at the shattered vase and felt herself begin to tremble as voices from the past reared up to taunt her. "You're too clumsy Abigail— must be punished. You've been a wicked girl Abigail—raise your petticoats and bend over. It's for your own good Abigail, maybe next time you'll not be so reckless." Then the pain would start—blinding white in its intensity, humiliating in its nature.

Abby watched Mr. Carlson disengage himself from the group and she struggled not to flinch when he reached for her.

"Are you hurt?" his voice was low, as he scooped

216

the flowers from her arms and handed them to Wadsworth. Already a young maid was tending to the shattered porcelain.

"I'm so sorry," her voice shook with fear. "You've been bad, Abigail, you know you must be punished." The words sounded over and over in her mind and as Mr. Carlson took her hand, Abby realized that this man had the power to hurt her far worse than all the others.

Christopher led her back into Nick's study with Sarah close on his heels. Thinking her about to faint, he urged her to a chair.

"I'm so sorry," Abby chanted, her breath coming in hiccupping gasps. "I'm so sorry."

Sarah knelt, thinking Abby looked more shattered than the vase. "Abby, it was an accident," she said gently. "Accidents happen all the time. You're not to become upset over it."

Abby twisted her hands in her lap. Her frightened eyes darting from Sarah to Mr. Carlson. "It was a costly piece, wasn't it . . ."

Sarah shook her head. "Nothing in this house carries a price greater than friendship."

Abby closed her eyes and wrapped her arms around the pain that coursed through her. "I didn't mean to do it," she whispered. "I'm just so clumsy." "You are clumsy, Abigail," the voices taunted. "And costly mistakes need a greater punishment." Abby opened her eyes and looked frantically about the well-appointed room. Objects in this house were worth more than any she had ever encountered. Her punishment would be worse than any she had ever received. Her stomach lurched and only the strongest will power kept her from being sick all over the Oriental carpet that covered the floor.

"Sarah, would you leave us for a moment?" Chris said.

Sarah turned and saw anguish cross Christopher's face. And as she rose, she couldn't help but wonder who was hurting more.

"I'll get everyone settled outside," she said softly giving Abby's clenched hand a reassuring pat. "Just open the door when you're ready." Her heart went out to Chris as he stood rigidly before her. "Just remember," she whispered, raising to kiss his cheek, "you love her and everything will work out."

Christopher watched Sarah leave and close the door firmly behind her. Turning back to Abby he felt his heart constrict. She sat perched on the edge of the chair, head bowed, shoulders rounded, carrying the weight of the world on her slender frame.

"Abigail, stand up," he commanded softly. He watched her jerk instantly to her feet but her eyes stayed locked on her shoes and her hands clenched so tightly he could see her knuckles whiten. "Give me your hand."

Abby fought back the terror that rose in her throat. The voice was no longer in her mind, and the time had come. Palm up to receive the first blow, she offered her hand and steeled herself for what was to come.

"Abigail," Chris took her fingers within his own and found them freezing. "Look at me please." Instantly her head snapped up to obey his command. Chris wondered how everything had suddenly gone so wrong. It's because you're forcing her to marry you, his mind taunted. She doesn't love you and you know it. But I love her, his heart answered, and she needs me. Chris tightened his grip on her fingers and tugged her gently closer, until his arm encircled her

218

shoulders.

"This is our wedding day." He searched for the words that would ease the way for her. "I want you to put this mishap from your mind. We can deal with the consequences later when we get home for there are many alternatives. We could offer to pay for the vase or even replace it."

Abby closed her eyes in resignation. She had ceased to listen after he had declared they would take the matter up later when they returned home. Well of course, her mind ridiculed, did you really think to take your punishment here and be done with it? Waiting had always been Malachi's favorite game. Ofttimes she didn't even know what she had done, but Malachi's fiendish smile would greet her even as she struggled from sleep. You've been clumsy again Abigail, he would taunt. You need another lesson at the woodpile tonight. Then he would leave her to fret the entire day until her nerves were raw before the beating even began. Every time she felt his eyes upon her, she looked up to see his sinister smile, and her anxiety would intensify until the waiting tormented as much as the beating itself. But when she thought of the value of the Beaumont's vase, she knew she deserved no mercy.

"Will you do as I ask?" Christopher tipped up her chin. "Will you put it out of your mind until we can deal with it in private?"

Numbly she nodded, knowing the fates would grant her no mercy.

Chris looked down and saw her chin quiver. Dear lord how he wanted to hold her close and protect her from all the injustice life had hurled her way. "And will you smile for me?" He struggled to keep the pleading tone from his voice.

"Yes, sir." Abby knew better than to refuse, but her smile took more effort than she possessed and ended as a lopsided grin that made him chuckle and cluck her under the chin.

"Good, and I think it is time you called me Christopher," he declared soundly, placing a quick kiss on her forehead. "You are about to become my wife and I find myself anxious to get this marriage underway." He felt his excitement return. "The faster we are married," He offered his own comical grin. "The faster we can take our leave to return home."

Chris felt his blood quicken with the thought of easing into her willing flesh. Tonight, when they were alone, he would demonstrate once and for all the depth of his love for her. Tonight, the final barriers would be cast aside and she would at last become his.

Chapter Thirteen

Gathering the last remnants of her courage, Abby stood with head held high as Christopher Carlson ushered her across the hallway to their waiting guests. A hushed silence greeted the striking couple as they entered the crowded room. Christopher's tall, lean handsomeness never failed to draw attention but this day all eyes were on the petite beauty that graced his arm. The harpsichord changed its tune to proclaim their arrival and a path magically cleared before them.

Abby watched the parting in stunned silence. Like Moses and the Red Sea, she thought daring to steal a glance at her intended. Gone were the sweat stained shirts and the plain brown breeches she had grown accustomed to. Expensively garbed in velvet of midnight blue with trim of ivory lace, his attire was the perfect compliment to hers. But the fine cut of his coat did little to disguise the well-formed muscles that lay beneath the costly fabric, and Abby shuddered with apprehension. Her feet felt like lead, the tight stays forced the breath from her body and the unaccustomed weight of the beaded gown felt like a millstone about her aching shoulders.

She would have faltered more than once as he purposefully lead them through the crowded room, but his hand pressed hers in reassurance as it rested on his arm, and oddly the warming touch brought comfort.

Tiny flames from a hundred candles illuminated the waiting minister and the costly scent of bees wax mingled with the heavy perfumes that already filled the air. The candle's heat stirred the mixture and Abby felt her head begin to spin in earnest. Her stomach churned and she would have given a king's ransom for a single breath of fresh air.

The Reverend Jeffers ended his prologue and Abby felt her knees begin to shake. Her time had come. There would be no miraculous reprieve. They were facing each other now, and she tried to focus on the large hands that held hers so gently. His thumb rubbed softly across her knuckles and as her eyes lifted to his, Abby felt a jolt akin to pain shoot deep within. Had her bodice allowed, she would have gasped from the heat that burned in his gaze; had her fear not been so great she would have noticed the throbbing emptiness in her soul that cried out for his touch. Her eyes met his and held firm.

"If there be one who objects to this union, or knows of reasons that these two should not be united in holy matrimony, let him speak now or forever hold his peace." The minister's words challenged the assembled group. All remained silent.

With a deep smile the reverend turned back to the couple before him. "Dearly beloved, we are . . ."

A shrill cry pierced the air, followed by the hearty sound of flesh striking flesh. The double doors to the parlor crashed open, bouncing back against the walls to tremble on their hinges. A small, thick-set woman clad in black from head to toe struggled with Wadsworth, the Beaumont's butler. His reddened cheek bore her hand print, and as her arms flailed, the sodden fabric of her cape showered those nearest.

"Stop the wedding!" Her shrill voice grated across the stunned silence.

Nick left his place at Christopher's side with menacing steps, planting himself directly before the intruder. "Madame, you encroach on a very private gathering. I must demand you leave at once."

"This wedding can't continue," she shrieked, dislodging her arm from the tenacious butler. "It is a travesty against all that is holy. That whore is already married."

The room gasped as one then filled with whispered speculation.

Abby felt her knees give way and had Christopher not pulled her close to lean against his chest, she would have sagged to the ground.

The softness in Nick's voice hushed the murmurs. "Explain yourself, madam, and do so quickly."

The woman threw back the hood to her cape revealing a hawk-like nose and narrow beady eyes that glinted over small wire glasses. Her white hair had thinned to let her scalp shine through until she tugged her wig low over her wrinkled forehead. Her finger raised in condemnation and it shook with fury as she pointed to the bridal couple. "She's a harlot, sent straight from hell, for she flaunts herself at any man who will cast his eye in her direction."

223

"Madam . . ." Nick's voice went softer still. "You try my patience with no just cause."

"Just cause," the woman shrieked. "Just cause! I'll give you just cause." Her blue white skin blotched red with indignation. "There can be no wedding, for that slut is married to my brother!"

Christopher felt Abby stiffen in his arms then struggle to be free. Reluctantly he loosened his hold.

"Marilla?" she questioned hesitantly, grateful Mr. Carlson's arm still supported her. "Marilla, is that you?"

The elderly woman started forward but Nick's unyielding stand blocked her way. "Tell them, Abigail," She commanded. "Tell them you're my brother's trollop."

Abby began to tremble. She had met Marilla only once, the first summer she and Malachi had been married. The woman had eyes like a hawk, the tongue of a viper, and a penchant for finding the slightest flaw. She had taken her pleasure in pointing out to her brother each and every short-coming his young bride possessed. Abby remembered all too vividly the excited gleam in Marilla's eyes when Malachi would hand down his punishments. Though she never stayed to view the deed, her smug look of satisfaction had said it all. Looking now on the aging woman, Abby saw only the face of her husband back from the grave. She struggled to keep her voice from betraying her fear.

"Marilla, Malachi is dead."

"And probably by your hand."

Magnus Webster and two magistrates now flanked Nicholas Beaumont's side.

224

"Madam," Webster interjected. "I caution you to consider well your words. I penned a letter to you some six weeks ago advising you of your brother's death . . . by accident."

Marilla's dark eyes scanned the well appointed room, appraising its wealth. The Chinese vase, she calculated, was worth a small fortune. "I must have misunderstood," she stammered. "Are you telling me my brother's dead?"

"I wrote, madam," Webster said firmly, "and if you will recall, you responded by asking for your portion of his estate."

Marilla nervously glanced about but found no sympathetic eye. "I don't recall . . ." she faltered. "But if it is as you say, then what of mourning? How is it that my brother's widow, now finds herself a bride before my dear brother is even cold in the ground?"

Chris heard Abby's soft moan and pulled her back against him.

"Madam," he said tightly. "Surely you don't expect Mrs. Barclay to carry the burden of overseeing the Stag's Head Tavern alone?"

"Well, I . . ."

"Enough," Julie pushed her way past the wall of broad shoulders. "Can't you see this poor woman is completely distraught?" She slipped her arm about Marilla's shoulders, grimacing only slightly as the wet cape brushed against her gown. "It is of no little matter, the death of a beloved brother. And then to find his wife about to become a bride? Hah!, it would be enough to torment the strongest of hearts."

She pulled off the woman's sodden cape and thoughtlessly tossed it to the glowering Wadsworth.

225

"Come over here, dear," she crooned, leading the stunned woman to a side chair. "Go back to your wedding," she commanded with a flick of her golden curls. "Surely no one can object to Abigail's sister-in-law remaining for the ceremony."

Chris looked down at Abby's pale face with reservation. "Do you find fault with her presence?" he questioned, angry over the words Marilla had used to describe his bride, yet unwilling to cause the ceremony further delay.

"Of course she doesn't," Julie interrupted, her arm now possessively around Marilla's shoulders. "The woman is family."

"She can stay," Abby squeaked, then gathering her resolve, "She can stay."

"Wonderful," the minister's sigh was echoed throughout the room, and gently he drew attention back to the front.

Abby watched the proceeding through a haze of fear. Her eyes burned from the candle's heat, and her throat tightened. She heard her voice parrot the minister's words but had no notion of what was said. Then an intricate golden band was placed on her finger and her fate was sealed.

"I now pronounce you husband and wife." The Reverend's voice boomed his verdict and Abby felt her world tip as Mr. Carlson took her firmly by the shoulders and placed his lips directly on hers. A burning ache shot through her, startling in its intensity, demanding in its need. Her resistance melted and as she leaned against him for support she felt his arms encircle her to pull her closer still. He was the only man who'd ever kissed her, and for the briefest moment she wanted nothing more than to crawl into his skin and find safety.

The boisterous cheering from the guests broke the couple apart. With his arm securely about his bride, Christopher grinned from ear to ear as he accepted the congratulations and well wishes heaped upon them. Glasses of hearty rum punch were passed and all drank a toast to the lovely bride and her fortunate husband.

Like starving ants, the guests moved to the next room then fell on the waiting tables where delicacies of every description awaited them. A large ham, a leg of lamb, and a great roast of venison graced the center of the table, with roasted chicken and ducks placed artfully around. Oysters with crab meat stewed in butter and a variety of fish were likewise provided. The oaken table groaned under the additional weight of the marrow puddings, mince pies, and a grand array of vegetables.

Not to be overshadowed by its mate, the sweets table held its place on the opposite side of the dining room and it, too, was a work of art. Filled with almond cakes and cinnamon biscuits, cheese cakes, fruit tarts, jellies, and syllabub, it boasted every fruit in season. Shiny red apples mixed with yellow pears, grapes, and pineapples filled the silver platters and spilled over in grand cascades, while sugared tarts and tiny spice cakes scented the air with their mouth watering aromas.

The hours slipped by and Christopher felt his impatience grow. Abby had not regained her color since Marilla's untimely entrance, and although Julie had succeeded remarkably at keeping the old woman at bay, he felt Abby tense each time she drew near.

The clock in the foyer struck ten and Chris decided to end their trial. With a grand farewell, the two made their escape.

Abby struggled to maintain her balance as the darkened carriage swayed on its short journey. Mr. Carlson had not bothered with the lantern but the gloomy interior fit her mood. Her fingers clutched at the window strap, and desperately she prayed he'd not try to pull her close. Her mind ran in circles and her eyes were again stinging and hot as she contemplated the hours to come. With Malachi, she had been able to go cold inside, taking herself off to another place while he inflicted his pain. But when she thought of her new husband standing over her in that fashion, hysteria threatened. Why, her mind argued, should it be any different? Why did it suddenly seem so much worse?

The carriage halted and Abby drew a shaky breath. She'd not cower, she promised herself. She'd broken the vase and knew the consequences. With limbs that trembled she allowed him to escort her inside.

Nanny and Obadiah had already returned and soft lantern light greeted them as they stood in the silent entrance way. She allowed him to slip the new cape from her shoulders and hang it on a peg beside his own. But when he turned her to face him, Abby felt the last of her composure vanish. The act would be bad enough but suddenly she knew hearing the words from him would forever defeat her.

"Abigail," his voice was gentle, almost hesitant. "You must . . .

"Nay," her fingers pressed boldly against his lips. "Please don't . . . I know what you must do." Turning, she fled down the darkened hallway.

Christopher entered the chamber he had claimed as his own and cursed himself soundly. The fire in the hearth glowed in welcome, but did little to warm his spirits. Why had he ever made such a rash promise? With angry motions he tossed his jacket on the bed and scowled at its wide expanse. The covers had been turned back so invitingly and as his palm skimmed the soft surface, he could feel the warmth from the heated bricks at its foot. What a joke, he thought shrugging out of his waist coat. The room had been cleaned and scrubbed and now housed only his furniture. Decorative branches filled the earthenware jug on the chest by the window and a decanter of fine brandy with two crystal glasses stood in wait.

"I've everything but the bride," he muttered darkly. Whatever had possessed him to tell her they would wait to consummate the marriage? Why had he ever agreed to let her decide when? He pulled a hardwood rocker closer to the fire but found himself too restless to sit. Instead he helped himself to a generous measure of brandy. The liquid burned his tongue but did nothing to extinguish the ache in his heart or the throbbing in his loins.

The hour grew late, and Christopher's mood turned blacker with each tick of the clock. "Condemned by my own gallantry," he swore, pacing the length of the chamber and back. "She finds her peace in her solitary bed while I am condemned to wait. But for how long? Only she can say." He took two more angry steps before pausing to shatter his goblet in the fireplace. It brought no satisfaction. He perched on the side of the bed. The one he had hoped to share with his new bride, and glared at the small bouquet of primroses he'd picked for her pillow. With the coming frost, they'd be the last of the season. Why had he ever thought the magic of the ceremony would soften her heart towards him?

"Everything but a wife." He rose to pace again. "The one thing I desire, is placed within my grasp, yet she bids me not to touch." The tall case clock struck midnight and as he listened to the last chime fade, his decision was made. He'd promised her time. Time in which to know him better, time to become accustomed to their hasty marriage. But time would mean nothing, he reasoned, if it was spent apart. She'd share his bed and his warmth, and when she was ready, she'd share her body. Until then, he'd make himself content just to hold her. But share his bed she would.

Smiling for the first time since their return, Christopher wondered which room she claimed as her own and how much she would struggle against his decision. Tossing another log on the fire, he decided it didn't matter. He was the master here and the sooner she recognized that fact the better.

On silent feet he made his way down the shadowy steps to the tavern's main floor. Instincts told him his modest bride wouldn't keep a room above stairs with gentlemen patrons. But he jumped with a start when Obadiah stepped out of the shadows directly into his path. The old servant carried a single taper, but his rage would have been evident even in the dark.

"I thought you different," the wizened old man spat his displeasure. "But you be even worse. What you trying to do, kill that child?"

Stunned, Christopher took a step back. "Stop prattling, man and speak plain. Who am I sup-

230

posed to be killing? For if it is your mistress you speak of, I'll tell you here and now that I am the one who aches."

"That so?" Obadiah took a daring step closer. He knew the penalty for striking a white man, but he was dangerously close to not caring. "You ache so bad that you gotta let her freeze before you finished the deed? That gonna make you feel better? You know, you let the skin get cold enough, when you hit it, it gonna pop open like a shattered melon. That what you want to do to that poor child? That little one ain't never been nothing but kind to you and this be how you thank her?"

Christopher felt a sickening premonition settle in the pit of his belly. His hand snaked out and gathered the old servant by the shirt. "Stop speaking nonsense, Obadiah" he warned, his voice a dangerous whisper. "Where is your mistress? And what's this nonsense about beating her? Did she tell you that?"

Obadiah had tasted fear many times in his life and knew the flavor well. Taking a breath he swallowed hard, praying he'd made a mistake. "She told me about the accident. Said, she broke an expensive vase."

"So?" In his anger and fear, Chris jerked the old man until his toes nearly lost the floor. "Where is she? Has she fled?"

"Miz Abby's no coward," he defended. "She's waiting for her punishment like the old master taught her."

Chris's fingers instantly slackened on the old man's shirt. "Barclay beat her?" he whispered, his voice filled with anguish.

Obadiah sank gratefully back onto his own feet

231

and nodded. "She come to the master when she was but ten and four. A shy little thing she was, like a young colt all arms and legs. He beat her for being clumsy or for being tardy with her chores. Sometimes he hit her for his own pleasure. But Miz Abby, she be stubborn, and no matter what he did, she'd never let him see her cry. Used to sent the old master into a rage, and often cost her dearly, but she'd never give in."

Chris felt his stomach turn from the images in his mind. "Did no one help her? Why didn't someone intervene?"

"Who gonna help, Mr. Carlson? You've seen with your own eyes what her father be like. Who gonna step in between a husband and his wife?"

Chris shuddered and swallowed back the bile that rose in his throat. In his youth he'd received his fare share of beatings, and usually deserved them. But they'd been from a loving hand meant to guide not to degrade. "Where is she?"

Obadiah watched the emotions flash across his face and felt a flicker of hope. "She's been out at the woodpile a waiting on you," he said softly.

"All this time?" Christopher felt a new fear spear through his heart, as the servant nodded. "Build up the fire in my room," he commanded, as he turned toward the door. "And stick the warming bricks in to heat."

Christopher took the last few steps at a run. The rain had stopped, but frost had already started to cover the ground when they had returned from the wedding. The wind stung his face as he stepped out the back door, taking the stairs two at a time. He found her, huddled in a ball on the frozen ground, seeking what shelter she could beside the chopping block. Her bridal finery had disappeared and now she wore only the flimsiest of gowns. Had this too been one of Barclay's obscene rules, to wait without adequate protection against the elements? His stomach turned at the thought of someone laying a hand on her. He would have been sick, had not the need to get her to safety been stronger.

"Abby," he said gently, pulling off his shirt to wrap around her stiff shoulders. "Wake up sweetheart, I've got ·to get you inside." She whimpered at the sound of his voice and tried to curl tighter for protection.

Christopher felt his heart break. All he had wanted to do was love and cherish her, yet now she was half frozen because of him. Gently, he gathered her stiff body, cuddling her close, whispering words of comfort she didn't hear. His lips brushed against the cold flesh at her temple as he carried her shuddering form into the tavern. Dear Lord, don't let me be too late, he prayed. Don't promise me heaven with one hand and then take away my only joy with the other.

He passed Obadiah on the stairs. "Don't wake us in the morning," he said quietly. "She'll need her rest after this and I intend to see that she gets it."

Abby floated in a sea of warmth and a smile touched her lips. She had been so cold, but now . . . She pressed her face against the soft pillow and inhaled the scent of fresh linens. Light filled the chamber, and though she kept her eyes closed, she could no longer deny its presence. Reluctant to leave her dreams, she snuggled deeper under the covers and basked in the heat that seemed to radiate about her as she drifted on the fringes of slumber.

Her awareness slowly returned and with it came the nagging feeling something was amiss. She blinked slowly, trying to make the pieces of the puzzle fit. This wasn't her hard pallet on the floor and never when she rose to greet the day was she as deliciously warm as she was now.

Her eyes blinked open and as the room came into view, reality came crashing back. The broken vase, the woodpile, the cold that had seeped into her bones until she knew no more. She turned her head to find Mr. Carlson, propped on his elbow smiling down at her, and realized he was the source of the wondrous heat.

"Good morning, wife," he said gently dropping a kiss on her forehead.

Abby froze, her body rigid with fear and her heart jumped in panic as she realized how intimately their legs were intertwined. Her hands took a death grip on the blanket's edge as she peered up at the crystal blue eyes that feasted down on her. Was the punishment not yet over?

Chris leaned closer and touched his lips gently to hers in a silent prayer of thanksgiving. Would she think him the fool if he declared his love? Should he blurt out the fact that without her, he would have no life? That in that brief moment when he'd feared her dead, his heart had stopped beating until he heard the soft echo of hers?

He had prayed for hours, holding her close willing the warmth of his body into her stiff limbs, and left her side only long enough to exchange the bricks that helped to heat the bed.

Now, as her soft brown eyes stared up at him, Christopher felt a joy the likes of which he'd never known. She was alive, she was awake, and she was his. Reverently, he placed another kiss against her lips and the softness of her skin sent his blood racing. He tasted the corner of her eye, the gentle curve of her cheek, the touch of vanilla behind her ear. Restraining the need to crush her to his chest, Chris struggled against the want that threatened to consume him.

Abby felt the stiffness in her bones slowly melt under the fiery heat of his touch. The intensity of his gaze turned her insides to jelly. He had urged her arms around his neck, and now as her universe started to spin, his solid form became her lifeline. His eyes met hers as his hand reached between them to push the covers aside. Then the hard muscles of his chest brushed against her nipples and her eyelids fluttered closed from the erotic sensation.

His mouth sought hers again, open and wanting, but as his tongue traced the tight seam of her lips, her eyes flew open with a start.

"What are you doing?" she gasped, trying to ignore the fact that his hot flesh now pressed from belly to thigh against hers.

Christopher only smiled. He knew he'd promised she could choose the time, but he could think of no better way to demonstrate intensity of his love. His finger traced the soft line of her brow then down to her nose. "Don't you like it?" he questioned softly, feeling the rapid beat of her heart against his chest.

Abby struggled to make sense of the riotous sensations that were coursing through her. "I don't know," she stammered, wondering if she dared to ask him to repeat it.

His smile deepened as his lips brushed coaxingly

235

against her. "Open to me, little one." His tongue met no resistance as it supped at the corner of her smile then slipped between her lips. Her arms tightened instinctively around his neck. With his breath deep and uneven, Christopher struggled to hold himself in check. But when her foot hesitantly caressed the back of his leg, he knew he was lost. "Abby," he sighed her name. "I've waited all my life for you."

His hands cupped her hips, then his impatient flesh sought release within her warmth. Too late, he recognized the resistance for what it was and arching back, his sigh of pleasure became an anguished groan as he felt her body go rigid with shock.

Caught in the haze of passion, Abby wasn't prepared for the wondrous shock of heat and wetness as his tongue plunged between her lips. Her resistance fled as rippling waves of pleasure that turned her body limp and pliant. His full weight settled over her pushing her deep into the bed and her toes curled in mindless anticipation. She could feel his breath against her neck as his hot flesh pressed so intimately against hers. Then his knee was wedging hers apart. She heard him whisper her name and the sound wrapped around her like a smile. Hesitantly, she let her fingers caress the silken hair at the back of his neck and felt his strength as she lightly traced the width of his shoulders. Then he was shifting, pressing closer.

A searing pain exploded as his body invaded hers. Stunned, Abby went rigid with shock and astonishment. Dear God, he was inside her. She struggled with little success to keep her panic at bay. But as he shifted against her, betrayal over rode the shattering humiliation he inflicted. He had lulled her into a sense of security, only to breach her defenses. Her eyes pressed closed and she bit hard on her bottom lip. The end was always the same, punishment after all.

Chapter Fourteen

Clad only in his breeches, Christopher stood before the dying fire. His hands gripped the mantel hard as he struggled to maintain his temper. From the corner of his eye he could see her quaking form curled away from him and his head dropped between his outstretched arms. Silently he cursed himself as every kind of bastard. And when his list ran out before his anger, he invented new combinations, but none came close to labeling him as vile as he felt at that moment. Why hadn't she told him?

He dragged the air back into his aching lungs, and his voice was tight as he approached the bed.

"Would you explain madam, how it is possible that after some nine years of marriage, you are yet a virgin?"

Abby flinched and pulled her body upright to face him. Frantically clutching the bed covers to hide her nakedness and her shame, she edged back against the headboard.

"You speak in riddles," her voice trembled with the after shock. "I don't know what you mean."

"My words are plain, madam," his tone turned menacing. "Was the thought of marriage to me so abhorrent that you felt the need to lie about your ability to carry my child?"

She flinched at the unjustness of his accusation. She had ached to find herself with child. But as months, then years had slipped by, that dream, like all her others, had been destroyed. "I told you I was barren." The words burned in her throat as she voiced her inadequacy.

"Did you think I would not notice?" he asked incredulously. "Or did you think that by telling me, you'd never need to share my bed?"

Abby clutched the sheet tighter to her breast and tasted fear the likes of which she'd never known. "I don't know what you mean?"

"You lied, madam," he roared.

Frantically she shook her head. "Never!"

Chris stalked angrily to the side of the bed and watched her press back until the headboard blocked her retreat. "How can you sit there and still play this charade? Did you think me to dense to suspect the truth? Do you expect me to believe your monthly course is the cause of this?"

Mortified he would speak of such an intimate thing, Abby dropped her head in shame and humiliation. "It is not my time," her voice was the barest whisper.

"Then madam," he challenged angrily. "Pray tell why you continue to profess yourself barren?"

Abby struggled to find a single remnant of strength to lean upon, as she raised her eyes to his. "I was married for nine years and produced no heirs for my husband." Her voice carried self derision. "I lied not, when I told you I am barren."

Christopher felt his control snap. "Madam," he snarled, "you carried no child because you were

239

still a virgin. And despite what you say, the proof of it now stains the bed." Angrily, he snatched away the coverlet, revealing both his wife and the scarlet stains that dotted the linen.

Abby's eyes flared wide with panic as he tore the last of her covering away, leaving her exposed and vulnerable to his angry tirade. She couldn't have been a virgin after all the obscene acts Malachi had inflicted upon her, her mind screamed. But now it mattered not for the vibrations of Mr. Carlson's anger scorched the air between them. Instinctively she fell forward over her knees, her body curled and braced for the first blow.

Christopher froze at the sight of her trembling form. But his heart stopped beating when the sunlight touched the smooth plane of her back. In the morning light, his eyes perceived what his hands had only guessed at the night before. He reached out to touch the faded white scars that crisscrossed the pale skin and felt her flinch at his touch. "Dear Lord," he whispered softly, "what did that monster do to you?" Carefully he sat on the edge of the bed beside her and watched her body curl tighter.

Overcome with emotion, Christopher leaned over and brushed his lips across the length of the deepest scar, wishing he had the means to erase all the hurt she'd been forced to endure. Gently he tried to gather her up in his arms, but she jerked upright to her knees, her body rigid, her eyes wild with fright.

"Hit me if you must." Her breath came in pleading gasps as her arms wrapped tightly about herself. "Or lock me in the fruit cellar. But don't do that to me again." Her eyes dropped briefly to his

240

lap then to her complete mortification filled with tears.

Stunned, Christopher watched her luminous brown eyes fill with pain as she rigidly held her tears in check. Obadiah's words from the night before echoed in his mind. "No matter what he did to her, the old master could never make her cry." Now as he watched her struggle, he felt like crying himself.

"Darling," he said gently, raising his hand to her cheek. She flinched then held herself in rigid check as his fingers brushed the tangled hair from her forehead. "I'm not going to hit you."

"Please," her voice was thick, her eyes pressed tightly closed. "Please . . . don't . . . please don't do that . . ."

"Abigail," he took a deep breath, and found his own voice unsteady. His finger raised her chin and his breath left his body. Hot tears streamed down her face and she began to tremble.

Quickly grabbing a blanket from the foot of the bed he pulled it around her shoulders and gathered her into his arms. With unsteady steps he moved to the rocking chair before the fire and sat keeping her bundled form securely on his lap.

"Shhh, darling," he said gently. "I'm not angry with you . . . I didn't mean to yell . . . it is just by not knowing . . . I could have eased the way a bit . . ."

Eyes filled with tears looked up at him. "I didn't know," her voice faltered. "All those years . . . I didn't know."

Christopher struggled to make sense of the madness. How could a woman, full grown, not know she was a virgin? But as he held her trembling

241

form, bits of Obadiah's story came back to haunt him. She hadn't known because she'd been but a child when the aging Barclay first got his hands on her. He felt his anger bloom anew.

Gently, he brushed his lips against her fevered brow. "Tell me love, what did I say to make you think I would punish you last night?"

"I broke the vase," she sniffed, hating herself for the tears that wouldn't stop. "I'm clumsy and careless and whenever . . ." she took a shuddering breath, "whenever I broke something, Malachi would . . . I just couldn't bear the thought of hearing you tell me to go out to the woodpile. I didn't mean to anger you, I only . . . thought to save you the embarrassment of saying the words."

Christopher fought back the tears that now welled in his own throat. "How ever did you manage to survive?" He hadn't realized he had spoken the words aloud until her voice quivered in answer.

"I could always find a place to hide within my mind," she said haltingly. "And I'd wait until the pain was over to come back. But with you . . ."

"With me?" he prompted.

He watched her shoulders slump in defeat and her arms wrapped around herself as if warding off a sudden chill. "I can't make it work anymore." Her words trembled with a hiccuping sob. "I hear your voice and my blood quickens. And try as I might, I can't make it go cold like I did with Malachi. I've no place to hide anymore."

Christopher felt as if he'd been kicked in the gut as he realized how innocently he'd stripped away her defenses. "Darling," he said hesitantly. "Mayhap your secret place doesn't exist anymore because you no longer have use for it." She looked up in

242

confusion. "It always hurts the first time, love," he said gently. "But there'll be no more pain."

Her eyes dulled with resignation as she shuddered. "Then you mean to do it again?"

He toyed with her clasped hands and fought back the need to slam his fist into the wall. "Would you believe me if I said it would bring you pleasure?"

Her head shook slowly from side to side. "Why me?" Her whispered cry tore at his heart. "I saw the way those young girls looked at you at the wedding. The one in the costly jade gown hungers desperately for your attention. Why must it be me? I've been used and I've nothing to offer in return?"

Christopher felt the pain of rejection rend through him. "Yours was the heart that called to mine," he offered lamely.

"But I did not mean to call your heart," she whispered desperately. "If I had but known, I would have . . ." Her eyes darted frantically about as she searched for the words. "I would never seek to bind someone as fine as yourself." Her head dropped forward and her eyes closed with defeat. "You're the first true gentleman I've ever known. You're talented and kind. You deserve so much more than I can offer." The tears started anew. "I'll always carry his mark as a reminder and the memories . . ." her body began to shake. "They make me feel so dirty . . . like I'll never be clean again . . ."

Christopher knew she meant the stripes across her back and felt his pain dissolve into anger. Carefully he turned her toward the fire and edged the blanket from her shoulders, exposing her pale flesh and Barclay's legacy. He felt her shudder and

243

shrink from his touch, but he was relentless. Slowly his lips brushed her shoulder then moved downward. She began to tremble and then collapsed completely, her body racked with violent sobs that would have knocked her to the floor had he not pulled her back against him.

He thought he wanted, nay, needed to know. But as her words started, Christopher closed his eyes and wished to God he'd never asked. She spoke of deeds and good intentions gone amiss and punishments that made the bile rise in his throat. He wanted to scream at her to stop, so he could push the madness from his mind, but he knew her salvation rested in how he handled her past. Her words tumbled faster now and her ribcage heaved as if she'd run for miles. Then she wept; hot bitter tears that had been carefully saved and stored away, tears for the death of a mother she couldn't remember, and for a father who's only attention had been violence, and tears for the humiliation and pain she had suffered at the hands of her husband.

He held her tenderly, crooning soft endearments against her hair. But the lump in his throat swelled making his voice jagged. Her tears soaked the blanket's edge and he gave up trying to dry them, pulling her instead closer to his chest to keep her warm.

Too weary to struggle, Abby couldn't resist leaning against the warmth and strength of him, ready to accept whatever crumbs of compassion he might offer. And as exhaustion claimed her, her last memory was of Mr. Carlson's arms tightening protectively about her.

Abby felt a gentle tickling against her nose and

fought against the darkness that cloaked her. Her eyes fluttered open in confusion and her head ached. The candles were lit and her mind swirled. What had happened to the day? Dusty shadows danced about and then she realized Mr. Carlson was kneeling before her as she sat curled in the rocking chair. He held a lock of her hair and once more brushed the curly ends against her cheek.

"Time to wake up, sleepy head, the day is almost over." He smiled.

Abby felt her stomach tighten, and desperately prayed her memories were but a dream. She had forsaken all, and cried like a baby, yet he was still here kneeling before her, toying with her finger that carried his ring.

"How do you feel?"

"My head hurts."

"It's little wonder." He brought her fingers to his lips and placed a kiss against her knuckles. "By my calculations, you've not eaten a decent meal in two days. Come, I've arranged for our supper to arrive shortly, but I thought you'd like the comforts of a bath first."

Abby started to rise, then stared in amazement. A huge brass tub the likes of which she'd never seen sat angled before the glowing fire. Even now she could see steam rising from its depths. Her eyes turned to his.

"They just finished bringing the hot water," he said easily. "I wanted you to awaken before it cooled."

Her head spun with confusion. A bath, inside, with hot water just for her? Surely it was still a dream for madness clearly surrounded her. Mr. Carlson rose to his feet and extended his hand.

Abby felt the color flare in her cheeks as her eyes dropped to the floor in shame. She had cried on his shoulder and confessed humiliation she couldn't even voice during the light of day. How he must hate finding himself bound to her. As if reading her mind, his hand reached out to cup her chin, making her skin tingle from his touch.

"It was not your choice to live with that madman," he said firmly. "But you survived and that's all that matters. You are brave, and strong, and beautiful. And I thank God that I've found you. Now," he pressed a finger to her lips when she would have protested. "You are going to have a slow, leisurely bath. Then we are going to share a meal."

"But . . ."

He dropped to one knee before her chair and took both her hands within his. "You are my wife." His eyes captured hers and refused to let her look away even as the heat glowed brighter on her pale cheeks. "And although you've no cause to think kindly on the word husband, that is what I am and shall be to you until our dying day." His fingers tightened about hers. "You promised before God to obey me, but I promised before God to cherish you." He watched confusion fill her eyes. "You have my vow, madam, that none shall cause you harm as long as there is breath in my body. And I shall spend every day of my life trying to make up for the wrongs that you've suffered." His lips brushed against the golden bands that encircled her slender finger.

Abby felt the lump in her throat grow larger as his head bent over their clasped hands nearly resting in her lap. Hesitantly, she loosened her fingers and with new found courage touched the back of his head and let her fingers smooth down the thick sun streaked locks he'd tied at the nape of his neck.

When he looked up, the heat in his gaze took her breath leaving a strange exhilaration in its stead. He stood easily and a smile touched his lips.

"Come," he urged her gently to her feet, ready with a strong supporting arm when she swayed. Slowly he led her to a small screen in the corner of the room. "I'll leave you to your privacy, for a moment." He placed a soft kiss near the corner of her mouth that left her wanting more, then with a wink, took his leave.

Abby clutched the screen, thankful that the room no longer spun and wondered how he could know her needs even before she did? She attended to the most pressing matters, then stepped from behind the screen and pulled the blanket securely about her shoulders. Her eyes grew wide as she surveyed the room.

She knew the bed had been exchanged, for she had supervised the procedure and spread the coverlets herself. But now a finely carved desk sat near one window and a broad chest on chest claimed a goodly portion of the wall. Branches of bittersweet, thick with bright orange berries filled the jug on a small chest and the air carried the scent of lye soap and cinnamon. Nothing of Malachi remained. A smile touched her lips when she spied the dish filled with rough chunks of cinnamon bark. Even the stale odor that always haunted the chamber had vanished. Was it not time to banish the memories of Malachi as well? Her fingers ran over the edge of Mr. Carlson's desk where the plans for his shop were stacked neatly. How, she wondered looking about, had all this been done without her knowledge? And how had the huge tub been carted in without her awakening? Thomas, for all his strength, couldn't walk two steps without making noise and Obadiah's thin shoulders and bad knees would never allow him to haul so many buckets of water above stairs. Her eyes fell on the bed and again grew wide when she realized that fresh linens had been spread. Her cheeks turned hot when she thought of the stains that all would see. Then the door clicked and Abby felt her heart stop beating.

Turning quickly, she stepped on the trailing end of her blanket and bumped into the small table that she hadn't noticed. It had been laid for an intimate dinner for two, but the tall stemmed goblets now wobbled precariously. Frantically, she grabbed for one nearest the edge, but the blanket only tangled further about her legs. Abby dropped to her knees catching the goblet against the folds in her lap as her heart leaped into her throat. Her body trembled as she clutched the blanket tightly with one hand and then carefully righted the goblet with the other. She would have climbed to her feet, but her knees simply refused to do her bidding and her head leaned forward against the table edge until her heart could find its way to beat again.

Strong arms scooped her up and suddenly she was resting high against Mr. Carlson's chest. One arm encircled his neck but she kept a firm grip on the blanket.

"Pick up that goblet," his words were quiet and Abby felt her panic flare anew. He dipped his knee slightly and her fingers shook as she clutched the delicate crystal. "Now toss it across the room," he said easily.

Taking a breath she met his gaze with question.

"I'll have nothing in this room that shall cause you such distress," he said solemnly. "I'll not watch you scramble in terror each time a goblet breaks or a dish falls. Toss it into the fire."

Abby pressed the goblet to her heart and felt a curious ache in her toes. "And if I say the piece brings me pleasure?" she questioned hesitantly.

A rakish smile tilted his brow. "Then I shall gift you with a dozen. That way you may break them at your leisure or treasure them as you wish."

She felt the tight panic in her chest drain away only to be replaced by elation that fluttered clear to her toes. "May I keep this one?" her voice trembled.

Christopher nodded solemnly and dipped low again so she could replace the glass. "Your wish is my command, m'lady." He moved easily across the room setting her down before the warmth of the fire.

Abby felt the absence of his arms and clutched the blanket tighter. Soundlessly she watched him lift another log onto the fire as the soft fabric of his shirt stretched against the wide expanse of his shoulders. But her mouth went dry when he turned back to her. The firelight cast bronze shadows on the angular planes of his face, and his eyes went dark with desire.

Capturing her gaze, Abby could only stare as he slowly removed the studs from the cuffs of his shirt. Placing the silver buttons on the mantel, his eyes never left hers as he purposefully began to fold the cuff of his sleeve back upon itself again and again until his entire forearm was bare to the elbow. His smile deepened as he repeated the process with the other sleeve. The firelight turned the hairs on his arms to gold, and Abby could see the veins that ran from elbow to wrist.

"Is my lady ready for her bath?" he questioned, with a rakish tilt to his brow.

A fluttering sensation akin to fear made her knees tremble and she stepped back even as he stepped forward. Surely he did not mean to stay and watch her bathe . . . but stay he did and more.

At first, the heat of the water had startled her. She would have drawn back, but Mr. Carlson was already lowering her into the foamy liquid. Now, as the warm water surrounded her, and the bubbles tickled her nose, Abby sighed deeply letting her body sink lower until the water reached her chin. She'd never taken a bath of leisure before. Bathing was done hurriedly at the creek during summer, or with a shallow wash basin before the fire in the winter. She wiggled her toes delighting in the gentle ripples of water against her skin. Her muscles lost their stiffness and, despite her earlier sleep, her eyelids grew heavy. What a wicked indulgence she thought, letting her arms float up to the surface.

Something brushed gently against her toes and she shivered in delight but, when the caress slid boldly up her calf to her knee, her eyes flew open.

Mr. Carlson's smile greeted her as he innocently rubbed a bar of scented soap against the sponge he held. Stunned, she watched his muscular arm dip into the water and felt the caress journey up her other leg.

"You looked like you needed some assistance,

250

m'lady," he teased loving the way her breast peeked at him from the water's edge.

Abby pulled her leg from his slippery grasp and sat up with a start, sloshing water over the tub's rim and onto her husband. He only grinned. "If you wanted me to join you madam, you had only to ask. No need to drown me." He plucked his wet shirt from his chest, then pulled the wet garment over his head tossing it carelessly to the puddles on the floor. The firelight played over the hard muscles that flowed from his chest and shoulders to the flat plane of his belly. "Don't you dare," she stammered, her eyes wide.

Christopher smiled and wondered if she realized it was the first time she'd ever talked back to him. "Nay, madam, don't distress yourself," he said groping in the water for the sponge, loving the way her brown eyes sparkled. "This one is for you alone. Although I dare say in the future it would be more prudent for us to share. But lean forward and let me scrub your back before you wrinkle and turn into a prune.

Abby froze, her arms carefully wrapped about her knees as he moved behind her. He would see them clearly now, her mind screamed in panic. The marks from Malachi that would scar her forever.

Christopher rubbed the soap against his hands and then touched the stiff shoulders, smoothing over the rigid flesh. "There are no secrets between us, Mrs. Carlson," he said easily. His fingers rubbing deep against her muscles.

"But they'll always be there," her voice held the threat of new tears and she felt his fingers slow.

"Then wear them as a badge of honor, madam," he said gently letting his hands slide down her ribs.

251

"Use them as proof you were strong enough to survive."

Abby let her head drop forward. "What a remarkable man you are," she said not daring to look back at him, for the tips of his fingers tracing along the sides of her breasts were creating havoc with her senses.

"Not remarkable, madam, only starving."

Abby jerked about in the tub, sending more water splashing over the side. "Why didn't you say something?"

Christopher's eyes rounded with a start as she all but flew out of the tub, nearly toppling over as her feet hit the wet floor. She had herself wrapped in a towel before he could blink and inwardly he groaned, knowing the hunger of which he spoke was not the one she sought to appease. The fantasy of slowly blotting tiny droplets of water from her skin would have to wait for another time.

She allowed him to help her into a wrapper of soft rose wool then discreetly turned away as he moved to shed the remainder of his own damp clothing. She had never seen a man in a dressing robe before, and the splendid sight of him in the midnight blue made her think of royalty and fairy tales. But when he guided her to the table and she caught sight of his bare calf, Abby blushed realizing there was nothing but her husband beneath the robe.

They ate by candlelight; steaming, fragrant peanut soup and chunks of fresh bread spread thick with butter. Christopher topped her wine glass again before leaning back in his chair. She was more relaxed than he had ever seen her. The tight lines of strain were gone from her mouth and her lips pouted full and inviting. Her hair the color of ripe wheat wet with rain hung in loose flowing curls about her back and shoulders. He sighed, thinking there could be no greater travesty in life than to keep those glimmering locks hidden under the ridiculous cap she wore. The muffled sound of merriment came from the tavern's rooms below and Christopher shifted in his chair. If she let her hair hang free, then all the tavern's patrons would be witness to her beauty. His jaw hardened and his smile fled. Tomorrow, he'd stop by Madame Rousseau's and order her at least a dozen new caps. She'd wear her hair down, but only for him. His smile returned and his contentment grew. Lord, she was beautiful.

Abby leaned back in her chair and felt a peace she had never known. This man, her husband, knew her darkest secrets yet he didn't turn away in contempt. He'd been angry, yet he'd sworn not to strike her. Silently she studied him over her wine glass. The strong curve of his jaw, the straight line of his nose and brow. His skin carried a rosy glow from his days in the sun but it was his hands that fascinated her the most. Broad, strong hands that forged delicate jewelry from chunks of raw metal . . . hands that could snap her in two if he wished . . . yet brought only comfort when they touched. She watched the candlelight touch the golden hairs that started just above his wrists and felt a curious sensation deep in her being.

The golden bands that ringed her finger glowed in the firelight and again she marveled at the complexity of the design. Her other hand reached up to touch the locket that rested in the hollow of her throat and a nagging suspicion took hold.

"Did you make this?" she questioned softly, extending her hand and letting the firelight intensify the metal's shine. Just for a moment, she thought he blushed, then she realized it was only the glow of the fire.

Christopher cleared his throat and shifted in his chair. "Do you like it?" he hedged.

Abby nodded slowly, her brown eyes soft. "It is beautiful. I've never seen anything like it."

Christopher relaxed back in his chair. "I wanted to gift you with something special, unique." Something as beautiful as you are, he continued silently, something to bind you to me forever.

She watched his eyes and felt the pull of his desire, but fear held her back.

All too soon the dishes and tub were cleared away. Abby stood before the fire and tried to ignore the wild beating of her heart. Behind her she could hear Effie's gentle hum as the servant carefully turned back the bed. Then the door closed and the click of the lock sliding into place echoed through the silent room.

"The hour grows late, Mrs. Carlson." The voice sounded at her ear and Abby jumped with a start. "I would seek our bed."

Turning she faced her husband and forced a smile. "Do not tarry on my account, sir," she said brightly. "But I fear after my long rest this afternoon I find myself not at all sleepy."

His smile grew and his eyes sparkled mischievously. "That suits my purpose well, wife, for sleep was not what I had in mind."

She swallowed hard realizing only too late the error of her words. Frantically she tried to think of a way to forestall him, but Mr. Carlson was not to be put off.

"I'll leave you for a moment's privacy, madam," he said gently taking her stiff fingers within his own to place a kiss within her palm. "So attend with haste whatever needs you would see to, for when I return, 'twill be for the night."

Abby curled her fingers around his kiss and watched his silent retreat. Her eyes darted frantically for means of escape, knowing even as she looked there were none. You've suffered worse her mind argued as she paced nervously before the fire, it is not as if the man plans to beat you. But as memories from the morning's humiliation pushed forward, her body began to tremble. Slowly she raised her clenched hand and hesitantly opened her fingers as if expecting to find some treasured object. But her palm was empty and her anxiety grew.

Chapter Fifteen

Christopher entered the bedchamber and closed the door firmly behind him. A single taper burned on his desk, but from the warm glow of the fire, he could see her slight form beneath the covers of his bed. He extinguished the taper and crossed the room on silent feet. A sad smile played across his face as he gazed down on the delicate features of his wife. Eyes closed, with the blanket clenched tightly beneath her armpits, her arms lay straight as ramrods at her side. He shook his head in resignation. If ever he'd seen a woman set on being an unholy sacrifice, she was it.

In all his life he'd never faced a situation such as this. He was a good lover and he knew it. He'd learned early on that the true source of his own enjoyment lay in the satisfaction of his partner, thus he'd never lacked a willing bedmate. But now as he looked down at Abby and desire coursed through his veins, he felt singularly protective. She, who had endured so much, was now his to do with as he pleased. And although pleasing her was his most fervent wish, she remained reluctant. He felt her vulnerability, and as he eased himself down beside her, it became his own.

"Abby, sharing love is not a punishment to be endured, but a pleasure to be shared . . . by both." Her brown eyes opened, her look full of doubt. "And I'll not take you quickly so you can crawl back into that secret place of yours and push the deed from your mind."

She shuddered and closed her eyes again. Her only hope, that he'd be soon done with her, had vanished and his silhouette in the firelight showed more than she wished to see. The bed dipped further as he slid under the covers and despite her resolve she stiffened.

He didn't grope blindly at her naked flesh as she expected but stretched full length beside her, emitting a sigh of supreme satisfaction.

She waited.

He didn't move.

She held her breath.

He searched for the words to ease her fright.

Cautiously she opened her eyes and stared at the shadows on the ceiling, hating the fear that prickled along her skin and burned behind her eyes. Why didn't he just do it and get it over with? Dear Lord, she prayed, surely he didn't mean to wait until morning.

Christopher scowled at the ceiling. The tension in her body had become a tangible force. Mayhaps I should wait until morning, and let her have the night in peace. After all, what's one night against a lifetime? But as the minutes ticked by, his frustration grew. The image of her bathing would not leave his mind. Droplets of water had glistened

257

from her silken skin enticing him to touch and taste. The rosy tips of her breast had peeked at him again and again from the water's edge and knowing now they lay within his grasp made him swallow back a groan of frustration. Of its own volition his hand reached over and captured hers pulling it to lay on the hard plane of his stomach. A log hissed and spit in the hearth, then the silence became deafening.

Keeping her fingers firmly within his own, Chris rolled to his side and propped his jaw on his palm. She bit down hard on her bottom lip to stem the fear that tightened her limbs.

"Do you like children, madam?" he questioned softly.

Her head rolled against the pillow to look at him, her eyes wary. "Of course, sir. Who would not like children?"

The indignant look on her face made him chuckle. "If you had met my sister Julie when she was a child, madam, you might carry a different opinion."

She stiffened thinking of her confrontation with the woman in Mr. Beaumont's office. Had she already voiced her reservations?

Christopher let his arm rest against her middle as his fingers toyed with hers. "When Julie was little, she was adorable. She'd bat her eyes and toss her curls and everyone, myself included, ran to do her bidding." His eyes dropped to their linked fingers and his thumb brushed over her ring. "We learned too late, my parents and I, that what was cute at three was much less becoming at ten and three. But by then the damage was done. Now that she's a

258

woman grown, I know that I am partially to blame for the creature she's turned into."

Abby stared at him in confusion. "I don't understand."

Chris locked their fingers together and let the back of his hand brush gently against the swell of her breast. "I just want you to know that I'll try my best not to repeat the mistake."

"You speak in riddles, sir. Do you mock the slowness of my wit?"

He watched a single tear escape to trace down her cheek and felt his chest grow tight. Then comprehension dawned and his smile returned.

"Abby," he whispered, "have you not realized it yet?"

"What?" She turned her face away and tried to swallow back the lump in her throat.

"You can't possibly know if you're barren because you were a virgin. We might be able to have a child after all."

Her head turned so quickly on the pillow he thought her neck would snap. "A baby?"

Solemnly he nodded, warning himself to tread with care. She'd had no women in her life to share the mysteries and the knowledge that he was to become her teacher pleased him more than he would have thought possible. "What we did this morning, well that is how babies are made," he continued, feeling his desire soar as her brown eyes gazed deeply into his, seeking the truth of his words.

"Then all that time . . ."

Awkwardly he shook his head. "The blame cannot be heaped at your door because Malachi never planted his seed. Without the seed there can be no child. Therefore Madame, the fault lay with your husband, not yourself."

"We could have a baby . . ."

Christopher gazed down at her. It was like watching a tight bud feel the warmth of the sun. The petals relaxed and slowly opened until it blossomed full, ready to share its beauty with the world. He felt her joy as the realization took hold and any doubts he might have had were wiped away.

Abby gazed at him in wonder. A baby . . . there was still a chance. Her limbs stiffened. If he spoke true, then he'd have to . . . she closed her eyes and tried not to shudder from the memory. But a baby, her heart pleaded, surely you can endure it once more to have a child. A gentle calm settled over her and she knew the decision was made.

"Sir, I would so like a baby . . ."

She blushed.

He smiled.

"Aye madam," he whispered, like children sharing secrets in the night. "But there is a price to pay."

Her brow wrinkled as she gazed up at him. "A price?"

"You insist on calling me sir," he lowered his head until his nose touched the side of her cheek. "I would hear my name from your lips to know that you wish *my* child."

Her blush grew deeper when she realized of what he spoke. "Surely, sir," she sputtered, "you can't mean to suggest that I would do," she faltered—searching for the word—"that I would do *that* with anyone save yourself?"

Chris bit back his laugh. She still looked upon the act as some heathen ritual to be tolerated. How would she feel when she knew different? "Did you enjoy none of it then?" he questioned. Her blush turned to fire beneath her skin and she would have looked away had he not caught her chin. "Well . . ."

"It was very pleasant when you placed your lips upon mine," she said primly. Her eyes looked at a spot beyond his shoulder. "No one, save you, has ever done that to me before either."

Christopher felt his restraint begin to crumble. "Say my name wife," he said, his voice hoarse with wanting.

"Christopher," she whispered, as her eyes captured his. "Christopher."

Fighting back the need to possess her quickly, Christopher breathed in the sound of his name on her lips. "You have no cause to think kindly on this act," his voice filled with emotion. "But know now that I will never hurt you. Let me show you the joy a man can share with a woman."

"And the baby?" her voice trembled from the intensity of his gaze.

"I shall do everything in my power, wife, to get you with child. But first I would bring you pleasure." His lips brushed against hers with the touch of a butterfly, hinting at the sweetness that lay just out of reach. He felt her tremble and at once his arms pulled her close to calm her fears. His breath soothed against her ear and slowly she began to relax.

Abby felt her head reel from the touch of his flesh against hers. But even as her mind urged cau-

261

tion, her body was pressing against his warmth seeking desperately to find fulfillment. Her hand reached up to cup his jaw. "I've never known a man like you. Have I died and gone to heaven?"

Chris brushed his lips against hers. "With any luck, my lady wife, we shall both be in heaven shortly."

Her arms stretched and wrapped around his neck as her fingers threaded through his thick hair. "Then begin this journey sir," she whispered. "For while you're with me, I shan't be afraid."

The acceptance in her voice shattered the last of his restraints and desperately he lowered his mouth to hers. Never had he tasted such sweetness, and knowing she belonged only to him made his thirst intensify. His tongue dissolved the hesitation he found and her lips opened to him. Like a parched man in the desert he drank. Like an eternal spring she provided. And when her tongue hesitantly ventured between his lips, Christopher knew that they would indeed reach heaven.

Hands skilled at shaping silver slowly began the ardent task of shaping trust as his fingers traced over her flesh, coaxing the tension from her limbs. His palm journeyed down her side to the sharp dip of her waist, then up to capture the swell of her breast. He swallowed her moan of pleasure as he cupped and caressed its weight. Impatiently he shoved back the covers, filling his eyes with the sight of her.

The dim glow of the firelight touched her skin with its rosy blush. "Dear Lord, how perfectly exquisite you are," he whispered in praise. And how tiny. He closed his eyes, thinking how he must have hurt her the first time. "I've been given a second chance, Lord," he whispered against her skin, "and for that I'll be forever grateful." His lips returned to hers with deep, drugging kisses meant to reassure as well as seduce until he felt the last of her resistance begin to drain away.

His knuckles brushed against the hardened peak of her breast and Abby felt the jolt of sensations shoot through her. How long had she stared at the ceiling, willing her stiff muscles to relax? Now his gentle touch achieved what her will had not. She felt limp and fluid beneath his hands, as if she floated on a sea of warmth. His fingers continued their exploration of her breast, mapping a journey for his tongue to follow. And when his lips encircled the turgid flesh she felt the gentle tug pull at the very depths of her feminity.

Looking down, Christopher again felt his breath catch in his throat at the sight of her. "Abby," he whispered against her flushed skin, "you are so beautiful." His hand slid down her stomach, his fingers touching lightly the golden curls below. Then his palm was dancing over her flesh, memorizing each graceful line, each gentle curve. He could feel her inner battle, the reluctance to trust, but even as her mind struggled against total submission, her body was betraying her. His head bent low and his lips touched her stomach, feeling the muscles jump and quiver in response. He kissed his way lower still, pausing at the top of her downy curls, moving on to the silken flesh of her inner thigh. She was quivering beneath his hands when his tongue journeyed upward to touch the mysteries of her womanhood. A strangled cry left her lips but his broad shoulders kept her legs from closing as again and again he tasted and tormented the core of her. Her breath quickened and he felt his own heart strain to keep the pace. Her soft moans were driving stabbing pains of desire into his loins and the intensity of his need multiplied a hundred fold.

When her moan turned to a cry of surrender, Christopher eased his fingers into her damp sheath and pushed her higher still. Like a child on a swing she flew above the tree tops and into the clouds. His hands and tongue became her life line urging her on until her soul broke free on its flight to ecstasy.

Despite the chill in the room her skin was slick with sweat as he moved over her. He could feel her tremors as he pulled her close and they stoked his own passion until he felt he'd be consumed by the heat of his wanting.

Soft brown eyes drugged with passion and filled with wonder opened to him and Christopher felt his heart turn over. "Now, my lady wife," his breath seared against her fevered skin, "now we make a baby."

Abby felt the heat and strength of him slide into her willing flesh as if her body's only purpose in life was to welcome him. She wanted to tell him about the magic but as he wrapped himself around her and started to move, all logical thoughts were scattered like leaves in the wind. Again and again he sent her flying, this time higher than before, through clouds of ecstasy too exquisite to imagine, and when the last shred of fear would have held her back, his words whispered in her ear.

"Don't be afraid, Abby," he urged, his body commanding her response. "Fly with me . . . fly with me now."

Her cry of fulfillment was echoed by his own. Christopher collapsed in a sated heap on top of her. His face pressed against her neck, his muscles lax, his senses stunned. He knew he should move, he could feel her shallow breaths and thought he must be squashing her. But when he would have shifted, her hands tightened possessively on his back.

"Stay," she whispered, letting her lips taste the salt of his skin. She tried to pull her thoughts together, but the act proved useless. The warmth of his body wrapped her in a cocoon of pleasure she never wanted to leave. It felt so right, his flesh pressed against hers. She could feel the rapid beating of his heart against her breast and knew it was matched by her own.

"Is it always like that?" she asked in amazement.

Chris summoned the strength to roll to her side and gazed down at her. "Never," he gasped trying to stem the rapid beating of his heart. "It's never been so good before." Bewildered, he tried to reason how such an innocent could have taken him higher than the most experienced courtesan in all of France. "You were perfect." He pulled her into the shelter of his arms and settled her against his shoulder.

"I had no idea such things were possible," she admitted shyly letting her fingers trace through the golden curls on his chest.

Christopher closed his eyes and rubbed his chin against her hair. "Oh Abby," he sighed. "Neither

265

did I . . . neither did I."

Her eyes grew heavy as she watched the steady rise and fall of his breathing. The embers of the fire grew dim and Abby let her eyes drift closed. She knew she should leave and return to her own pallet below stairs, but even as she shifted, his arms tightened spasmodically, pulling her closer. His hand soothed down the back of her head, his fingers tangling in her hair. Then he was still. Thoughts of her cold room and hard pallet on the floor made her shiver. Surely he wouldn't mind if she stayed just a while longer. As if hearing her silent plea, Christopher shifted in his sleep. Rolling to his side, with her back tight against his chest his legs curling up to cup around hers spoon fashion. His muscular arm encircled her waist locking her to the heat and warmth of him.

Abby brought her own hands up to clasp the fist that rested possessively against her breast and hugged him closer still. Thoughts of leaving her warm nest were banished by his embrace. Her lips curved in a satisfied smile even as sleep invaded her senses. Perfect. He'd called her "perfect" . . .

The moon danced within the silver storm clouds as it climbed to its peak in the southern sky then, enticing them to follow, started its western descent. Birds fluffed their feathers against the new chill in the morning air and shifted closer beneath the eaves. The stars winked out one by one as streaks of pink foretold the coming of the sun and the rooster behind the woodshed issued his welcome.

Abby shifted, snug in the cocoon of warmth that

surrounded her. She could hear the rooster's cry and knew without opening her eyes that morning had arrived. But thoughts of leaving her snug nest to venture into the cold room made her brow wrinkle. Just two minutes more, she promised herself, pressing her face against the soft down pillow. The muscular arm that encircled her waist tightened and she felt her senses leap. Gently she was turned until she lay on her back, and her eyes slowly opened.

"Good morning wife," Christopher pressed a kiss to her forehead.

"Has the light of day ruined your aim, husband?" she challenged.

He cocked a brow. "Do you find fault with me so early in the day?"

A slow, easy smile touched her lips as his legs rubbed sensuously against hers. "Never with you, m'lord. Perhaps a bit impatience, but never would I find fault." Feeling a surge of self-confidence, Abby reached up and encircled his neck. Little urging was necessary to receive the kiss she desired, but when she would have moved closer, he held her off. Immediately she stilled with embarrassment.

Christopher sighed and pulled her close. "Stop it," he said giving her a firm shake. "You can't freeze up each time I say something wrong. I'll not live my life walking a tightrope."

Abby fought back her tears. Damn it all, she never cried. What was it about this man that brought her emotions so close to the surface and gave her no control? "I didn't mean to be so forward," her voice betrayed her mortification.

Chris tipped her chin up with his finger. "Look

at me," he commanded sharply. Her eyes flew open from the angry sound of his words. "The day you can't be forward with me is the day I die. Do you understand?" Her confused look clearly said she didn't. He dropped his forehead to touch hers and their breaths mingled. "You are my wife," he said gently. "The keeper of my house and my heart." His eyes gazed down at her. "I love you more than life itself."

Abby felt her blood race in anticipation. "Then why . . ."

His lips brushed against hers. "You're going to be sore this morning," he said gently. "And as much as I want you, I'll never willingly cause you pain."

She shook her head in denial as a blush touched her cheeks. Twice in the night she had awakened to find him gazing down at her and the memory of what came after made her skin glow hotter.

Christopher chuckled at her look. "We have a lifetime, little one. We don't need to do everything in one day."

Abby stretched and knew he was right. But the tenderness between her legs was insignificant compared to the yearning in her heart. "And if I say that I want you?" she challenged. She watched his eyes grow dark and knew his need matched her own.

"Then your wish must be my command, madam." He settled over her and their lips met, the intensity of their kisses sending both minds spinning. "Why is it that with you, madam, I can't seem to get enough?" His flesh slipped into hers making her flinch as he knew it would. "You leave me burning for the want of you even as you grant me satisfaction."

Abby felt her head reel as if she'd consumed a bowl of Nanny's legendary punch. There was pain, as he said there would be, but the ecstasy that taunted the edges of her mind overrode the minor discomforts of her flesh and impatiently she urged him on.

But her husband, she found, would not be hurried. He loved her gently if purposefully, restraining his power and his needs, cradling her as one might handle a fragile bird's egg. He teased and tempted, refusing to bid release from the growing passion that licked through her veins like a flame. Her head thrashed against the pillow, but his hands kept her hips steady, refusing to allow the frantic motions that would push her past the top. With each gentle touch, each tender caress, he carried her higher until Abby thought she would surely die from the wanting. Her legs lifted and encircled his hips in a desperate effort to pull him deeper within and she felt his control shatter.

"Now, Christopher." Her whispered command breathed against his ear. "Take me now." His hips flexed in the motion older than time and Abby felt her world explode.

When the frantic beating of her heart began to slow and her breathing again returned to normal, she opened her eyes to find her husband gazing down at her. "You, sir, are a devil," she groaned, trying unsuccessfully to roll from his grasp. His grip was gentle but unyielding.

"Aye, madam," he winked with smug male pride. "And next time when I bid you nay as to not cause you pain?"

If a look could turn wicked, Abby's did. "Then I would do all in my power to demand your immediate performance, sir, for you like to steal my very heart away."

Christopher wearily placed his head beside hers on the pillow. "Know then madam, that I've replaced it with my own."

Abby smiled and pulled him close as the student became the teacher, the victim the one to dispense comfort. "You're too good to me, sir," she whispered as her hand caressed the back of his head as it rested against her shoulder. "Sleep now, you've earned your rest."

She felt his breath grow even and knew he slept, but her own mind reeled with questions. How many different ways were there she wondered, thinking of the passions they had shared. Was there a number one could count on two hands that once learned could be practiced over and over? Or was it like the patterns made by white clouds against the azure sky, ever changing and constantly alluring?

The insistent tap of the woodpecker broke her thoughts and Abby sighed with resignation as she carefully slipped from her husband's arms and reached for her new woolen robe. Her toes curled on the bed's rope frame and hugging herself against the chill she gazed down at him. The desire to press a kiss to his flesh was strong, but afraid the touch would wake him she turned away.

A gasp left her lips as her bare feet hit the icy floor and muscles she never knew she had groaned in protest from the night before. Her hand pressed to the small of her back as she hobbled about searching for her stockings to warm her frozen feet, but needs came before comfort and again she gave silent thanks for the privacy awarded by the corner screen.

Forcing her body erect. Abby's fingers shook as she poured water from the pitcher into the porcelain basin. And her teeth chattered as her hands scooped the frigid water against her face. Quickly she washed the last traces of sleep from her eyes, then turned to search for her clothing. Desperately she prayed she'd not have to venture through the hallway in naught but her robe, for she could already hear the stirrings outside.

Relief was hers when she spied her best petticoat folded on a chair near the bed and found the new chemise from her bridal gown under it. Quickly she shed her robe and pulled on the sheer garment, then wondered why she even bothered, for the delicate fabric offered no warmth against the chill in the room. Still, as she fastened the tiny buttons and tied the last of the yellow bows, she couldn't help but let her fingers smooth over the costly fabric. Her own tattered petticoat seemed worse by comparison but at least the added layer offered warmth, she thought, tying the knotted string snugly about her waist. Turning she caught a glimpse of herself in the new looking glass and a gasp caught in her throat from the sight. The air had turned her nipples hard as pebbles and they pressed wantonly against the sheer fabric, leaving naught to the imagination. Quickly she reached for her old chemise, then hesitated even as her hands started to untie the yellow bows. A gleam touched her eye as she looked from one to the other, then the decision was made and the old chemise was pulled on top of the new and tucked into the waistband of her petticoat. She stepped into her skirt and reached for her new apron. A smile touched her lips as she felt the freshly pressed fabric. Nanny must have made a new batch of potato starch after all she thought, slipping the garment over her head then tying the bands behind her waist.

Stepping lively she hurried to the hearth and searched for life among the dying embers. She raked the coals then picked a handful of kindling from the basket to tempt the flames. Her efforts were rewarded as tiny flames glowed and spit then grew in strength as the dry twigs were consumed. Carefully she placed a log across the grate and stepped back holding her cold fingers to the heat. She wrestled a second larger log into place then taking a small brush from the basket she stooped down and swept the ashes back into the hearth, enjoying the growing heat that bathed her face. Satisfied that all was as it should be, Abby rose just as a knock sounded at their door.

"Coming," she whispered loudly as she dared glancing over her shoulder to her husband's sleeping form. The click of the latch echoed through the room and Abby muttered a silent curse as she edged the door open.

Obadiah held a heavy pewter tray laden with coffee and bread but hesitated in the doorway. "The master he says not to come," the servant whispered nervously, "but there's trouble. Miz Beaumont just sent a messenger."

"What's wrong, Obadiah?"

Abby jumped at the sound of her husband's voice and wished desperately she'd had time for a sip of coffee before she had to face the world. The sight of her husband's bare chest in the firelight was one thing, but to see him naked in the light of day was quite another. Taking the tray from Obadiah she placed it on the side chest and poured two mugs of the aromatic drink.

Obadiah moved quickly to the bed and handed the master his breeches from the chair. "Jamestown is on fire, sir," his words tumbled one upon the other with his agitation. "Miz Beaumont sent Luther with the message. She said Mr. Nick had business that needed him spending the night there and now she's feared for his safety."

"The entire city?" Christopher gasped flinging back the covers.

"Luther said the new Statehouse and others, is what they heard. Miz Beaumont's worried cause Mr. Nick's office be not that far from the powder magazine."

"Dear Lord," Abby gasped, watching her husband's face go pale as he hastily pulled on his shirt and shoved it into his breeches. Obadiah helped with stockings even as she stepped closer with his coffee.

"Be careful, it's hot," she warned handing him the mug. "What can we do to help?"

Gratefully Christopher accepted the drink and slipped into his shoes. "Send someone to fetch Jimmy and have him rouse the men from the shop. Obadiah, I'll travel now with Luther. You have Thomas harness both wagons for my men when they arrive."

273

"And me?" Abby urged helping him into his coat as Obadiah turned to go.

Christopher pulled her into his arms for a fierce hug. "You're not to set one foot in the direction of Jamestown until I return. Is that clear?"

"But . . ."

He halted her words with a desperate kiss. "If I thought you in danger," he said quickly, "I'd be worthless to them. The hours ahead will be bad enough. At least grant me peace of mind knowing that you are safe."

Her hand reached up to smooth the frown from his brow. "As long as I have your word that you'll not do anything foolish."

Christopher grinned and placed a fleeting kiss on her forehead. "Madam, I am not the one with a penchant for rushing into burning buildings or breaking windows with my bare hands."

But when he would have turned to go, Abby caught his hand with a desperate hold. "But you will keep safe won't you?" Her voice was suddenly thick and her throat burned with the memory of consumed smoke.

Touched by her concern, Chris again pressed her close to his chest and breathed deeply hugging her scent to his mind. "Madam, with you to return to only a fool would dance in harm's way, and I assure you I am no fool. Now, let me be gone so I can return all the sooner." Reluctantly Abby stepped aside then hurried after him.

Obadiah stood waiting in the back yard holding the reins to a massive black horse. As if sensing the excitement the stallion sidestepped with anticipation. Christopher took the reins and swung skillfully into the saddle. Nanny stepped as close as she dared to the dancing horse and offered up a bound sack.

"There's three roasted chickens, fresh bread and cheese," she said sternly. "Don't you forget to eat something. A new husband's gotta keep up his strength."

Abby's eyes grew wide as a blush touched her husband's cheeks. Their eyes met for an instant before he turned to leave; hers begged for caution, his promised passion. Then he was gone.

Chapter Sixteen

Abby shivered in the windy yard as she turned to Obadiah. "I know Mr. Carlson told you to have Jimmy fetch the men, but don't the Richardson's live out past the edge of town?"

Obadiah nodded and rubbed a finger against his nose. "I don't believe the Master was thinking right when he said to send Jimmy with the word. It'd sure be quicker if I was to go myself."

Careful to conceal her stiff muscles, Abby retraced her steps up the back porch and ticked off in her mind what needed her attention first. "Obadiah, you go directly to the shop and inform the overseer, Mr. Williams. Then stop by the Raleigh Tavern and share the news. The more hands we can send the better chance they'll have." Grateful to be momentarily out of the cold Abby pulled on her old woolen cape. "Thomas, you rouse the men that are staying here. They can eat in the wagon on the way down."

"Mayhap some of the students will want to venture down also," Thomas added.

"As long as they mean to help, not just spectate," Abby called from the doorway. "Someone tell

Nanny I've gone to the Richardson's to fetch Jimmy and I'll be back as soon as I can."

Obadiah hesitated. "Miz Abby, it be seven miles to Jamestown. If the fire's bad, then it's likely to have burned everything to the ground before they even gets there."

Abby shuddered. Obadiah had just voiced her very thoughts. "We'll do what we can, Obbie, and pray for the rest. Now hurry, Mr. Carlson needs all the help he can get."

Tightening the cape around her shoulders, Abby left the inn. Her muscles sang in protest, slowing her usually spry step. At first determination alone kept one foot moving before the other, but after covering half a mile, her muscles eased and her pace increased.

The sky was clear and fallen leaves rustled in great abundance about her ankles, but the wind carried a bitter chill and by the time the Richardson's cottage was in view, her feet in their cloth slippers were stiff with cold.

A dog barked in the yard as she pushed open the gate and picked her way down the cobbled path, noting the well tended beds that flanked both sides of the front entrance way. Abby raised her hand, but before she could knock the door swung open.

"Mrs. Richardson?" she ventured, taking in the woman's tear streaked face. "I'm Abigail Carlson. I'm sorry to call at such an inconvenient hour, but is Jimmy about?"

Gracie Richardson opened the door further and wiped her eyes with the edge of her apron. "He's in trouble, isn't he," she sniffed, closing the door and

277

leading the way into a sparsely furnished but well-tended parlor. "He's a good boy but I knew he was in trouble when he didn't come home." She gestured to a straight back chair for Abby to sit. "He's just not been himself lately." Gingerly she perched on the edge of a low wooden stool. "What's he done?"

"No, no Mrs. Richardson," Abby said quickly. "I didn't come because Jimmy's in trouble. But what do you mean he hasn't been home?"

Gracie's eyes welled with fresh tears. "Jimmy hasn't come home since the day of the wedding. The first night I got angry, 'cause he's never done nothing like that before. But then I says to myself, he's a growing lad and if he's had too much to drink he probably found a place to sleep it off 'cause he knows I don't tolerate drinking. But when he didn't turn up yesterday morning, I sent Jessie to the shop to find him."

"And . . ."

"He wasn't there," a young voice piped in.

Abby turned to see a small girl leave the doorway and move to lay a comforting hand on her mother's shoulder. Clad in an immaculate gown of jade green, the child's resemblance to Jim was unmistakable.

"I'm Jessie," she said formally, giving a short curtsy that made Abby blink with a start. "When Jimmy didn't come home or send some word, Ma had me take his lunch up to the shop. Mr. Williams told me Jim hadn't come at all that morning. He said it was a good thing the master was busy with other things else Jimmy would have gotten a good walloping for being so tardy."

Abby felt her cheeks grow warm for she knew exactly what "other things" had claimed her husband's attention. "And no one has seen Jimmy at all?"

Jessie shook her golden curls. "We ain't' seen him since the day before yesterday. He's been gone two whole nights."

Abby pressed her fingers to her eyes. Had Jimmy run away because of what happened at the wedding? She tried to think back on his exact words, but her own memories of the day were hazy at best. Frustrated, she shook her head and rose. "Mr. Carlson's gone to Jamestown today. We got word there's a fire."

"Dear Lord." Gracie clasped her hands tightly as if in prayer. "Were many hurt?"

Abby drew a shaky breath. "I don't know. What I do know is that we need to find Jimmy before Mr. Carlson returns. You and Jessie find out where he's hiding and send him to me. Tell him there's nothing that's gone before that can't be put to rights again, but running away won't solve anything."

"I'll find him, Mrs. Carlson," Jessie said with quiet determination.

Abby patted the young girl's shoulder. "Then good luck to you, Jessie."

Gracie sniffed and drew herself erect. "Thank you, Mrs. Carlson. I'm truly sorry to burden you with our problems, you being newly wed and all."

Abby blushed and moved to the door. "I'm sure everything will work out. You just find Jimmy."

* * *

Abby kept her shoulders straight and her step even until the Richardson house was no longer in view. Dear Lord what next, she thought trying to ignore her frozen feet. Jamestown in flames, Jimmy missing . . . she knew the incidents weren't connected. The fire in the silver shop had been an accident. An accident that was *your* fault, her mind taunted. If the boy hadn't been trying to make you a gift . . . her brow knotted in thought. Had she ever done anything to encourage feelings on his part? Her foot hit the rough edge of a stone and she stumbled. Abby muttered a curse under her breath then hobbled on ignoring the ache of her bruised feet.

She was but a yard length from the inn when she heard her name called. The market street was crowded, but Abby had no difficulty recognizing Michael Danvers as he crossed the road to greet her.

"Good day to you, Mrs. Carlson," he said cordially. "It's a fine day for a walk is it not?"

"I hardly think so, sir. Have you not heard of the fire in Jamestown?"

Danvers shrugged. "The fire is there and I am here. I can't truly say I've given it much thought."

Abby stiffened as he grasped her arm and urged her about. "Take your hands from me this instant," she hissed under her breath.

"Now, now, Mrs. Carlson, is that any way to greet such a dear friend?" His grip on her arm tightened. "I just want to walk with you a piece. You see, I wasn't invited to the wedding so I've had no opportunity to offer my . . . congratulations."

"Thank you," she replied briskly. "But you must excuse me. I am very busy just now."

"I'll only take a moment of your time, m'lady," he continued easily, forcing her to meet his step as they wove their way back toward the market square.

His sly smile made Abby's skin crawl and a nagging fear settled in the pit of her belly. "Loose me this instant, or I shall call for help."

Danvers only smiled and tightened his grip. "Help from who, madam, and for what?"

Her eyes anxiously scanned the busy market street for a familiar face. "I'll call for the magistrate," she threatened desperately.

"Madam, madam," he chided, "must I keep reminding you that I am a respected attorney in this fair town? Who would believe that I would wish you harm? Especially when I say that you looked so distraught, I only sought to assure myself of your well being. Nay, madam, you'll not call out for you've too much to lose if you do."

"What do you want, Mr. Danvers?" She jerked hard, freeing her arm from his grasp.

"You don't have to be shy with me," he reached to touch her cheek, but she drew back sharply.

"Let me pass, sir. . . ."

Danvers stepped closer, blocking her path. "You needn't play the outraged victim with me, Mrs. Carlson." He drew out the sound of her name like a threat. "For I know too well what you are about. I just wanted to let you know that I'll be watching you very closely. And if you try to cut me out," he paused for effect, "you'll be very very sorry, as will those you carry such an unusual affection toward."

Fear tempered her words and she tried to conceal her panic. "You speak in riddles, Mr. Danvers. If there was business between you and my husband, then it is dead and buried with him."

Danvers grin turned malicious. "I thought you'd say that." Again he caught her arm in a cruel grasp causing her to cry out in alarm. "Don't be foolish, Mrs. Carlson," he threatened giving her a shake. "Don't do anything to draw attention to yourself. Your husband wouldn't like the consequences if you do."

Abby's face paled further. "Leave Christopher out of this." Anxiously she glanced about but no one paid any heed to the odd couple they made.

"You listen and you listen good, my little mouse," he said softly. "I'll be patient until you make your move, but then I want my cut, just as usual."

"Your cut of what? Malachi never shared his business with me. If you knew my husband you would know that too."

"I thought I did," Danvers conceded. "But then I never realized you were the mind behind his schemes."

"I'm what? I don't know what you're talking about."

Danvers eyes sparkled with amusement as he shook his head. "Who would have thought Malachi Barclay's mousy little widow would possess the talents to trap the most eligible bachelor in the county? You might fool others with that act of innocence, Mrs. Carlson, but not I. As your attorney I've come to know you too well. I believe you have some runaway slaves do you not? I'd be happy to

282

place an advertisement that offers your reward for their return.

"No," Abby gasped. "You can't do that. I've issued no such reward."

"Ah, but Mrs. Carlson, I have receipts from payments made by yourself to prove otherwise. And if it came down to it, the matter of who authorized the advertisement would be of little consequence in the business of runaway slaves."

"You wouldn't . . . "

Danvers smiled and looked past her shoulder. "Do you know what they do to teach runaway slaves a lesson, Mrs. Carlson? After the public lashing that is?"

Abby felt his words like a fist to her gut. She'd heard of cutting off toes or crushing feet, and the thoughts of it happening to Harley or Celie made her knees crumble.

Danvers grabbed her arm to keep her from falling. "You do that so well, my dear," he taunted. "Practice often do you?"

"You are despicable."

"Perhaps," he said easily. "But more, I'm determined. I deserve more out of life than the miserly coins that are tossed my way, and I intend to get it." He half turned and raised a hand in greeting. "Reverend Jeffers, might I have a word?" He glanced back at Abby with a satisfied smirk and tipped his hat. "Until we meet again, little mouse. Remember, I'll be waiting."

Stunned, Abby watched him cross the square to the Reverend, who waved a greeting in her direction. She tried to swallow back the fear that now lodged firmly in her throat but with little success.

Panic surrounded her and for a fleeting instant she wanted to run as far and as fast as her feet would carry her. Instead she turned and made her way back toward the Inn. Dear Lord what was she going to do? Thoughts of Celie and Harley being hunted down like dogs made her stomach churn and her head go light, but she hadn't a clue as to the schemes that Danvers spoke of. She tried to remember if Malachi ever mentioned his name, but thoughts of her dead husband only increased her distress.

"Miz Abby . . ."

Abby screamed and jumped as a hand reached from behind to touch her shoulder.

Obadiah jerked back, his dark eyes wide. "Darn, Miz Abby, you plum took the starch right out of me."

Abby struggled to catch her breath as her eyes nervously scanned the street. "I'm sorry, Obbie," she gasped, "you startled me."

Obadiah cocked a brow. "That be true, but then you sure paid me back." Hesitantly, he stepped closer. "You feeling all right? You be paler than parchment. You're not gonna faint is you?"

Giving her shoulders a shake, Abby took a deep breath and managed a quivering smile. "I'm fine, Obbie."

"That's good," he replied anxiously, "cause we gots trouble at the tavern. Big trouble."

Abby climbed the steps to the tavern's front door and found Marilla Barclay waiting impatiently in the foyer. Clad in her mourning black she glared over her glasses.

"What a disgrace," the older woman snapped. "I travel all this way to see you and you don't even have the common decency to be home for my arrival."

The woman's resemblance to Malachi was striking and Abby's hand trembled as she removed her cape. "I'm sorry, you were inconvenienced, Marilla, but I didn't know you were expected."

"Bah," Marilla snorted. "I came to your wedding didn't I? Who did you think I was coming to see if not you?"

Abby rubbed the growing ache in her temple and wondered how a day could go so quickly from bad to worse when the clock had yet to strike the hour of eight. "Marilla, I'm deeply honored that you've traveled all this way, but what do you want?"

"I told her we don't have rooms for no ladies," Obadiah chimed in. "But she wouldn't believe me."

"You insolent man," Marilla glared. "How dare you interrupt your betters. It's a good thing I arrived when I did, Abigail, for you are in a sorrier state than I thought."

"Marilla, Obadiah meant no disrespect and you must not take it as such." Abby watched Obbie tense and touched his arm, praying he'd not reveal their secret. Marilla was like a dog with a bone. If she thought something amiss, she'd badger everyone until she knew all, and if she was to uncover the truth about the freedom papers . . . Abby fought back a shudder. "Now, what can I do for you?"

"You can show me to my room, Abigail, so I can get settled. Traveling is quite exhausting."

"You want to stay here?" Abby squeaked.

285

Obadiah's "I-told-you-so" look turned cold as he glared back at Marilla. "I told Miz Barclay we don't house no ladies," he replied tightly. "I even offered to carry her bags over to Mrs. Warren's boarding house."

"Marilla, Obadiah's right. You know the Stag's Head doesn't offer rooms to ladies."

"I'm not a lady . . . I'm family."

Abby caught Obadiah's eyes and flashed a silent warning. "Marilla, we don't have any empty rooms."

"I find that hard to believe." Her eyes narrowed. "There's not a soul about."

"They've gone to Jamestown," Abby explained. "There is a fire and they've gone to lend a hand."

"Everyone?"

"All except a few of the students from the college," Obadiah offered. "The younger ones didn't want to miss their classes."

Marilla pressed her hand to her heart and huge tears filled her eyes. "I don't believe it," her voice went meek with distress. "My dear brother dead less than two months and already I'm not welcome in his home. What is to become of me?"

Abby grabbed her arm as the woman swooned and Obadiah quickly pulled a chair close. Together they lowered Marilla's trembling form. "Marilla, why don't you stay and break the fast with us? Then Obadiah can carry your belongings over to Mrs. Warren's. You'd be so much more comfortable there," she offered, kneeling beside the woman's chair.

"Abigail," Marilla sniffed, dabbing at her eyes with a lace handkerchief. "You're my only living

286

relative. Is your heart so cold you would condemn me to live my last days with strangers?"

"Last days?" Abby ignored Obbie as he stood behind the old woman and vehemently shook his head. "What do you mean 'last days.' Are you ill?"

Marilla let her head drop forward. "I'm old, Abigail. The doctor told me I'd probably not last the winter. Now with the shock of losing my dear brother . . . oh please don't cast me out." Two tears traced slowly down the woman's wrinkled cheeks.

Abby felt her heart soften, though for the life of her she couldn't remember Malachi ever being dear to anyone. "Marilla, I would not turn you away, if I had a choice. But the tavern is full up. Only one space is left and I suspect it is because Mr. Simmons is on the portly side that none have chosen to share a mattress with him."

"Then put someone else out and give me their room," she suggested quickly.

Abby shook her head. "The men sleep two and three to a bed as it is. I've no private rooms to offer you."

"If you really wanted me to stay," she sniffed again letting her voice fade, "you'd find a way. Why, I could stay in your room with you. Surely if your husband's a gentleman, he'd not mind giving up his bed for a relative so dear to your heart."

Obadiah snorted and earned a glare from their guest. "Why don't we just waits and ask Mr. Carlson when he returns," he offered, remembering the master's reaction to Miz Barclay's ill spoken words at the wedding. "We should just let Mr. Carlson decide."

Abby shook her head. Christopher had enough

287

to worry about without adding Malachi's sister to the heap. "Wait," she said coming to her feet. "Obadiah, we could give Marilla my old room. It's below stairs so she'd not be bothered by the men, and she *is* family . . ."

"I'd rather have my brother's room, Abigail," Marilla said meekly. "That way I'd be closer to his memory."

"That be the master's room." Obadiah watched the anger come and go in the old woman's eyes and wondered what mischief she was about.

"Couldn't you and your husband move into your old room so I could be in Malachi's?" she prodded. "I wouldn't think you'd be comfortable sleeping in the same room with a different man, Abigail. At least I know my genteel nature would not allow for such."

Abby felt her head begin to swim and wondered how everything had suddenly gotten so confusing. "I don't think . . ."

"Then it's settled," Marilla interrupted. "We'll simply have your things moved. I'm sure I'll be contented as a clam."

"Miz Abby, since Miz Barclay here want's to be near to her brother's memories, she don't want the master's room 'cause there ain't nothing of Mr. Barclay's left in there. Mr. Carlson had it all removed before he put his own furniture in."

"He what!" Marilla gasped with outrage. "Abigail how could you ever allow such a thing to happen?"

"Everything's safe, Miz Barclay," Obadiah added. "It's stored out in the hayloft."

"That's it," Abby exclaimed. "Marilla you shall

288

have your room after all. Obbie after we finish clearing away the morning meal, get Thomas and bring down Malachi's bed and chest and put them in my old room."

"Thomas be out with Mr. Carlson," Obadiah reminded.

"I don't think this is a good idea, Abigail."

"It's an excellent idea," Abby brushed aside their protests. "Obbie, get Effie to help you, but save the heavy pieces until Thomas returns. Marilla, you just make yourself comfortable. The morning meal will be ready soon and then we'll get you moved in."

Marilla clasped her hands across her wide bosom and scowled. "I really wanted my brother's room. Him being my only relative."

"Well, you shall have his bed and chest," Abby said firmly pushing the memories of Malachi firmly aside. "Now I must see about the morning meal."

Abby leaned over the vat of boiling water and skimmed the impurities from the wax that settled on the top. Effie had finished twisting the first batch of wicks the afternoon before, and the last of the honey had been drained. Still it would take the rest of the afternoon to finish the first skimming. The dipping wouldn't commence before tomorrow at best.

The sweet scent of honey filled the air and Abby pressed a hand against the ache in her back as she watched the simmering mixture. Malachi's furniture had been carted down from the hayloft and installed, but Marilla's howls of disapproval had echoed for hours. The room was too small and too chilly without a hearth of its own. And once the furniture had been set in place, her protests had only grown louder. The room was too crowded, she couldn't move. The complaints had gone on until Abby felt she was walking on egg shells from trying to keep everyone at peace. Obadiah was barely speaking to her for all the insults he'd suffered, yet she couldn't tell him the source of her fear lest she confess his freedom papers were a fraud. Marilla had banished the twins, Wesley and Willie, for running down the stairs, making Effie huff in parental indignation until Abby had sent her out with her boys to collect bayberries and milkweed puffs for the candle wicks. And Jessie Richardson had arrived in tears to say that no one in town had laid eyes on Jimmy.

Carefully, Abby gently swung the kettle away from the flames and scooped the cleaned wax into the waiting container. The mixture still held its yellow pallor and she knew there would be no help but for a second skimming. Her shoulders ached from the growing tension and as she heard Marilla's shrill voice from the yard, she knew not if it was fear or compassion for the old woman that had made her bid her stay.

The last rays of the sun were fading from the sky when Christopher wearily drew his mount to a halt in the yard behind the tavern. Soot streaked his face and clothing but to Abby he'd never looked so good. The wagons had returned more than an hour before and her impatience had grown with each passing minute. But now as her eyes feasted on the sight of him, she was filled with hesitation. Her heart yearned to approach him but her feet were unsure of the journey. Christopher solved the problem without a second thought. In two steps he was at her side then she was in his arms.

He held her close, desperately needing to reassure himself she was safe after the devastation he'd been forced to witness. He breathed her scent through the acrid smoke that filled his lungs and relaxed for the first time in hours.

"Was it bad?" she questioned. "Is Mr. Beaumont safe?"

The haunted look in his eyes answered. "Nick is fine but most of the city was destroyed," he said, gratefully taking a chair just inside the doorway. "The new Statehouse is completely gone as is the jail, and more than half of the private homes."

Abby dropped to her knees beside his chair and pressed a mug of ale into his hand. "Was anyone hurt? Does everyone have some place to stay? We could always double up here to lend a hand if needed."

Christopher tried to smile but took a greedy drink instead. His throat was so parched he felt as if he'd carried half the fire's smoke home in his lungs. "When I left, everyone had shelter," he said hoarsely. "And there's already talk of moving the capital. Some say that the town is cursed because of so many fires and that the colony will never succeed as long as the capital resides there."

"That's ridiculous," Abby snapped. "How can a piece of land be cursed?"

Chris gave a weary shrug. "The land is too low. The tide constantly eats at the shoreline making dock repairs a never-ending battle and the mosquitoes are abominable." As if to prove his point he rubbed at two red welts on his neck.

"But what would happen?" She helped him pull off his boots and then stood to take his soot streaked coat.

Chris gave a weary stretch. "Nick seems to think the time is right to move the House of Burgess here, to Middle Plantation."

"Have the government here, in our town?" Abby gasped. "But we've no harbor for trading. Wouldn't everyone object?"

Chris shrugged and shed his waist coat, then pulled his shirt from his breeches. "I don't know. I do know that it would be good for business, and some are already quick to point out that the college is thriving. But still, who's to reason with those who love politics?"

The door to the hallway swung open and Marilla Barclay filled its entrance. "Well," she huffed looking down her nose. "I heard the commotion and had planned to invite you to be my guest at the evening meal." Her eyes raked over Christopher's form from head to stocking toe. "But I had expected to find a gentleman, not some vagabond. I withdraw my invitation and advise you to visit the river before the stench of your clothing permeates this entire establishment." With her edict hanging in the air like Christopher's jaw, Marilla spun about and departed as silently as she came.

Anger pushed aside his fatigue and Christopher turned on Abby. "What is that bitch doing here?"

292

She flinched but held her ground. "She arrived this morning with no place to go." Abby took a deep breath. "So I agreed to let her stay here."

"You what?" Chris exploded and his frustration from the fire fanned his ire. "I won't have that bitch in my house."

Abby took a step back before she could stop herself and watched his scowl go darker still.

"I'm not going to hit you," he snapped. "Stop comparing me with that bastard."

"I didn't think you were," she retorted, her own frustration rising to the bait. "But you want me to pretend Malachi didn't exist and as much as I might wish it, I can't do that."

"Then work on it," he snapped.

Abby could sense pain beneath his anger. "Christopher, my heart knows you're not the same, you're gentle and loving and kind; everything Malachi wasn't. But my senses spent nine years ducking his wrath, and it's not something I can just turn off at will." Bodies tense with anger, they stared at each other in silence.

Christopher let his hands drop wearily to his sides and leaned back against the opposite wall. "Did I ever tell you how proud I am of you? When I think of all it took for you to survive . . ."

She came to him then, needing his touch as much as he needed to give it. Her arms wrapped tightly around his neck and her feet left the floor from the exuberance of his embrace. "I was so worried about you," she gasped. "I kept remembering the night the shop burned and I'd picture you rushing into the flames to help someone and . . ."

His kiss stopped her words and Abby surrendered. She savored the touch of his lips on hers and the warmth that glowed deep within her. He was safe; he was home; and he stank to high heaven. Reluctantly, she eased from his embrace.

"You need a bath, sir,"

Christopher lifted his arm, took a whiff, then grimaced.

Abby chuckled. "You didn't need to do that to find the smell," she teased stepping back and fanning the air before her face. "You reek of smoke. Come, my lord," she extended her hand. "Your bath awaits."

Chapter Seventeen

Christopher stared through the darkness that filled the bed chamber and wondered what had pulled him from his sleep. He had been dead to the world upon his return from Jamestown, and reasoned only blind luck had kept him upright on his mount. Abby had had steaming water waiting for his bath and then had urged him to bed. He rubbed a hand across the stubble on his chin. He didn't even remember climbing under the covers or closing his eyes. But now, as the coals in the hearth burned low, he was wide awake and the hairs on his neck bristled. Carefully he identified the sounds; the hiss of the fire, the wind in the eves. Something was definitely amiss.

Abby snuggled closer and he tucked the quilts more securely about her shoulders, then edged himself upright on the bed and reached for his breeches, easing them on as he stood. His eyes grew accustomed to the scant moonlight that filtered through the window but he saw nothing amiss. Ignoring the freezing floor beneath his bare feet, he crossed to his desk, opened the tinderbox and took out the flint.

It came again, the slightest of sounds, but it made his heart stop and his hand freeze as the click of the door latch echoed softly through the darkness. Silently he moved back against the wall as he watched the door to their chamber edge open. His mind scrambled for a reason for the intrusion, but none came. It was too early for the servants to be about and no one else in the household would dare to enter without permission.

In the shaft of light from the doorway, he watched the form of a woman appear. Clad in a voluminous white gown, a black shawl pulled about her ample shoulders, Marilla Barclay stole further into the room.

Christopher folded his arms across his chest and waited until she stood near his desk before speaking. "Do you have a problem that requires my attention, madam?"

Marilla's scream rocked the rafters, sending Abby straight up in bed with a scream of her own.

Christopher took the opportunity to light a taper then leaned back against the wall, his eyes sharp and his anger ready.

"Marilla, what are you about?" Abby cried, struggling into her dressing robe and giving her husband a generous glance of milky white thigh in the process.

"You uncivilized heathen," Marilla gasped, trying to stem the frantic beating of her heart and the lightheadedness that came with it. "You could have scared me to death."

Christopher felt no sympathy and held his ground.

Abby took the old woman's hand and found it frozen. "Christopher, what is going on?"

"I think you should ask our house guest that." His voice was deathly quiet. "And I for one am most anxious to hear the answer."

Abby turned and found four of the tavern's patrons in various stages of night wear hovering in the opened doorway. "Is something amiss, Mrs. Carlson? We thought we heard a scream."

Marilla swayed and grasped Abby's hand for support. "I must have gotten turned about in the night and thought this chamber my own. But before I could realize the difference," she glared over at Chris, "he liked to steal the very breath from my soul."

Relieved, Abby looked back to the men who had now doubled in number. "Everything is fine," she said struggling to keep her voice calm. "Mrs. Barclay just got turned around a bit. I'm sorry you were awakened."

Muttering words like "sleepwalking" and "nightmares," the group in the doorway stumbled back to their beds. Abby knew Christopher was angry. She could feel his tension from across the room. But if there was to be a confrontation, she didn't want Marilla as a witness.

"Come Marilla," she said gently. "Let me take you down to your own room." She waited for Christopher to object but he remained silent as she helped the trembling woman down the stairs. Minutes later, Abby climbed the stairs again and found herself anxious. The door to the chamber remained open and Christopher leaned against the wall just where she'd left him.

"It's gotten chilly tonight, don't you think?" she asked nervously. She heard the click of the door latch and the sound of the bolt sliding home as she moved to the hearth.

Christopher reached it first. His muscles flexed as he lifted a thick log and placed it securely on the coals. Brushing his hands against his breeches he

297

turned back to his wife whose brown eyes were wide with apprehension.

"Are you going to tell me now the real reason Marilla Barclay is under my roof?"

Abby wasn't fooled by the quiet sound of his voice, for she could see the tension in his muscles. "I don't know any more than you," she offered lamely. "She arrived this morning and said she had nowhere else to go."

Christopher watched her shift nervously from foot to foot, then shook his head even as he scooped her into his arms. "Why can't we send her back to where she came from?" he growled.

Abby let her arms loop over his neck and wondered how he could possibly stand in a freezing room without his shirt and still manage to be warm. "Christopher, I think she's ill. She told me the doctor said this might be her last winter. We can't send her off to die alone."

Christopher cocked a brow as he sat on the bed with her on his lap and reached to rub warmth back into her frozen toes. "Marilla Barclay not only looks like a horse, but she has the constitution of one as well. I'd lay odds she'll see each of us in our grave before the Lord is desperate enough to call her home."

Abby shuddered at the thought of Christopher dying and her arms about his neck tightened. "Do you really think Marilla is dangerous?"

He hugged her close and felt the chill on her flesh. "If I thought her a threat to you, my lady, she'd be out in the snow before you had a chance to blink. No, I simply don't believe the fable of her being ill any more than I do that cock and bull tale she told just now."

"I could understand one waking in a new place and becoming disoriented in the dark."

"Abby our room is on the second floor. Are you going to tell me that Marilla is so addled that she forgot even as she climbed the stairs that her room was on the ground floor?"

She rested her head against his shoulder. "It is a rather feeble excuse isn't it."

Christopher nodded and flopped back, taking her with him. "It certainly is." He pulled the covers over them and gave a sigh. He'd have to keep a much closer eye on Marilla than he'd planned and Obadiah would be just the one to speak to. He nestled Abby more securely against his chest. He'd not worry her with his suspicious thoughts, not until he had some proof of Marilla's trickery. Her hair brushed against his cheek and his body responded.

"Tell me about your day, madam," his breath was warm against her ear. "For I find that circumstances have left me wide awake."

Abby stifled a yawn. Thoughts of Jimmy Richardson intruded and selfishly she pushed them aside. Her fingers traced across his chest loving the changing textures they encountered, wiry hair, hard muscles, smooth skin.

"Do you really want to know about my day?" She arched against his chest, tantalizing them both with the promise of things to come.

Chris flipped her onto her back and his eyes narrowed in passion. "Maybe after."

Abby smiled in her sleep and rolled over on her stomach. Her face pressed against the soft down pillows and her arms stretched lazily working the kinks from her shoulders and neck. But as her hand stretched further and encountered only emptiness, her eyes flew open. She was alone. Sitting up she rubbed the sleep from her eyes and scowled. The pillow still carried the impression from his head, but the sheets no longer held the warmth of his body. Abby wrapped her arms about her knees as she sat in the center of their bed. A huge fire glowed warmly in the hearth and she knew Christopher had been responsible, for the servants would never have been so lavish with the wood. A puzzled smile stole across her lips as she watched the flames. He had seen to her comfort, but chosen not to wake her and she realized it was disappointment that now taunted.

Frustrated, she flopped back against the pillows and heard a crackling sound. Rolling over, she found a folded sheet of parchment resting half beneath her. She recognized the style of Christopher's strong hand and the letters that formed her name on the top, but her ignorance allowed for no more. Desperately she stared at the note, tracing her fingers over and over the swirls and patterns the letters made, but the message stayed firmly beyond her grasp. Frowning she tried to think of who she could ask to read it to her. Obadiah and Nanny knew fewer letters than she did, and although she knew Marilla could read, thoughts of hearing her husband's private words from Marilla's lips did not bear contemplating.

"I'll just have to ask him myself," she reasoned with new enthusiasm. And as the clock struck half past six, Abby didn't even care that she had overslept and the morning meal was going to be late . . . again.

With the last of the breakfast cleared away and

300

Nanny started on the afternoon meal, Abby stared at the bushels of apples that covered the floor. How had she gotten so far behind? It would soon be time to tend to the butchering and she'd yet to even start on the applesauce. Nanny caught her look as she perched on her stool, snapping beans into a wooden bowl.

"Not having Celie and Harley about, that's what did it. That and Thomas and Effie going off for a time. Once you gets behind, you stays behind."

"Well Thomas and Effie are back now and I mean to catch up." Deftly she peeled and cored the first piece of fruit and tossed it into the waiting pan. "Effie can lend a hand here when the rooms above stairs are tidy, and we've got to finish the candles this afternoon. The wax has been skimmed twice and the second batch of wicks are ready, so the dipping should go smoothly."

"Shame Miz Marilla can't see her way to lend a hand. The way that tongue of hers cuts through folks, seems to me she should be able to wield a pretty fair paring knife."

"Tell me true, Nanny," she chuckled. "Do you really want Marilla in here giving you her opinions on how things should be done?"

Nanny set down her bowl with a stern look. "The day that woman starts bossing in my cookhouse is the day Obadiah and I takes ourselves elsewhere."

Abby felt her humor disappear and her stomach tighten. She knew Nanny exaggerated, but what if Marilla did push beyond their limit? What would she do if they decided they truly wanted to leave?

"You feeling poorly child?"

"I was just thinking," she hedged.

"Well it sure wasn't no good thoughts then,"

Nanny said taking up her bowl again. "You been worrying too much. You should be thinking about that new husband of yours, not about making candles this afternoon. See," she gave a toothy grin as Abby blushed. "I knew that Mr. Carlson could put the roses back in your cheeks."

Abby's guilty grin went from ear to ear. "He sure is something, isn't he Nanny."

The old woman nodded her head. "Almost as good as my old Obbie there, and Missy, that's saying something."

"He left me a note this morning before he left." Her hand pressed against the letter that rested in her pocket.

"Hum?" Nanny rocked slowly back and forth as her fingers made short work of the beans.

Wiping her hands on a rag, Abby gingerly removed the folded parchment. "See, it has my name right up at the top," Carefully she unfolded the treasure. "Problem is I can't read what it says." Her hands lovingly smoothed over the fold lines.

Nanny gave the parchment a quick glance. "Says that he ain't coming home for the noon day meal. Gonna be too busy trying to make up for yesterday."

Abby's eyes went wide in amazement. "How do you know that? You can't read . . . can you?"

"I know cause the man told me this morning when I caught him stealing my biscuits." She shifted from her chair and dumped the beans in a kettle with a hunk of sizzling fat-back. "He said, 'Nanny I gots ta eat something 'cause I be so busy today, I probably ain't even gonna have time ta come home for dinner.' "

"Mr. Carlson said all that?"

Nanny nodded and started peeling the beets. "Yup."

"And what did you say?" Abby prodded, thinking back to the night they had snuck into the cookhouse to steal fresh bread and butter. He had kissed her that night for the first time and just the thoughts of it now made her stomach curl and twist with desire.

Nanny looked down her nose. "I told him that if he wasn't fixing to come home for my dinner then he'd just better take some ham to go with that biscuit so he didn't fall over from starvation. I ain't gonna have no one think I can't cook good enough to keep a body upright, especially with him being a new husband and all."

Abby's soft laughter filled the cookhouse and she carefully refolded the letter and slipped it back in her pocket. I wonder if he'd teach me to read, she thought suddenly, then we could send messages back and forth all the time.

"You gonna peel those apples girl, or just sit and daydream all morning?"

Ignoring the gentle rebuff, Abby's eyes grew soft as she thought of being able to read. And more than once as she worked, her elbow pressed against her pocket making the paper rustle.

Her wrists ached by the time the fourth bushel was completed and Abby stood and stretched her back. She placed clean straw in the bottom of the first kettle and then heaped in the apples.

"Be sure you put the sour ones on the bottom. You know they take longest to cook."

"Yes ma'am, and I lined the kettle with straw so the apples don't stick or burn. This batch is ready." Abby dumped the last of her bowl in and swung the kettle over the fire. Deciding she needed a change of pace, she began threading apples they planned to dry on a heavy linen string. These would hang in the cookhouse attic until they were needed later in the winter.

Nanny dumped the beets into another kettle of boiling water and almost immediately their pungent odor filled the cluttered room.

"I don't see why something so pretty has to give off such a sour smell." Abby grimaced at the steaming kettle.

"You not gonna mind after these get in the pickle. We got mace and ginger to add to that horseradish Thomas ground yesterday and these beets is gonna taste just fine."

Abby held up a hand of protest as she looped another string of apples over the pole. "You can have my portion any time."

The apples were nearly half finished when preparations for dinner claimed all their attention. And as the clock struck two, platters heaped with a variety of vegetables and meats were whisked into the dinning room for the waiting patrons.

Abby tucked a thick cloth over the top of her basket. "Are you sure you can manage without me?"

Nanny rolled her eyes. "Who you thinks was feeding these folks before you was born child? Now you gets. Miz Marilla don set herself up as the hostess in there. I say let the woman earn her keep."

Abby placed a kiss on the old woman's weathered cheek. "I won't tarry and I'll be back to help with the cleaning up."

"You take your sweet time," Nanny called after her. "It won't do Effie no harm to help with the washing up. Think she so high and mighty being the above stairs maid. Do that child good to remember where she come from."

Abby settled her basket over her arm and waved and she hurried out the door. The November wind whipped her cape about her legs and stung her cheeks, bringing tears to her eyes. She turned her face against the onslaught and thought gratefully that her afternoon chores would at least keep her indoors today.

Her fingertips and toes were frozen by the time she reached the new shop, and her eyes went wide with awe as she viewed the massive structure. She could understand why Christopher was pleased with the progress for the walls were nearly completed.

"You looking for the master?" a voice called.

Looking up, she spied a lone workman perched high on the rafters where the ceiling would eventually be. The sight made her dizzy and Abby forced herself to look away until her stomach settled.

"Is Mr. Carlson about? I've brought his dinner."

The man gestured down the street. "He's working over at the Livery today. If he hasn't left for his midday meal, he'll still be there."

Abby waved her thanks and continued down the street on feet that now felt like blocks of ice. Why was it, she wondered, that the stones in the road hurt so much more when her feet were cold? And how was she going to tell Christopher so early in the marriage that her slippers were worn through again in two places?

The yawning mouth of the Livery beckoned, the acrid odor of smoke mixing with that of heated iron and horses. Grateful to be out of the bitter wind, Abby paused as the jarring twang of the hammer rang out. Closer inspection showed horses stalled against the left wall while the forge occupied most of the right, but Christopher was not to be seen.

Enticed by the glowing coals, she stepped closer to the waist high fire place. The heat rushed against her face and she basked in the warmth of it.

"Ya don't want to get too close now miss."

Startled she spun about to find Mr. Knapp, the blacksmith, had stepped behind her and was reaching for the handle to the bellows. "Them coals look inviting, but they spit a cinder at you and you're gonna have to set aside some time for mending. Now, what can I do for you Miss?"

"I'm looking for Mr. Carlson." Intimidated by his size, she tried not to stammer. "They told me at the shop he was working here today."

The burly man nodded toward a door on the far wall. "He's in there Miss, but he's real busy so don't you stay too long."

Abby nodded and pulling her cape close, scurried down the shadowy corridor. The door stood ajar affording her a view of her husband as he worked. Perched by a low window, Christopher had tacked the hem of a leather apron to the wall and wore the bib of it around his waist. His head bent in concentration over his work, and Abby watched in amazement as his hand moved a saw no thicker than an apple stem flawlessly through the metal to cut an intricate pattern.

Christopher paused and scowled then turned to the doorway. The lines on his face were instantly erased by his smile as he saw her.

"I hope I'm not disturbing you," she hedged.

He raised a brow and looked pointedly to the spot of ground beside his chair, pulling her closer with the force of his will alone. His arm snaked around her

306

waist as, still sitting, he hugged her to his side. "The sight of you, madam, is never an interruption, but I'll love you forever if you've brought me food."

She nodded eagerly. "Why didn't you come for dinner?"

Chris carefully untied the leather apron from his waist and then, curling the garment, let the silver shavings slide into a waiting dish. "I'd promised this piece to the Attwaters," he said, handing her the base of a delicate egg cup. "I think they mean it for a gift."

Abby let her fingers smooth over the intricate filigree pattern he'd created and marveled again at his talent. "How do you know where to cut?"

Christopher took the base and set it beside the drawing on the shelf that held his tools. "It's sketched first and then I follow the design on the metal. What smells so good?" Taking the basket from her hands he groaned from the weight of it, making her laugh.

"Nanny seems to think you need to keep your strength up," she teased watching him peek under the checkered cloth that lined the top.

He sent her a leering grin and offered a chicken leg. "Have any ideas what I should do with that strength once it's up?"

Her eyes went wide and her cheeks burned. "I think I'd better leave you to your eating or you'll end up with indigestion."

"I'd rather end up with you," he teased, grabbing a handful of cape to prevent her exit. His eyes met hers and held her captive. "Have you eaten?"

Not thinking she shook her head. "I left as soon as the meal was served."

"Couldn't wait to see me?"

She blushed again and wondered why every word from his mouth seemed to have two meanings.

"Christopher . . ." a gruff voice sounded down the hallway.

"Come on back, Jeremy." The door pushed all the way open to admit the bulky frame of Jeremy Knapp. "Have you met Mrs. Carlson?" Chris tucked his free arm around his wife. "She brought me dinner. Care to join us? We've enough to feed half the town."

The blacksmith nodded cordially to Abby. "I'd like nothing more, but I've come to beg a favor. The misses has just sent our youngest down to fetch me for dinner. Usually I close up when I'm gone, but I was wondering if you would mind keeping an ear open instead. I'm not expecting any business this hour, but the Thurmonts have a rigging to return and I'd hate to see them have to come back twice."

Christopher nodded. "After all you've done for me, I'm happy to repay a small part of the favor. Enjoy your meal and your family. I've enough work to keep me the better part of the afternoon and I'll take advantage of the forge in your absence."

Jeremy tipped his hat in appreciation. "Nice meeting you, Mrs. Carlson. Thanks Chris. I'll be back within two hours."

Christopher tugged Abby's arm and together they followed the blacksmith and waved to him from the doorway.

"This is heaven sent." Tossing the chicken bone aside he grabbed her by the waist and spun about in a circle.

"You're making me dizzy," she cried clutching his shoulders.

"I plan for more than that, madame. Would you

308

accompany me up to the hayloft?" Her look of complete innocence only made his blood quicken faster. "I've a surprise I've been wanting to share with you."

Abby cast him a dubious glance even as she moved to the wooden ladder. "Then why didn't you just bring it home?"

His grin turned wicked as he watched her climb. "I'll explain everything once we get up there."

The loft was warm and cozy. Sunlight poured in from the high open window and dust spores danced in the afternoon glow. The scent of fresh hay filled the air and Abby watched in confusion as Chris perched on a tied bale and started to remove his coat.

"What are you doing?"

He beckoned with a crooked finger. "I plan to kiss my wife. Now would you come over here so the deed is possible?"

"Here? Now?" Totally amazed she could only stare at him.

"And pray tell, why not madam?"

Abby looked about the secluded loft. True from the ground no one could see them, still a customer could enter at any moment through the wide open doors.

"I'll hear anyone who enters," he said grabbing her hand and reeling her closer. "And they'll think nothing amiss when I go down." He pulled her onto his lap and eased the cape from her shoulders. Hands that could fashion the most delicate of silver, made short work of the ties and bows on her chemise. "The most noble thing I ever did was leaving you to sleep this morning." His lips brushed down her neck leaving a trail of damp kisses in their wake. "And I've been paying for it ever since."

309

Her hesitation gone, Abby startled them both when she straddled his lap to face him.

"Does it ever end?" she whispered as his knuckles brushed against the tips of her breast through the thin fabric of her chemise. "Does this wanting ever end?"

Christopher felt the tips harden and cupped the fullness of her breasts. "Never," he swore, teasing the corners of her mouth with his own. Pushing the fabric away he freed his treasures. "When I'm a feeble old man, I'll still look at you and feel my blood race with need."

Christopher kissed the soft skin between her breasts making her squirm. Then taking a nipple between his lips, his assault began in earnest.

Abby tossed back her head to give him better access and felt the delicious tension begin to build. Her fingers ran through his hair even as she pressed him closer. Each tug of his lips tore at something deep within until she felt her insides melt with want.

Her elusive scent captivated his senses even as his clever fingers tugged her skirt from beneath, settling her against him with naught but his breeches between. Then he was releasing the buttons and flesh pressed against willing flesh.

A low moan escaped his lips as she enfolded him. Christopher threw back his head exhaling sharply. For a heartbeat both were still, lost in the intense pleasure of their joining.

Abby placed her arms on his shoulders to steady herself and watched him with eyes radiant with love. "You fill that part of me that's been empty for so long," she whispered against his lips. "You make me feel whole."

His hands settled on her waist to hold her steady

as he arched even deeper, making her cry out in pleasure. Then the fragile restraint shattered and they surged together, seeking to please, needing to love, reaching fulfillment.

Like a wilted flower, Abby sagged across his chest, her fingers still tangled in the hair at the nape of his neck. She felt his breathing slow and her lids grew heavy. But the afternoon sun warmed her back and the gentle neigh of the horses below titillated, and she wanted more of this forbidden fruit.

"You've just sent me to heaven," her fingers slipped within his shirt and brushed against his flat nipple. "But like my father with his bottle, I find that one sip is not enough. I'm addicted to the feel of your flesh against mine and the taste of your smile on my lips."

Christopher looked down at her in wonder and felt himself harden again. "Then it is a good thing, madam," he shifted within her. "For I fear it will take this lifetime and most of the next to satisfy my need for you."

Chapter Eighteen

Abby floated back to the Tavern on feet that never touched the rough rocks that lined the pathway. The bitter wind felt deliciously cool against her fevered skin and the day carried a crispness she noticed for the first time. Tilting her head back she gloried in the beauty that surrounded her. Had the sky ever been so blue, the golden leaves so bright, the scarlet holly berries so thick? Contentment wrapped about her like an expensive cape and even Nanny's troubled face didn't dim her smile as she reached the tavern.

"I'm sorry I took so long." She glided in to the cookhouse, shed her cape, and looked about as if she'd never seen the room before. She stared with confusion at the stack of clean plates and cups waiting on their tray for Obadiah to carry them back into the tavern.

"I already finished," Effie huffed, tying off another string of apples. "I thought you was gonna take Mr. Carlson his lunch and then be right back."

"Effie!" Nanny scolded. "That ain't no way to speak to Miz Abby."

Effie looked down at her feet but her scowl stayed. "If I'd knowed Miz Marilla was gonna be taking over the taproom I'd not worried Thomas

312

to come back. That woman is a beast."

"Child, you hush now. You gonna stir up all kinds of trouble."

"Then you tell her, Nanny. Miz Abby's gotta right to know."

Abby smiled absently. "Know what?"

"Miss Marilla's done rented out a room while you were gone. She's in there right now, playing like she owns the place."

Abby's smile brightened. "Then at least she's earning her keep."

"Miz Abby," Nanny said slowly. "She rented out the last space to Mr. Bloom."

"Cyrus Bloom?" Abby's eyes went wide in astonishment. "Why on earth would the man want to take a room at the Stag's Head? He owns his own home."

Effie heaved an angry breath. "I heard him tell Miz Marilla his house was being done over. He said the workmen were making too much noise and dust was everywhere. Said a body shouldn't have to put up with such nonsense."

Abby shrugged with resignation. "Well he is gentry, so at least we know he'll pay his way." Her misty smile returned. "Have either of you been outside yet? It's the most beautiful day."

Effie's scowl would not be appeased. "Miz Abby it's freezing out there."

"Oh . . ." She hefted the heavy kettle and strained the beet juice into a waiting crock. "I was going to suggest that you take the boys and go off for a few hours. You know how they love to hunt bayberries and we could always use another basket or two."

"Miz Abby," Nanny interrupted before her daughter could agree. "You need Effie's help cause you gots candles to dip this afternoon."

Abby brushed aside the protest. Setting the heavy

313

kettle on the table she took a ladle and began to transfer the cooled beets to the waiting pickling mixture. "I can manage the candles," she said easily, feeling she carried a strength that would last forever. "I think . . ."

A piercing shriek filled the yard and the door to the cookhouse slammed open. Two brown streaks flashed through crashing into Abby with a force that sent her and the beets to the floor in a tangle of arms and legs and seven-year-old bodies.

"Don't let her get us, Miz Abby," Wesley pleaded, scooting behind his mistress' back.

"She said she's gonna skin us alive," Willie cried, taking refuge under the table.

Abby had barely a minute to look at her ruined apron and gown before the door swung open again and Marilla, belt in hand, filled the entrance way.

"Where are those heathens?" she screamed, making the dishes rattle. "I'm going to teach those little monsters a lesson they'll never forget. Abigail, what in heaven's name are you doing on the floor? You've got beet juice all over you. I declare I've never seen a body as clumsy as you are."

Abby scrambled to her feet and plucked the cloying fabric from her legs. "It was an accident."

Marilla huffed and crossed her arms over her ample chest. "With you it always is. Now where are those demons?"

Abby dropped her skirt and wiped her sticky hands on her ruined apron. "What happened?"

Drawing herself erect, Marilla looked down her nose and her gray eyes narrowed. "Those monsters put salt in my punch."

Struggling not to smile Abby turned to the twins who now stood plastered to their mother's legs. "Did you do that?" she questioned.

314

"How dare you ask them, when I've already told you what happened," Marilla shrieked.

Thomas and Obadiah rushed into the cookhouse. "What's wrong?" Thomas gasped. "I heard the screaming all the way down the street."

"It was her, Daddy," Willie pointed. "She's gonna skin us alive."

"Willie," Abby bent over and looked directly into the dark frightened eyes. "Did you put salt into Miz Marilla's punch cup?"

The boy hesitated only a moment before nodding. His eyes filled with tears and he pressed his face to his mother's skirts. "Wesley made me do it," he sobbed.

Abby turned to Wesley whose eyes had also filled with tears. "Is that true?"

"I told you, Abigail," Marilla's voice pierced the air. "And it wasn't just a single cup of punch. The little demons poured salt in the entire bowl, now the entire batch is ruined."

Huge tears rolled down Wesley's round cheeks. "We was just watching her mix the punch," he sniffed. "And she kept taking a taste whenever she thought no one was looking. Willie thought it'd be funny to see her face wrinkle up like a prune."

"They need to be punished, Abigail," Marilla threatened.

Abby straightened with a sigh. "I know, but not by you." She plucked the belt from the startled woman and turned to Thomas. "Their father will handle this."

Thomas' eyes went wide as Marilla screamed.

"That's the most ridiculous thing I've ever heard of. He's not going to do anything to those boys."

Abby looked at the huge man standing before her. "You're wrong," she said gently, her eyes on Thomas.

"He's their father, and he wants them to grow up good. He'll see that the punishment is given with a hand meant to teach rather than humiliate." She offered the belt on her opened palm.

Thomas hesitated, then nodded his eyes full of respect and gratitude.

"No," Effie pressed the boys closer to her legs. "Nobody's gonna take a belt to my babies."

"They be my boys too," Thomas said quietly, taking a twin by each hand. "And like Miz Abby said, we wants them to grow up right. There ain't nothing right about wasting salt or ruining good punch."

Captivated by her husband's simple words, Effie released the children who both started to scream.

Nanny put a comforting arm about her shoulder as Thomas led the boys away. "Thomas is a fair man, girl. He'll teach them and they won't forget. But he loves them and that they'll remember."

Marilla snorted. "As if that makes any difference. Abigail your apron is ruined."

Abby looked down and felt her heart sink. "Maybe if I put it to soak in some buttermilk . . ."

"You want to use some salt, Miz Abby," Nanny said turning to get the bowl. "Rinse it out and then rub it with salt and put it in the sun to bleach."

"Harrumph, as if we haven't wasted enough salt already. That's not going to work, Abigail. You need to use lemon juice on a beet stain."

Abby watched the two women square off and knew nothing good could come from another confrontation. "Marilla, thank you," she said firmly. "Your help has been appreciated but you can go back in the tavern now. Effie, get these beets cleaned up and when Thomas is finished, take the boys off for bayberries."

Marilla's eyes widened with surprise at the authority in Abby's voice, but she took her leave.

When the door closed behind her Nanny touched her mistress' arm. "You did real good child," she said proudly. "You did real good."

Abby moved slowly to the door and wondered why she no longer felt good. "I'm going to go and change."

"We will get that stain out," Nanny declared. But as their eyes met, both women knew that the apron and gown were ruined.

Standing behind the bar in the empty tap room, Abby counted the coins and tobacco vouchers in her money box for a second time. Carefully she stacked the month's rent in a pile. She would ask Christopher to drop it off at Mr. Webster's in the morning. She critically eyed the remaining amount. Her most important need was sugar so she separated the price for a new loaf and also set that aside. Disheartened, she stared at what was left. When the foodstuffs were purchased for the coming day there would hardly be anything left, and slaughtering day was fast approaching. There was no way a piece of new fabric could be worked into her budget. She placed all the vouchers and coins back in the box. The notion of asking Christopher was discarded as quickly as it came. She already knew that she'd need to approach him soon for new slippers, and the thought of begging for a new apron at the same time was too much to contemplate. Mayhap in another few weeks she thought, tucking the box away on the shelf. With Mr. Bloom in residence, they were now full up and things had to get better . . .

Christopher fastened the last button of his waistcoat as he entered their bedchamber. "You're not ready," he said, finding her in her night robe sitting before a spinning wheel he'd never seen before. "And where did that come from?"

Abby looked up from her spinning. "The wheelwright came today and mended this," her head nodded to the spinning wheel as her fingers expertly worked the flax. "Didn't Obadiah tell you to go ahead without me?"

"I want you to come with me," he said stepping closer, making her fingers go clumsy on the wheel. "I told you that Nick and Sarah invited both of us for the evening. Now leave that for the morrow. After all you've done today, you deserve a few hours of peace and relaxation. Come I'll help you pick out something to wear. But not this rag," he said with a grimace, carelessly dropping her only gown onto the floor.

Abby rescued the garment then stood frozen as he opened each of the drawers in the chest on chest. "Madam?" Puzzled he started to turn when the last drawer produced what he sought. "Here," he pulled out the heavy beaded gown then looked back with a frown.

"That's my wedding gown," her voice was the barest whisper.

"And the rest of this?" he questioned poking through what he knew to be undergarments.

"They're the petticoats that go beneath."

Christopher's scowl deepened as he stood. "Abby, I specifically asked you to move your things into this room. Now where are your clothes?"

Her cheeks burned scarlet and her head bent forward in humiliation. "There was an accident this afternoon and my new apron was stained. I've put it into soak with lemon juice and salt, but there wasn't enough time to fix it before dinner."

He looked at the extravagant gown he still held and the rag that she clutched tightly in her fingers and a sickening dread settled in the pit of his belly. "Where did you get your wedding gown, Abigail?" His words were soft, but he saw her shudder.

"It was a gift from Mrs. Beaumont," she whispered, her voice full of self reproach.

"And the robe you now wear?"

"A gift from Madame Rousseau."

He looked about the room and realized for the first time she owned no other garments. "Do you have any shoes?" he questioned, dreading the answer.

She nodded, but her eyes stayed locked on the ground.

"Where are they?"

She scurried to the side of the bed and withdrew a worn pair of slippers. Her hand trembled as she offered them for his inspection.

Christopher looked at the tattered fabric she called shoes and wanted to weep at his thoughtlessness. He knew she had no money, that was why she had married him. Yet she'd never asked for anything personal and he'd never thought to offer it. He closed his eyes tightly and tried to swallow the lump in his throat. His ladies had always let their needs—no, their *wants*—be known, and he'd been generous and obliging. But with Abby all had changed. She haunted his every waking hour, yet never once had he thought past how happy she'd made him. He watched the silver tracks on her cheeks and knew them for tears.

"I know I shouldn't have accepted such a grand gift," she said miserably. "But I didn't want to shame

319

you. I can recut the wedding gown and I'm sure in a few days, I could have a new dress ready. Mayhap you could go alone this evening and then extend an invitation for the Beaumonts to join us here at the end of the week?"

The lump in his throat grew bigger. Even now, she didn't ask. He'd been blind to her most obvious practical needs and she worried about shaming him.

"Abby come here." He felt his chest grow tight when she started to flinch, but held herself in check. "Abby, please." When she stepped close enough, Christopher gently enfolded her within his arms. "If you don't mind I think I'll send a message to the Beaumonts and beg off for the evening."

She looked up then, her eyes luminous, her lashes spiked with unshed tears.

"I'd rather stay home and make love with my wife."

Her smile was hesitant. "You're not angry?"

He scooped her into his arms. "With you, madam? Never. But I fear we must go shopping on the morrow. I should have taken you to Charlotte's long ago."

Abby looped her hands about his neck, her brow wrinkled with thought. "Madame Rousseau has been most kind and her work is exquisite, but I fear her prices will be dear. If you could but see your way clear to purchase a length of fabric from Mr. Wilkins' store, then I could fashion a new apron in no time."

"You shall have anything your heart desires, madam." He crossed to the bed.

Abby looked deep into the blue of his eyes and felt her excitement perk. "Anything . . ."

"If it is within my power to grant it, your wish is my command." He sat on the edge of the bed and tried to guess what color gown she would ask for.

"Would you teach me to read?"

Christopher blinked in confusion. "What?"

Immediately cowed, Abby folded her hands and her gaze dropped to her lap. "I'm sorry," she whispered. "You probably didn't mean something as grand as that."

"I didn't realize. . . ."

She felt the tears burn behind her eyes. Why had she ever voiced such a ridiculous notion? She wasn't smart enough to learn to read.

Christopher silently cursed himself for having the sensitivity of a goat. The joy on her face had vanished and he realized yet again he'd taken more than she had to spare from her small store of self-confidence. He watched her struggle to appear aloof.

"Never mind, it was a foolish notion." She blinked back her embarrassment and tried to smile.

"I said your wish is my command, madam," Gently he reached out and cuddled her close.

"Then you think I could . . . learn to read, that is?" Her excitement grew until her entire body vibrated within his arms. "You don't think me too dimwitted?"

"Dimwitted? You madam? The only dimwitted fool in this room seems to be myself. But if you'll have me, I would be honored to teach you."

She threw her arms around his neck. "I can't believe it," she cried hugging him tight. "Just think," she gasped looking deep in his eyes. "You can leave me messages like you did this morning and I would know what they said . . ."

He felt his chest swell with emotions. "We could start tomorrow evening if you wish."

"What ever did I do to deserve you?" she sighed, basking in the pleasure of his hands on her flesh.

"It is I who am the lucky one, madam." He followed her down on the bed.

Abby glanced toward the fireplace. "But my spinning . . ."

"Will just have to wait."

They lay facing each other, sharing the same pillow, their fingers locked between them. Christopher brought their clasped hands to his lips and kissed her knuckles. "You know what I like best about being married to you?"

A rich smile covered her face and her eyes twinkled. "Yes."

"Besides that," he laughed pulling her into the crook of his shoulder. "I like thinking about talking to you. Knowing that when the day is over, I have someone to share things with."

Abby propped her head on her arm and gazed down at him. "It seems to me that last night after Marilla woke us up, you asked me about my day and then abruptly changed your mind."

He gave a sheepish grin and looked over at the tall cased clock. "I think you have about ten minutes before I want you again," he teased. "So tell me, how was your day, Mrs. Carlson?"

Abby laughed out loud and hugged him close, feeling for the first time the tension he had managed to hide so successfully. "You first."

A worried look commanded his face. "Jimmy Richardson is still missing."

She pushed back up on her elbow to look down at him. "Did you speak with his mother?"

He nodded. "She told me you'd been there, and how you offered to help him." He kissed her knuckles again. "I appreciate your doing that. I just don't know where the lad could be or what could have happened to make him run off. He seemed genuinely pleased to be working with me." His brow wrinkled. "I don't think I was too hard on him, but then I've never had an apprentice before and there's a lot to learn."

Abby stared down at her husband and felt her heart swell with love. Instead of ranting about his own inconvenience because his apprentice had disappeared, Christopher worried as to why the boy left. She took a deep breath for courage. "It is not your fault that Jimmy ran away, but mine."

"What?"

She nodded slowly. "Jimmy was upset that you married me."

Chris brushed aside her words with a shrug. "I knew he had taken a fancy to you but that's hardly enough reason to disappear. I'm beginning to think the lad might have stumbled into foul play."

Abby stared hard at their clasped hands. "Would you take him back if he could be found?"

"Of course," he nudged her chin up so their eyes met. "If you know something, Abby you must tell me. The boy might be in danger."

"Would you take him back even if you discovered he had something to do with the fire that destroyed your shop?" She waited for the explosion . . . none came.

"I can see from your eyes there is more to this story, Abigail, so start at the beginning."

"I don't know everything." Desperately she tried to remember all of Jimmy's words at the wedding. "I do know that he told me he was in the shop when the fire started." Her eyes filled with guilt. "He was trying to make me a gift and there was some kind of accident."

Christopher jerked from the bed and heedless of his nakedness began to pace. "That little fool," he ranted. "He could have gotten himself killed! He wasn't ready to work on his own. He barely knew how to begin."

Her eyes filled with tears. "I'm so sorry," she stammered. "I didn't do anything to encourage him . . . at least I don't think I did. I can't remember . . ."

Chris saw the tears on her cheeks and his mood instantly softened. "You're not to blame, love," he sat on the bed and gathered her close. "It is the randy notions of youth that got him into this fix." He wiped her tears with his thumb. "But when did you learn this?"

Abby scrubbed her face with the back of her hand. "Jimmy found me in Mr. Beaumont's study just before the ceremony. I don't think he meant to say what he did but once done . . ."

"And now he's afraid to come back." Christopher stood and eased into his breeches. "I'm going to have to go out for a while," he said dropping a kiss on her forehead. "If Jimmy is afraid of repercussions he's likely to do something foolish and the boy's too young to be going off on his own."

She watched in silence as he pulled on his shirt and stockings. "But what can you do at this hour?"

He stood and slipped into his shoes fastening the buckles with careless ease. "I'll stop by the Raleigh Tavern and seek out a few well chosen friends. They'll keep an eye on the wharf. If he hasn't departed by ship already, he'll have a difficult time of it. If he's gone by road, then it might take a bit longer." He turned and saw the anxiety in her eyes.

"It's not your fault, love, so put the notion from your mind."

"But . . ."

"Abby, accidents happen to all of us and we all make mistakes. But it's how we deal with those mistakes that makes the difference. Jimmy is a bright boy but he's not had a father's guidance in years. He's worth the effort and I'm going to find him." He urged her back under the covers and tucked her in as one might a child. "Get some sleep," he growled. "For you'll not get any when I return."

Despite her resolve to stay awake, Abby felt her eyelids grow heavy. Her day had been long and the next one was fast approaching. Within minutes she slept. She roused slightly when Christopher climbed back into bed with her and pulled her close. He tucked her against his chest spoon fashion and whispered something in her ear, but knowing he was home and safe, her muscles relaxed against him and exhaustion claimed her again.

She dreamt of sitting on a grand chair, a book of letters in her hand, a glass of the finest claret at her side and a smile touched her lips. Then the light faded and screams pierced her hazy vision. Dark, menacing shapes reached out with their tangled fingers to pull her down and Malachi's face loomed before her.

Abby woke, shivering and rigid with terror, only to find Christopher already clothed and striding to the door.

"Stay here and don't get out of bed," he commanded from the door way. "There is something wrong down below. I'll be back when I know what is amiss."

Abby watched in horror, then heard the door lock behind him. Frantically she clutched her pillow. She knew she should rise and go down, but the violent shudders that racked her body made the notion impossible. She pressed her head to her knees and rocked in abject misery. Malachi is dead, she whispered over and over. He can't come back because he's dead. Frozen in terror and despising herself for the weakness, she counted each agonizing minute until Christopher returned.

It seemed like a lifetime, but moments later Christopher opened the door to their chamber with a disgusted sigh. He locked the door and tossed the key to his desk, shaking his head.

"Marilla was sleepwalking again." Wearily he sat on the bed to remove his breeches. "What did you serve for dinner tonight?"

She stared in confusion, easing over as he came under the covers. "I don't understand. I thought I heard a scream."

"You did," he sighed, pulling her close and closing his eyes. "Cyrus Bloom was also sleepwalking, seems they gave each other quite a start. Bloom claimed his dinner hadn't settled well, then Marilla said there was nothing wrong with the meal. I left them arguing in the tap room."

Abby sat upright. "But how did they get in the tap room to begin with?"

Chris gave a sleepy yawn and pulled her back down. "I don't know. But you should have seen Bloom. He wears a pink night cap to bed, I think the man is bald as a turnip under that massive wig he wears."

Her thoughts scattered in a million directions. What were they doing in the tap room? Marilla's room was on the other side of the tavern and the tap room wasn't on the way to the privy . . .

Chris nuzzled against her neck. "You run a fine

326

tavern, Mrs. Carlson," his words began to slur with fatigue. "But I can't say I'll mind when we leave."

Abby bolted upright on the bed. "You want to leave the tavern?" she gasped, watching Chris press his face deeper into the pillow.

"It only makes sense," he replied, his eyes still closed. "Why should we stay here and pay rent? When the house and shop are complete we'll move there. Surely you'll not mind giving up all the extra work the tavern demands of you."

But Abby's thoughts had turned to panic. A new renter would demand to see the slaves listed in the property agreement and Obadiah and Nanny would learn their freedom papers were a fraud. Anxiety seeped back into her frozen limbs as desperately she tried to find a plan.

Christopher's breathing turned deep and even, but for Abby the hours of sleeplessness had just begun.

Chapter Nineteen

Abby heard the clock strike half past five and pried her eyes open. If she had slept at all she couldn't remember, yet she was still no closer to solving her problem. It had never occurred to her that Christopher might want to leave the tavern and she chided herself for not thinking of something so obvious. You are so ignorant, she thought miserably. Her head pounded in protest as she scrambled into her robe and forced herself from the bed.

The frigid water from the pitcher washed the sleep from her eyes but offered little else in the way of comfort. With a heavy heart, Abby turned back to the chair that held her clothes. She jumped with a start to find Christopher stoking the fire.

"I thought you were still asleep," she gasped, pressing a hand to her heart.

He turned and placed the iron poker on its stand. "It's freezing in here. Why don't you get back in bed until the fire takes the chill from the room."

Despite her headache, she smiled. "If I get back in bed, breakfast will be late again."

He chuckled, reaching for his clothing. "And would that be a tragedy?"

Abby didn't respond, for her eyes had come to rest on the chair that held her clothing. "What is this . . ." her words were breathless as she lifted the new gown.

Christopher grinned and tucked his shirt into the snug waistband of his breeches. "I would have thought that obvious. Come, I'll play your maid and help you dress."

Her fingers smoothed over the rich brown fabric delighting in the velvet's soft nap. "But where did this come from?"

Chris stood near the fire for warmth and held up her new chemise. "I got them for you last night. Now will you get over here before you turn to an icicle before my very eyes."

"But where . . . when . . ." she shivered as he peeled off her robe then tugged the chemise over her head and fitted her arms into the sleeves.

"I stopped by Madam Rousseau's last night while I was out." Expertly he guided another petticoat over her head and turned her to tie the fastenings at her waist. "I wasn't sure what trim you would want, so I told Charlotte to leave it plain. We're going back this afternoon and she'll add the decorations then."

"But it's beautiful as it is." Her voice was muffled beneath a second petticoat as she struggled to get her head free.

"I knew the color would go well with your hair and eyes," he said holding the bodice like a coat for her to slip her arms into. "But I just didn't know what type of lace you would prefer." He turned her, nimbly fastened the front hooks, then reached for the skirt.

"You certainly do this well," she said, imagining just where he might have gotten such experience.

Christopher only grinned. "Just consider it practice so I would be an expert for you my love."

"I think I'd rather have you stumble a bit," she said dryly.

He urged her onto a chair and produced a pair of sheer stockings. "Charlotte assures me that these will keep you warm, but I must admit I have my doubts.'"

Abby tugged the delicate stockings over her slender calves and secured them with the ribbons provided. Never, except on her wedding day, had she worn such finery.

"You are too generous, sir."

"And you are going to be late for breakfast if you continue to look at me that way, madam," he teased, taking in the gentle smile of gratitude that touched her face. "Here, there's even a new apron to go with it."

Abby stared at herself in the tall looking glass and found a stranger looking back. The gown hugged the curves of her bodice and showed the slender length of her arms, then flared slightly over her hips. And the velvet's rich brown color made her hair look like spun gold even as it hung in wayward curls about her shoulders.

She felt a lump of gratitude swell in her chest as she turned back to him.

"None of that," he said simply, taking her hand. "You can thank me properly tonight when I have you at my leisure."

"Can I not even thank you a little now?" she whispered.

Christopher shook his head. "If I give in to my need for you now," his lips brushed against hers, "your prediction will come true but breakfast will never be served at all."

Abby laughed and hugged her arms about herself. She felt so deliciously warm, and she wondered only briefly if it was because of her new gown or her husband's words.

"I plan to go to see Magnus Webster this morning," Chris said over breakfast. "He'll set up a line of credit for you with any of the merchants you wish. This afternoon when I return, we'll go to Madam Rousseau's together. But in the meantime, you must send someone to the print shop to secure paper, quill and ink for me. We shall need them for our instruction this evening."

Abby felt as if her heart would burst with pleasure. He hadn't forgotten. "Would you do an errand for me?" she asked shyly. "Mr. Webster said the rent must be paid by the fifth of each month. And while I know today is only the second, I'd like to see the payment made. Would you give it to him for me? I have it all counted out and ready in a pouch in our chamber."

Christopher finished the last of his coffee. "I'll fetch it before I leave. Now, can you get away about noon?"

Her hands smoothed over the soft fabric that covered her lap. "Would you think me ungrateful if I asked to keep the gown the way it is, without lace or beads?" She looked up at him though the thick lashes that fringed her eyes. "It is the grandest garment I've ever owned."

"Then this one shall stay as it is." He smiled. "But you'll want to choose the others yourself."

Her eyes widened with confusion. "Others . . ."

"Gowns," he said patiently rising from his chair. "I think one of deep forest green would also complement your hair but as to the others, the choice will be yours. Now give me a kiss so I can go." And heedless of the patrons who still dallied with their morning meal, Christopher kissed his wife full on the lips.

Abby felt like royalty as she glided through the dining room in her new finery. She smiled at everyone and even Cyrus Bloom earned a soft word of good morning.

Obadiah whistled through his teeth when she entered the cookhouse. "Whoo weee, Miz Abby, you sure are something in that new gown."

"You can't help with the washing up in that," Nanny stated. "You let Effie do it. You sit down and decide what we needs from the market."

Abby all but floated through her morning. And even when Obadiah confided he had found Cyrus Bloom wandering through the pantry just before daybreak, her good mood would not be daunted. He was probably just hungry, she explained. After all, the man is used to living under his own roof. More than likely he just forgot where he was. He and Marilla should get along fine, she thought with a grin.

Christopher waved aside the offered drink and sat before Magnus Webster's cluttered oak desk. The portly man fussed with his wig and then grimaced with disgust.

"Would that I had your courage, my boy, or that fine head of hair of yours. This thing is giving me a devil of a time this morning." He poked at the elaborate chestnut curls that hung well past his

332

shoulder. "I took it to be cleaned and damn it all, I think they shrunk it."

Christopher tried not to laugh. Webster might carry the airs of a bungling fool, but a keener mind he'd never seen. He waited patiently until the attorney located his glasses and perched them on his nose.

"Now," Webster said, settling in his chair. "What can I do for you this fine morning?"

"I'd like you to set up some lines of credit for Mrs. Carlson," Chris said. "Today if possible."

Webster nodded and sorted through the litter on his desk. "I see no problem with that request. I'll attend to it straight away. And if you don't mind me saying so, we truly enjoyed attending your marriage celebration. My wife's talked of nothing else for days. The food was delicious, especially those floating islands." The portly man kissed his fingertips in appreciation. "Makes my mouth water just to think of it. And your new missus, she's a real beauty if I do say so myself."

Christopher's smile came easily. "She certainly is." He rose to go and then slapped his head. "Damn," his hands fruitlessly patted the deep pockets of his coat. "I knew I forgot something. Abigail had the rent payment ready and she asked me to bring it over."

Webster instantly straightened in his chair. "For the Stag's Head?"

Chris nodded from the doorway. "I know it's not due until the fifth, but she was so pleased with herself for having it early, I promised to bring it round. Damn," he hit his palm against the door's edge. "I knew I was forgetting something."

"But sir," Webster stuttered.

"I know," Christopher turned back. "Just trans-

333

fer the funds from one of my accounts. I'll send a servant down later with the Abigail's payment."

"But why would you want to do that?" Webster's eyes narrowed.

Chris grinned. "You've been married what twenty, thirty years, you know the consequences if you don't please your wife."

Webster only looked more confused. "My boy, why would you want to transfer money from one of your accounts to another?"

Chris stepped back into the office and closed the door. "What are you saying?"

"You own the Stag's Head Tavern. I thought you knew that. It was in that batch of properties that you acquired when you purchased the silver shop from Walter Johnson."

"Wait . . . you mean to tell me I was about to pay rent to myself for a property I already own?"

Webster had the grace to look contrite. "Please accept my apology, sir," the attorney blustered. "But I understood that you and Mr. Johnson discussed all the aspects fully."

Stunned, Christopher could only shake his head. "In my haste and exuberance to own my own shop, I'm afraid I let the business end of it go by the wayside. The talks I had with Mr. Johnson always returned to the best proportions to use in a pickle mixture or which hammer to use for an edging."

"Then I have been greatly remiss as your attorney, sir, and I beg your indulgence. You own the Stag's Head Tavern, the silver shop, part of Knapp's Livery, as well as several plots of prime land in the heart of town itself." Webster looked up. "Should I go on, sir?"

Christopher waved him aside, as he tried to imagine Abby's reaction when he plopped the rent money back in her lap. "I'll come back next week when things are more settled and we'll go over everything then. I've pressing business this morning."

"Is there any way I might be of assistance, sir?"

Chris' eyes narrowed in consideration. "Yes, Magnus, you can and I'm sorry I didn't think of it sooner. I want you to hire several discreet men and have them search for my wayward apprentice. The boy is not to be harmed in any fashion, but I want him returned."

"I heard he'd gone missing."

Chris turned for the door again. "The poor lad thinks himself guilty of mischief and it is not the case."

"Ahhh," Webster replied knowingly. "And now he's afraid to come home?"

"Exactly. Pick carefully for I don't want the lad scared anymore than he already is."

Webster folded his hands and rested them on the clutter. "I shall attend to that and the lines of credit for Mrs. Carlson immediately."

Christopher nodded his goodbye and stepped into the crisp fall wind. He owned the Stag's Head. His step was brisk as he walked to the silver shop. The first thing he was going to do was to get Abby more help.

Abby stood patiently at the kettle and dipped another rod of strings into the hot wax. She had removed her new gown lest it became spattered with wax, but the new apron over her old gown hid a multitude of sins, and her good mood thrived. She had been dipping for nearly an hour when Effie came rushing into the cookhouse.

"There's a Mrs. Morgan in the parlor wanting to

335

see you," she gasped. "Thomas said she come in a private coach and I ain't never seen someone dressed so fine."

"Mrs. Morgan?" Abby frowned and searched her memory.

"Real pretty, with yellow curls and big blue eyes. The same shade blue as Mr. Carlson's."

"Oh oh," Abby felt her stomach tilt. "I think it might be Mr. Carlson's sister. Did she ask for him?"

"No," Effie frantically shook her head. "She asked for you by name. You better get in there Miz Abby. I don't think she's the type that likes to be kept waiting."

Abby started out but Nanny caught her arm. "Effie will take her a tray with hot cider. You go up and put that new gown on and tidy your hair."

Abby reached up and realized her hair hung about her face in limp strands from standing over the kettle. Under Nanny's scrutiny she took a deep breath, and put her shoulders back.

"You be one of them now, Miz Abby," Nanny scolded gently. "And don't you forget it."

Ten minutes later, Abby found Julie Carlson Morgan seated comfortably beside a roaring fire sipping one of Nanny's secret recipes.

"Mrs. Morgan," she said, walking calmly into the room while her stomach tied itself in knots. "How nice of you to come to call."

Julie set down her cup but made no move to rise. "I wanted to speak with you. Is Christopher about?"

Determined to ignore the woman's manners, Abby took a chair. "He'll be home at noon. We're . . . we have an appointment."

Julie looked at the clock on the mantel then

leaned forward. "I came to apologize for my words at the wedding. I was tactless, rude, and utterly insensitive. I'd like to beg your pardon for my thoughtless behavior."

Stunned, Abby missed the way Julie shuddered over the last words. "You have it, Mrs. Morgan."

"Julie," she admonished. "After all we are sisters of a sort and you mustn't be so formal with family."

Abby felt the tight knots in her stomach begin to ease. "I'd like very much for us to be friends. For I find your brother magnificent."

"I'll just bet you do." Her smile took the sting from the words. "So tell me, Abigail, how have you and Christopher been keeping?"

"Might I join you?"

Abby looked up to find Marilla already coming through the parlor's doorway. "Marilla, perhaps another . . ."

"Nonsense," Julie interrupted rising to fondly greet the older woman. "How good to see you again, my dear. Here, take this chair close to the fire so you'll be warm."

Abby looked at the pair with confusion. "I didn't realize you had met."

"At your wedding," Julie smiled. "And I must say you were a beautiful bride. Didn't you think so, Marilla?"

Marilla accepted the cup Julie offered and gazed at Abby over the rim. "Without a doubt. But then Mr. Carlson was a most handsome groom."

"Ah, Christopher," Julie sighed leaning back in her chair. "The ladies have been after him for years. Tell me Abigail, how did you do it?"

Suddenly uneasy, Abby set her cup back on the tray. "I'm not sure I know what you mean, Mrs.

Morgan. But I consider myself most fortunate that Mr. Carlson found me." A knock sounded and Effie entered the room carrying a tray laden with sweets. "Pardon me, Mrs. Carlson," she said formally carefully setting her tray on the table nearest her mistress. "But Mr. Carlson just sent a messenger. Said he'd gotten word about Jimmy and he was going to investigate. He said for you to go on to Madame Rousseau's without him."

Abby tried to hide her disappointment. "Thank you Effie, and thank Nanny for the pastries."

Julie waited until the servant had closed the door then leaned forward. "I don't mean to criticize, my dear, but you really shouldn't thank them that way. They'll get a false sense of importance and then you'll have nothing but trouble."

"So you're going to Charlotte Rousseau's this afternoon?" Marilla interrupted, before Abby could speak.

"How marvelous," Julie reached for Abby's hand and gave a reassuring squeeze. "For I must admit I was a bit surprised when I first saw you today." Abby's blank look prodded Julie further. "Your gown," she said gently. "At first I thought . . . no never mind. I realize now that this is your costume for doing the wash. Am I right?"

Abby looked down at her new treasure with confusion. True it didn't compare with the creation Mrs. Morgan wore but . . .

"Oh dear," Julie's face filled with remorse. "I didn't mean to distress you. There's absolutely nothing wrong with greeting family in such a gown. But tell me, what have you planned for when the Governor comes to dine?"

"The Governor?" Abby stammered, her brown eyes wide.

338

Julie looked to Marilla then back to her hostess. "Darling don't you have any idea how truly important your husband is? Why Christopher is respected in the highest social circles. I'd bet my fanciest hat pin that the governor himself will invite you to Jamestown within the week."

Abby felt the knots in her stomach return. "A week?"

"Well a fortnight at the very most. What do you plan to wear?"

"I don't know . . ."

"Why of course, how foolish of me," Julie rolled her eyes. "That was why you were going to Charlotte's this afternoon, am I right? Of course," she chatted on not waiting for a reply. "But you don't want to pick out a gown alone, do you my dear?"

"Madam Rousseau . . ."

"Wants to make a sale," Julie interrupted. "Oh the woman is talented, I give you that. But sometimes I think she's too caught up in the Paris fashions. Did you see that monstrosity she created for Sylvia Myerson? The poor woman thought herself the height of fashion but even her husband was embarrassed to be seen with her. Of course no one would say anything outright, but the looks said it all. Poor George was beside himself with humiliation and there was nothing he could do about it."

"I wouldn't want to embarrass Christopher," Abby whispered.

"Then I shall go with you and help you choose." Julie stood and spun around for their inspection. "I do have a taste for fashion wouldn't you agree?"

"You look magnificent, my dear," Marilla offered.

Abby stared in awe. Mrs. Morgan's gown was the exact same shade of blue as her eyes and the cut of

339

the bodice emphasized her delicate curves and womanly shape. In truth, she did look breathtaking. Abby's hand trembled as it smoothed over the soft nap of her skirt and a sense of inadequacy filled her. I would have chosen another like this, she thought miserably. And Christopher would have been too kind to bid me nay. She remembered how he wanted the gown to have lace and decorations and then how he'd bowed to her wishes.

"I would truly appreciate your advice, Mrs Morgan. If you can spare the time to accompany me."

"I'll come too," Marilla offered.

"Wonderful," Julie clapped her hands together. "We shall make a grand afternoon out of it. My carriage is ready, let's go now."

Abby felt herself being swept away.

"But wait," Julie turned in the doorway. "I have an even better idea. Let's go to Yorktown. It is not that far and my own seamstress resides there. Her name is Josephine Francoise and she is magical with needle and thread."

"But . . . Madam Rousseau . . ."

Julie took Abby's arm and ushered her into the foyer where the footman stood with her cape. "Charlotte is wonderful, my dear, I'll not argue that. But," her voice dropped to a whisper. "Josephine charges only half the price. And while my brother is quite well off, I know he's had to spend quite a bit to have his shop rebuilt. Wouldn't he be pleased to learn you'd saved him a coin or two?"

Realizing how tattered her cape looked compared to Julie's, Abby relented. How she must have embarrassed Christopher, yet never once did he reprimand. Then her eyes narrowed suddenly with thought. If the gowns were truly inexpensive, and she didn't purchase more than one for herself, she could get one for Nanny and Effie too. Excitement sparkled from her deep brown eyes. "Let's go," she stated with determination. "As long as we can be back before the evening meal, I say on to Yorktown."

"Wonderful," Julie cheered. "To Yorktown."

Cyrus Bloom entered the foyer with cape in hand and doffed his hat with a courtly bow. "Have a most pleasant afternoon ladies. Did I hear you say you were off to Yorktown?"

"We're going shopping," Marilla huffed, her cheeks turning pink.

Bloom smiled and winked at the older woman. "Then as I said before, have a pleasant afternoon."

The trio reached the carriage and Abby was already inside when Julie doubled over in pain and frantically clutched Obadiah's arm.

"What's wrong," Abby cried in alarm.

"Oh no," Julie wailed her eyes luminous with tears. "I'm going to have a bout of stomach flu. I can feel it coming."

"Then we're staying home. You need to be in your bed not rattling about in a carriage," Abby started to descend, but Julie threw out an arm that prevented her exit.

"Abigail, I would never forgive myself if the governor was to call tomorrow and you had nothing to wear because of me. You and Marilla go. My driver knows the way. I'll just lie down until you return."

"I can't leave you here alone and ill."

"I'll be fine," Julie promised. "I just need a bed. Perhaps you'd let me use yours?"

Marilla nudged Julie aside and pushed her way into the carriage. "Let her stay and rest Abigail. Don't cause the poor girl any more distress. I

341

might be old fashioned, but I assure you that I can help you pick out gowns that will do your husband proud."

Julie caught Abby's hand from the doorway and pulled her close. "Trust Josephine's taste," she whispered giving Marilla a dubious glance. "She knows what she's about. Now you leave and I shall go and rest for a few hours. I'll be anxious to hear all about it when you return."

"I don't think . . ." But Abby's words were cut off as Julie slammed the carriage door shut. There was a shout and even before she could reclaim her seat, the carriage was moving.

"Do you think she'll be all right?" Abby tried to settle on the wide leather seat.

Marilla wedged her bulky form more securely into the corner. "Stomach flu is never pleasant, but I think Mrs. Morgan would have been more distressed if she had caused us to miss the outing. Could you put that flap down, Abigail? This cold is piercing my bones today."

Abby immediately secured the window flaps, closing out the bright sunlight. Heated bricks lined the floor for their comfort and she pressed her head back against the cushions to help against the rolling motion of the carriage.

"Do you know where we are going?" she questioned softly.

"I know the street mentioned. And although I've never met Madame Francoise, if Mrs. Morgan's gowns are any indication of the woman's talents, she's a genius." Marilla settled back and closed her eyes indicating the conversation was now over.

Abby clung to the window strap and wished she could see the passing country side. She'd never

342

been to Yorktown and as the carriage moved on, she felt her excitement begin to grow.

Within minutes, Marilla's snores filled the small interior and Abby tried not to laugh. Carefully she leaned over and tucked a heavy robe about the woman's lap. Then moving closer to the window, she edged the flap up ever so slightly. The wind brushed against her face and she delighted in the scenery that rolled by.

They hadn't traveled far when she felt the carriage slow and Marilla came instantly awake. Abby lifted the window flap and secured it upright, but frowned in confusion. She had expected to see a street lined with houses and shops like Middle Plantation, instead she saw only forest.

Marilla, too, looked about with alarm. Angry shouts sounded then a shot rang out and the door to the carriage was yanked open.

"Dear Lord, we've been set upon by highway men," Marilla gasped.

"Out ladies."

Unwilling to converse with a man holding a gun, Abby assisted Marilla from the carriage. But her cry of alarm could not be contained when she saw their driver slumped over the seat, his chest covered with blood.

"What do you want," she stammered, realizing their assailant had two partners.

"Get in the wagon." His words were muffled by the woolen scarf tied over his mouth and nose, but the dark eyes that peered out at her were hard and cold.

"Tie them and blindfold them first," came the orders from one perched on a tall, prancing bay. "The man don't want them to know where they're going."

343

"But why are you doing this?" Marilla pleaded as her wrists were pulled behind her back.

"Shut up old woman, or we'll leave you here for the wolves."

Marilla cried out in pain as the rough hemp was tightened.

"Now just stop that," Abby commanded, shouldering the man aside. "There's no need to hurt her."

A large hand caught her square across the face, and for her effort, Abby saw stars. She fell to the ground and her assailant followed her down. "Listen here, Missy," he threatened pulling her own hands together. "Spout off again and you'll get more of the same. Now shut up."

Abby bit back her whimper of pain as the rope cut into her flesh. A filthy cloth was tied around her eyes then she was carelessly tossed like a sack of grain into the empty wagon bed. Her shoulder took the force of the fall and tears stung her eyes as she struggled to pull herself into a sitting position. She felt something heavy collapse against her legs and grunted from the pain. Then they were moving. If she had thought the carriage ride rough, Abby realized it was nothing compared to an open wagon. With her arms bound behind her and her sight obliterated, she could find no way to brace herself against the constant jolts that tossed her about. The wagon traveled at a terrifying speed. The wind stole her cap and tore her air free to whip about her face. The rope cut off the circulation in her hands and Abby felt a terror worse than any she had ever known. Christopher, she cried silently, please find us.

* * *

The clock had just struck noon when Christopher entered the tavern.

"We wasn't expecting you 'til later, sir." Obadiah took his cape and hung it on the peg.

"It turned out to be a false lead," he said wearily. "Is Abby about?"

Obadiah shook his head. "She sure is going to be sorry she missed you, sir. They done gone off to Yorktown to get new dresses."

Christopher paused at the bottom of the stairs. "They?"

"Mrs. Morgan came today sir. She and Miz Marilla talked Miz Abby into going to Yorktown."

"Julie came here?"

"Yes sir, fact she's still here. Just as they was ready to depart, Mrs. Morgan, she gets a fierce bout of stomach fever. So Miz Marilla and Miz Abby go on without her."

Christopher frowned. He couldn't imagine Abby leaving someone so sick to go shopping for herself. That was a stunt his sister would pull.

"Mrs. Morgan made her go, sir," Obbie said as if reading his mind.

"Where is my sister now?"

Obadiah looked at the stairs. "She be in your room sir and she wants to go home something fierce. She's been a begging us to find you ever since Miz Abby's carriage rolled out of sight."

"And you say she's sick?"

Obadiah nodded quickly. "Poor little thing is as peaked as they come."

Christopher took the stairs two at a time. She'd better be sick, he thought darkly for if she's up to trouble I'll wring her neck. But the sight of Julie crumpled on his bed immediately erased his anger.

"Oh Christopher," she cried looking up as he en-

345

tered. "I thought they would never find you. I'm sick."

"I can see that." He brushed a hand across her brow but found it cool to the touch. "Have you sent for the doctor?"

Julie shook her head and her eyes filled with tears. "It's stomach fever. Nanny made me some peppermint tea, and it's helped greatly but Chris I want to go home. I want to be in my own bed." She collapsed against his chest and sobbed.

"Hush, Julie," he soothed. "You can spend the night here and I'll take you first thing in the morning."

"No . . ." Her tears came faster. "Don't you understand? I need to go home now. Oh Chris how can you deny me this when I feel so wretched? I thought you cared for me."

Nanny knocked softly then entered on silent feet carrying a fresh pitcher of water. Her eyes filled with sympathy as she took in Mrs. Morgan's crumpled form. Her dress was wrinkled beyond repair, her hair hung in tatters about her face, and her eyes were swollen and red from crying.

"If Mrs. Morgan wants you to take her home, sir, then I thinks you should do it."

"Nanny, it's nearly six hours in a carriage."

"But it's just past noon now. Oh Christopher please? If we left immediately, I could sleep in my own bed tonight. How can a loving brother deny such a simple request?"

"I'll explain to Miz Abby when she comes home, sir," Nanny offered, giving Julie's hand a gentle pat. "I'm sure she'll understand."

Christopher stared hard at his sister's swollen face and knew he had no choice. "You stay here and rest and I'll get a carriage harnessed. We'll fix

346

a makeshift bed for you on one of the seats."

"Oh thank you," Julie threw herself into his arms and started to cry again. "I just know I'll feel better when I'm back home again."

Christopher patted her back and rolled his eyes, thinking of the tedious carriage ride to come, and already missing Abby.

Chapter Twenty

Trapped in a world of darkness Abby sat—cold, damp, and consumed by terror. Her shoulders ached from the pull of her arms tied behind her and every inch of her body felt bruised from the frantic wagon ride. She'd received two vicious blows for not moving quickly enough to please her captors and promised a third if she made a sound. And so she sat, desperately trying to fight back the panic that would render her useless.

She knew she had been left in a shelter of sorts, for the wind no longer pricked along her skin with its icy fingers. But her senses warned she was not alone and fear held her tongue. Cautiously she drew her heels toward her and then lowered her head to rest on her knees. When no rebuff came, Abby slowly rubbed the side of her face against her knees, praying no one would notice her subtle motions. Little by little the fabric loosened and she gasped with relief when the blindfold was finally pushed from her eyes.

Blinking in the dim light, she found her prison to be a crude, one-room shack. Broken glass filled only parts of the windows and a rough-hewn door gaped crookedly on its hinges. But as her eyes searched further, her terror increased as she spied Marilla's crumpled form. With no thought to the consequences, she awkwardly scooted across the dirt floor toward Marilla.

"Please let her be alive," she whispered frantically. With her hands useless behind her, she used her head and teeth to roll the old woman over and sighed with relief at her groan of pain. "Thank God, you're alive," she sobbed, unable to stop the tears that ran freely down her cheeks. "Come on, Marilla," she coaxed scooting as close as she could. "Wake up, now. We need to get out of here."

Marilla groaned again but her eyes fluttered open. "Abigail?"

"That's right, dear," Abby coaxed. "Are you hurt? Can you try to sit up?"

Marilla struggled to sit, but without her arms to help her she toppled over and her eyes filled with terror. "Abigail what happened? Where are we?" Her voiced turned shrill with panic. "Who were those terrible men? What are they going to do with us?"

"Hush, darling, hush," Abby soothed anxiously. "They don't seem to be here right now, but you must be quiet."

"My arms hurt," Marilla started to wail in earnest. "And I'm cold."

"Marilla, shut up," Abby demanded sharply. "They might be just outside that door. Do you want them to come back in here?"

Marilla bit back her sobs and tried to look indignant. "There's no need to be rude, Abigail," she sniveled.

"That's right, Marilla, get angry," Abby taunted. "Get furious. But not at me. Use that anger to push yourself up." Taking a mouthful of the woman's cloak, Abby tugged with all her strength until Marilla sat upright.

"I can't even feel my fingers," she complained. "And I think my toes are frozen. I don't like this Abigail, I don't think I like this one bit."

Abby struggled to right herself again loosing her breath in the effort. "I think they've left us alone," she gasped softly. "I haven't heard anything for the longest time."

"Use your head Abigail," the old woman looked down her beaklike nose. "Why should they freeze their privates off? Trussed up like a turkey for the spit, we certainly aren't going anywhere."

"That's just it," Abby whispered urgently. "We've got to get away from here."

"Abigail you don't even know where 'here' is," Marilla huffed. "And with our hands tied, how are we going to manage? Besides, it's starting to snow."

Abby's heart sank as she gazed through the open doorway. White crystals drifted through the gray sky. They danced with the wind then came to rest on the frozen ground. "Marilla, we are going to get out of this place, and right now," her voice held conviction for the first time.

"How?"

Abby felt the old woman tremble and knew it was from cold as much as fright. "Put your hands back towards me. I'm going to try to untie the ropes."

But as she worked, Abby found frozen fingers had little dexterity and no strength. Tears of frustration filled her eyes but she angrily blinked them back. "I'm not going to just sit here," she swore. And as the minutes turned to hours she continued

350

to work at the rough knots.

Christopher groaned with relief as he stepped out of the carriage and onto the familiar ground of his parents' plantation. But his eyes darkened as the hazy glow of twilight revealed the property's neglect. The formal gardens filled with shrubs and larkspur that graced the front of the house were overgrown with weeds dead and dying and in the distance he could see tobacco fields long past their time for harvest.

"What is going on here?" he demanded turning toward his sister who now carried a remarkably healthy glow. She had slept for most of the trip, and for that he'd been grateful. But now, sick or not, Julie was going to give him answers. "I've been gone just under three months and look at this." He gestured toward the ill-kept yard.

Julie took her brother's hand and tugged him onward. "The air is too cold, Chris. Come inside and let me explain."

Chris looked about the vast horizon and wanted to weep from the sight of it. All the years his father had worked and slaved to build a home of beauty . . . the hours his mother had toiled side by side with the servants over her garden. Now it lay in ruins. Taking his sister none too gently by the arm, he helped her up the steps and into their childhood home. Here at least everything remained the same.

Once seated in the parlor, with a fire to warm them, Chris took the offered mug of ale and firmly dismissed the young maid he'd never seen before. His sister, now clad in her dressing robe, reclined regally on the settee and daintily cradled a glass of brandy.

"I'm so glad you're home, Christopher," she sighed with a contented smile.

"And you have exactly one minute to tell me what is going on," he threatened.

Julie shrugged. "Clarence and I have decided to live separately," she said, carefully gauging her brother's reaction. "I've been staying here and he resides at Tall Oaks."

Stunned, Christopher could only drag a hand down his face. "Why didn't you tell me?"

"That's why I came to see you."

"Julie you arrived in Middle Plantation nearly two weeks ago. Yet today was the first time you chose to call."

"You had just gotten married," she countered.

"You're my sister," he argued. "You should have come to me straight away."

She smiled, loving the guilt that covered his proud face. "I didn't want to impose on your happiness." Her voice faded to a martyr's sigh.

"But Julie, all this," he gestured, "didn't happen in the last two weeks. The front yard hasn't seen a hand since the day I left."

Waiting until her eyes had filled with tears, she turned to face him. "I just can't live with him, Chris," she sobbed. "He wouldn't let me get any new gowns; he complained constantly that things were a mess, but he did nothing to help me. Clarence even turned the slaves against me."

"What?" His voice filled with disbelief. "Where are they?"

Her lip pulled into a pout. "Most of Momma and Daddy's old hands are with Clarence. They won't come back here with me. And the new ones

352

are just hopeless. They don't season my food properly, they scorch my petticoats on purpose, and they never have what I need when I want it."

Christopher tried to assimilate the information but his senses were deluged. "You mean to tell me you've been living here with no help? That does it," he rose with angry motions.

"Where are you going?"

"To fetch Clarence and make him face up to his responsibilities."

"Wait," frantically she clutched his sleeve. "You don't have to go tonight. We can discuss this further in the morning. I'm too tired for a confrontation."

"Well I'm not." Shaking her grip from his sleeve, Christopher angrily strode to the door.

"Wait!" she shrieked, growing more frantic by the minute. "Perhaps Clarence isn't only to blame."

Christopher recognized the tone the moment it left her lips. That—*well just maybe I'm about to become trapped in a lie, let me quick think of another story*—tone.

He let her lead him back into the parlor and wearily took his seat. "What's really going on, Julie?"

Sheepishly she stared at the ground. "Clarence and I have separated, but it was my choice more than his. He's begged me to come home but I just couldn't stand listening to him harp all day. You'd have thought each coin I spent came directly from his own pocket. The man is tighter than a virgin's knees."

"Julie, running two plantations is not a picnic. And sometimes the cash isn't available until the crop comes in. You know that."

"But if I want a new gown, I don't see why I should have to wait." She began to whine.

"And how many have you purchased since August?" he questioned.

She folded her arms angrily across her chest and her foot began to tap in agitation. "I don't see what bearing that has on anything."

"How many?"

Julie rolled her eyes and flopped back down on the settee. "Perhaps a dozen or so . . ."

"Two dozen?" he gasped

"More or less. But what should that matter? I needed them."

Chris leaned forward and wearily propping his elbows on his knees, he rubbed his face with his hands. How was it he wondered, that Abby could survive with nothing and turn out so remarkable, while his sister who had everything had turned into such a shrew?

"You're going to need to be more thrifty, Julie," he said stiffly. "Or Clarence is going to end up in the poor house and you'll be there beside him."

Sensing her brother's mood was not in her best interest, Julie yawned. "I'm grateful you brought me home, Christopher," she said quietly. "But the journey has left me exhausted and I fear I must seek my bed. I know you'll be able to sort through all of this in the morning. Charlotte Rousseau wouldn't dare refuse me credit if you were to ask for it."

Christopher rose and shook his head. "I'll not be here to deal with anything, sister. I'm returning tonight. I suggest you invite your husband over for breakfast and try to make your peace with the

354

man."

"But surely you'll not desert me when I need you to stay."

Chris leaned over and placed a fleeting kiss on her forehead. "I'll be taking a fresh horse from the stable. I'll send someone back with him by the week's end."

"But I need you here," Julie wailed. "You can't desert me. What would Momma and Daddy say?"

Christopher's gaze turned sad. "That you should deal with your husband and start taking responsibility for your actions."

She stamped her foot and let her tears gather again. "I'm useless without you to help me," she pleaded. "Surely Abigail can do without you for a few days. After all she managed the tavern without you before."

Chris smiled, thinking of the grand news he'd still not had time to share with Abby. "You'll have to manage the best you can," he said. "I'm leaving now. There's still a bit of daylight left and I mean to make the most of it."

Julie whirled from the doorway. "Well you'll not get far for it's started to snow."

Christopher felt the news like a blow to the gut. But as he watched the flakes lazily float to the frozen ground, he knew Julie would get her way one last time. Traveling at night was dangerous at best. But traveling at night in a snowstorm was suicide. "I'll stay the night," he relented grudgingly. "But I'll say goodbye now as I'll take my leave at first light."

Julie offered her cheek for his kiss. We'll just see about that, she smiled with satisfaction as she watched him climb the stairs to his old room.

Much can happen before morning.

Obadiah stepped into the cookhouse and dusted the snow from his head. His face wrinkled with worry as he extended his hands to the warmth of the fire. "There's something wrong, Nanny I can feel it in my bones."

"What you feel is that joint fever that comes with the snow," Effie offered a reassuring smile. "Miz Abby can take care of herself. If the roads be bad she and Miz Marilla will just find a place to spend the night and stay in Yorktown. She ain't foolish enough to try to come home in this." She gestured outside.

Nanny ladled the last of the vegetables onto the waiting platter and covered them with a pewter top. "Here, now you gets these into the dining room before they starts to cool." She slid the platter across the worktable toward Effie. She waited until the girl was gone before turning back to her husband. "Obbie, you getting one of those funny feelings again, you best tell me. I don't want nothing happening to that child. Miz Abby just found her happiness, I ain't gonna let nothing take it away from her."

"It just hits me, Nanny. Remember at the wedding how Miz Marilla says all those things about Miz Abby? Well I gots to thinking back and I don't think Mr. Carlson's sister was none too keen on the wedding either."

Nanny's eyes narrowed. "Them two spent a powerful lot of time hovering in that corner."

Excited, Obbie nodded his head. "Right and then all of a sudden Mrs. Morgan shows up a-wanting to be friends . . . something ain't right here. Now, Miz Abby's gone missing and Mr. Carlson ain't around to go find her. I think that Mrs. Morgan's up to some no good mischief."

Nanny hefted her bulk off the stool. "Let's get into the tavern. I thinks we let too much time go by already. We need to get out and look for Miz Abby."

Cyrus Bloom shook the snow from his cape as he entered the tavern. Cold and hungry, he stepped into the dining room expecting to find his dinner waiting. Instead he found the food cooling on the side bar and a noisy crowd with everyone speaking at once.

"What is the meaning of this," he snapped, his voice crackling through the group like a whip.

"Beg pardon, sir," Obadiah stepped forward as the room grew still. "Miz Abby and Miz Marilla went to Yorktown this afternoon and they ain't back yet. We's afeared they had an accident and we's going out to find them."

Cyrus looked at the boisterous group. Most of Carlson's building crew, a few students from the college, as well as the tavern's servants stood about in total confusion.

"Then get yourselves organized," he charged. "How long have they been missing?"

"Miz Abby said she'd be back before supper," Effie whispered suddenly fearful.

"Then we must search. You three," he gestured toward men he knew to be in Christopher's crew. "Get your lanterns and go down the main road to Yorktown. I've horses stabled in the barn, take any but the black stallion."

Obadiah watched with relief as Mr. Bloom issued

his orders. He never would have thought the man capable of such, but within moments the room was clearing out and each had a direction in which to search. Even Nanny had been sent back to the cookhouse with orders to stay there and set the kettles on to heat water.

When the room was empty, Obadiah stepped hesitantly toward Bloom. "Thank you, sir, he stammered. "Miz Abby sure be precious to us. And I don't wants to think of her coming to no harm."

Bloom's face drew taut. "She's precious to me too, you old fool. Now get your carcass out there and start looking."

Obadiah nodded. "Thank you sir, I'm on my way." Leaving Bloom to see to his own horse, Obbie paused in the cookhouse only long enough to fetch his jacket. Then with Nanny's threadbare cape over his shoulders for extra protection, he took his lantern and departed.

Cyrus Bloom watched out the back window until Obadiah's figure blended into the darkness. His full lips pulled into a smile that never reached his eyes. He planned to search all right, but he was not going out into the freezing night to do it.

"Don't give up, Marilla, you can do it. Just take your time." Abby fought back her tears as she felt Marilla struggling with the broken glass to free her bonds. It had taken hours and her fingers were raw from the effort, but she had managed to free Marilla's hands. But now, as the freezing cold seeped in to steal the last of their strength, even with the glass, Marilla was failing. They had moved closer to the door, hoping the glare from the snow would shed some light on the stubborn knots, but so far all it had done was make them colder.

Marilla's impatience had turned to whimpers of pain and Abby winced in sympathy each time the old woman made a sound. And as the night ebbed slowly by, her fear that Marilla would give up grew with each heartbeat.

When the ropes at last were free, Abby let her tears come. Shooting pain racked her shoulders as she pulled her arms before her and hugged her frozen fingers close to her body. But as the fiery pain stabbed each finger making her tears increase, she gave thanks that at least they had not frozen solid.

"What are we going to do now?" Marilla's desperate whisper echoed in the empty shack.

Abby forced herself to stand and felt her head swim from the effort. "Come," she reached for the older woman, "we've got to get away from this door and find a corner to get warm in."

Marilla's knees buckled as she tried to stand. "Abigail, I don't think I'll ever be warm again."

"We're going to make it, Marilla. Those men left us because they thought us helpless, but they were wrong. Just look at us."

Marilla's reed-thin laughter started small then grew to hysterical proportions. "Abigail, you are priceless. We are stranded in a shack in the middle of a snowstorm. We have no fire, my feet and hands are frozen solid and I can hardly stand, and you say just look at us."

Abby helped the old woman to the far corner where they both collapsed to the ground. "I'm not going to sit here and wait for them to come back." Abby wiped the tears from her cheeks so they wouldn't freeze.

Marilla took a deep breath of the frigid air and pulled her rounded shoulders back as much as she dared. "I never thought I'd say it Abigail, but you're right. I'm tired of being useless to everyone including myself. But what should we do? We'll never make it if we try to leave."

Abby struggled to keep her teeth from chattering. "Christopher must be frantic by now, but he'll probably not be able to mount a search until daylight. As much as I hate to say it, I think we should just stay here and wait for the sun to rise. At least in the shack we're somewhat protected." Abby felt Marilla stiffen as they huddled together.

"Christopher won't be coming," said Marilla, her voice quivering with fear. "Oh, Abigail, what have I done?"

"Hush," Abby soothed, fighting back the dread that was seeping into her bones with the cold. "Why on earth would you think Christopher reluctant to find us?"

"Not reluctant," Marilla sniffed, "unable."

Abby's heart leaped into her throat and her chest pulled tight as dread turned into panic. "Marilla, explain yourself and quickly. Do you think Chris in danger?"

Marilla shook her head and tried to wipe the tears from her eyes. "Mrs. Morgan asked me to help her," she whimpered. "She said she'd give me a hundred pounds if I would help her get you to Yorktown. We were to shop and then return home."

"But how would that affect Christopher?" Abby interrupted.

Marilla took a deep breath. "While we were gone, Mrs. Morgan was going to talk Christopher

360

into returning home with her."

"Thank God," Abby felt relief like a tangible force. "I thought you meant Christopher had fallen into dangerous hands too."

"But don't you see, Abigail," Marilla whispered impatiently. "Christopher is probably at their plantation by now. He won't even know we're missing."

Abby smiled and hugged her arms to her chest. But he's safe, and that's all that matters she thought. "Well, then we shall just have to think of a different plan. But tell me, why would Mrs. Morgan journey all that way if she just wanted Chris to go back with her? Why not send a letter. He does know how to read you know," she stated proudly.

"Mrs. Morgan thought you were a bad influence on her brother. She said you'd bewitched him and he'd never listen to her if you were about. But I swear, Abigail, I never knew she intended this."

"Witchcraft! Me?" Abby sputtered with disbelief. "That's pure nonsense. And Marilla, surely you can't believe Julie had anything to do with this? My God, they killed the driver and the footman. No, I think we were victims of highwaymen set on procuring a ransom. I just pray they won't harm Christopher."

"I'm sorry, Abigail. I should have never agreed to her plan."

"Well, what's done is done, Marilla. And if we can't depend on Christopher to rescue us, then we will just have to rescue ourselves."

"But how? We've no horses, it's snowing, and those dreadful men could come back at any time."

Abby pulled herself into a tighter ball against the cold. "We have to make a plan . . ."

361

* * *

Christopher paced impatiently in the dining room. Dawn had never been so slow in coming. The young girl from the night before placed his breakfast on the table and then lit another candle.

"Is there anything else, sir?"

Chris shook his head and took his place. "Thank you Aggie. I appreciate you rising so early to accommodate me."

The young girl blushed beet red from the compliment. "Thank you, sir. And the mistress instructed me to give you these first thing." Her hand trembled as she pulled two folded letters from her pocket. "The mistress says you was to open this one first."

Christopher nodded his thanks and the young maid scurried away. With his coffee in one hand and the letter in the other, Chris scanned the contents and felt his muscles tense. *My dearest brother,* it read. *I would do anything to spare you the pain of this letter, but I fear that is not in my hands. As you probably already guessed I was not truly sick yesterday, but merely desperate to have you home again. You see, I have some disastrous news to share with you and I felt that the surroundings of our childhood home might help soften the blow. When I arrived at the tavern yesterday, I found the bride you love so dearly packing her trunks to leave. She said she'd decided that married life was not for her and she was leaving. Dearest brother, believe me when I say I pleaded for her to stay. I implored her on all things holy not to set aside her vows and betray you, but she would not be swayed. I watched her pen a letter to you and then make her departure. I assure you I begged and pleaded until her trunk was placed in the carriage and the carriage was out of sight. Seeking only your best interest, I confiscated the letter she left for you and then convinced the servants I was ill. My only thought was of you, dear brother, and the pain this parting would cause you. I hope you will forgive me for wanting to protect you. I know after you read Abigail's letter your pride will not allow you to return to the tavern, and the memories of a woman who spurned your affections. Please know that I would deem it an honor to have you living back under this roof again. The plantation thrived once before under your careful handling. I know it will again. You loving sister . . .*

Christopher set the first letter slowly on the table then picked up the second. Betrayal sliced through him like a hot knife, dulling his senses, leaving only pain. How could she claim to love him and then do this? The second letter fell to the table as his hand clenched with the need to do damage. With angry steps he went to his father's study and removed quill and ink. His hand moved swift and sure over the paper then he walked stiffly back to the dining room. Placing his own letter over the ones from his sister, Christopher glanced around then took his leave in the predawn light.

Chapter Twenty-one

Cyrus Bloom wiped the last of his biscuit through the gravy then stuffed the morsel into his mouth. Through blood-shot eyes he surveyed the weary group that surrounded him. They had searched through the night but Abigail Carlson and her sister-in-law had not been found.

Exhausted and haggard the searchers had straggled back to the tavern one by one as the hour had approached midnight. Regretfully acknowledging that it would be fruitless to continue the search through the storm each had retreated to his bed, to seek whatever comfort he could find. But now, as the morning sun shone bright upon the pristine snow, hopes dared to surface.

Downing the last of his hot cider, Cyrus pushed back from the table and tugged his brocade waistcoat down over his protruding belly. "It's time to leave," he commanded gruffly, thankful that no one challenged his orders. "Mrs. Carlson and that poor old woman must be found today." He watched Nanny sway as she cried silently into her apron and was grateful for the added touch of urgency. "Now, I propose we each search the same area that we did last night. Look for tracks in the snow or anything that seems unusual. Does anyone object?"

He was met only by silent stares from tired faces. "Good. Now I challenge each of you not to return for at least four hours. Mrs. Carlson's life is in our hands and I for one don't want to face her husband without knowing in my soul I did all I could." There was a mumbled agreement, then chairs scraped and weary bodies rose. "You girl," he turned to Effie. "You walk down to the orchard and then slowly make your way back. Stop at each house and inquire if they've seen Mrs. Carlson. Don't mention she's missing, just that Mr. Carlson wondered where she'd gone off to."

Effie twisted a napkin nervously in her hands. "Wouldn't it be better, sir, if I was to say that Miz Abby was missing? Then we'd have more help to find her."

Cyrus drew himself erect on his stacked heels and glared. "Do you mean to question my judgment?"

"No sir," Effie shook her head frantically. "Everyone's saying how lucky we are that you was here to get things organized the way you did."

"Then get about your business," Cyrus snapped. "I've more important things to do than justify my actions to you."

Julie glided down the wide staircase bathed in a path of sunlight and felt her heart sing. Her brother was home at last and everything was going to be wonderful. Her smile deepened when she thought of Charlotte Rousseau. That snooty dressmaker would regret the day she'd refused credit to a Carlson when Christopher got through with her. Waltzing into the dining room, she rang the golden bell on the side bar, then stood at the tall window and let her eyes feast of the beauty of the snowfall. It covered the ground in a quilt of white and clung to the trees giving the landscape a mystical appearance.

"Yes madam?" Aggie struggled to curtsy.

"You can bring my breakfast," she sighed contentedly. "And I want you to tell me the minute my brother wakes."

Aggie shifted nervously and edged carefully out of reach. "Mr. Carlson's already left, madam."

"What?" Julie spun on her heels her face contorted with anger. "Did you forget to give him those letters?"

Aggie pointed quickly to the table as her Mistress advanced. "No madam, they're still there on the table where he left them."

Julie turned and spying the letters for the first time snatched them up as Aggie scurried from the room.

Her face went red with fury then blanched white with fear as she scanned Christopher's parting note. He'd written just five words across the page in his anger and Julie felt the agony of defeat as she read them:

Abby can't read or write.

Julie's scream of anguish filled the empty dining room, but no one came to her aid.

Abby blinked back tears as the glare from the

366

snow stung her eyes and made them burn. They had waited for the first rays of sunlight to make their escape. Now, as they trudged slowly along the road, they prayed they journeyed in the right direction. Exhaustion wrapped them in a cloak of despair that neither would voice, but each step became a conscious effort as fatigue weighted their limbs.

At first she thought she was dreaming. Wiping the tears from her eyes Abby blinked against the glare. "Oh thank God, Marilla," she cried, her voice hoarse from cold and thirst. "Look . . ." Her finger trembled as she pointed to a lone horseman coming toward them. "We're going to make it."

"Saints be praised," Marilla whispered, leaning heavily against Abby for support. "But wait," she cautioned, pulling down Abby's arm. "What if he's one of those that put us in that terrible shack?"

Abby's heart flipped over and her grip on Marilla's hand tightened as the horseman bore down upon them. Frozen in fear with no strength to run, they watched in terror until the man dismounted. "It's Cyrus Bloom." Abby's yell of joy came as a squeak. "Marilla, it's Cyrus Bloom." Of all the faces she had hoped to see, this was one that had never come to mind. His cape flapped in the wind revealing a coat of sky blue against a waistcoat of pink and a tall hat perched precariously atop his thick, brown curls, making him a comical sight at best.

Bloom tightened his grip on the reins as his stallion snorted and pranced nervously behind him. "Well ladies, it seems you are more resourceful that I thought."

"Mr. Bloom," Marilla sank to her knees in the snow. "Thank God, you've found us."

"Thank God, indeed," he turned toward Abby only to see comprehension beginning to dawn. "And you're also quicker than I gave you credit for, aren't you my dear."

"You had something to do with this," she challenged.

Bloom moved toward her with a steady step. "A tedious plot my dear, but very necessary."

Marilla looked from one to the other in confusion. "Abigail, what are you saying?" She tried to climb to her feet but without Abby's support the effort was too much.

"Why did you do it?" Abby edged steadily backward. "Why did you have us kidnaped?"

Bloom shrugged his shoulders. "Not kidnaped my dear, simply detained for a while."

"But we nearly died." Marilla, filled with righteous indignation, struggled to her feet. "What madness are you about?"

"I had some unfinished business with Malachi Barclay, and decided the time was right to see it ended."

"By leaving us to die?" Abby gasped.

"No, no, my dear. After I found what I needed, I was going to gallantly rescue you. But alas that is not to be."

"I don't understand," Marilla wailed, her sanity fleeting. "What do we have to do with Malachi?"

"It's his letters that I am in need of," Bloom said looking back at the old woman. "Isn't that what you were searching for when you made up that ridiculous story about sleepwalking?"

Marilla shook her head in denial and Abby interrupted. "Malachi didn't leave any letters. If he had I would have found them. You've been searching in vain for something that doesn't exist."

Bloom's face turned red with fury. "Oh they exist all right, Mrs. Carlson. I'm not so gullible as to believe your simple tale. Now, step over to my horse. You and I are going back to the tavern and you are going to produce those letters."

Abby folded her arms over her chest in a show of courage she was far from feeling. "And if I refuse?"

Cyrus only smiled. "Then I shall have to shoot Mrs. Barclay to persuade you."

Her eyes went wide as he pulled a small gun from within his coat. "But you're a gentlman from a fine family . . . surely you wouldn't." Her breath caught in her throat as she watched his eyes and saw the madness.

His smile turned cold. "I've already killed her brother, so I don't think I'll have any trouble with a sniveling old woman."

"You killed Malachi?" Abby felt her breath escape. "But the carriage accident . . ."

"Was a convenient way to obscure the truth. Now move to the horse. And I'll warn you only once, Mrs Carlson; make one false gesture and Mrs. Barclay will not live to draw her next breath."

On leaden feet Abby moved toward the prancing stallion. The horse looked big and hot tempered and his black coat glistened with sweat. "But what about Marilla?" she questioned as Cyrus pushed her onto the saddle.

With an agility that defied his bulk he swung into the saddle behind her. "The old biddy stays here. The horse can't carry three."

369

"But she'll die out here," Abby cried trying to twist back.

"No, you can't leave me here," Marilla's thin scream tore through the air.

"Be still," he hissed, taking the reins. "If she freezes that's one less body I have to worry about." Then giving the stallion a sharp jab, they were off, as Marilla's anguished cried echoed in her mind.

They reached the tavern quicker than Abby would have thought possible, and her hope surfaced. Surely, Obadiah or Thomas would notice something amiss. But as they entered the tavern a curious silence hung in the air.

"Where is everybody?" She tried to speak loudly but only a hoarse whisper sounded.

Cyrus took her arm in a crushing grip. "Why, out looking for you my dear. I organized a very careful search party."

"But they're going to come back . . ."

"And by then we'll be gone. Now you have two choices my dear. You get those letters without a fuss and I'll see your death is quick and painless. Cross me and it will take you a very long time to die. It took your husband more than two days."

Abby felt her knees crumble. "But the carriage accident . . ."

"Like I said before, it was a very tidy way to hide the truth. No one questions broken bones when you're found lying under an overturned carriage."

She felt her stomach heave and needles of pain filled her fingers and toes. "Cyrus, please believe me. If I knew where my husband kept correspondence I would gladly give it to you. But I've never found anything. I don't know what you're talking about."

"That's not what Danvers thinks."

She would have fallen if his grip on her arm hadn't kept her upright. "He's in this too?"

Cyrus pulled her into the dining room where the breakfast dishes still sat unattended. "As you can see," he said easily, "everyone is out looking for you and they won't be back until noon. So stop stalling and get me what I want."

Abby never saw the hand that lashed out until it caught her face and sent her crashing to the floor. Her senses whirled and everything spun as she crawled to her knees. A shiny black boot settled over her splayed fingers on the floor, but exerted only enough pressure to keep her still.

"The choice is yours, my dear, but you're going to be very sorry if you make the wrong decision."

"I don't . . ." Her words froze in her throat when Christopher's voice rang from the back of the tavern.

"Abby, where are you. What the hell is going on? Where is everyone?"

"Warn him and he's a dead man," Bloom promised grabbing a thick silver candlestick and stepping behind the door.

Abby struggled to kneel upright as Christopher came striding through the door. But her scream of warning came a breath too late. Cyrus brought the candlestick down on Christopher's head with an echoing thud and he crumbled in a heap to the floor.

"That wasn't very wise, Mrs. Carlson." His smile was gone and the icy coldness that remained chilled Abby further. Carefully stepping over Christopher's body he picked up a knife from one of the tables. "Mayhap I've been threatening you in the wrong way. I wonder how many of your husband's fingers I have to cut off before you remember where the letters are?"

The blade of the knife caught the sunlight that streamed in the window. "You're mad if you think to get away with this."

Cyrus only shrugged. "We shall see." Carefully he stepped back to Christopher's unconscious form. "Mayhap a little slice across the face would be the best place to start." Abby watched in horror as he took a handful of hair and flipped him over.

"Wait," she screamed. "I'll give you the letters. But they're in my chambers above stairs. I'll go get them."

"And I'll come with you, my dear."

A deadly calm took over her mind. She'd not let him harm Christopher, no matter what the cost. Her blood raced but her steps remained steady as they climbed the stairs, then entered the master chamber at the end of the hall.

"Tell me something," she turned to face him. "Is there really work being done on your home or was that just an excuse to take a room here without raising suspicion? It was quite clever if that was your plan. I never suspected a thing. Not even when you bumped into Marilla in the night." Abby felt her stomach turn over when she thought of Marilla, half frozen and left in the snow. "But tell me, how are you going to explain Marilla's death?"

"No explanation is necessary. Everyone thinks that you both were in some type of accident. When they find Marilla's body she'll be long past dead and they can come to any conclusions they wish for none will turn in my direction. After all, I was the one who organized the search party in your husband's absence."

Abby felt her courage like the time slipping away. "But how does Danvers fit into the scheme? I've never understood that."

"Because he doesn't," Cyrus snarled. "Malachi was blackmailing me and Danvers suspected something. He convinced Malachi to give him a share. Whether he was successful or not is immaterial for Malachi never gave him the letters. You still have them and I want them now."

Abby thought her eyes were playing tricks when she saw Christopher standing drunkenly in the doorway. Bloom turned, gun in hand, and without thinking Abby lunged for his legs. Then everything happened at once. A shot rang out. She saw Christopher's look of surprise, then he was falling. Abby felt a crushing weight, then she knew no more.

Christopher sat beside the bed and bathed her face gently with a damp cloth. Her dark lashes were a startling contrast to her pale skin and his thumb brushed ever so softly over the violet smudges that ringed her eyes.

She surfaced slowly fighting against the exhaustion that threatened to pull her under again. He saw the look of terror fill her eyes and quickly gathered her into his arms to stop her scream.

"It's all right," he soothed rocking her close. "Bloom's gone. The magistrates have already taken him away."

Afraid to believe, Abby struggled from his grip and leaned back letting her fingers touch his face and shoulders searching for the bullet wound.

373

"He didn't shoot me," Chris assured. "Although I have a hell of a headache."

"But I saw you fall," her voice rasped.

Chris leaned over and retrieved a mug then pressed it to her lips steadying it as her hands trembled. "I didn't fall," he said simply as she drank. "I lunged for Bloom the same moment you did. The shot went wild but the bastard fell on you in the process."

Tears swam in her eyes. "Chris, I was so scared he would hurt you. He left . . . oh dear God," the last of the color drained from her pinched face. "Chris, he left Marilla out in the snow. We've got to find her."

Taking the mug from her fingers he pressed her firmly back against the pillows. "They've already found her and brought her back. We've switched beds around a bit so she could be in a room with a fireplace and no one's complaining, not even Marilla."

"Is she all right?"

Christopher nodded. "The doctor said she'll ache for a few days and it will take a few days more to get her strength back. But Nanny's tucked her in bed with hot bricks and brandy and I'll wager she'll be her same disagreeable self before we know it."

Abby struggled to sit up. "I need to see for myself," she whispered. "Please?"

She could have asked to go to the moon and Christopher knew he would have somehow found a way. Wrapping her in a quilt he carried her across the hall to Marilla's new chamber.

Effie met them and smiled with relief. "I'm glad you've come. The doctor said she should stay abed,

374

but she's been a struggling to get in to see you, Miz Abby, ever since the doctor left."

Chris stepped through the door and took a chair near the bed keeping Abby firmly on his lap.

"Thank God you're going to be all right." Abby let her tears come.

Marilla reached out a shaky hand and captured Abby's. "I've brought you nothing but trouble and now I owe you my life."

Abby shook her head. "You just need to get well, Marilla."

But the old woman would not be put off and struggled to sit more erect against the pillows. "I've said and done things that I'm ashamed of, Abigail." Her voice trembled but she forced herself on. "And I can only say that I deeply regret the problems and pain that I've caused you. I hope you'll accept my apology." Abby squeezed her hand in reassurance and Marilla continued. "I didn't know that Malachi was blackmailing people. I only know that he once told me he could live in style for the rest of his life because of the money in his book. That's why I came. At first I was going to demand my share, but when I saw the straits you were in, I knew you either hadn't found the book or didn't know about it. At any rate, I decided to search. And I can't honestly say that I would have shared it with you if I had found it." She sniffed and a single tear ran down her wrinkled cheek. "I had become desperate, you see. There are creditors in Maryland who are looking for me and I had no place to hide. That's why I jumped at the chance when Mrs. Morgan offered me money to take you off to Yorktown for the afternoon. But I never had any idea that we'd come to harm. I swear to you I didn't."

"Don't distress yourself, Marilla," Chris spoke for the first time. "Bloom admitted that he arranged for you to be taken when he heard you making plans in the foyer. Julie's plan was for you to take Abby away so she could convince me to return home with her."

"But what will happen now?" Abby's troubled eyes turned to her husband.

"Bloom will be prosecuted for kidnaping and murder. I was in the hallway outside trying to clear my head when he told you about Malachi's death.

Abby sighed, then her eyes brightened. "I don't have any letters, but I do know where the book is. She pushed herself from Christopher's lap wincing only slightly when her sore feet hit the floor. "You both wait here, it's just across the hall."

She returned within moments carrying a narrow ledger bound in leather. "I overheard Malachi say the same thing, Marilla," she offered the book to Chris. "But there's no money in there. I shook it every way I could when I found it and no money ever fell out."

Christopher looked up from the pages, his eyes full of disgust. "There is money here all right, but not in coin. This is the information Cyrus Bloom was searching for. If this information got into the wrong hands, his family name would be ruined forever." Chris thumbed through several more pages and his scowl darkened with each passing glance. "This book holds information on almost every prominent person in our town."

Marilla crossed her arms over her ample chest and looked pointedly toward the doorway. "I don't want to know what's in there. I won't tolerate blackmail. Even I won't stoop that low."

"Could we not tear out the pages needed to prosecute Cyrus and destroy the rest?" Abby offered.

Christopher looked up from reading a passage on Sarah Beaumont that stated she'd been accused of witchcraft in the colony of Salem. He made no protest when Abby closed the book within his hands.

"I don't think the prosecutor needs to see any of this," he said with disgust. "With us as witnesses, his case against Cyrus is clear cut. I say we burn this now before it causes more harm."

Abby looked to Marilla and together they nodded.

Christopher gazed down at Abby and watched her sleep. Her eyes had closed before her head had hit the pillow. And although his need for her was strong, his love for her was stronger. Cradled in his arms she snuggled closer even as she dreamed and Christopher filled with contentment. His had been the only eyes to feast on the dark secrets hidden within Malachi Barclay's book and they had watched with satisfaction as the pages burned until only ashes remained. Neither Abby or Marilla had asked him what he had read and he knew they never would. Cyrus Bloom was confined in the jailhouse and if rumors were true, Michael Danvers would be joining him by daybreak. Their punishment would be severe but Christopher felt no pity when he thought of what their greed had nearly cost him. And he wondered if he'd ever find it in his heart to forgive Julie for her interference. If

377

he'd stayed just a few hours more, he would have lost Abby forever.

He felt her stir and snuggled her closer. Then her eyes opened and Christopher felt his heart burst with love. "How are you feeling," he whispered.

She smiled and stretched against him. "Like I should stay abed for a week."

He kissed her nose. "You'll get no objections from me on that count."

"There are meals to see to," she smiled wearily then her brow wrinkled. "Did someone attend to the dishes from breakfast? What time is it? Has dinner been served? Dear Lord, Christopher how could you let me stay abed when there is so much to do?"

She started to rise but he pinned her flat. "It's two in the morning, so the only one hungry is me and you'll not have to leave this bed to satisfy my appetite."

She blushed and turned her face to his chest, but this time it was Christopher who pulled away.

"I have a surprise," he teased, taking a leather pouch and dropping it on her belly.

Abby recognized the pouch immediately but her eyes held only confusion as she looked up at her husband. "Did you forget to pay the rent?"

"I just did," he smiled. "With all that's happened, I've not had time to share my news. We own the tavern."

"What?" she gasped, her eyes wide with wonder.

He nodded. "It turns out that Malachi sold it to Walter Johnson some five years ago. It was in the group of properties I acquired when I purchased the silver shop. I didn't find out until I went to pay the rent."

Abby started to giggle. "I'll bet Mr. Webster thought you were a mite strange," she teased, realizing that Nanny and Obadiah would now be safe. She looked deep into her husband's eyes and knew she would tell him all, but first they had some unfinished business.

"Have I told you that I love you, Mr. Carlson," she whispered.

Christopher pulled her closer still, his lips a hair's breath from hers. "Not nearly often enough, Mrs. Carlson," he replied. "But now would be a good time to start."

Abby rocked contentedly before the fireplace in their new home. The building had been completed and they had welcomed in the year 1699 under their new roof. Her fingers smoothed over the tiny flowers she'd embroidered. Marilla had recovered with lightning speed and to the amazement of all had turned into a different person. She had cried with gratitude when Christopher had asked her to stay at the tavern and run it for them, but since he had hired so much new help, Marilla had only to direct the activities. Even Nanny had approved the decision, and in spite of their beginnings, she and Marilla had become fast friends.

Abby gazed dreamily into the fire but her smile began to fade when she thought of Jimmy Richardson. Despite all Christopher had done to search for the boy, it was as if Jimmy had disappeared off the face of the earth. Abby sighed. She knew Chris sent money to Mrs. Richardson each month, and that he'd never truly give up the search for Jim, but he had Effie's twins working with him now in the silver shop. She let her mind wander and thoughts of Suzannah surfaced. She hadn't seen her sister since the night of the fire. Abby's hand touched her stomach; did Suzannah know already?

Christopher burst into the bedroom, still carrying the cold winter air on his coat. "It's official," he beamed. "The capital is to be moved from Jamestown to Middle Plantation. And we're to have a new name — Williamsburg — after the King." Shaking off his coat he turned then halted, midstride. He knew she was excited about his news, but her face held a joy and radiance he'd never seen before. "Is all well with you, wife?" He dropped to his knee beside her chair.

Abby smiled and offered the tiny garment she'd been sewing. "It's official," she smiled, loving the expectant look in his eyes as he held the delicate garment. "We're going to have a baby. You're about to become a father."

Author's Note

Readers familiar with Colonial Williamsburg will find that I have taken some liberty with the historical development of the city. In the year 1698, the town of Middle Plantation consisted of the College of William and Mary, a church, several stores, a few houses and an inn or two. There was one main street that ran from one end of town to the other. For purposes necessary for the story, I have described the town as it might have flourished a few years after the capital was moved. The fire in Jamestown on October 31, 1698 actually happened as stated and was the major influence for moving the capital in 1699 and renaming the city Williamsburg.

Special thanks must go to the following people — Linda Couch, who portrays the widowed tavern owner Jane Vobe in Colonial Williamsburg, for the hours she so freely shared; Alison Hentges for her hospitality; Lois Anderson, my traveling companion, whose support never wavers; Mary Jane

Nauss, researcher extraordinaire; Dorothy Leverett, the librarian who could find dates when all else failed; Craig Davies for his help putting out fires; Nancy Anderson for her wonderful connections; and last but not least to RHAPPS.